FORGIVING

FORGIVING

LaVyrle Spencer

G. P. PUTNAM'S SONS   NEW YORK

G. P. Putnam's Sons
Publishers Since 1838
200 Madison Avenue
New York, NY 10016

Library of Congress Cataloging-in-Publication Data

Spencer, LaVyrle.
    Forgiving / LaVyrle Spencer.
        p.   cm.
    I. Title.
PS3569.P4534F6   1991   90-42821 CIP
813'.54—dc20
ISBN 0-399-13599-5

Printed in the United States of America
1   2   3   4   5   6   7   8   9   10

This book is printed on acid-free paper.
∞

TO STEVEN AXELROD
    my agent

    Steve, you're the best!

Many thanks to Nita Celeya and Fred Brian
for providing helpful background information
while I was researching this book.

L.S.

CHAPTER 1

Dakota Territory, September 1876

*T*HE Cheyenne stage was six hours late, putting Sarah Merritt into Deadwood at ten P.M. rather than in the late afternoon. The rig rumbled away and left her standing in the dark on a muddy street before a crude saloon. Several crude saloons. An entire streetful of them! The noise was appalling—a mixture of shouts, laughter, banjo music and brawling. And the smell—ye gods! Did nobody pick up the animal dung? Horses and mules lined the hitching rails; nearby, one of them was snoring.

Sarah backed up and squinted at the sign overhead. Eureka Saloon. She glanced down at the place—a frame building, unpainted, roughly constructed and crowded by a similar structure on the left and a log building on the right. The door to the Eureka was closed, but through its window murky coal-oil lantern light tumbled down a set of wooden steps leading directly from the building to the mud, without the benefit of a boardwalk.

Sarah glanced down at the trunks and bandbox sitting at her ankle, wondering what to do. Before she could decide, three gunshots cracked, a mule brayed, the door of the Eureka flapped open and a crowd of rowdies burst from inside and stumbled down the steps into the street. Sarah snatched her bandbox and scuttled to the shadow of the saloon wall. "Kill that claim-jumper, Soaky!" someone bellowed. "Fix his face so only his mama could love him!"

A fist smacked against a jaw.

A man stumbled backward and somersaulted over Sarah's trunks, picked himself up and vaulted at his opponent without noticing over what he'd stumbled. The rabble milled this way and that, shouting, brandishing their fists and beer mugs. A man thumped into the side of a mule, which brayed and skittered sideways.

"Kill the sonofabitch!"

"Yeah, kill him!"

Two onlookers clambered onto Sarah's cowhide trunks to get a better view.

"No! Get off there!" she shouted.

When she moved, one of the drunken revelers spotted her.

"Mother of God, it's a woman! You hear me, boys, it's a *woman!*"

The fracas ended as if a firebell had clanged.

"A woman . . ."

"A woman . . ." The word was passed from one man to another as, like fog, they crept close, hemming her in.

She stood with her back to the saloon wall, the hair on her nape prickling, clutching the ribbons of her bandbox while the men gawked at her skirts, hat and face as if they'd never before seen a female.

Summoning a note of bravado, she greeted, "Good evening, gentlemen."

Silent, they continued gawking.

"Could anyone tell me where to find the home of Mrs. Hossiter?"

"Hossiter?" a croaky voice repeated. "Anyone heard of a woman named Hossiter?" The crowd mumbled and shook their heads. " 'Fraid not, ma'am. What's her husband's name?"

"I'm afraid I don't know, but my sister's name is Adelaide Merritt, and she works for them."

"Nobody named Merritt around here. Nobody named Hossiter either. Can't be more than twenty-five women in the whole gulch, and we know every one of 'em, don't we, boys?"

A murmur crescendoed and faded.

"What's your sister do?"

"Domestic work, and she distinctly said the name of her landlady was Mrs. Hossiter."

"Landlady, you say?" A spark of deeper interest perked up the fellow's voice. He spread his arms wide and pressed back the throng. "Here, boys, don't crowd the little lady, let her move out into the light where we can see her better. My name is Shorty Reese, miss, and I'll do what I can to help you find your sister." He doffed his hat, took her elbow and drew her to the foot of the steps where the lantern light ranged from the open door. By it she noted he was middle-aged, with dirty clothing, seamed face and one missing tooth.

"If you'll let me through, those trunks are mine. I have a picture of my sister. Maybe one of you will recognize her."

They stepped back and allowed Sarah to open the buckles of one of her trunks, from which she produced a sepia daguerreotype of herself and Adelaide, taken five years before. She handed it to Shorty Reese. "She's twenty-one and has blond hair and green eyes."

He turned it toward the light, cocked his head and studied it. "Why, this is Eve," he pronounced, "one of the upstairs girls at Miss Rose's, and she don't have no blond hair. Her hair's as black as the end of Number Fourteen stope."

"Eve?"

"That's right. Ain't this Eve, boys?" The picture was passed around.

"That's Eve, all right."

"Yup, that's her."

"That's Eve." The picture returned to Sarah. "You can find her up at Rose's, the north end of Main Street on the left. You mind my asking, miss, if you plan to work as an upstairs girl, too?"

"No, sir. I plan to start publishing a newspaper."

"A newspaper!"

"That's right, as soon as my press arrives, if it hasn't already."

"But you're a woman."

"Yes, Mr. Reese, I am." Sarah returned the picture to the trunk and buckled the straps. "Thank you very much for your help. Now if you could point me in the direction of a hotel, I'd be ever so grateful."

"Help her with her trunks, boys!" Reese shouted. "Let's get her over to the Grand Central!"

"No, please . . . I . . . ."

"Why, it'd be our pleasure, miss. We don't get a chance to see a lady hardly at all. Like I said, can't be more than a couple dozen of the fairer sex in Deadwood, if that."

Though she little relished making her entrance into Deadwood in the company of the Eureka Saloon's clientele, she had no idea how she'd carry two trunks to the hotel on her own. It struck her, too, that as a newspaperwoman, she would be prudent to avoid alienating any of the townspeople on her first night in town. This was a gold town. Gold spelled money, and money meant rowdiness. Any one of these men could be the owner of the lot she might want to buy, or the building she might want to rent, or a member of the town board, for that matter.

"Thank you, Mr. Reese, I appreciate your help." She found herself buffeted along by the noisy lot, who hoisted her trunks onto their shoulders and escorted her to the other end of the block.

"You're in luck," Reese said, climbing the steps of a tall, false-fronted building with the first boardwalk she'd seen. "The Grand Central just opened last week." They took her right inside, across a Spartan lobby to the desk where they formed a circle around her, grinning, while presenting her to the night clerk. "Got a customer for you, Sam. This here's Miss Merritt, just came in on the Cheyenne stage."

"M–miss M–Merritt." His face grew scarlet as he extended a hand which was limp and moist as cooked cabbage. He was a chinless little man with round spectacles and an effeminate manner, dressed in a brown plaid suit with his hair parted in the middle. "I'm happy to m–make your acquaintance."

"This is Sam Peoples," Shorty filled in for Peoples, who was too flustered by her appearance to supply his own name.

"Hello, Mr. Peoples." His blush made him look combustible and for a moment he forgot to withdraw his hand. Self-consciously, Sarah withdrew hers, unaccustomed to creating such a stir.

"She's gonna start up a newspaper."

"A newspaper—my, my. Then we'd better take good care of her, hadn't we?" Peoples forced a nervous laugh. He dipped a black pen and extended it her way while revolving the hotel register to face her. Signing, Sarah felt the entire gallery of men watching.

When she finished she gave Peoples a smile and the pen.

"Welcome to the Grand Central," he said. "That'll be a dollar fifty for the night."

"In advance?"

"Yes. In gold dust if you please." He touched the gold scale at his elbow and left it nodding.

She stood straight as a lodgepole and fixed her eyes on the clerk's spectacles. "Mr. Peoples, I've just spent six nights and five days on the stagecoach from Cheyenne. Given all the robberies that have been happening along the stage routes, do you honestly believe I'd be fool enough to carry my money with me in the form of gold?"

Peoples' face turned brighter and he glanced helplessly at the men. "I'm s–sorry, Miss Merritt, I'm just the n–night clerk here. I don't own the hotel. But it's our p–policy to accept only guests who pay in advance, and gold dust is our legal tender out here."

"Very well." She set her bandbox on the desk and began untying its ribbons. "All my money is in the form of Wells Fargo certificates. If you can cash one into gold dust, I'd be happy to pay in advance." From a black organdy pouch she extracted a one-hundred-dollar certificate and offered it to Peoples.

Again, he glanced at the men, his face crimson. "I don't keep that k-kind of gold around either. You can c-cash it in the morning at the bank, however."

"And in the meantime?" She fixed him with a determined stare.

One of the onlookers said, "You gonna let a lady sleep on the street, Peoples?"

"Mr. Winters g-gave me orders." The more flustered the clerk became the more he stuttered. "Sh-she c-could sleep in the l-l-l-lobby, but it's the b-b-best I can d-do."

"Lobby!" A leather pouch landed on the desk beside the gold scale. "Take it out of there." Another pouch joined it—"Or out of here"—and another and another until there were nearly a dozen lying on the high counter.

Sarah turned to the men behind her, with a hand spread on her chest. "Thank you all so much," she said sincerely, "but I can't accept your gold."

"Why not? There's plenty more where that come from, ain't there, boys?"

"Hell yes!"

"El Dorado!" They punched the air in hallelujah and let out a roar. Several of them *hoo-rahed*, lifting their beer mugs, then took swigs.

Sam Peoples selected a pouch and carefully weighed out the gold—at twenty dollars per ounce, a dollar and fifty cents' worth scarcely looked like enough to have created this embarrassing contretemps. When the pouches were reclaimed by their owners, the gold proved to have come out of the sack owned by a tall, lanky man with thinning dark hair and a bleary-eyed smile. He had a prominent Adam's apple, watery red eyes, and he wove back on his heels as if struck by a wall of wind.

"Thank you, Mr.—?"

The man continued weaving and grinning in his alcoholic euphoria.

"Bradigan," Reese told her. "His name's Patrick Bradigan."

"Thank you, Mr. Bradigan."

Bradigan listed toward Sarah wearing an expression like a scratched cat, his squinting eyes scarcely registering what he saw.

"I shall repay you tomorrow as soon as I've visited the bank."

He gave a floppy salute and someone stuffed his gold pouch into his pocket.

"Where can I find you?"

"Least I can do fer a pretty lady," Bradigan mumbled.

"Bradigan tipped a few tonight," one of his cohorts explained. "He won't know the difference whether you pay him back or not."

They would have carried her trunks upstairs to her room but for the protests of Sam Peoples. "You'll w–wake up all my customers! Gentle-men, pl–please—get back to the saloon where you belong."

"All your customers are still *in* the saloons!"

"Then get back and j–join them." He sent the boys shuffling off with a doffing of hats and a chorus of goodnights for "the pretty little lady," which Sarah was not. She was five foot ten in her stocking feet, with plain brown hair, a nose she considered a trifle too long and lips too thin to be remarkable. She did have passably attractive blue eyes, vivid and thick-lashed, still nobody with all their faculties would mistake her for pretty. She was a long-faced woman who in all her life had never attracted as much male attention as during the last quarter hour.

"I'm giving you a room on the third floor. It's warmest up there," said the ingratiating Peoples, carrying the first of her trunks. He led her through a building whose primary recommendation was size. Big it was, but raw in every sense of the word, without a plastered wall in evidence, not even in the lobby, where the windows were bare of curtains and the only spots of brightness were provided by the china cuspidor and the calendar behind the desk, sporting the picture of a waterfall. The floors were constructed of bare pine planks, still emitting the smell of newly milled lumber. The walls were of green studs still oozing sap, between which the clapboard siding showed, replete with knotholes that seemed to peer back like empty eye sockets.

The stairs, situated just behind the desk, led up to the mouth of a dark, narrow hall. Midway along it, a single coal-oil lantern hung from a wall bracket; on the floor beneath it sat a covered china slop jar. He led her to a room a third of the way down on the left and opened a door made of planks on a Z-shaped frame.

"Water's in the c–can outside the door, mornings only, and you can dump your sl–slop in the jar down the hall. Matches are on the wall to your left. I'll be right back with your other trunk."

When he was gone, she found the tin match holder and lit the lantern beside her bed. By its smoky orange light she perused the room. *Lord in heaven, what have I gotten into?* The walls were as stark as those in the lobby, bare planks pocked by knotholes through which drafts blew. Overhead, the ceiling rafters showed. The window and floor were un-adorned, the bed made of tubular brown tin, the ordinary table beside it holding only the lamp—no runner or doily, nothing to appeal to the feminine eye. Not even a coverlet on the bed, only the spruce green woolen blanket and a pillow which—thank heavens—had a muslin slipcover. She turned back the blanket and found muslin sheets and a real mattress stuffed with straw and cotton, and breathed a sigh of relief.

There was a commode stand with a pitcher and bowl on top. She opened the door beneath and peered inside to find a covered china commode.

She had just closed the door when Sam Peoples returned with her second trunk. "I haven't eaten since noon," Sarah told him. "Would there be anything to eat?"

"Our d–dining room is closed, I'm sorry. But we'll be open for breakfast."

"Oh," she said, disappointed.

He backed toward the door. "There aren't many w–women in Dead-wood, as you know. You'd best b–bar the door." He indicated a heavy wooden four-by-four standing in the corner. "Good night then. May I say it's a pl–pleasure having you."

"Thank you, Mr. Peoples. Good night."

When he closed the door she studied the crudely hewn wooden brackets on either side. The bar was heavy. She struggled to lift and drop it into place, then turned to face the room with a sigh. She dropped to the edge of the bed, bounced once tentatively and fell back with one arm crooked above her head. Her eyelids closed. Of Sarah's five nights on the road, only two had been spent in beds. Two she'd slept wrapped in her own blanket, on the floors of log shacks serving as stage relay stations, and one on board the stagecoach itself, folded like a carpenter's rule on the hard horsehair seat. Her last filling meal had been yesterday noon at Hill City, where she'd had bread, coffee and venison. Today's fare had been bacon and cold coffee at breakfast, and at noon dry biscuits accompanied by water from Box Elder Creek. She'd taken her last bath in St. Louis nine days ago and smelled—she real-ized—like an old horse's hoof.

Get up, Sarah. Your day's not over.

Suppressing a groan, she forced her tired body to bend and shoved herself to her feet. The pitcher and bowl were empty. Out in the hall, the water tin was, too: *mornings only,* she remembered and went back inside to whack the dust from her woolen suit as best she could, recomb the sides of her hair and wipe off her face with a dry cloth. She replaced her hat, rammed the pin through her chignon, took her organdy pouch containing the Wells Fargo certificates, her father's watch, and her pen and ink, and left the room.

As she passed through the lobby, she startled Peoples, who advised, "Ma'am, you shouldn't be out on the street alone after dark."

"I've traveled clear from St. Louis alone, Mr. Peoples. I'm perfectly capable of taking care of myself. Furthermore, my sister is someplace in this town and I haven't seen her for five years. I intend to do so tonight if I have to wake her up to do it."

Outside, the din from the saloons still rattled up and down the thoroughfare. The boardwalks proved intermittent, built or not built at the whim of each lot-owner who'd erected a building. Striding down the center of Main Street, she made a mental note to write an editorial about standardizing the height and width of the boardwalks and making them compulsory for every building along Main. And streetlamps—the town needed streetlamps and a paid lamplighter to tend them at dusk and dawn. Ah, her work was cut out.

In spite of the clamor, the town had an eerie feeling lit solely by blobs of light from the saloon windows falling onto the rows of sleeping horses. She looked up. Only a narrow corridor of starlight shone overhead. The sides of the gulch hung like a widow's curtains, closed against intrusion, isolating Deadwood from the rest of the world. In the dark she made out the blacker shapes of pines high on the steep slopes, separated from town by the paler spots where the hills had been denuded. A few pines straggled in places to the very edges of the street. The wind whistled through them and down the ravine, a cold late-September wind that fluttered her skirt and stirred the scent of fresh animal droppings. Sarah covered her nose as she hurried along, formulating yet another editorial.

She passed a tin shop, grocer's, barber's, tobacconist, hardware, uncountable saloons and (surprisingly) a huge theater, the Langrishe, where lamps were lit and the bill announced "Flies in the Weed" by John Brougham. Smiling, Sarah paused and reread the bill. A hint of culture, after all. To her amazement, in the next block on the opposite side of the street she passed *another* theater, the Bella Union! Her spirits took their first upswing since she'd arrived in Deadwood. But where was the church? The school? Surely in a town this size there must be *some* children. She would make it a point to find out how many.

At the far end of Main, where it took a swing to the right, the wooden structures petered out and the gulch bottlenecked from three streets into one. Beyond that point fires glimmered in the distance, dots of hazel light between the paler squares of lantern-lit tents that lay scattered along the cut like the beads of a broken rosary. Where the three streets of town merged, foot traffic picked up. Men . . . all men. They stared at Sarah and stopped in their tracks as she passed. Men . . . noisy men, milling about the last string of buildings on the left whose doors opened and closed constantly, releasing peals of piano music and laughter.

All six buildings looked alike—narrow, unadorned, with heavy draperies drawn across the windows; windowless doors. There must be some mistake, she thought, stopping before Rose's, glancing at the names of the adjacent establishments—The Green Door, Goldie's, The Mother Lode, The Doves' Cote and Angeline's. They appeared to be saloons.

Nevertheless, she decided the safest course was to knock on the door of Rose's. She did, then clutched her money packet against her jacket buttons with both hands and waited. Given the noise inside, it seemed little wonder nobody answered. A creek purled somewhere behind her. A man left the place next door and disappeared into the dark in the direction of the tents. Unaware that she stood behind him, he broke wind noisily, pausing and canting his left buttock before the sound died and he moved on.

She knocked again, harder.

"Nobody knocks on the door at Rose's," a deep voice said behind her. "Go right on in."

She jumped and spun, pressing a hand to her heart. "Good heavens, you scared me!"

"I didn't mean to." A tall man stood close behind her. The dark hid his face.

"Tell me . . . is this the only Rose's in Deadwood?"

"The one and only. You're new in town," he speculated with a grin in his voice.

"Yes. I'm looking for my sister, Adelaide. I'm told she's an upstairs maid at Rose Hossiter's, but it seems she's changed her name to Eve."

"I know Eve."

"You do?"

"I know Eve very well, as a matter of fact. So you're her sister."

"Yes—Sarah Merritt. I've just arrived from St. Louis." She extended her gloved hand. He took it in a hard, protracted squeeze while she peered up trying to make out his face in the deep shadow of his ten-gallon hat.

"Noah Campbell."

"Mr. Campbell," she returned politely. When she would have withdrawn her hand he continued gripping it. "Well, Miss Merritt, this is an unexpected pleasure. Allow me to escort you inside and introduce you to Rose. She'll know just where your sister is." As if executing an allemande-left, he opened the door and swung her inside, dropping her hand as the door thumped shut behind them.

"Welcome to Rose's, Miss Merritt," he said at her shoulder, flourishing an open palm at the room.

As if plunged into a nightmare, she stood rooted, absorbing impressions—hazy lantern light, garish parlor furniture, a parrot sidling left and right on a perch, squawking, "Dollar a minute! Dollar a minute!" Thick, tassled draperies, the smell of stale whiskey and hard-boiled eggs, the sting of cigar smoke, a lot of men in stages of semidrunkenness and one blowsy woman dressed entirely in emerald green with carmine lips and a feather in her red hair. She possessed an acre of cleavage resembling a baby's bare buttocks: an obese woman with a smoking cigar between her teeth who stood with her arm around the shoulders of a big, bearded man while he fondled her rump.

Sarah spun to Noah Campbell. "There must be some mistake. This isn't a private home."

"No, ma'am, hardly."

For the first time she saw his face. He had a bushy auburn mustache, a roundish nose with a faint dent at the end and grinning gray eyes that lighted on Sarah's and lingered. "Come along, I'll introduce you to Rose."

He put a hand on her spine and she balked. "No! I told you, my sister is an upstairs maid and her landlady's name is Mrs. Rose Hossiter. And please remove your hand from my back!"

He obliged, then stood back, studying her indulgently while his grin lingered. "Getting last-minute jitters, are you?"

"This place is horrible. It looks like a brothel."

He glanced idly at the woman in green, then back at Sarah. "Tell you what." His eyes roved lazily down her torso and back up. "I'm a pretty conventional fellow—Rose will vouch for me. I like it straight, no rough stuff, no more than two or three drinks beforehand. I pay good, in pure gold, I don't have any diseases or lice. *And,* I already took my bath. You can tell Rose that you've already lined up your first customer. How would that be?"

"I *beg your pardon!*" Sarah felt the blood surge to her face. The skin across her chest felt taut as a sausage casing, and it took superior poise to keep from slapping his face.

"I understand," he added in a confidential tone, taking her arm as if to guide her toward Rose. "Your first night in a new place and you're bound to be nervous—but there's no reason to make up stories about Adelaide being your sister."

"Adelaide *is* my sister!" She wrenched her arm free and turned upon him furiously. "And stop touching me, I said!"

He raised both palms as if she'd drawn a six-shooter. "All right, all right, I'm *sor*ry." His voice turned irritated. "You women are all so damned quirky. Never met a one of you who wasn't."

"I am *not* one of *those* women!" she spit, mortified.

Several men had risen and encroached. "Hey, Noah, what you got there?"

"Hooey, she's a tall one . . . nice long legs . . . I like them long-legged ones."

" 'Bout time we was gettin' some fresh flesh around here."

"What's your name, sugar?"

One of them with a beard like a billy goat reached out as if to touch her and Sarah recoiled, bumping back against Campbell, who gripped her arms to steady her. She lurched from his touch and hid a shudder, fighting the urge to crouch and raise her fists. The men inched closer. They were for the most part loud and ogling, with wet lips and florid cheeks; hair that needed cutting, nails that needed cleaning and necks that needed scrubbing. Most were old and brazen, but some were pitiably young and blushing as much as she.

At the sudden stir Rose glanced over and raised one eyebrow.

"Hey, Noah," one of the men asked, "where'd you find her?"

"Out on the street," Noah replied, "but back off, Lewis, tonight she's spoken for."

Rose was bearing down on them with one hand on her fat hip and her breasts leading the way like a pair of pink cannonballs. Her face wore an expression of hauteur and she carried her cigar in the crook of one finger. She parted the crowd as a plow parts soil, stopped before Sarah and assessed her coldly—one pass, down and up—with contemptuous, putty-colored eyes. She drew a mouthful of cigar smoke, let it slither up her nostrils and spoke, breathing a gray plume like the top of an Indian teepee.

"What've you got here, Noah?"

Sarah spoke up angrily. "Are you Rose Hossiter?"

At close range Rose's skin had the texture of cottage cheese, and her mouth was ludicrously enlarged. The kohl on her eyelids had gathered in the cracks and oozed to the inner corners where it collected in two black beads. One of her teeth was cracked off and her breath stank of cigars, though the smell was muddied by that of lily-of-the-valley perfume.

"That's right. Who wants to know?"

"Sarah Merritt. I'm Adelaide's sister."

Rose's hard eyes perused Sarah's flat brown felt hat and high-collared wool traveling suit, pausing on her inconsiderable breasts and hips. "I'm not looking for any new girls. Try next door."

"I'm not looking for a job. I'm looking for Adelaide Merritt."

"There's nobody here by that name." Rose turned away.

Sarah raised her voice. "I was told she goes by the name of Eve."

Her remark stopped Rose. "Oh?" The madam turned back. "Who told you that?"

"He did." She nodded sideways at Campbell.

Rose Hossiter flicked the wet tip of her cigar with a thumbnail and considered a while before asking, "What do you want with her?"

"I came to tell her our father died."

Rose took a pull on her cigar and swung away. "Eve is working. Come back tomorrow afternoon."

Sarah took one step forward and demanded, "I want to see her now!"

Rose gave Sarah a view of her broad posterior and her brassy Grecian topknot. "Get her out of here, Noah. You know we don't allow her kind in here."

Campbell took Sarah's elbow. "You'd better leave."

She swung around and swatted his hand with her money packet. "Don't you *ever* touch me again, do you understand?" Her eyes grew dark with indignation. "This is a public place, as public as a restaurant or a livery stable. I have as much right to be here as any man in this room." With one finger she drew an invisible arc spanning half of them.

"Rose wants you out."

"Rose will have me out when I'm satisfied about whether or not my sister works here and what she does. You expect me to believe that an upstairs maid works at this hour of the night? I'm not quite that naive, Mr. Campbell."

"Upstairs *girl,* not upstairs maid," he said.

"There's a difference?"

"In Deadwood there is. You're right. Your sister is a prostitute, Miss Merritt, but around here we call them upstairs girls. And Rose"—he nodded at the woman—"we call her kind landladies. This end of town is referred to as the badlands. Now, do you still want to see your sister?"

"Yes," Sarah declared stubbornly and marched away from him to take a seat between two very bad-smelling men on a horrid beet-colored settee with carved mahogany arms. One of them smelled like dried sweat, the other stank like sulfur. She perched stiffly, folding her hands over her money packet on her knees. She was neither a tearful nor a fearful type, but the realization that her sister was upstairs at this moment, probably servicing a man, brought a lump to her throat. The men beside her began crowding her thighs, and her heart started hammering.

The fellow on her left took out a twist of chewing tobacco and gnawed off a piece. The one on her right stared at her while she fixed her eyes on the parrot.

"A dollar a minute! A dollar a minute!" he squawked.

Presently Noah Campbell cut off Sarah's view of the bird. Her chin snapped up and her lips pruned. He hadn't even the grace to remove his hat or gun indoors, but wore the one pulled low over his eyes and the other strapped low on his hip.

"If you're not one of the upstairs girls," he advised, "you don't know what you're up against here. Since I'm the one who brought you in, Rose asked me to escort you out. Now the choice is up to you, but if you don't leave, you'll have to tangle with Flossie." He nodded at a figure moving toward them. "I doubt that you'd want to do that."

The Indian woman appeared silently, an amazon well over six feet tall, with a face that looked as if it had been hewn from a piece of redwood with ten whacks of an ax, then set afire and stomped out by hobnail boots. Her eyes were tiny, black and expressionless. Her skin was as coarse-grained as a strawberry, her stringy hair clubbed at the nape, her arms the circumference of a Civil War cannon.

"You," she pointed. "Get ass out."

Fear burned a hot path up Sarah's chest. She swallowed and stared into Flossie's unwavering, compass-point eyes, afraid to look away.

"My father has died. I haven't seen my sister in five years. I want to talk to her, that's all."

"Talk tomorrow. Now, get skinny ass out." Flossie leaned forward, gripped Sarah's upper arms and lifted her bodily from the red couch, extending her arms parallel to the floor until Sarah hung like a union suit on a clothesline.

"Put me down, please," Sarah requested in a trembling voice, her shoulders meeting her earlobes. "I'll leave on my own."

Flossie opened her hands and dropped Sarah like a discard. Caught unprepared, her knees buckled and she stumbled forward before catching herself on the arm of a chair and regaining her balance.

"Flossie!" a new voice shouted. "Leave her alone!"

Sarah straightened, tugging at the peplum of her jacket. Halfway down the uncarpeted stairs that dropped from above into the middle of the room, a woman stood with one hand on the rough rail. Her hair was jet black, hacked off parallel with the earth at jaw and eyebrow level, flaring out at the bottom as if its ends were split. Her skin was white as cornstarch, her eyes ringed by kohl and her lips a slash of scarlet. She wore a chemise and pantaloons of white covered by a transparent black kimono sporting two large red poppies, strategically placed. Wearing an expression as cold as Rose's, as foreboding as Flossie's, she advanced toward Sarah and stopped before her.

"What the hell are you doing here?" she demanded icily.

"I believe I should be the one asking that question."

"I work here, and I don't like to be bothered when I could be entertaining customers."

"Entertaining! Adelaide, how could y—"

"My name is Eve!" she snapped. "I've done away with Adelaide. As far as I'm concerned she never existed."

"Oh Addie, what have you done to yourself?" Sarah reached toward the brittle black hair at her sister's jaw.

Adelaide jerked back. "Get out of here," she ordered through set teeth. "I didn't ask you to come here. I don't want to see you."

"But you wrote to me. You told me you were here."

"Maybe I did, but I never thought you'd come traipsing after me. Now, get out."

"Addie, Father is dead."

"Get out, I said!"

"Addie, did you hear me? Father is dead."

"I don't give a damn. Now get out!" Addie spun away.

"But I came all the way from St. Louis."

Sarah found herself reaching for Addie's retreating back as her sister moved toward a cluster of men swilling whiskey at a round table.

"Snooker—you're next, honey. Sorry for the delay." Addie ran her palm across the shoulders of a middle-aged man wearing a red plaid shirt and suspenders. He craned his head around to peer at Sarah. Addie put a hand on his cheek and turned his face toward her own. "What're you gawking at her for? She's nothing." She leaned down and opened her garish red lips over Snooker's much older ones and Sarah turned away.

Noah Campbell reached for her elbow as if to escort her out.

"Don't touch me!" she ordered, once again jerking away from the man who, apparently, was another of Adelaide's customers.

Gathering her dignity and her broken heart, she headed toward the door.

CHAPTER 2

*B*ACK at the hotel, she lay in bed, wide awake, stiff beneath the blankets. She was not a green waif, ignorant of what went on in the world. Hadn't her mother run off with a lover when she was seven and Addie three, never to be seen again? Hadn't she learned young that carnality can drive people to extremes?

Furthermore, she was twenty-five years old and had begun typesetting for her father at the age of twelve, writing articles at the age of fifteen. In the years since, she had been exposed to every kind of repugnant story imaginable. She had learned to control her personal reactions to them, to release her choler or her compassion only in ink on newsprint. *To care too much is to lose your objectivity,* her father had warned, and because there was not a person ever walked the earth whom she had respected more than Isaac Merritt, she had absorbed his every word. In doing so, she had become inured to the seamy side of life, to the frequent cruelties of humankind, to their immorality and greed and callousness and lust.

But this was personal. This was her little sister, Adelaide, with whom she'd shared a bed as a child, with whom she'd had the mumps and the chickenpox, and to whom, in lieu of their mother, she'd taught the basics of reading, writing, manners and housekeeping. Adelaide, who had always had such difficulty being happy after Mother left. Adelaide, in that repugnant place, doing repugnant things with repugnant men.

She pictured the brothel again with its wet-lipped clientele, its cigar-smoking madam and its degeneracy. What had prompted Adelaide to work there? How long had she been there? Had she been a prostitute ever since running away from home?

Five years. Sarah closed her eyes. Five years and all those nights and all those men. She opened her eyes: five years or five nights—was there a yardstick by which to measure depravity? She relived the initial rush of shock upon seeing Addie in those unchaste clothes, a good twenty pounds heavier, with her face painted and her hair dyed black, gone wiry. The last time Sarah had seen Addie, her sister had been a trim young girl with elbow-length silky blond hair and a shy smile she rarely showed. She had been a devout Christian, an obedient daughter and a loving sister. What had changed her?

By the devil, I aim to find out!

In the morning Sarah awakened to the tinny clang of someone replacing the cover on the water canister in the hall. Her eyes snapped open to the sight of the naked ceiling joists above. The memory of last night returned, and with it a zeal to get her sister out of Rose's.

She bolted from bed, flung open her trunk, rooted for clean clothes and tossed them across the bed. She unbarred the door, peeked into the hall and, with her enamel pitcher, hurried to the water tin. Poking a finger inside, she muttered wryly, "Oh, grand . . . just grand," dipped her pitcher anyway, carried it back to her room dripping, and in spite of the cold water, put the soap and the privacy to good use. Thirty minutes later, still shivering, with her hair in a doughnut at the back of her head, dressed in high-top black shoes, a brown broadcloth skirt, a no-nonsense brown shirtwaist and a double-breasted wool jacket, she stepped out of the Grand Central Hotel.

The September morning was chilly. Standing on the shaded boardwalk, she shuddered again, squinting up and down the street, drawing on her gloves, her money pouch clutched beneath one arm, a two-penny notebook between her teeth. She walked to the end of the boardwalk, her heels playing a tomtom beat on the hollow floor, and peered up a side street. It ended behind the hotel where Whitewood Creek brattled along just beyond the point where Deadwood Creek fed into it. On the far side of the water the gulch wall rose sheerly, holding back the sun. Taking a bearing from the shadows, she deduced the gulch ran in a northeasterly by southwesterly line. She and the Grand Central were at the southwest end; the "badlands" and her sister were at the northeast.

Out on the street, she lifted her eyes to the cerulean sky and turned in a circle. The canyon walls were dizzying, leading to a brownstone ledge high above the creek bed, and on one side, a stretch of towering white rocks, like great shark's teeth taking a bite out of the blue firmament. The rocky outcroppings were connected by stands of ponderosa pines blanketing the hills in great rolling stretches, then trailing down ravines and draws in jagged green-black fingers. Alive, the pines towered; dead, they crosshatched the depression in thatches of gnarl, lending Deadwood Gulch its name.

The town itself looked like an extension of the deadfall, as if tumbled down the ravine by centuries of weather. It started as a collection of tents and huts high up in the hills and straggled down to a bottleneck wide enough at one point to accommodate only a single street—Main— and it a disappointment. Its buildings were a sorry lot, thrown up hastily by the prospectors and merchants who'd come to cash in on the gold rush begun only that spring. Before coming out here, Sarah had read articles in Eastern newspapers claiming that Deadwood cabins were springing up faster than teepees on the Little Bighorn. There were accounts of lots being purchased on Monday and by Saturday holding frame buildings open and stocked for business. They looked it! Between these unpainted structures, brush wickiups and canvas tents served as temporary shelters for new arrivals who waited their turn for lumber or logs. Adding to the haphazard appearance of the town were the sluice boxes that poked their long snouts down the hillsides into the creeks, looking like giraffes with their feet splayed and their heads dipped to drink.

Sarah walked the length of Main Street, whose only spots of color shone from the shingles of newcomers heralding their practices and products: butchers, lawyers, doctors, a second hotel (The Custer), assayers, gambling halls (the Montana Club and the Chicago Room proving to be two of the largest buildings in town, filling the full size of their lots—which she estimated at twenty-five by one hundred feet— and boasting signs saying their doors never closed); gunsmiths, barbers, brewers, saloons (she lost count of these after thirteen); bakery, hardware and, of course, the badlands. As she had feared: everything for the adventuring male, but nothing for his lady. Not even a single mercantile store.

The two theaters, however, offered the promise of refinement, though by daylight the Langrishe proved to have wooden walls and a canvas roof! The liberty pole down on the corner of Main and Gold Street gave evidence that the country's centennial had been celebrated in some way on the Fourth of July. Also encouraging was the fact that someone had begun constructing what appeared to be wooden water ditches to convey water from some unseen spring to the town for domestic use.

Already at seven-thirty Deadwood was busy. Everywhere Sarah went, men's heads snapped around for a second look. Some of their mouths dropped open. Some flushed. Others mechanically doffed their hats. Along the creek men were working with cradles over open placer mines. All-night gamblers stumbled from the gaming houses with bags beneath their eyes. From the bakery came the smell of bread baking, making Sarah almost light-headed from hunger. Wranglers were hitching up horses at a livery stable. Out in front of a miners' supply store, a man with the longest arms Sarah had ever seen was hanging out gold pans on an overhead wooden grid where the breeze set them tinging like glockenspiels. Up the street she discovered a bathhouse—a bathhouse! she rejoiced. In the empty lot beside it two men were lighting a fire under an enormous black pot. She paused and watched awhile, coveting the idea of hot water—enough hot water to submerge oneself in. She was surprised when she saw them drop clothing into the pot and begin stirring it with long sticks.

"Good morning!" she called.

The pair turned and reacted like all the others, gaping as if she were an apparition.

"Good morning," they chorused after an awed pause.

"Are you a laundry or a bathhouse?"

"Neither, ma'am. We sell rags," said the shorter of the two.

She would need rags; there was always ink around a printing press.

"Oh, wonderful. That's what you're boiling there?"

"Yes, ma'am. The miners they come into the bathhouses carrying new clothes and they leave their old ones behind. Same up at the whore-hou—" His buddy punched him with an elbow. "Ah, up at the bad-lands, that is, if you'll excuse our saying so. We pick them up free and delouse them and sell them again."

"How enterprising. I'll most certainly be one of your customers. Well, have a nice day, gentlemen."

"Wait!" they shouted when she turned away.

She paused and faced them.

"Who are you? That is, I mean to say . . . I'm Henry Tanby and this is Skitch Johnson." Tanby, the shorter of the two, removed his hat and held it in both hands over his chest. He had the features and neckless build of a bulldog.

She approached them and shook hands. "Mr. Tanby, Mr. Johnson." Johnson was young, skinny, pimply-faced, and apparently tongue-tied.

"I'm Sarah Merritt from St. Louis. I'll be printing the first issue of my newspaper as soon as I locate my press."

"Newspaper. Well, I'll be. You come in on the stage?"

"Last night."

"Well, I'll be," Tanby repeated, then seemed to go blank, smiling into her face, forgetting to don his hat. Finally he remembered. Johnson was still standing with a gaping smile. Tanby nudged him in the ribs. "He's got no manners. Gawks like he never seen no woman before. Course the truth is we don't see many of 'em up here in the gulch."

"So I've heard." A self-struck woman would have reveled in all the attention she was getting; it merely amazed Sarah, who'd never before in her life made heads turn. "Well, I must move on, gentlemen."

As she turned away Tanby called, "You need anything, just ask! Always happy to help a lady!"

"Thank you, Mr. Tanby! Nice to meet you, Mr. Johnson."

Johnson came out of his stupor long enough to return her wave. Walking away, Sarah felt a fresh flash of surprise at receiving so much male attention. She was honest enough, however, to realize the underlying reason for it. She'd known there was a dearth of females in the goldfields, but had never guessed its extent. It put her in a rather advantageous position, she admitted, and decided she wasn't above utilizing that advantage when necessary. As a single woman in a new town, inaugurating a newspaper, there'd be times when she'd need help, guidance and support. Tanby, Johnson, Reese and Bradigan: she would remember the names of those who'd shown overt friendliness.

The town, she learned during her walk, held several faro banks but only one for use by the general public. She found it with no difficulty. It went by the very high-sounding name of Pinkney and Stahl's Merchants and Miners Emporium of Gold, Bills and Exchange. Its verbose marquee also boasted, "Greenbacks Exchanged . . . Loans Given . . . The Only Large Sized Iron Safe in the Diggings . . . We Take Gold Dust for Safe Keeping." She was waiting when its doors opened at the odd hour of eight-twenty. A short, overfed man dressed in a pressed black suit and four-in-hand tie unlocked the double-paned door and his eyebrows flew up when he saw her outside.

"Whu—am I seeing things?" He was bald and pink as a June plum.

"Not at all. I've come to cash some Wells Fargo certificates."

"Well, come in, come in." He ushered her in solicitously and extended his hand. "My name is Elias Pinkney, at your service."

He fixed her with an eager smile, though he was forced to look up to do it.

"I'm Sarah Merritt."

"Miss Merritt . . . well, well . . .."

Again she was compelled to extricate her hand. Pinkney seemed to follow the hand as she withdrew it, moving so close she took a step backward. "I must say you're a welcome sight. A welcome sight."

Did he repeat everything?

"I've just arrived in town and I need some gold dust so I can buy a meal."

"You don't need gold dust at all if you'll allow me to buy you breakfast. I'd be honored. Most honored."

His undisguised pressing startled Sarah, who was totally unversed in rejecting men's advances. She groped for a gracious refusal. "Thank you, Mr. Pinkney, but I have a lot of business to transact today. I'm going to be printing Deadwood's first newspaper."

"A newspaper. That *is* good news. Very good news. In that case, I could introduce you up and down the street."

"Thank you, but I don't want to take up your valuable time. And I do need gold dust, if you'd be so kind."

"Of course, of course. Right this way."

She saw immediately that Mr. Pinkney, in spite of his overt interest in her, was a shrewd businessman. She exchanged one of her Wells Fargo certificates for gold dust, which she accepted in a buckskin pouch, Mr. Pinkney having extracted the customary five percent for the bank's fee; she deposited the remaining certificates in the bank safe, agreeing to pay a rate of one percent for the first month's service. Before leaving, she struck a barter with Pinkney whereby in the future she would have the use of his safe without charge and he would have free advertisement in her newspaper.

"So you're a woman with a good head on her shoulders."

"I hope so, Mr. Pinkney. Thank you."

She would have foregone a parting handshake, but he forced the issue, extending his hand first in a small breach of etiquette. Once he captured her hand, he retained it beyond the point of discretion, looking up at her from his diminutive height.

"The invitation to dinner stands open, Miss Merritt. You'll be hearing from me soon. Very soon."

With gold dust in hand at last, she escaped, hurrying, breathing easier once she was out of the bank. What a repugnant little man. Rich, no doubt, and wearing fresh laundry, but so certain that his money and social position would woo the first single woman to hit town. She found herself relieved that she'd been wearing gloves during all that handshaking.

With her stomach growling, she stopped at the first eating establishment she could find, a crude frame building called Ruckner's Meals. The place was filled with men who, by turns, stared, murmured, whistled, passed close to her chair for no good reason, doffed hats, spoke in undertones with their heads close together and chuckled. None of them, however, settled in the tables adjacent to hers, but left a ring of unoccupied chairs with her highlighted in its center.

A boy of perhaps sixteen came to take her order, grinning all the while.

" 'Morning, ma'am. What can I get for you?"

"Good morning. Could you fry a beefsteak so early in the day? I haven't eaten since yesterday noon."

"No beef, ma'am—sorry. Not much space for the beef to graze around here. We've got buffalo, though. It's just as good."

She ordered a buffalo steak, fried potatoes, coffee and biscuits, realizing every man in the building heard her do so. After the boy went away she donned a tiny pair of oval spectacles, opened her notebook, extracted a pen and a vial of ink from her organdy pouch and, trying to ignore the fact that she was being openly ogled, began composing her first article for the *Deadwood Chronicle*.

"$1.50 In Gold Dust Welcomes Editor of Deadwood Chronicle." In it she paid credit to all who had been solicitous in helping her the previous evening.

She was still writing when her food arrived.

" 'Scuse me, ma'am." A suspendered man stopped at her elbow with a platter of sizzling meat that smelled heavenly.

She glanced up and closed her notebook, removing it from the tabletop. "Oh, excuse *me*. Mmmm . . . that looks delicious."

"Hope you like the buffalo. You could sure have beef if we had it." He set down the plate and remained at her elbow while she capped her ink and removed her spectacles. "My name's Teddy Ruckner, ma'am. I own this place." He was thirtyish, blond, dimpled and handsome in a boyish way. He had bright blue eyes and a likable smile that never wavered from her face.

"Mr. Ruckner." She extended a hand. "I'm Sarah Merritt. I've come to Deadwood to publish a newspaper."

When their hands parted he remained, wiping his palms on his thighs and nodding at her notebook. "Figgered you for a smart one when I saw you writing. It's sure good to see a woman around here. Where are you setting up business?"

"I'll have to locate a place. For now I'm staying at the Grand Central."

"There's one boardinghouse. Loretta Roundtree's. You could try there."

"Thank you, perhaps I will."

She picked up her fork, hoping he'd leave—her stomach positively ached—but he lingered, asking her several more questions, until she began to feel additionally conspicuous as the focus of his overeager attention. Though she was not a woman prone to blushing, she blushed. Finally he realized he was delaying her meal and backed away. "Well, I'd better let you eat. Anything else you want, you just let me know. There's plenty more coffee where that came from."

She was in the restaurant for the better part of an hour and during that time not one customer left. More came in, however; perhaps two dozen more—quietly, unobtrusively, slipping in like children to see a sleeping infant, pretending to pay her no mind when it was obvious the word had spread she was there and they'd all come in to give her a gander. The chairs filled and still they came, standing to drink their coffee while in an immediate circle about Sarah the chairs remained vacant. Their furtive glances made her feel dissected. She kept her eyes on her plate and the article, on which she continued to write as she ate. Others—she could feel their eyes—studied her more overtly, probably assessing her as the sister of "Eve" from up at Rose's. Her coffee cup couldn't get a quarter empty before Teddy Ruckner refilled it: the only one brave enough to venture near her. When her plate was empty he came again with a piece of dried-apple pie. "On the house," he said, "and it's the house's pleasure—the whole meal, as a matter of fact."

"Oh Mr. Ruckner, I couldn't possibly accept without paying."

"No, I insist. You're about the most welcome thing we've seen around here since the last piece of fresh fruit came in. Enjoy the pie."

Self-conscious once more at being the center of attention, she concentrated on her pie. She had eaten half the slice when she heard repeated greetings of "Mornin', Marshal."

"Mornin', boys," came the reply as the newcomer moved through the crowd. He shuffled to a stop on the far side of Sarah's table, taking a stance with his feet set wide and his hands on his hipbones. Even with her eyes downcast, Sarah saw his black trousers and the gun at his hip and sensed who stood before her.

She raised her eyes slowly to the silver star on his jacket, the rusty mustache, the black cowboy hat he declined to remove. In the clear light of day he was freckled as a tiger lily—she'd never been partial to either mustaches or freckles. He looked strong as a mule and about as pretty, with gray eyes and that notch at the end of his nose. She supposed some women might find it boyishly attractive. She, however, was put off by everything about the man, starting with his effrontery.

"Mr. Campbell," she said, cool, even as her blood began to rise.

He touched his hat brim. "Miss Merritt. Just wondering what all the hullabaloo was about in here."

"Hullabaloo?"

"Anytime the men start flocking to one spot it's my job to find out what's drawing them. Usually it's a fistfight."

Her blush continued glowing, fired by the realization that the marshal of Deadwood frequented its whorehouses, had carnal knowledge of her sister, and had offered to buy the services of Sarah herself last night within an hour after her arrival in town. Distasteful and cocksure, he stood before her with his Colt .45 strapped to his hip, daring her to make something of it.

"So it's Marshal Campbell, is it?"

"That's right."

She laid down her fork and met him eye to eye, speaking loudly enough to be heard in every corner of the room. "Is it common out here on the frontier for the town marshal to frequent its whorehouses instead of trying to shut them down?"

The big ox hadn't the grace to be affronted. Instead, he threw back his head and laughed while half the room laughed with him. When he'd finished, he pushed his hat to the back of his head and hooked a thumb over his holster belt.

"You're a regular little spitfire, aren't you?"

Incensed by his cavalier attitude and his amused eyes, she removed her spectacles and rose to her feet. "If you'll excuse me, Marshal, I've got a newspaper to get started." She gathered her belongings, stood beside her chair and raised her voice. "Gentlemen," she announced to the room at large, "my name is Sarah Merritt. I've just arrived from St. Louis and I plan to publish a newspaper here in Deadwood. I'm looking for two things, and I'd be very grateful if any of you could help me find them. First, I need a building to either rent or buy—preferably one made of wood instead of canvas. Secondly, I need news. No editor can print a newspaper without it, so please . . . feel free to stop me wherever you see me and tell me what's happening up and down Deadwood Gulch. I want the *Deadwood Chronicle* to be *your* newspaper."

When she finished speaking, someone in the far corner cried, "What do you say, boys, how's about a welcome for the little lady?" A cheer rose from dozens of male voices (all but Campbell's) and at last they closed in, offering their hands to be shaken, introducing themselves—

men with names like Shorty and Baldy and Colorado Dick and Potato Creek Johnny; men with broken teeth and unwashed clothes and hands as rough as the terrain they mined; men with tintypes in their pockets and wives back home; women-starved men offering obeisance.

They told her where to find Craven Lee about available property, Patrick Bradigan about the $1.50 he'd loaned her, and where to find her printing press, which had arrived by mule train and was stored at the freight office run by a man named Dutch Van Aark.

Throughout their welcome, Marshal Campbell stood by observing, leveling her with his distracting watchfulness, speaking one last time as she headed for the door.

"See me about getting a license for that newspaper of yours."

She flounced out disregarding him, thinking, *I'll see you in hell first, Campbell!*

She began with Craven Lee, who'd laid out the lots for the town and acted as its realtor. She found him in a log cabin on Main Street, but learned he could do nothing for her at the moment. The list of prospective buyers, it seemed, was as long as a Norwegian winter, and the best he could advise was for her to stay where she was. At least she had a roof overhead and a bed at night.

She went next to find Bradigan at the Buffalo Hump Saloon, where he had begun his morning imbibing to ward off the trembles from the previous night's round. She marched in and once again made heads turn—all but Bradigan's. He was facing the bar with a glass in his hand.

"Good morning, Mr. Bradigan," she said behind his shoulder.

He cranked his head around slowly before removing his elbows from the bar and straightening in the bone-by-bone way of the seasoned drunk.

"Good morning, Miss Merritt." She was surprised he remembered. He aimed for his hat but never quite touched it.

"I owe you a dollar and a half in gold dust." She found her pouch and tugged at the drawstring.

He watched her with bloodshot eyes, digesting her message for some time before replying in a heavy Irish accent that came as slow as a spring thaw. "No, pretty colleen. Mine was the lucky pouch. 'Twas my pleasure, most sortainly."

Not by the longest stretch of the imagination did Sarah consider herself a pretty colleen. "Mr. Bradigan, please . . ." she returned quietly, flashing a glance at the bartender and several patrons who were watching and listening. "I pay my debts, and last night I wasn't altogether sure you knew your money was being taken."

He lifted a forefinger, gave a wobbly smile and turned back to his glass of whiskey. Hoisting it, he saluted her. "Welcome to Deadwood, Miss Sarah Merritt."

Realizing she would not get Bradigan to accept her gold, she handed the pouch to the bartender. "Here. Please take out a dollar fifty's worth and buy Mr. Bradigan whatever he wants."

Before she left, she said, "Thank you again, Mr. Bradigan." He faced her foursquare and silently bowed over his whiskey glass.

It was one o'clock by the time she stepped back onto the street. One o'clock and hopefully the residents of Rose's were up. Sarah headed toward the badlands with great trepidation, doffing her jacket and carrying it on her arm. It had warmed considerably and flies buzzed above the dung in the streets. A constant stream of wagons moved up and down Main Street competing with the foot traffic. Of the dozens of faces she saw, none were female. She began to understand why both she and girls of her sister's ilk were such attractions in Deadwood.

At Rose's the front door was unlocked—a surprise. She'd expected to have to find a rear entrance or bang on the door until her knuckles were bruised to get an answer. Instead, it opened at her touch and she entered the same dim, smoky room as last night. Not a soul was in it. The smell of stale whiskey and unwashed cuspidors permeated the place, accompanied by the the strong sulfuric stench she'd detected last night. The room was unlit. The red tassled draperies were drawn against the noon sun with only a thin triangle of light filtering in at the bottom where the tassles brushed the floor. In the gloom, Sarah looked around, observing what she'd only glimpsed last night: the picture of a fleshy nude reclining on a fainting bench with a veil twined between her thighs and her private hair showing; a sign on the wall with a finger pointing toward the hall, saying BATHS REQUIRED; another with the heading MENU. She moved up close and read it.

THE BATH
THE TRIP
THE FRENCHY
THE HALF & HALF
THE SHOW DATE
THE OUT DATE

Startled, Sara realized the menu had nothing to do with food. Feeling debauched, she looked away.

A door to the left of the stairs stood open and she proceeded through it, to a long hall with an opening at the far end where voices, window light, clinking dishes and the smell of food announced a dining room. As she moved toward it, the sulfuric smell grew stronger. She reached its source—a room off the hall to the left, with a huge copper bathtub, wooden barrels of water, an iron stove for heating it and damp wood floors. Her revulsion freshened when she realized the required baths were laced with carbolic acid . . . for delousing.

With pinched nostrils she continued toward the far end of the hall, where she stopped just short of the doorway and listened.

". . . could tell he never did it before. The bulge in his pants was bigger than a ham bone, so I says to him, I bet you hung like a bull, sugar. Get that big guy out here and let's have a look at him."

"Did he?"

"Too scared. Just stands there with his Adam's apple jumpin' and his face redder than a branding iron so I had to take control. I take his hand and put it on hisself, just to see what he do and he—"

Sarah stepped to the doorway. "Excuse me."

The story stopped. Everyone turned to stare at Sarah in the doorway.

Adelaide sat at a table with four other women—Flossie among them—wearing a royal blue dressing gown and eating chicken stew and dumplings. At a cast-iron stove on the far wall a fat woman tended a coffeepot. The black woman who'd been speaking let her glance move from Sarah to Eve and back.

"Adelaide, I'd like to talk to you."

Adelaide's face hardened. "What are you doing here! I told you last night I didn't want to see you. Now, get out." She resumed her eating.

"I've come a thousand miles to find you and I'm not getting out until we've had a chance to talk."

"Flossie." Adelaide signaled with her fork. "Get rid of her."

The Indian woman pushed back her chair and Sarah experienced another bolt of fright. But her father had taught her a newspaper-woman's first qualification must be courage. "Now, just a minute!" she said firmly, entering the room with her heart clunking, pointing a finger at Addie. "I'm not one of your customers you can have bounced onto the street. I'm your sister, and I'm here because I care about you. You can have me thrown out or probably beaten if you wish, but I'm not going away. Our father is dead and I've brought you your share of the inheritance. I've also brought his printing press and I'm setting up business in Deadwood, so you can either talk to me now or have me plaguing you persistently. Which will it be?"

Her show of bravado stopped Flossie and emboldened Sarah, who pinned her sister with an unremitting gaze. When Addie stared back stubbornly Sarah said, "Furthermore, I have a message for you from Robert. In that regard you have three choices. I can deliver it to you in front of your friends, or print it in the first issue of the newspaper, or you can take me to someplace where we can talk privately. Which will it be?"

Adelaide set her teeth, threw down her fork and lurched to her feet, rocking her chair onto its back legs. "All right, dammit, but five minutes and that's all! Then you either get out of here under your own steam or Flossie will help you out. Is that understood?" She stalked out the kitchen door, down the hall and up the stairs with her royal blue wrapper flapping, leaving Sarah to follow.

Before leaving the kitchen, Sarah pointed a finger at Flossie's nose and said, "You ever lay a hand on me again and you'll be sorry."

Upstairs, Addie led her along a skinny dark hall into the third room on the left. The door slammed behind them and Addie swung to face Sarah, her arms crossed tightly beneath her breasts.

"All right, make it quick."

Since temerity had worked so far, Sarah tried a little more. "If this is the room where you do your work, I refuse to speak to you in it."

"This is my own room. I work next door." She nodded sideways. "Now get on with it because I'm getting mighty impatient with you, big sister or not!"

"This is where you live?" Sarah surveyed the grim little room with its single cot, a curtain of the roughest unbleached muslin on the window, theater posters tacked to the rough walls. There was a rug, a coverlet, a cheap dressing table, mirror and one chair, a commode stand, and on the floor beside the door a china washbasin. A line of hooks on the wall held a collection of sleazy, bright-colored costumes much like the one Addie had been wearing last night. The only objects to warm the room in any way were some faded paper roses on the wall and, on the bed, a stuffed cat made of red, shaggy fox fur. The sight of it plucked at Sarah's heart: it was the only hint of the Adelaide she remembered: as children they'd never been without a pet cat.

"I see you still have a cat," she remarked with a reminiscent smile, shifting her regard to Addie, who raised one eyebrow and kept her arms crossed.

"Say what you have to say."

What Sarah wanted to say was, Why? Why this place? This profession? This apparent hatred for me, who never did anything but be the mother you never had? But she'd get no answers yet; that was clear.

"Very well, Addie." She spoke quietly, all traces of harshness gone.

She opened her organdy pouch. "Father died last spring. I sold the house and the furniture and the Market Street Building. All I kept was the press and his desk and the few things I'd need to set up business. Here is your half of the money."

"I don't want his money!"

"But Addie, you could leave this place."

"I don't want to leave this place."

"How could you not want to leave this place? It's horrible."

"If that's all you came for, you can take his money and get out."

Sarah studied her sister sadly. "He never got over your leaving, Addie."

"I don't want to hear about him!" Addie insisted. "I told you I don't give a damn about my father!"

In spite of Addie's virulence Sarah forced herself to continue. "He contracted the bronzed disease about a year after you left. At first I only noticed that he was looking a little feebler, but then his mind became weak, his appetite grew capricious and in time his digestion ceased functioning. By the end he was unable to hold anything down and he suffered an extreme amount of pain. The doctors treated him with everything that's been rumored to help—glycerine, chloroform, chloride of iron—but Father's debility only grew worse until he shriveled up like a baby bird. He was always a proud man; it was very hard on him. I was managing the paper alone by then. Before he died, he made me promise I'd try to find you. He wanted us to be together, as we should be." With added tenderness Sarah said "Addie, you're my sister."

"An accident of birth." Addie turned away and stared out the window.

"Why did you run away?" When Addie refused to answer, Sarah entreated, "Was it something I did? . . . Please, Addie, talk to me."

"Women who work in places like this don't talk to outside women. You'd best learn that."

Sarah studied Addie's shoulders for a long time before asking softly, "Was it something Robert did? He's wondered just as I have."

The back of Addie's hair was coarse as boar's bristles, uncombed, showing sections of her skull where her natural blond showed like the white at the throat of a purple iris. The sight of it brought a sorrowful expression to Sarah's eyes.

"You hurt Robert so badly, Addie. He thought you loved him."

Addie said, "I wish you'd go." The choler had left her voice; it was as quiet as that of a doctor asking a visitor to leave the bedside of one gravely ill.

After a stretch of silence Sarah said softly, "Robert has never married, Addie. That's what he wanted you to know."

Facing the window, with her arms crossed stubbornly, Adelaide Merritt felt threatened by tears, but refused to let them form. Behind her, she heard Sarah move toward the door, heard the doorknob turn and the hinges squeak. She knew Sarah was standing in the open door studying her, but she refused to turn around.

"I haven't found a building for the press yet," Sarah said, "but I'm staying at the Grand Central. You can come there anytime to talk to me. Will you do that, Addie?"

Addie gave no indication she'd heard.

Sarah studied her sister's blue wrapper and felt an immense clot of sorrow settle in her throat. On this mortal coil there was no other blood relative than Addie, and Sarah needed very badly to touch her once. They had sprung from the same womb and been sired by the same father. She crossed to Addie, laid a hand on her shoulder blade and felt it stiffen.

"If not, I'll come back again soon. Goodbye, Addie."

When the door closed, Addie stood a long time, staring out the window at a dry buff ledge where a poor misguided kinnikinnik bush had taken root far from its usual habitat. Its few berries were withering from waxy white to brown, unlike Addie—poor misguided Addie—who had gone from a healthy brown to a waxy white, living within walls where the sun never touched her skin, shut away from decent people, a prisoner by choice if not by circumstance. She had changed her name, and her hair color and her mode of dress and her persuasions. She had run half the length of the country, hoping never again to confront a soul from home. Now here came Sarah to unearth the past with all its promise and sordidness and secret guilt. To bring word of Robert, that wholesome young man of the clean skin and the sinless spirit who had seen in Addie only what he wanted to see. Robert . . . who had kissed her once with lamblike innocence . . . Robert . . . who had not married.

Tears were a luxury Adelaide had given up years ago. What good were tears? Could they change the past? Could they heal the present? Could they alter the future?

Blinking away the few that had formed, refusing to reach up and dry even the corners of her eyes, Addie dove onto her bed and curled her body around the fox-hair cat, clenching up until her knees nearly met her forehead. With her face against the furry stuffed animal she squeezed her eyelids tightly shut. Her bare, dirty feet were overlapped, her toes were curled and her stomach muscles quivering. For minutes only her fingers moved in the cat's fur. Then, still coiled, she made a fist and drove it into the mattress. Again. And again. And again.

CHAPTER 3

IVE minutes after leaving Rose's, Sarah found Dutch Van Aark's freight office. It was located in a log building which served as a miner's supply, grocery and, today, a post office. A corpulent man with a walrus mustache was serving a cluster of customers gathered beneath a sign announcing, LETTERS—JUST ARRIVED—25C. When the group became aware of Sarah's presence they parted to let her near the counter.

Van Aark saw her and smiled. He had yellow teeth and a bun-sized lower lip that drooped, exposing his gums.

"I'll bet you're Miss Merritt and you've come for your printing press."

"Yes, I am."

"Well, it's here, out back. Come in on a ox train couple weeks ago along with all the rest of your stuff. I'm Dutch Van Aark."

He introduced her around and explained, when she inquired, about the mail. It had come in on yesterday's stage and since the town had no post office, anyone could buy the mail from the stage driver, then sell it to the recipients for a small profit. She recorded the interesting tidbit in her notebook along with the correct spelling of Van Aark's name. While she was writing, a woman entered the store—wide-beamed, with a workaday face, around thirty-five years old, wearing a homemade dress and cotton bonnet. It took little more than a five-second glance to ascertain she was a typical housewife.

The two women smiled at one another like long-lost cousins.

"Mrs. Dawkins, come in and meet the newest lady in town."

Sarah moved toward Mrs. Dawkins and the two clasped hands. "Mrs. Dawkins and her husband run the bakery here in town."

"Hello, I'm Emma Dawkins."

"And I'm Sarah Merritt."

Their joy in meeting was genuine and the two exchanged a flurry of questions and answers. The Dawkins lived above their bakery and had three children. They had come to Deadwood from Iowa, leaving their families behind. Emma Dawkins was in the freight office today, hoping to find a letter from her sister back home.

"No letter, Mrs. Dawkins, I'm sorry," Van Aark told her. "But now that Miss Merritt is here, maybe we'll have more than letters to read." After the exchange of pleasantries the entire troop went outside to inspect Sarah's printing press. They found it in a wagon, covered by canvas, broken down into pieces, the smaller of them crated but the largest—the frame—standing free, lashed to the side of the wagon with leather straps.

When the canvas was folded back Sarah touched it reverently—her father's old Washington Hand Press—a thousand pounds of steel on which she'd learned her trade side by side with him. With it were his massive rolltop desk and packing crates containing the type cases, furniture cabinet, newsprint, ink and other paraphernalia she'd packed that summer in St. Louis. She counted the crates and found them all accounted for. Her eyes took on a glow of excitement. "I'll need a block and tackle to unload it tomorrow."

"I've got those in the store," Van Aark replied.

"And a tent, and a lantern and a few other things. If I make you a list can you have them ready in the morning?"

"You bet, Miss Merritt."

After the arrangements were made, Sarah spent a long while talking with Emma Dawkins, learning a great deal about the town and its residents and accepting an invitation to have supper with the Dawkins family the following night. Upon leaving Emma, she looked up the boardinghouse of Loretta Roundtree, located on a path that angled up the west side of the gulch where the buildings were perched on narrow terraces with their rear ends buried in the mountain. Though Mrs. Roundtree, bluff and big-faced, said she'd have loved to rent a room to Sarah if only for the female company, she regretfully turned her away, claiming she had a waiting list of over fifty.

Sarah made a note to that effect, and spent another hour walking up and down Main Street asking questions and taking additional notes on the status of the town before returning to her hotel room in the late afternoon.

There, once again she took out pen and ink, drew her bedside table near the window and sat down to keep a promise.

Dakota Territory.
September 27, 1876
Dear Robert,

I take pen in hand as I promised I would when I arrived in Deadwood, which I did yesterday. This is a particularly sordid settlement which, like a boy of fourteen, is outgowing its breeches and experiencing growing pains. If all is true that I've heard, the population of this gulch and all its tributaries is presently around 25,000.

Many of the men are rich, but more have not struck the big gold. These struggle along doing whatever jobs they can find. Others are now mining high-grade quartz, pulverizing it by hand using mortar and pestle. I have thought how odd that a town so rich resorts to such archaic methods.

But enough about the commercial aspects of Deadwood. You asked me to tell you if and how I found Adelaide, my dear sister and your remembered sweetheart.

She is here in Deadwood, but how my heart breaks to tell you what I must. Oh Robert, I fear our hopes for her were optimistic. She is not the same winsome young girl we last saw when she was sixteen. Dear Robert, do fortify yourself for a cruel blow which I so extremely regret delivering. Your fear was that I would find Adelaide married, but the truth is much worse. My sister has become a prostitute. Here in Deadwood they call her kind upstairs girls, soiled doves, similar euphemisms, but the unvarnished truth is as I said. Adelaide has become a prostitute.

She has changed her name to Eve and works for a procuress named Rose Hossiter, an uncivil and odious bawd who raises shivers along my arms as I force myself to recall her. Our Adelaide has blackened her hair, kohled her eyes, rouged her lips and allowed herself to grow obese during her prodigal years. I shall not torment you with details of her reprehensible mode of dress. These external changes are, however, only manifestations of the inner, more disturbing metamorphosis from the darling we once knew to a woman of granite expression and stone heart.

Though she has resisted my every overture, I will be here for Adelaide and will make every attempt to win her over and with the power of the printed word, to close down these dens of vice and corruption that turn decent, wholesome young girls like Addie into the poor, misguided, morally impoverished souls who deserve our pity.

I grieve for your disillusionment and sorrow upon receiving this letter, and for the loss of your dreams which you have held so long and faithfully, but in all earnestness, I implore you to move forward with your life, find some deserving young woman worthy of your devotion and, of Addie, to carry the memory, not the dream.

I shall post this by the Pony Express, which is much faster than the Cheyenne Stage, whose service is still only bi-weekly into Deadwood, and hope that it reaches you in all due haste. May your spirits not languish long, Robert, for you are too kind and good a man to suffer so unjust a sentence.

Yours in friendship,
Sarah Merritt

After she'd folded and sealed the letter she sat a long time, despondent, looking out her third-story window in the direction of Rose's. She thought she made out the tip of the building's false front, though Addie's window faced one side.

Oh Addie, you could have had such a fine life with Robert. How I envied you his favor, but he had eyes for no one but you. Even after you left, his mourning allowed him to see no other woman. You could be married to him now. Instead, there you are, in that horrid place, having run off just like our mother did, abandoning Father and me. After the hundreds of times you and I talked about the hurt she caused us, I could not believe you'd do the same.

The memories of those first days after her mother's abandonment were still vivid to Sarah. She had been sleeping soundly on a gray morning in November when her father, instead of her mother, had come in to awaken her for school.

"Where's Mama?" she'd asked, rubbing her eyes, and he'd told her Mama had gone away to visit her sister in Boston.

"In Boston?" There had never been talk of any aunt in Boston. "When will she come back?"

"Oh, I'm sure she'll be back in a week or so."

But a week had passed, then another; a month, and Addie started wetting the bed again, and crying for their mother at bedtime, and Sarah stood for hours looking out the window up Lamply Street, watching for a glimpse of the familiar dark-haired figure. A woman named Mrs. Smith was hired as their temporary housekeeper, but stayed on, and Father grew dour and his back became bowed, though he was still a very young man. Not until Sarah was twelve did she learn the truth from Mrs. Smith, who told her one day in the kitchen where they were pickling beets. "Your mother won't be back, Sarah," Mrs. Smith had said. "It's time you knew the truth. She ran off with a man named Paxton—Amery Paxton—who worked for your father as a typesetter. Where they went, nobody knows, but she left a note saying she loved Paxton and was going off to marry him. Your father never heard from her again, and of course he's never remarried, because he has no idea whether it would be bigamy or not."

Sarah had started collecting words that day, an acquaintanceship that would become the backbone of her life's work. *Bigamy,* she had entered in a blue-lined journal, *when one woman is married to two men. I know now why my mother left us.*

To this day Sarah could not eat beets or tolerate the smell of vinegar.

Sitting in her dreary bedroom in the Grand Central Hotel, she looked down at another journal, filled with notes she had taken since her arrival in Deadwood. She sighed and drew out a clean, loose sheet of paper. When things are troubling you, her father had often said, write.

She wrote, laboring under an intense commitment to create as accurate a picture of today's Deadwood as it was possible to paint with words. The inaugural issue of her paper would undoubtedly be preserved for all time. In a town where history was being made, this was bound to be true.

She worked until midnight, composing the articles for her first issue of the *Deadwood Chronicle.* Along with the one she'd begun in the restaurant at breakfast, the headlines included, MAIL ARRIVES AT VAN AARK'S STORE; CHEYENNE STAGE—DAILY SERVICE TO DEADWOOD EXPECTED BY OCTOBER; TELEGRAPH LINE COMPLETED AS FAR AS HILL CITY; SCARCITY OF WOMEN PREVAILS IN DEADWOOD; GRASSHOPPERS STILL PRESENT IN MINNESOTA; SEVEN BUILDINGS UNDER CONSTRUCTION ON DEADWOOD MAIN STREET; MSS. BELDING & MYERS CONSTRUCTING WATER CONVEYANCE DITCH FROM WHITETAIL TO THE HEAD OF GOLD RUN; PROSPECT ON #82 WHITEWOOD: $200 PER DAY. On her own behalf she composed a want ad announcing that the editor of the *Deadwood Chronicle* was looking for a place to set up her business and to lodge. But she worked the longest over an editorial entitled "Close the Heathen Brothels of the West." It was lengthy and impassioned and ended by saying, "We must purge this city of this scandal and bring the keepers of these houses under the lash of the law. But how shall we do so when the very representative of the law itself is frequenting the fair and frail? Surely public opinion can be brought to bear against this source of moral and physical disease."

By the time Sarah removed her glasses her eyes burned and her shoulders ached. Addie would be angry when she read the editorial, but that was a risk Sarah had decided she must take when she made her decision to attack the disease rather than the symptom. Shut down the houses and you shut down the prostitutes. Not a popular stand, given the conspicuous acceptance of the brothels, but a journalist's call—Isaac Merritt had taught his daughter—was not to be popular, but to be effective in forcing change where change was necessary.

In the morning Sarah stepped outside to discover there'd been rain— both a bane and a boon, for though the streets had turned to Dakota gumbo, the absence of dust, to a printer, was the greatest blessing of all. She was surprised to find she'd missed the storm, which had left tree limbs in the street, but a blue sky above and the promise of a perfect autumn day. The smell of the newly moistened dung in the street, however, had intensiifed.

She picked her way around it and posted her letter at the Pony Express office, then headed for Van Aark's store, gathering up an entourage on the way. They followed like children after the Pied Piper: Henry Tanby, Skitch Johnson, Teddy Ruckner, Shorty Reese and finally Dutch himself, all of them eager to help her move her printing press.

"Where do you aim to put it?" Dutch asked as he hitched a horse to the wagon.

"Follow me," she said and led them to the spot she'd chosen beneath an immense ponderosa pine whose bole was imposing enough to have put a gooseneck in Main Street down near the Number 10 Saloon: public property, she was sure, yet protected from traffic by the tree trunk itself and shaded by its branches.

"Here," Sarah proclaimed, looking up.

"Here?"

"We need a branch sturdy enough to support the weight of the press. That one will do."

"On the street?" Van Aark's lower gums showed pink as his mouth hung open.

"Until I can find an office, yes, this will do fine."

"But it's practically the middle of the street!"

"Public property though, right? And am I not the public? Are not you and I—all of us—the public? Who does a newspaper serve if not the public? Now if you'll help me, gentlemen, I'll have your first edition thumping off the press before nightfall."

They raised a cheer while a crowd gathered to watch Skitch Johnson swing himself from Henry Tanby's shoulders into the tree. Within minutes the block and tackle were mounted and the rope was reeved. As it dropped down through the sheave, eager hands waited to catch the steel hook and attach it to the frame of the printing press. The frame swung up and others leveled the earth beneath with flat spades and laid down a square plank as a stabilizer. The men strained at the ropes and, piece by piece, the press took shape: legs onto frame, frame onto plank, track onto frame, tympan frame onto track. Sarah gave instructions, lifting her arms to guide the pieces into place, securing them herself with shear pins and bolts. Some shimming was required before the entire setup stood firm and level, but when it did, she demonstrated the ease of operating the machine by cranking the empty bed and lowering the platen one time. Another cheer rose.

"All we need now is type, paper and ink and we'll be in business," Sarah declared.

"How about your tent, Miss Merritt, you want we should set that up, too?"

"I'd be so grateful if you would."

In no time they had her small tent standing taut and inside it her newsprint up off the damp earth. Outside, in bolder light, they uncrated all of her typesetting paraphernalia: furniture font, typecase, composing stick and leather apron. Once it was unearthed and arranged on the packing crates, she glanced around in satisfaction and brushed off her hands. "Thank you so much." She shook hands with each man who had helped. Meanwhile, the crowd had multiplied until it hampered traffic movement in the street. Fascinated, they remained, ogling the press, waiting to see it in operation. "I appreciate the muscle and the goodwill. You've given me a very warm reception, all of you."

"When will the first copy come off the press?" someone shouted.

"Find me another typesetter and I can be rolling ink by noon."

When the crowd failed to disperse, she removed her jacket, rolled up her sleeves and began setting type while they watched. If they had been fascinated before, they were transfixed now. Her right hand moved so fast the onlookers could scarcely follow it with their eyes. Over the years, setting type had become second nature to Sarah, and she did it in whirlwind fashion, often plucking the individual characters from the grid-shaped typecase by feel. She filled the composing stick in a matter of seconds, transferred the block of three lines to a flat tray called a galley, and began again.

Meanwhile, the crowd grew.

Two blocks away, Marshal Noah Campbell sat in his tiny office filling out more stinking licenses. Damn, how he hated paperwork! But when the town government was officially formed two weeks ago he'd agreed to take on all the duties of city marshal as prescribed by the newly drafted ordinances. Among them was the issuing of licenses and the collection of taxes from every company, corporation, business and trade in Deadwood.

Beaudry, Seth W., Gunsmith, he wrote arduously. *$5.00 Licensing Fee, Fourth Quarter, 1876, City of Deadwood.* He sat back, mumbling, scratching his mustache, eyeing his work. Shit and shit twice. Looked like a drunk chicken had walked through the barnyard and across the form. He could handle a gun and a horse and any drunk who wanted to start slinging fists, but a pen and ink had the power to discommode him.

Noah Campbell, he signed, then blew on the ink and added the license to the finished stack. He was dipping his pen to fill in the next one when he heard an ox whip. His head snapped up and he listened. The sound came again. There was no mistaking it, nor the bellowing of the skinners that drifted in through the closed door. Noah dropped his pen and his chair screeched back. In a half-dozen long strides he plucked his black Stetson off the wall hook and reached the door.

Smiling and eager, he stood on his front step, facing the opening of the gulch, watching the lead pair of dun-colored oxen plod toward him while the sound of the ox whips cracked against the gulch walls—*fap! fap! fap!*—like a stack of lumber dropping. They snaked along, ten, twelve, fourteen spans, while the cartwheels creaked and the lead bull-whacker let fly a string of profanity.

"Gee, I said, you sons of a whorin' bitches! You mothers of whorin' bitches! You grandmothers of whorin' bitches! Whaddya need, gun-powder up your asses b'fore you'll move! I'll ram it in with my own fist and light the fuse with this here cigar between my teeth if you don't—"

The rest was lost in the echoing crack of an ox whip as Noah leaned back and laughed. Good old True Blevins, he knew how to put on a show. Kept the whole street laughing every time he pulled in.

Noah and his family—mother, father and brother—had made the trip into the Black Hills beside True's ox train in May. It was a common practice for families unable to hitch up with a wagon train to move through the hostile Indian territory in the company of one of the bullwhackers, who charged a price for the concession.

In Noah's case the price had been worth it: he and True had become friends.

True wouldn't be too happy, though, to hear the news that he'd have to pay a license fee of $3.00 per wagon before he could unload his freight.

The cavalcade drew abreast of Noah and moved on as he waved to True and the drivers of the successive carts. Suddenly, up ahead, he heard the bawling of the oxen and the unmistakable voice of True, cussing fit to kill. The oxcarts halted and there was more cussing down the line. From the step of his office Noah could see a bottleneck up the street near the Number 10 Saloon. Leveling his hat, he leaped into the mud and headed up that way.

"Let me through," he ordered, squeezing between men's shoulders, bumping people aside as he forced his way through the crowd. He saw, even before he reached her, what was causing the traffic jam. None other than Miss Sarah Merritt, with her printing press set up practically in the middle of Main Street. Damn, but the woman was an aggravation. Dressed all in brown, with her sleeves rolled up and her hair in a doughnut, tall and skinny as a bean pole, she was busy dropping type into a metal stick while the onlookers appeared to have settled in for the day, waiting to see history in the making.

"What the Sam Hill is going on here?" He scowled and broke through the edge of the crowd.

Sarah glanced back over her shoulder and kept clicking pieces of type into place.

"I'm laying out a newspaper."

"Have you got a license to do that?"

"A license?"

"I told you yesterday you needed one."

"I'm sorry, I forgot."

"Furthermore, you're holding up a whole freight train and causing a road jam. You'll have to get this stuff out of here."

"I'm on public property, Mr. Campbell."

"You're a public nuisance, Miss Merritt! Now, I said you'll have to move!"

"I'll move when I find a building to rent."

"You'll move now or I'll throw you in jail!"

"This town hasn't got a jail. I've walked every inch of it and I know."

"Maybe not, but it's got an abandoned tunnel dug into the side of the hill behind George Farnum's grocery store and don't think I won't throw you in it—woman or not. I've got a job to do, and I intend, by God, to do it."

"Incarcerating me might prove to be an unpopular move on your part." She glanced at the onlookers. "These men are anxious to see the first copy of their town paper come off the press."

Campbell turned to the crowd. "You men, move on! You're holding up traffic here. Go on now, git!"

A miner with a gold pan and wheelbarrow raised his voice. "You really gonna throw her in jail, Noah?"

"Absolutely, if she doesn't obey the laws."

"But, hell, she's a woman."

"We made the laws for women as well as for men. Now move on so True can lead his train on through!"

He turned back to Sarah, standing with both hands akimbo, his big black Stetson worn level with the earth. "Miss Campbell, I'll give you one hour to get this paraphernalia packed up and moved off the street."

"I'm not in the street." She finally stopped setting type and swung to face him. "I'm beside it on public land."

"If you're not gone in one hour, I'll come back and see to your removal myself. And the *next* time I see you set up for business . . ." He pointed a finger at the bridge of her nose. "You'd better have a city license hanging on your wall."

He pivoted on the ball of one foot and stalked off with his cowboy boots rearranging the mud on the street. Glaring at his back, with her lips curled tight, Sarah gave one frustrated kick that fanned her skirts. Before the brown muslin had settled into place, she was back at her typesetting.

"Show's over, folks," Campbell cried to the malingerers. "Go on back to work." Waiting for the crowd to disperse, he drew a dollar-sized stem-winder from his vest pocket and checked the time: 11:04. He'd be back under that pine tree at four minutes after twelve, and that tall, bullheaded pain in the ass had better have pulled up stakes or there'd be hell to pay. She'd end up in a hole behind Farnum's grocery and he'd have every woman-starved male in the gulch harassing him for arresting her. But what choice did he have? He couldn't have her setting up her business anyplace she damn well pleased, stopping traffic, clogging up the street, thumbing her nose at their ordinances. Let her get by with that and the next thing he knew there'd be fistfights breaking out and men shot. In a town that lacked women the way this one did, it was bound to happen sooner or later. It might anyway, even after she moved her rig. Any way he cut it, Campbell realized he stood to look like a heel for stopping Sarah Merritt from printing the town's first newspaper. Sonofabitch, this was going to get sticky.

The crowd began breaking up.

Stalking toward the lead oxcart, Noah faced his next unpleasant task. "True!" he bellowed, reaching the bullwhacker, "True, I've got to hold you up a minute."

True stopped his freight wagon and spit a stream of tobacco juice into the mud, then swiped his stained mustache with the edge of one cracked hand. He had skin like venison jerky and only one eyebrow. He'd lost the other one in a close call with a bullet some years before.

"Noah, how're you doing, boy? How's your ma and pa?"

"Last time I saw them they were fine, but the Indians still raise occasional hell out there in the Spearfish, and to make matters worse, the farmers out there have to go out of the stockade to harvest. I worry about them some."

"Yuh." True adjusted his sweat-stained hat. "Bet you do. Well, you tell 'em hey from old True."

Noah nodded, rested a hand on the cart and squinted up at True. "Listen, True . . . the town set up some ordinances since you were here last, and I've been appointed the marshal."

"The marshal!" True raised his face and bellowed with laughter.

"What's so funny about that?"

"Why, hell, you ain't mean enough nor ugly enough to be no marshal. Well, on second thought, you just might be ugly enough."

"At least I got two eyebrows."

"You better watch what you say or you won't for long." True took aim at Noah's brow with a forefinger.

Noah laughed, then got serious. "Listen, True, I've got to charge you three dollars a wagon to let you unload your freight."

"Three dollars a wagon!"

. "That's right."

"But we been hauling freight in here since spring. Hell, if it wasn't for us skinners this town wouldn't have windows or stoves or beans to boil! For that matter, if it wasn't for us, who would you and your ma and pa have rode up here with last spring when the damned Indians were trying to keep everybody out?"

"I know, I know. But I didn't make the ordinances, I just enforce them. Three dollars per wagon, True, from every one of you, and I've got to collect it."

True spit. Wiped his lip. Scowled at the ox yoke. "Well, shit and dance around it," he mumbled. He picked up his ox whip, made it whistle and smack, and bawled, "Git goin', you lazy no-good hunk of guts!" As the train began to move, he said without glancing at Noah, "We'll pay up at the freight house."

It took Noah the better part of an hour to collect the license fees from the entire ox train. The drivers had to be contacted and their gold weighed out, their names taken down and recorded for the city clerk and treasurer.

It was one minute after twelve when he left the gold at the city treasurer's and headed down the street toward the pine tree, where a crowd was again gathered watching Sarah Merritt defy his orders. He shouldered his way through the throng, tall enough to see above the surrounding heads that she was rolling ink, loading the press and cranking it by hand. When the process was finished she lifted a printed sheet. A roar of applause rose: shouting and handclapping and hooraying enough to be heard on the other side of the mountain.

"Gentlemen! The first copy of the *Deadwood Chronicle!*" Sarah shouted. "It's only a single page but the next issue will be bigger!" The cheers doubled as the sheet, with its ink still wet, was passed from hand to hand. Those who couldn't read asked those who could what it said. The men whose names were mentioned for helping Sarah on her first night in town became fleeting celebrities, patted on the back by their fellow townsmen. The editorial about the brothels was eclipsed by the feeling that each man there had taken a personal part in bringing the press to Deadwood.

Sarah Merritt had produced a second copy and was rolling ink for the third by the time Noah reached her.

"Miss Merritt," he shouted above the din, "I'm afraid I'll have to put an end to this."

She set down her brayer, closed the frisket, cranked it into place and lowered the platen with a lunge of one hip. "Tell *them!*" she challenged. She opened the press, plucked another printed sheet from it, the ink still gleaming, and handed it to him. "Tell them why you want to shut me down, Marshal Campbell! Tell them where I saw you the first time, and what you were there for, and why you want to restrict my freedom of speech!"

He glanced at her headlines. One jumped out at him. CLOSE THE HEATHEN BROTHELS OF THE WEST.

Before the blood hit the crown of his head she was appealing to the crowd. "Gentlemen! Marshal Campbell is here to arrest me because he claims I'm on public land. But ask him what his real reason is! Ask him!

I'm not the first newspaper publisher to be silenced because I speak the truth, and I won't be the last."

"What does she mean, Noah?"

"Let her be, Noah—"

"Town needs a paper, Noah—"

Noah knew the signs. Covertly he reached down and unsnapped his holster strap while shouting to them, "I warned her an hour ago she couldn't set up this press in the middle of the street. We've got new laws and I've been hired to see that they're obeyed."

"But you can't arrest no woman!"

"I don't like it any more than you do, Henry, but I took an oath to faithfully and impartially perform my duties, and she broke two ordinances that I can see. Ordinance number one, section two, regarding licenses, and Ordinance number three, section one, on nuisances and junk in the streets and alleys, to say nothing of disturbing the peace and obstructing traffic—which she and every one of you are doing when you refuse to break up this gathering."

"All we come to do was see the first copy getting made!"

"All right, you've seen it, now move along!"

"What's she talking about, Noah? You got other reasons to shut her down?"

"I'm not shutting her down, only forcing her to move!" Turning to Sarah, he ordered tightly, "Get your jacket and come with me."

"No, sir, I will not."

"All right, have it your way." He grabbed her by the back of the neck as if to shepherd her away.

"Get your hands off me!" She struggled.

"Get those feet moving, Miss Merritt!" He pushed.

"But my ink! My press!"

"Throw the canvas over it if you want to, but that's it. I gave you an hour to move it and you chose not to. Now get going!"

He pushed her.

A hunk of horse dung hit him on the shoulder.

"Let her be, we said!"

"Yeah, let her alone! She ain't hurting nothing!"

Another chunk of dung knocked Noah's hat off. He released Sarah and spun to face the crowd. They were surging forward, expressions black, fists clenched.

"You men, get back! She can run her press. She just can't run it here!"

"Get him, boys! He can't manhandle no woman like that!"

Everything happened at once. The sky began raining horse dung.

The militants shoved forward. Noah drew his gun. Someone's fist struck him on the jaw. Sarah screamed and Noah stumbled back. His pistol fired and a half a block away True Blevins slumped over and fell across the freight he'd been unloading. Noah went down on his back, crushing his hat. Like a disturbed anthill, the men swarmed, fists first.

Sarah screamed, "Stop this! Stop!" and fell into the fray, grabbing an arm, hauling back on it. She caught glimpses of fists smashing into Campbell's face and screamed again, trying to protect the downed man. "Stop it! Oh please, no . . . Listen to me!" She screamed till her veins bulged.

"Listen to me!"

Her screaming finally registered, and the inner circle of attackers heeded. Their shouts stilled. They looked about for her. She knelt among them with her face ferocious, her hair awry.

"Look what you're doing!" she screamed raspily. "He's your friend, your marshal, and he was only doing his job! This is my fault!" She pressed her open hands to her chest. "Mine! Please, let him up."

Several men still crouched above Noah, their fists poised. They glanced from Sarah to the lawman. Realization filtered through them. Their hands relaxed. Murmurs began. "Let him up . . . yeah, let him up . . ." Sheepishly they shuffled to their feet. "You all right, Noah?" One of them offered Noah a hand. He knocked it aside and struggled to his feet, bleeding from one ear and his nose and mouth, cradling his ribs with his left arm. Already his face was beginning to swell.

In the stillness a voice called from down the street. "True Blevins has been shot!"

"Oh Jesus," Noah whispered and began shoving his way through the crowd, which parted as he came. Before he reached True, he was running. He vaulted onto the oxcart and took True's shoulders, turned him over gently on the sacks of cornmeal he'd been unloading.

True's eyes were bleary, but he gave a murky grin.

"Y' got me, boy," he croaked.

"Where?"

"Feels like everywhere." True's weak voice ended in a cough, followed by a groan as his eyelids closed.

"Get a doctor!" Noah hollered, and saw the blood on True's dirty leather vest. Softly he said, "True, I'm sorry. Hang on now, buddy. Don't you go die on me." Frantically, Noah stood and shouted, "I said get a doctor, goddammit!"

"He's coming now, Noah," someone beside the oxcart said in a hushed voice. "Here, you want to use this?" A handkerchief was handed toward Noah.

"No! Nobody touches him with anything dirty!" Dan Turley approached at a run, carrying his black bag. "Hurry, Doc!" Noah cried. "Help him up!"

A tall, gaunt man in shirtsleeves clambered aboard the oxcart and bent over True. "Get this cart rolling," Turley ordered as he turned back True's vest and unbuttoned his shirt. "Take us to my place. Noah, how about you? You need attention, too?"

"No, I'm all right, Doc." An ox whip cracked. The cart lurched and began rolling.

"Then I believe you've got business to attend to. You won't be any help hovering over me, so go keep yourself busy. I'll send word to you as soon as I know anything."

"But Doc, I'm the one who shot him!"

"He's in good hands, Noah." Doc took a moment to raise a no-nonsense gaze to Noah. "Go!"

Noah took one last look at True, touched the skinner's hard hand, and said, "True, you hang on, hear?"

Noah jumped off the oxcart and watched it roll up the street. His Adam's apple bobbed twice and his chest felt like drying rawhide. *Don't you go and do anything foolish, True.*

In time he sniffed, rubbed the back of one hand beneath his nose, and felt his concern for True give way to furor. He turned toward the great ponderosa pine where the crowd waited, becalmed by tragedy. As he strode toward them, their eyes dropped guiltily. They shuffled in place and joined their hands like mourners around a grave. A path cleared as he hit straight for Sarah Merritt, feeling rage building with each footstep. In his entire life he'd never felt the urge to strike a woman, but he felt it now, the unholy lust to drive a fist into that long, skinny face in retaliation for True. To see her crumple and whimper and be laid low just as True had been. What a stupid, senseless loss, if True died, all because of this self-righteous do-gooder who refused to obey a simple city ordinance.

She waited, stilled like the others, standing straight as the liberty pole behind her, holding Noah's Colt .45 Peacemaker on the flat of her hands as he approached.

"I'm so sorry," she whispered, solemnly handing him the gun. His left eye was swollen shut and rivulets of blood had painted rusty tracks down his chin.

"Shut up!" he barked, grabbing the Colt, suppressing the urge to crack it across her cheek. "I'm not interested in your pitiful condolences."

"Is he dead?"

"Not quite." He rammed the gun into his holster and bent over to sweep up his flattened hat. "But you'll have some answering to do if he gets that way. *You men!*" he roared, whirling on them, fanning at them with the hat. *"I'm telling you for the last time—clear out of this street!"* Like disturbed roaches, they scuttled off. Campbell punched a fist into the crown of his Stetson and it popped out, a mangled mess. "Sonofabitch," he mumbled, disgusted. When he spoke, the skin around his lips quivered and he rested his eyes anywhere but on the woman. "Sarah Merritt," he pronounced, glaring at the liberty pole in the distance, concentrating on what it symbolized in an effort to control his urge to drop her where she stood, "you're under arrest for disturbing the peace, operating a business without a license, and inciting a riot, and I hope to hell you put up another fight, because nothing would please me more than to tie and gag you and drag you through the streets by your hair!"

"You won't have to do that, Mr. Campbell," she returned meekly, picking up her notebook, jacket and organdy pouch. "I'll come with you."

His cork finally blew. *"Now* you'll come with me!" he shouted, glaring at her, pointing to where the oxcart had stood several minutes earlier. "Now that my friend's been shot, you'll come with me! God *damn* it!" He threw down his hat. "What ever happened to public whippings!"

She stood before him chastised, her mouth drawn, waiting. Beside her, her printing press was already covered by canvas.

"I can only repeat, I'm sorry, Mr. Campbell."

He studied her for several beats of silence and she thought she had never seen hatred more clearly illustrated than by his grim expression.

"If I have my way, you'll be a lot sorrier before this is over. Get moving," he said coldly.

She did as ordered, allowing herself to be ignominiously herded down the length of Main Street while the townpeople stared and whispered in her wake. He took her to a wooden frame building fronted by a set of steps and a covered boardwalk.

"Inside," he ordered, nudging her between the shoulder blades. They entered a store where customers stood as motionless as the cracker barrels around them, only their heads turning to follow Sarah's passage. A sleeping dog rose from behind a potbellied stove and nosed their heels desultorily as Sarah advanced through the premises with Marshal Campbell one step behind. They passed fresh apples and eggs, tinned goods and sacks of dried beans. And farther along, a vinegar barrel with a wooden spigot giving off the acrid smell Sarah so disliked. At the rear of the store a long counter faced the front and behind it stood a bearded man wearing a white apron, suspenders, sleeve garters and a dapper black derby hat.

"Noah," he greeted gravely.

"George," the marshal returned, "I need to use your tunnel for a while."

"Of course." There was no question: everyone in the place knew what had happened on the street and that the downed man was a friend of the marshal's.

"Is the lantern still back there?"

"Hanging on the hook in the passageway."

Campbell gave Sarah another nudge and followed her around the counter, through a back door into a short windowless walkway that smelled like a potato bin. When the door closed behind them, absolute blackness descended. Sarah felt a shiver of fear and balked. Campbell poked her again, propelling her forward three halting steps.

"Wait there."

She heard the clink of a lantern handle, then a match whisked and flared, illuminating his face as he plucked the lantern from the nail and lit the wick.

He nodded sideways and said, "In here."

She proceeded timorously into the abandoned mine. It was no bigger than a pantry and contained a wooden chair and a pile of straw covered with a holey horse blanket. It took a valiant effort to keep her voice steady as her eyes darted around the dirt walls.

"This is your jail?"

"This is it." He set the lantern on the floor beside the chair and headed for the door.

"Mr. Campbell!" she called, panicked at the thought of being left alone.

He turned and fixed his cold gray eyes on her but refused to speak.

"How long do you intend to keep me in here?"

"That's up to the judge, not me."

"And where is the judge?"

"Haven't had one assigned yet, so the town appointed George out there as acting judge."

"George? You mean the *grocer?*"

"That's right."

"So I'm to be tried by a kangaroo court?"

He pointed a finger at her nose. "Now, listen here, sister! You come in here and cause a man to get shot and now you're not happy with the accommodations. Well, that's just too bad!"

"I have rights, Mr. Campbell!" she shot back, her spunk returning. "And one of them is to present my case before a territorial court."

"You're in Indian territory now, and the territorial government is powerless here."

"A federal court then."

"The closest federal court is in Yankton, so all we've got is George. But the miners themselves picked him as the fairest man they know."

He turned toward the door again.

"And a lawyer!" she interrupted. "You cannot incarcerate me without a lawyer!"

"Oh, can't I?" He glanced back over his shoulder. "You're in hell-roaring Deadwood now. Things are done differently here."

On that ominous note he walked out and closed the door behind him. The last thing she heard was the key turning in the lock.

CHAPTER 4

SHE stared at the door and listened to the hiss of the lantern, the only sound in the silence. Her pulse thumped, filling her throat. The top of her head felt tight. The backs of her arms felt tingly, a sure sign of impending panic. How long would she be left here? Would anyone come to check on her? What kind of vermin lived in that straw pile? What if the lantern went out?

She fixed her eyes upon it, the only other semblance of life in the room, and perched as near to its warmth as possible, on the edge of the chair seat. With her hands pinched between her knees, she concentrated on the flame until her eyes began to ache, then tightly closed them and chafed her arms. It was so cold in here, and she was hungry; she had not eaten at noon.

Who cared enough to come to her? Addie didn't seem to, and anyway, who'd tell Addie? What would happen to Father's printing press, sitting there under the tree? And her precious newsprint, which had survived the trip clear from the railhead without getting wet, and the type she valued so dearly because it was the same her father had used all his life? Neither it nor her brayer had been cleaned. There hadn't been time in the chaos. The brayer would be ruined.

When she was released from this mineshaft, what would she face? Suppose the oxcart driver died, could the blame possibly be pinned on her even though she hadn't touched the gun? What recourse had she if Campbell failed to send a lawyer? And what would happen if she had to face their "judge" unaided? Was the assault on the marshal serious enough be called insurrection, and would she be liable for that, too?

She kept seeing his face with the knuckles battering it, feeling anew her horror at how spontaneously things had gotten out of hand, hearing the voice from down the street crying that a man had been shot. *I didn't mean to cause all that! I only meant to stand up for my rights!* Again the squeezing began, in her throat and scalp and down her arms, which began to feel numb.

Remember a newspaperman's first qualification, Sarah.

Resolutely, she found her father's watch, opened it and laid it on the floor beside the lantern. She rose from the chair, fetched the horse blanket and shook it. Lifting it to the light, she checked it for movement and saw none discernible. On the chair again, she draped it over her lap, removed her spectacles from the organdy pouch, donned them and opened her notebook and ink vial.

She contemplated a long time before dipping the pen and writing her first words.

Riot in the Street: Man Shot, Newspaper Editor Jailed.

With the unshrinking veracity instilled by her father, she set about writing an impartial account of what had happened on Main Street during the last two hours.

Doc Turley's office was a frame structure which doubled as his house. It was located a short distance beyond Loretta Roundtree's, where the buildings began to climb the steep sides of the gulch. The path to it angled up the side of the sheer slope like the footpath of a mountain goat. After the rain it was slippery, but Noah Campbell negotiated it with long strides and arrived at Turley's door worried. He entered without knocking, directly into Doc's waiting room, which was furnished with a few pole-and-hide chairs, all empty.

"Doc?" he called, advancing toward the rear.

"Come on in, Noah!"

Noah followed Turley's voice into his examination room, which had walls finished with a layer of pine boards over the studs—a rarity in Deadwood. A glass-fronted cupboard held probes and pinchers and a bevy of other intimidating instruments. In an enamel basin a bullet swam in some bloody water along with a needle and a pair of tweezers. On a leather-covered examination table lay True, out cold while Doc cut bandages for his right shoulder.

"How is he, Doc?"

"I had to chloroform him to take the bullet out, but unless I miss my guess, he'll be cussing at those oxen within a week or so."

Noah blew out a huge breath and felt the tension leave his shoulder blades.

"That's the best news I've had today."

"He's a crusty old bugger. His hearty condition will stand him in good stead now. Come and help me roll him over while I tie this gauze strip. I made an alum poultice to stop the bleeding."

Horsehair stitches held True's skin together and protruded like cat's whiskers in the area where Doc had done surgery. Noah had to cock his head to one side and watch with his good eye while Doc covered the wound with a white pad and looped gauze strips over True's shoulder and around his trunk.

"How long will he be out?" Noah carefully rolled True onto his left side.

"Chloroform only lasts ten or fifteen minutes at most. He should be coming around soon. He'll be groggy, though." Doc completed the bandaging and poured water in a clean basin before beginning to wash his hands. "He'll need someplace to recuperate. You got any ideas?"

"He can have my room at Mrs. Roundtree's."

"Where would you go?"

"Hell, I can sleep anyplace. I can bunk on the floor of my office or even throw up a tent for a couple weeks. The weather's warm enough yet."

"He's going to need some attention, and I doubt that Loretta Roundtree's got the time to be looking after a convalescent on top of running that boardinghouse. Furthermore, knowing True, he'd come to his senses at Loretta's and get up out of bed looking for his ox whip before the blood is dry in these wounds."

Noah considered for several seconds. "You think he could make the trip out to the Spearfish?"

"After a couple days he could."

"Then put him at Loretta's for now and I can look in on him a couple times a day when I'm making rounds to see how he's doing. Maybe you can do the same."

"I can."

"When you think he's well enough I'll run him out to the valley. My ma will pamper the piss and vinegar out of him." Doc laughed, drying his hands. "Matter of fact," Noah continued, "she'll give me a dressing down if she finds out True needed help and I didn't give her a chance to provide it."

Setting aside his towel, Doc said, "As long as you're here, I'd better take a look at that face of yours."

Noah submitted to Doc's examination while Turley asked, "What about those Indians out in the Spearfish?"

"Well, on that score, we just have to hope for the best. The treaty is signed, now we'll just have to see if they honor it. Oww! What the hell you doing, Doc?"

"Making sure you can still see out of that eye."

"I can see! Now let go!"

Doc released Noah's eyelid and peered into his ear. "Might have punctured the eardrum. Usually that's the case when you bleed from the ear. Cover the other one and tell me if you can hear me. Eardrums heal, though, most of the time. They get a little scar tissue that cuts down the hearing somewhat, is all."

"I can hear."

"Good. Did you lose any teeth?" Doc reached toward Noah's mouth, but the marshal reared back.

"I've got all my teeth, now quit your infernal prodding!"

"Testy, aren't you?"

From the patient came a mumble as his eyes fluttered open, then closed. Noah turned to the table and stood beside it, waiting. After several seconds True mumbled again and opened his eyes. They were blue as cornflowers, surrounded by deep grooves.

"Hey, you old hornswoggler. 'Bout time you were waking up."

"Take more'n a bullet t' put me t' sleep." His words were slurred.

"Doc's got the damn thing out. He's makin' soup with it."

True managed a weak grin. "What the hell'd you run into—Sitting Bull?"

"You just shut up about what I run into or I'll have Doc plaster a little more chloroform against your mouth, you old buffalo hoof." Noah smiled the best he could with his puffy lips, then said, "Listen, True, we're going to put you at Mrs. Roundtree's till you get a little stronger, then I'm going to take you out to the valley and let my ma feed you some of her good cooking and sass you back, just the way you like. How does that sound?"

True let his eyes close and spoke sleepily. "Can't. Got a train to unload."

"Oh, no you don't! You just forget about unloading trains for a while."

True's blue eyes opened quite wide this time and fixed on the younger man leaning over him. He spoke with surprising irascibility. "Some sonofabitch charges me three dollars for a license to unload my freight, now he says forget about it. What kind of town you running here, boy?"

"The unloading's all taken care of. You need rest now."

"Rest, hell . . ." True grunted and attempted to rise. Only one of his shoulders cleared the examination table before he fell back, panting. The marshal and the doctor exchanged glances.

Turley stepped forward. "True," he ordered, "you lay still or I'll tie you down. You want that?" True waggled his head while his eyes remained closed. "All right then. Sleep while you can, because that shoulder's going to hurt like a son of a gun tonight. Noah will come back later and help me get you over to Mrs. Roundtree's, then in a couple days when you're stronger he'll take you out to the Spearfish."

Noah thought True had drifted off again and said quietly to Dan Turley, "I'll be back. I've got to clear that woman's stuff out of the street."

True opened his eyes. "Met your match with that one, didn't you, boy?" he said.

"Yeah, well, she's not talking so smart right now. I've got her locked up behind Farnum's."

True smiled and nodded as if speculating to himself. "Yup," he said, "she's a hellcat. Look out you don't get scratched."

Heading away from Doc's, Noah considered True's words. Sarah Merritt was a hellcat, all right, and though his wrath had diminished somewhat upon learning True would live, he had every intention of letting her mildew in that mole hole until she'd learn a damned good lesson about the value of freedom, *and* about harassing the local lawman! By now she was bawling so hard she was probably treading brine. Well, let her tread! Let her consider what kind of a disaster her bullheadedness had nearly caused. Let her wonder when she'd see the light of day again, and how hungry she was going to get, and how long it would be before anybody remembered she was in there! No damned gangly female troublemaker was going to sashay into Marshal Noah Campbell's town and get by with the kind of shit she'd pulled.

So just what in thunderation was he supposed to do with that rig of hers anyway? He should be making his rounds right now; instead he had a thousand pounds of steel to get moved, and a tent to fold up and all that other paraphernalia she'd unloaded in the middle of . . .

Where the hell is it?

Rounding a corner onto Main Street, he gaped at the big pine tree. Her outfit was gone! Press, crates and tent . . . gone! Nothing left but the depressions in the mud where they had stood, and those obscured by boot- and hoofprints.

His pulse began to thump as he glanced up and down the thorough-fare. She'd have something to say about this. Somebody stealing her equipment from the middle of Main Street, where the marshal should have set somebody to guard it. But who'd think anyone would have the audacity to take something so big from such a public spot? And how hard could it be to find? The press alone was as tall as a man and weighed half a ton! *Goddammit!* As if he didn't have enough to contend with today, now this!

He spent an hour searching and turned up nothing. Not in alleys or at the freight office or at his own office. Grumpily, he plunked down in his chair and filled out a few of the sonofabitchin' licenses—what they needed licenses for was beyond him. He knew every person who'd paid their tax and every person who owed.

In the middle of the third form he threw down his pen and cursed silently, wrapped one fist around the other, forgot he was hurt and pressed them against his mouth; yelped and cursed once more. Checked his watch. Going on five-thirty and Farnum would close up at six.

All right, so she'd requested a lawyer. Given his druthers, he'd leave her to stew till morning, but it might not look good, his jailing her without legal counsel. Section two of the Deadwood City Ordinances laid out clearly what constituted the Common Council of Deadwood City and its legal ramifications. Not only was it made up of the mayor and six of his fellow townsmen, it stated unquestionably that the council could sue and *be sued.* It wouldn't bode well if within two weeks of the town's official formation its marshal got the city council sued. And he had no doubt that self-proclaimed muckraker would do it.

So he'd find her a damned lawyer. The town was full of them—seven licensed at last count—all hard-up for business because of the absence of an appellate court and the fact that there were no lawbooks in town yet.

He made a grab at the coat hook, but his hat was missing, left in the mud after that fracas. Cursing, he stormed outside and headed for the office of the closest lawyer, a bearded, sniffling fellow named Lawrence Chapline, who had set up shop in a tent. When Campbell turned back the flap and entered, Chapline was in the midst of wiping his nose on a damp handkerchief. He took one look at the marshal and exclaimed, "What in blazes happened to *you!*"

"Got tangled up in that street riot earlier today. The woman who started it wants a lawyer. Are you interested?"

Chapline had his hat on before the question cleared Campbell's lips. They walked back to Farnum's store and found it full of curious customers who knew there was a female incarcerated in the mine out back. Some of them nodded silently as the lawman and the lawyer passed. Others called, "What you going to do with her, Noah?" and "Are you defending her, Chapline?"

Businesslike, they proceeded through the store into the passageway leading to the tunnel. Campbell opened the door expecting to find Sarah Merritt engulfed in tears. Instead she was sitting on the hoop-backed chair, diligently writing in her notebook. She looked up, and the picture she made riled him all over again because there were no oceans of tears in sight. No weak, wailing female terrified of her straits. Instead she sat calmly on a chair and looked up through small oval spectacles that magnified her blue eyes and gave her the appearance of a schoolmarm correcting papers. Her lap was covered by the horse blanket, and her brown hair had been neatened as best she could manage. She might have been sitting at a table on a raised platform with five rows of school desks before her. Calmly, she closed her book, capped her pen and laid them on the floor. Her militancy had disappeared and in its place was strict politeness.

"Marshal Campbell, you're back," she said, removing her spectacles.

"I brought you the lawyer you asked for. This is Lawrence Chapline."

"Mr. Chapline." She rose, folded the horse blanket over the back of the chair and extended her hand. Immediately when she'd taken care of courtesies she asked of Campbell, "How is your friend?"

"Alive and ornery."

She rested a hand on her heart. "Oh, thank the Almighty. He'll live, then?"

"Looks that way."

"I *am* relieved. I've been so upset thinking I might have been responsible for an innocent man's death. And what about you? Are you all right?"

"Nothing serious. Maybe a punctured eardrum."

"Oh," she said, her mouth a small circle of regret while she looked up at his eye, which had swollen up like a toad's throat at twilight. And after a lull, "I stand before you remorseful and prepared to pay whatever fines may be imposed."

Oddly, Campbell had been more comfortable with her ire. Her new-found contrition put him on uncertain ground. He shifted his weight and said, "You'd better talk to Chapline while you have the chance. I'll be back in a while."

Left alone with the lawyer, Sarah said, "Thank you for coming, Mr. Chapline. What's going to happen to me?"

"Why don't you sit down, Miss Merritt, while I give you a little background about the law here. I think it will help you to understand."

"I've been sitting for quite some time. If you don't mind, I'll stand."

"Very well." Chapline rubbed his nose with his damp hanky and studied the floor for several seconds. He was perhaps thirty-five years old, bony and round-shouldered, with thinning brown hair as fine as a one-year-old's. It drifted above his dome as if it hadn't enough weight to lay flat. His nose was red and his eyes watery—a man who presented not at all the picture of one in whom you'd place your confidence when your well-being was threatened. But he had a voice that rumbled with authority. It vaulted up from his depths like the resounding crash of falling timber and seemed to shake the very sand loose from the walls of the mine as he continued speaking.

"We have a rather peculiar history of the process of the law here in Deadwood. The stampede of gold prospectors brought population before civilization, you might say, at a rate so incredible it nurtured lawlessness along with it—claim-jumping, saloon brawls and theft, to name a few.

"So the residents instigated a miners' court and decided that each session would be presided over by one of the seven lawyers in town, with the 'judge' changing from session to session."

Chapline again scrubbed at his nose and paced.

"You heard about the unfortunate shooting of Wild Bill Hickok here last month, I presume?"

"Of course."

"It was a shock to all of us, and if ever there was a town that wanted to see justice done, this was it! However, the trial turned out to be a travesty of justice in spite of all our efforts at jurisprudence. Better than half the men on the jury were suspected of having been part of the bunch who hired Jack McCall to kill Wild Bill. They handed down a verdict of not guilty and we had to let McCall go scot-free. Nobody liked it, but what could we do?

"A lot of us weren't happy about our court system, but before we could come up with a better one we had another homicide take place, this one three weeks ago. Fellow named Baum was shot. This time all seven of us lawyers volunteered our services, and my colleague, Mr. Keithly, acted as judge. Trouble was, we didn't have any lawbooks, and it created one heck of a predicament.

"It was decided then and there that not only would we order a complete law library for Deadwood, we'd suspend all trials until they got here. In the meantime we've begun organizing ourselves as a city, which is the only way we can expect to have an appellate court established here with a real federal judge."

"Have your lawbooks arrived yet?"

"No, they haven't."

"Oh." Sarah's shoulders wilted slightly. "Then it sounds bad for me."

"Not necessarily, because in the meantime small disputes are being settled by our new mayor, George Farnum, and that was agreed upon by the whole town when they elected him. Now, before you jump to conclusions, why don't you give me your version of the events leading to your arrest."

"That's easy." Sarah picked her notebook off the floor and handed it to Chapline. "I've written it all down for my next issue of the newspaper. This is exactly how it happened."

Chapline spent the next several minutes sitting on the chair, reading the account, his shoulder slanted toward the lantern light. When he finished, he wiped his nose and looked up.

"Did you refuse to move your printing press?"

"Yes."

"Were you operating it without a license?"

"Yes."

"Were you informed by the marshal that you needed a license?"

"Yes."

"Did you incite a riot?"

"Yes."

"Intentionally?"

"No."

"Did you yourself strike Marshal Campbell?"

"No."

"Did you encourage others to do so?"

"No. I tried to stop them."

"Did you see the freight driver, True Blevins, get shot?"

"Yes."

"Who shot him?"

"Marshal Campbell."

"It was an accident?"

"Absolutely."

"Were any other guns drawn?"

"No. It happened too fast."

"Did you resist arrest?"

"The first time, yes. The second time, no."

"Would you be willing to pay any and all damages, get a license to operate your newspaper, and agree to put off further publication until your equipment is under proper cover on private land?"

"Absolutely."

Chapline studied her silently for some time, sitting on the chair with his knees apart, clasped by his bony hands. Finally he inquired, "Do you think you can repeat those answers verbatim if I asked you the questions again?"

"Yes."

"Do you have the money to pay for the damages?"

"Right here." She patted her waist above her left hip.

"Excellent." Chapline rose to his feet. "Then what I think we'll do is appeal to Farnum's sense of fair play, making no excuses for what you've done, simply pointing out that your intentions were not dishonorable, nobody was irreparably hurt, and you are remorseful—which you've already demonstrated to Marshal Campbell. When we go out there, just make certain you keep the same contrite tone you've displayed so far. Regretful but not groveling."

She nodded.

"All right, let's see what we can do." He gave her a bracing smile while rapping on the door.

Campbell opened it.

"We'd like to talk to Farnum," Chapline told him.

"Come on out." He stood back, waiting for Chapline and Sarah to precede him through the tunnel. To Sarah, the light at the end of it looked like the exit from purgatory. The sound of voices was as welcome as a spring thaw. From the musty smell of sunless earth she emerged into that of coffee beans and smoked jerky and vinegar (which seemed less offensive than before). From dark into light; from dampness into freshness; from solitariness into a crowd whose murmurs silenced as she appeared.

Behind the counter, Farnum stood, watching the procession move through the back door. Campbell halted just inside. The other two went around to the front of the counter.

"Mr. Farnum," Chapline said, "in view of the fact that our law library hasn't arrived yet, and a decent jail hasn't been built, and the town has voted you the authority to settle minor disputes, Miss Merritt asks if you would do so now, so she won't have to spend an indeterminate length of time locked in that abandoned mine."

Farnum replied, "Well, I don't know. That's sort of up to the marshal here, whether he thinks the charges against her need those lawbooks or not. Marshal?"

Campbell uncrossed his arms and cleared his throat. Before he could answer, Chapline spoke up. "Miss Merritt has no intention of under-playing her guilt, but neither does she consider herself a dangerous criminal who deserves being jailed without recourse. Perhaps you would both read this and then decide. It's an article she wrote for her newspaper, and I think her candidness will speak for itself."

Farnum removed his white apron and laid it across the counter with all the pomp of a judge donning black robes. Campbell moved behind the mayor's shoulders and the two read the article together. When they finished, they traded glances and in the following seconds each seemed to be waiting for the other to speak first. Again Chapline filled the gap.

"As you can see, Miss Merritt is not trying to whitewash her role in today's unfortunate incident, indeed, she's prepared to report it to the entire town in her own newspaper. Gentlemen, if you'll allow me, Miss Merritt has agreed to answer a few simple questions, and afterward you can make your decision."

"All right," Farnum said, "go ahead. I don't see what harm it can do to listen."

Chapline ran through his questions, ending by extracting from Sarah the promise that she would be willing to pay any and all damages, including the doctor bills for True, and for Marshal Campbell, if there were any; she would pay whatever fines were imposed, and would get a license to operate her newspaper, and agreed to put off doing so until her press was under proper cover on private land. In that regard, Chapline asked them to consider that she had valuable property sitting out in the street and exposed to the elements and which needed her immediate attention.

At the mention of her property, which he still had not located, Noah shifted his feet. He glanced past Sarah at the curious faces watching and listening and realized a detailed description of these events would spread up and down this gulch faster than an epidemic of smallpox. Not a soul who heard it would feel Noah was in his rights to keep this woman locked in a hole in the ground when none of what had happened was provoked by her intentionally, and when she had virtually thrown herself on their mercy and was offering to make recompense to whatever extent was fair. None of that spoke as loudly, however, as the fact that she was female, single, and a non-prostitute—a rarity in Deadwood. Wouldn't he have a time explaining her incarceration to twenty-five thousand woman-starved miners?

The proceedings were moving on. Where the *jumping hell* was her press? For a moment he was tempted to lock her up simply to give himself time to find it.

"What do you think, Marshal?" the mayor was asking.

"She's caused one devilish amount of trouble today."

"Yes, she has, but I believe in this case the real court might be lenient. After all, she is a woman, and that mine is no place to stick a member of the fairer sex."

"How and when is she going to pay?"

"Here and now," Sarah interjected, slipping her hand into the side placket of her skirt and coming up with her buckskin sack of gold dust. "Just tell me what I owe."

Campbell's eyes met Sarah's. She had the damnedest, most disconcerting way of looking straight at a man. He had a feeling she knew he'd been standing there hoping she couldn't come up with the dust on such short notice. He was the first to look away.

"Whatever you say, Mayor," he allowed grudgingly.

Farnum imposed a twenty-dollar fine for disturbing the peace and another ten-dollar fine for operating a business without a license. He said he'd trust Sarah to pay the doctor bill and that she could settle that with Turley tomorrow. When the gold was weighed out, including an additional ten dollars' worth for her first quarter's license to operate a printing office, Sarah put away her gold dust and extended her hand to Farnum.

"Thank you, sir. I would have disliked spending the night in that mine." She pumped his hand hard, once, and turned immediately to Campbell. "Marshal."

She didn't offer her hand. Instead she hit him with a hard, direct gaze. It struck him how different she was than her sister—direct, focused, a fighter.

"I suppose it's something in my nature, but I expect we'll bump heads again," she told him.

In about two and a half minutes, he thought uneasily, watching her turn toward Chapline as if this meeting were concluded and she had been the one controlling its tempo all along. "Thank you, Mr. Chapline. I'll come by tomorrow and settle up with you." When she was halfway to the door Campbell called, "Miss Merritt, wait." Again she faced him squarely, putting him on edge. At times she seemed able to control her very impulse to blink, as now, when she simply stood waiting for him to move toward her. "I, ahh . . . I need to talk to you about another matter. Outside," he added, conscious of the onlookers.

"Very well. We'll walk together." She turned and led the way from the store, opened the door herself without waiting to see if he'd do it (he had no such intention), stalked out into the middle of the street without concern for her hems (he'd never seen a woman so indifferent to mud) and headed in the direction of the ponderosa pine with her notebook pressed to her left breast (what there was of it). Here, too, she was different from her sister—not much in the way of femininity at all.

They advanced up the street and he spoke up before she could catch sight of the tree.

He said it straight out, as if it were no fault of his, because he knew damned well it was.

"Someone stole your printing press."

"What!" She halted and spun on him.

"It disappeared while I was at Doc Turley's checking on True."

"Disappeared? Half a ton of machinery *disappeared*? What are you trying to pull here, Campbell?"

The thought had never occurred to him she'd suspect him of skulduggery.

"Me? I didn't—"

"Where have you hidden it?"

"Now, listen here—"

"Don't tell me this isn't your doing—!"

"I was down at Doc's—"

"Because nobody else in this town—"

"You can ask him!"

They stood in the middle of the street, shouting at each other, nose to nose. It was nearly suppertime; the streets were busy with hungry men heading for the food saloons; many stopped walking to rubberneck.

". . . have no right to impound my press!"

"I didn't impound it. Someone stole it!"

"What for?"

"Hell, I don't know!"

"What about my type and my ink and paper?"

"It's all gone, even the tent."

Her mouth tightened and she looked as if she'd like nothing better than to sock him in his other eye and give him a matched pair.

"You're the most unscrupulous reprobate in this town, and the pity is you've got them all bamboozled! To think they all elected you!" She tromped off angrily, still clutching her notebook, her free hand curled into a fist. By the time he reached the tree she was standing beneath it throwing glances in a wide circle.

"You'd better find it, Campbell, and do it quick!"

"That'll take some time."

"Then spend it."

"And search every building in this gulch?"

"You're the marshal, aren't you? That's your job! That press means my livelihood, and the type is the same my father began on. They mean far more to me than just the tools I work with, but of course you wouldn't—"

"Miss Merritt?" The youthful male voice interrupted Sarah's diatribe. A boy with a curly crop of black hair had approached. He was about sixteen, comely, with a shy mien and the first shadow of a beard beginning to sprout beneath his nose. He wore dome-toed boots, worn wool britches and a shabby green plaid jacket. His hands were in the jacket pockets.

"Yes?"

"Mr. Bradigan sent me. He's got your press and he says you should come with me."

"Mr. Bradigan!"

"Yes."

"But why? And where?"

"He'll explain if you'll just come along."

Sarah looked to Noah but he only shrugged. "I'd better come along and see what Bradigan is up to."

"What's your name?" Sarah asked as they struck off behind the lad.

"Josh Dawkins." He glanced back briefly.

"Dawkins? Are you Emma's boy?"

"That's right."

"Oh, goodness, I just remembered, I'm supposed to be at your house for supper. It must be almost that time now."

"She'll hold it till we get there. You've got to do this other first."

"Do what?"

"You'll see."

He led them to a small frame building on the southwest end of Main Street. Facing east, it was already blanketed in shadow from the canyon wall; within, lantern light glowed. Inside, Sarah came to a halt while her glance snapped from wall to corner to wall. There before her were all her prized possessions—her press, her furniture cabinet, her typecase, her father's desk, the crates containing her ink, brayers, newsprint and wood engravings—all set up in perfect working relationship to one another. The oily smell of ink combined with the tang of turpentine hung in the air like printer's perfume. On a wooden table along the right wall four stacks of printed pages were drying. At the press, wearing a black-blotched leather apron, Patrick Bradigan was cleaning today's type with a turpentine rag. He turned when they entered, gave a slow, wobbly smile, and an even slower, wobbly bow.

"Miss Merritt," he said in his rich Irish brogue. "Welcome to the office of the *Deadwood Chronicle.*"

She moved forward as if mysticized, her eyes taking a more lingering tally of the setup before returning to him. Stopping before him she said, "Mr. Bradigan, what have you done?"

"Found you a building and gotten your first issue ready for the streets, with the help of young Dawkins here. Patrick Bradigan at your sorvice, ma'am. Have composing stick, will set type." He whisked his composing stick from a breast pocket as if it were a cigar. She could tell immediately he was inebriated. Nevertheless, she was grateful.

"Mr. Bradigan, Master Dawkins, though it's inexcusable in a newspaperwoman, I must admit to being speechless."

Young Dawkins stood by beaming while Bradigan sported a pie-eyed grin.

"We ran three hundred twenty-foive copies."

"Three hundred twenty-five!"

"You'll sell every one of them, just wait and see. Tomorrow young Dawkins intends to help you."

She turned her full attention on the boy. "Thank you for the help you've already given."

"Ma sent me over when she heard about the fracas in the street. Word got to the bakery that Mr. Bradigan was going to take over getting the first issue out, and she said I should come and help however I could. I put the paper in the frisket while Mr. Bradigan rolled the ink. It was fun!"

She smiled, recalling the first times her father had allowed her to do that, how fun it had been for her, too.

"Perhaps we'll teach you the rest and make an apprentice out of you—would you like that?"

"Yes, *ma'am!* Would I ever!" he exclaimed with a huge smile.

She took another scan of the premises—raw wood walls, but four of them, sturdy, with a solid roof overhead, and a wide front window facing east for good morning light during her favorite composing time of the day. "Is the building yours, Mr. Bradigan?"

"The building's yours, to rent or buy, whatever you choose."

"But why . . . and how?"

"A gesture from the townspeople who want their first newspaper to begin operating full steam ahead as soon as possible. You can see Elias Pinkney about it. His bank built it on speculation."

"But aren't there others waiting in line to buy it? That's what I was told."

Bradigan cleared his throat and scratched the back of his neck. "Ahh . . . well, you see, those others were men, Miss Campbell, not eligible young colleens like you."

The implication left the unpretentious Sarah at a loss for a reply. *Gracious,* she thought. *Mr. Pinkney again.* Fatter than a Christmas goose and forty years old if he was a day, with his glowing pink head upon which Sarah looked down from her superior height. How discomfiting to rationalize Mr. Bradigan's remark while Marshal Campbell looked on, drawing his own conclusions.

She quickly changed the subject. "Well, luckily for all of us, I've paid my licensing fee. Marshal, have we done everything legally this time?"

"As far as I can see. If you have no complaints about Bradigan usurping your press, I'll leave you."

"No complaints at all."

He turned toward the door and she called, "Just a moment, Marshal." From the table she swished one of the newly inked sheets and folded it in half with the edge of her hand. "Any changes in the content, Mr. Bradigan?" she inquired.

"No. Just as you laid it out."

"A complimentary copy, Mr. Campbell," she said, offering it to him with the editorial faceup. Given all the hubbub today, she knew he hadn't read it. Her contrary side felt a thrill of satisfaction when he took it and said, "Well . . . thank you."

He glanced down and she watched his eyes find the headline. He read a line or two, then lifted his eyes. They were gray and flat as riverbed stones. "You do enjoy butting heads, don't you?"

"It's my job, Marshal."

He regarded her for several seconds before handing the newspaper back to her. "Give it to someone who's interested," he said, and left.

CHAPTER 5

ROM the moment Sarah entered Emma Dawkins' kitchen, she knew she'd found a friend.
Emma flew from her black iron range across
the room and enfolded Sarah in her arms.

"Mercy, what you've been through today. I heard it all, and no
woman should have to go through that. Well, you just sit right down
and have a good strong cup of coffee while the girls help me dish up.
A nice hot meal will take the jitters out of your stomach. These are my
daughters, Lettie, she's twelve, and Geneva, ten, and this here is my
man, Byron. Everybody," she addressed the group, "this is Sarah Merritt, the new woman I told you about."

Lettie was a thin, black-haired beauty with skin like eggshell, a feminine version of her brother. Geneva still wore her adolescent fat and had
overstated dimples that would soon be beguiling the young boys around
town. Byron looked as ordinary as a fresh-rolled noodle, his skin so
naturally pale it appeared to carry a dusting of flour from his day's work.
He was thin, with even paler skin along the insides of his wiry blue-
veined arms, and had lanky brown hair and a clean-shaven face. Looking
at him and Emma, Sarah wondered where Lettie's and Josh's dark-
haired beauty came from. Byron came forward and shook Sarah's hand
with a diffident nod of his head, then rested his hands along his thighs.

"Welcome," he said simply. "Won't you sit down?"

The meal was delicious, cabbage rolls filled with a mixture of venison
and rice, richly flavored with onion and allspice, accompanied by an
endless supply of warm bread. There was, however, no butter. Emma

explained that the shortage of grazing land made dairy farming impossible except in the upland valleys, thus goat milk was widely used. The dearth of cattle created a butter shortage, too, so the town made do with salted lard for their bread.

Sarah made a memorandum to this effect in her notebook, adding that the butcher shop handled mostly wild game and fowl.

For dessert they had a marvelous tart stuffed with cinnamon and apples, accompanied by coffee.

The girls did the serving and clearing, without waiting for orders from their mother, and Sarah found herself impressed by their good manners and willingness. The Dawkins were a warm family who talked and laughed at the table; Sarah's presence was accepted as if she were a longtime friend. During the meal Sarah learned that all three of the youngsters helped their parents in the bakery and that none of them had attended school since the previous year in Iowa.

Sarah added another scribble in her notebook on a page with a heading, *Need for School.*

"How many children would you guess are in the gulch?"

This led to a ticking off of family names in which all the Dawkins took part while Sarah wrote down a list, including the locations of their homes.

When all but the coffee cups were cleared away, Sarah said, "I want to thank you both for sparing Josh to help Patrick Bradigan get my office set up."

"No need to thank us. He was only too willing, and the day's work was done at the bakery."

"Nevertheless, it was very kind of you to send him over. He did a respectable job, too. He helped Bradigan handle the press, and together they turned out three hundred twenty-five copies of the newspaper."

"Three hundred twenty-five!"

"That's what *I* said. But Bradigan assures me there'll be no trouble selling them all. As a matter of fact, Josh has applied for a job as my newsboy."

Across the table, Josh's brown eyes widened. When nobody spoke, Sarah went on. "Josh tells me he's interested in learning the printer's trade. If you thought you could spare him from the bakery, I'd be willing to pay him fifty cents a day to help around the newspaper office."

Josh's jaw dropped. His parents exchanged glances while Sarah pinned her earnest gaze on the boy. "He's a willing worker and Bradigan seemed to think he had a good, steady rhythm at loading the paper. On the day an issue comes out I could use him selling copies on the street if he wanted to. Also, once frost comes, I'd need him to go down to the office and start the fire early in the morning to thaw the ink."

"Pa, could I?" Josh's eyes shone with excitement.

Byron glanced from his son to his wife. "Emma, what do you think?"

Emma turned to Josh. "You'd rather learn that than be a baker like your father?"

Josh leaned forward eagerly. His glance darted between his parents and came to rest on Emma.

"Fifty cents a day, Ma," he said longingly, "and Miss Merritt says she could teach me how to set type."

"And perhaps to write articles, in time," Sarah added. "It's not school, but until we can get one here in Deadwood, it's as close as he can come. He'll be working with words, and—think!—is there any power greater than the power of the written word? My father always said, a man who can make words behave can make men behave. You would be giving Josh a wonderful opportunity."

"Well . . . I suppose since we still have the girls to help in the bakery . . ." Emma remarked as if convincing herself.

Byron said, "If that's what you want, son, I guess we have no right to stop you."

Josh pushed back his chair and leaped up, beaming. "I can do all those things and more. I can sell subscriptions door to door, and sweep up the shop at the end of the day, and shovel out front for you in the winter and carry in your wood and take messages for you when you're out. I promise you won't be sorry you hired me, Miss Merritt!"

"I'm sure I won't," Sarah told him with a smile.

Later, when Sarah and Emma had the kitchen to themselves, Sarah said, "I'm awfully lucky to have met Josh so soon after I came to town. He's going to be an asset to me, I can tell."

Emma was darning a sock stretched on an old wooden bed knob. She wove her needle in and out between the hand warping and spoke without lifting her eyes. "It's sad to see your young ones grow up. You know you've got to let them go, but when it happens, you're not quite prepared for it. Josh now, leaving us to earn his first money on his own . . ." She stopped darning for a moment and let the thought trail off.

Sarah leaned forward and covered Emma's hand. The women's eyes met.

"Should I have asked you first?"

"Aw no, it's not that. Josh is a real bright boy. If you want to know the truth, I never thought mixing bread dough would be enough for him."

Relieved, Sarah sat back. "Watching his eagerness tonight brought back memories of how I first helped my father. I was twelve when he first allowed me to set type. The piece was a very short filler about how to dry flower seeds for winter storage, and it had about fifteen lines or so. When I was done setting it my father was full of praise and he asked me how I'd done it so fast. Well, the secret was, I'd been 'playing printer' whenever I could sneak into his office and do so. He'd be busy at his desk or pulling a proof and I'd be doing what most children do—imitating. He'd hear the type clicking and he'd call to me, 'Be sure you put them back in the right places, Sarah.' So by the time he let me do it officially for the first time, I already had a rudimentary knowledge of the typecase layout and could actually find some of the letters without looking."

"So you were close to your father then?"

Sarah's expression became tender with reminiscence. "Always."

"And your mother?"

Sarah looked down into her coffee cup. "My mother ran away with another man when I was seven years old. I have only vague recollections of her."

"Oh Sarah. Oh my, how sad."

"We got along. We had a housekeeper, and Addie and I still had Father."

Emma studied her with sympathetic eyes before returning to her darning. "So you do have a sister." From Emma's tone it was clear she'd heard rumors.

"Yes."

"Is it true that you came here to look for her and found her working up at that place called Rose's?"

"It's true." Sarah's gaze became distant. "I just wish I knew why."

"Forgive me for asking."

"No, Emma, I don't mind, and what's the difference? The whole town knows anyway."

"Isn't it odd how two children can end up so different from one another?"

"Mmm . . . my sister and I were always different." Sarah brushed absently at the tablecloth, remembering. "From the time I first became aware that there was such a thing as physical beauty, I knew that was the biggest difference between Addie and me. It went without saying— she got the beauty and I got the brains. All through school, all through our growing-up years, she was the one old ladies patted on the head and I was the one they patted on the shoulder—there's a difference, you know."

Emma glanced up and waited for Sarah to go on.

"Children always wanted to be her friends, boys and girls both, while they somehow always stood back from me as if I cowed them. I never meant to. It was just the way I was. When the others would go out to play, I preferred to read. Boys pulled Addie's pigtails but they asked me how to spell the hard words. Addie won the prize for the prettiest-child contest and I won the spelling bees. Father even treated us differently. He babied her. I'm the one he took to the printing office with him. I'm the one he taught to set type. I'm the one who became his apprentice, his right-hand man. And don't get me wrong—I was proud to be. But I used to wonder sometimes why Addie didn't have to go to the office and work, too. Now, of course, I realize I was the lucky one. If Addie had learned a trade she might not be doing what she is."

"It's not your fault she ended up at Rose's."

"Isn't it? I sometimes wonder. Was it something I did or didn't do that made her run away from home? She wasn't happy there and I knew it, but I was so busy helping Father that I didn't take time to sit down and talk to her. From the time Mother ran away she was a sad little girl, but during her teen years she became even more quiet and withdrawn. I thought it was just growing pains."

"Now, don't you go blaming yourself," Emma said. "I haven't known you long, but what I do know tells me you had a hard row to hoe, growing up without a mother."

Sarah sighed and sat up straighter. "Goodness, haven't we gotten morose?"

Emma brightened and refilled their coffee cups. Clacking the pot back on the stove, she inquired, "So what do you think of our marshal?"

Sarah shot a glance at Emma. "Did you just see the hair bristle on the scruff of my neck?"

Returning to her chair, Emma laughed and took a sip of hot coffee. "There are a lot of rumors flying around about the two of you."

"They're not rumors. They're all true. We quite despise one another."

"What started it?"

"*He* started it!" Sarah became incensed. "The first night I came into town looking for Addie, who do you think was the first man I encountered going into Rose's? Your honorable marshal, that's who!"

"He's single, in the prime of life. What did you expect?"

"*Emma!*" Sarah's eyes and lips opened in astonishment.

"I'm only being realistic. We just got finished naming the families in the gulch. Us few married women, plus you and the upstairs girls are the only females for three hundred miles around. And men will be men."

"He's paid to uphold the law, not to flaunt it!"

"That's true, and I'm not excusing him. I'm talking about the nature of men."

"You are *too* excusing him!"

"Well, perhaps I am."

"Why?"

"Because I think he's a fair man when it comes to the law and he's got a hard job, taming this town."

"What if it were Byron who was frequenting Rose's? Would you be so forgiving then?"

"But it's not."

"But if it were."

"Byron and I have talked about it. He's happy at home."

Sarah had no idea married people discussed such subjects. She found herself discomfited and hid behind her coffee cup.

"Well." Emma set down her mending and slapped a hand down on the tabletop. "It seems we've had our first disagreement. This will tell us how good a friends we can be."

"I espouse causes, I know. Sometimes I become too zealous."

"I suppose that's how it ought to be for a woman in your business. But for a woman in mine it pays to look plainly at the temptations the world holds for a man and to see to it that *my* man has no reasons to seek them out."

They grew quiet for a while, studying each other, realizing they had been uncommonly frank with one another in this first private discussion.

"So . . ." Emma said.

"So . . ."

"Friends?"

"Yes, friends."

Emma squeezed the back of Sarah's hand on the tabletop.

The exchange lingered on Sarah's mind as she walked back to her hotel. Before coming to Deadwood if she had bumped heads with a woman over the subject of men frequenting brothels she'd have shunned the woman ever after. But she liked Emma, respected her in spite of her outlandish stand, and valued her newfound friendship, which Sarah was sure would grow in the years ahead. Emma was a wife and mother, a respectable woman who had a respectable marriage, and still she took a liberal stand on the issue of the marshal's peccadilloes.

How surprising that Sarah still respected Emma.

Perhaps she was still growing up.

The thought came with some surprise, for she had always considered herself years ahead of her age in maturity, thrust into it by the early loss of her mother, her sister's dependence on her at home, and her father's dependence on her in business, and he certainly had depended on her, more and more the older she got. Oddly, however, by depending, he had made her independent, for he had afforded her the opportunity to demonstrate her capabilities at an age when most young girls were still at home stitching samplers. Serious-minded as she was, she had thrived upon both the challenge and the success. The more her father praised her, the more diligently she had worked, in the end acquiring a master trade, a rarity for a woman.

So it was true; she'd been playing a grown-up role for so long she hadn't realized she had some maturing to do. Yet within two days of arriving in Deadwood she had bumped up against situations and people who had already begun to force her to a new plateau of growth.

Adelaide, of course—and who knew what mellowing would be required on Sarah's part before coming to terms with Adelaide's situation?

The marshal—she'd already run such a gamut of emotions due to that man, she felt years older after the confrontations.

And now Emma—a good, wholesome wife and mother who had reached out a hand in friendship but who—Sarah was certain—aimed to teach Sarah a thing or two about tolerance.

Well, she'd concede that Emma had the right to hold whatever views she chose about Deadwood's representative of the law visiting whorehouses instead of shutting them down, but she, Sarah, intended to use her considerable power as both a woman and a newspaperwoman to bring him to heel *and* to shut down the houses and clean up this town.

The following morning she awakened early, took a set of clean clothes and went to the bathhouse, where she sank into a copper tub of hot water to her armpits. Reclining, she let her hair trail into the water behind her and emptied her mind of all but the unaccustomed luxury of being warm, clean and drifting. She washed her hair, toweldried and twisted it into a knot, dressed, and rolled up her dirty clothes to be dropped off at the laundry. She opened the door, stepped out into the hall and came face to face with Noah Campbell, holding his own roll of dirty clothes.

They both came up short.

He looked like a herd of buffalo had stampeded his face. It was eight shades of blue, purple and rose. His left eye was split like an outgrown tomato skin and his lower lip was bigger than Dutch Van Aark's. No hat in sight either, to help hide the damage. A single glimpse of Campbell and Sarah felt her collar grow tight.

"Marshal," she said stiffly.

Campbell nodded, stiffly, too.

"I'm sorry about that."

"I'm sure you are," he replied sarcastically.

"How is your friend Mr. Blevins?"

"Let's get one thing straight, Miss Merritt." Beneath his mustache his mouth was shrunken into a tight knot. "I don't like you and you don't like me, so why pretend to make polite chitchat when we run into each other? Just stay out of my way and let me do my job, and we'll pretend to tolerate each other."

He turned and stalked off up the hallway, leaving her to stand red-faced with embarrassment.

When he disappeared her mouth got just like his had been. *Insufferable, despicable, freckle-faced boor!*

She was so angry she went to Emma's to blow off steam. Emma wiped her hands on her white cobbler apron and said, "What's got you upset this morning?"

"The marshal, that's what!"

"You run into him already this morning?"

"At the bathhouse. He's despicable!"

"He probably thinks the same thing about you. Here, have a warm bun and cool down. You two are going to be bumping into each other pretty regular in a town this size, so you might as well get used to it."

Sarah tore off a mouthful of bun and chewed it in a totally undignified manner. "I'm going to put a stop to him or to the brothels or both, Emma, mark my words!"

Emma laughed and said, "Well, good luck."

Josh appeared and Sarah was forced to cool down.

"Morning, Miss Merritt."

"Hello, Josh. Why don't you call me Sarah."

"I'll try."

She smiled. Emma and Byron had raised some fine kids.

"I was just heading for work," Josh said.

"So was I. Let's walk together."

Sarah took some extra buns and the two headed toward the *Chronicle* office. It was a pretty day, the town was bustling, and she forced the marshal from her thoughts.

"I've been thinking," she said to her new apprentice, "this first issue of the paper—it might be good for business to make it a complimentary copy. What do you think?"

Josh was surprised at being consulted. "But—gosh!—if you sold them for a penny apiece you could make three dollars and twenty-five cents!"

"But if I gave them away free, and gained goodwill in return, then went to two sheets next issue, I could perhaps get three cents, or four, or even a nickel. Now what do you think?"

They decided the first copy would be complimentary.

At the office Sarah fixed Josh up with a canvas shoulder bag to carry the papers. As he headed out she ordered, "Leave one on every doorstep, and at every business, then go up and down the gulch and give them to the miners."

"Yes, ma'am." He opened the door.

"Oh . . . and, Josh?"

"Yes?"

"Every business but the badlands. I don't want you anywhere near those buildings."

"Yes, ma'am." He turned to go.

"And one more thing," she called. "Make certain that the marshal gets one. You hand it to him personally, do you understand?"

"Yes, ma'am."

When Josh was gone, Sarah checked her watch. She had agreed to give Patrick Bradigan a try as a typesetter and had made arrangements to meet him at the office at eight A.M. It was already eight-twenty and no Irishman in sight.

He arrived at eight-fifty, red-eyed and affable, dressed in a brown tweed frock coat with his composing stick in his pocket and a red muffler tied jauntily around his throat.

"Top o' the morning to you, Miss Merritt," he offered, doffing an aging black top hat and bowing from the waist.

"Good morning, Mr. Bradigan. Am I mistaken, or did we agree on meeting at eight o'clock?"

"Eight o'clock, is it?" He pronounced his *t*'s crisply. "I thought it was nine. I says to meself, a pretty young thing like Miss Merritt must be getting at least that much beauty sleep to have eyes as bright as highland bluebells."

"And you've been kissing the Blarney stone, Mr. Bradigan." He was a likable fellow, but she took his flattery with a grain of skepticism, realizing that the footing upon which they started was the one upon which they would proceed. In a tone of light reproof she told him, "If you want to work for me you'll have to understand from the start that I won't abide your oversleeping, or arriving late, or missing appointments. When I commit myself to printing two newspapers a week I must know that I can rely on my staff to be here when I expect them."

He doffed his hat again and held it over his heart, bowing deep. (She already recognized he was a great one for bowing.) "My apologies, young miss, and I'll remember."

"Good. Then permit me—may I ask a few questions?"

Returning his hat to his head and tapping its top, he said, "You may."

"How old are you, Mr. Bradigan?"

"I'll be thorty-two on the Feast of St. Augustine."

"You're a journeyman printer?"

"I am."

"Where have you worked before?"

"From Boston to St. Louis and a dozen towns in between."

"What kind of presses have you worked with?"

"The wee ones—Gallys, Cottrells, Potters—and the big ones, too—the Hoe Ten Cylinder. I've even had a chance to operate one of the new Libertys that won the gold medal in Paris last year."

"Ah, and how was it?"

" 'Twas a beauty. Printed clear as a Kilkenny brook and distributed the ink perfectly. And that treadle saved on me poor tired back."

"Then why did you leave it?"

"Well now, you see . . ." He cleared his throat and scratched his temple. "There was a sortain young lady who broke me heart." He placed his hand over it and gave the ceiling a gaze of dejection.

A likely story, thought Sarah. *He probably showed up inebriated for work once too often and got fired. Or woke up in a stupor at noon one day and decided it was time to move on.*

"How fast can you work?"

"I can set two thousand ems an hour."

Her left eyebrow rose. "Two thousand." That was fast.

"Mignon," he added, naming the style of type.

"As you saw yesterday, I use Caslon, primarily, for the body type. It's what my father used."

"Caslon's all right. I've worked with it, too."

"I'll give you a try, then, Mr. Bradigan, at a dollar fifty a day if that's agreeable, and you'll work from eight until six."

"Those terms are acceptable."

"Agreed, then." She extended her hand. When he took it she felt the early-morning tremor in his. "To the success of the *Deadwood Chronicle,*" she said, giving two hard pumps.

"To the success of the *Chronicle,* " he seconded, and she withdrew her hand.

Leading the way toward the rear, she said, "Before we do anything else I want to get Father's clock hung up. I learned to the sound of its ticking, and I miss it."

"I spied it yesterday, when we were setting up. I'll be knowin' just which crate it's in."

With Bradigan's help, Sarah unearthed the familiar Waterbury in its fine walnut case, with its eight-day movement, ornamented pendulum and detailed hand carving. When it hung on the wall she set the hands to 9:09, closed the glass door and set the pendulum swinging. Standing back, she looked up at it.

"There, that's better. Wait until you hear it chime. It has a splendid cathedral gong that strikes on the quarter hour."

"Ahh," he responded, rolling back on his heels.

For several seconds they listened to the *tick-tocks,* then Sarah inquired, "Is there any plaster in this town, Mr. Bradigan?"

"Plaster, you say?"

"The clock looked so much better on our plastered walls in St. Louis. I miss them."

"Not that I know of. Not a soul I know's got plastered walls."

"Then let's be the first," she proposed. "I shall order some by Pony Express Mail today. Have you had your breakfast, Mr. Bradigan?"

"Me breakfast?"

"I've brought some buns from the bakery. Would you like one?"

When she offered one, he backed off with both palms raised. "No, no, none o' that for me. Me belly can't take it so early in the mornin'. But if it's all the same to you I will have a tot o' the rye—to oil the hinges, don't you know." From the capacious pockets of his frock coat he withdrew a small flask of whiskey and, with two fingers raised, took two deep swallows.

Watching him, she knew it would be useless to protest. Much as she disliked his imbibing, especially in so forthright a manner, she suspected that if she remonstrated with rules about his alcohol consumption she would lose a 2,000-em-per-hour typesetter. He was what she'd suspected—a tramp printer who'd wandered in off the stage with his composing stick in his pocket, and who would wander off again without notice, in a year or less, following the pattern of the majority of his ilk. The country was full of them, men who by virtue of the tedium of their trade had turned to the "ardent spirits" to break the monotony of routine, talented men who could set type like dervishes once they had several shots under their belt, but whose hands, without benefit of alcohol, shook as if palsied. She'd seen dozens of them come and go from her father's newspaper office over the years. Since Patrick Bradigan had seen the need to "oil his hinges" before so much as touching type for the first time today, she supposed he'd need the same lead time every day to allow the insidious stuff to calm his hands.

She turned away to find the article she'd written about yesterday's riot and subsequent arrest. Handing it to him, she inquired, "Can you read my writing?"

"As clear as me old mother's prayer book."

"Good, then I'll leave you to your task, since you know where everything is."

Covertly she glanced at the clock—9:13—and set about unpacking her books and small tools while pretending to pay him no mind. He did all the proper things, all in the fashion taught her by her father: removed his outerwear and rolled up his sleeves, a must where restricted movement meant inefficiency and a starched cuff could cause pied—spilled—type. He measured the width of yesterday's columns; set his composing stick to the correct length; dropped in the proper-length slug; settled it in his left hand with the thumb inside, fingers folded across the bottom—faultless form. Though Sarah turned away, she was wholly conscious of the *snick, snick, snick,* as he began plucking type—left elbow tilting, bringing the stick to meet the type in the most proficient fashion. *Snick, snick snick:* spacing, justifying, with scarcely a syncopation in rhythm.

He hadn't been lying. He was fast. Three lines were filled and transferred to the galley before the clock struck the quarter hour. Even the sound of the chime didn't distract him.

"You're right—splendid," he remarked at the reverberation, his hands flashing.

Patrick Bradigan went on creating the music Sarah loved while she unpacked her possessions and smiled at her good fortune. She thought of her father and how they'd worked together companionably this way, years ago; of her future and all she hoped to build here with this newspaper.

She thought of Noah Campbell and wondered if he'd read her editorial yet.

She thought of Addie, probably asleep in her room after a night of men like Campbell.

There were reforms needed in this town and she, Sarah, was here to make them.

Bradigan finished typesetting the article and slid it onto the composing stone, framed it with the chase, filled it with the furniture, locked it into place with quoins and tilted it to check the justification before carrying it to the press and pulling a proof. He used a pallet knife to spread a strip of ink, rolled it even on the brayer and inked his type with exactly four passes of the tool—the perfect number for greatest efficiency. He loaded the frisket, pulled the proof and brought it to Sarah for inspection.

"Thank you," she said quietly, then put on her spectacles and looked it over slowly. He had chosen Gothic Sans Serif for the headline—an appropriate matchup for Caslon body type. His indentations were uniform, justified edges clean; no misspellings or omissions. Flawless, fast work.

She removed her glasses, returned the proof and gave him a smile. "I think we'll get along just fine, Mr. Bradigan."

Sarah spent the morning setting up the remainder of her shop and greeting townspeople who came in to welcome her and the newspaper to Deadwood. Josh returned from distributing the papers and said he needed more, so he and Patrick got the press running again while she went to make calls on Lawrence Chapline and Dr. Turley. She paid the doctor and learned that True Blevins was progressing nicely. She went next to Elias Pinkney's bank to withdraw some gold dust and inquire about the wording on his advertisement. When he saw her enter the building he leaped from his desk chair and met her with his hand extended.

"Miss Merritt, my my, how lovely to see you again."

"Thank you, Mr. Pinkney." His name truly was appropriate: his cheeks, pate and mouth were all as pink as a baby's belly; pinker than ever as he continued smiling ingratiatingly and appropriating her hand.

"Everyone is talking about the first issue of your paper. Everybody. We're awfully proud to have it *and you* in Deadwood."

"I understand I have you to thank for making it possible."

"It is absolutely my pleasure to be of service to you."

She forcefully freed her hand from his grip and discreetly wiped it on her skirt. "The building is perfect and I'd love to keep it on whatever basis it's available. I can either rent or buy."

"Come, Miss Merritt." He appropriated her elbow. "Have a chair, please." He seated her beside his desk and concentrated on her eyes as if they were pools of blue water and he a man finishing hard labor on a hundred-degree day. For a moment she imagined him shucking off his clothes and getting ready to jump. The picture was distasteful. He was pudgy all over and had hairless, pink, feminine hands to go with his hairless, pink, feminine face.

"The rent, Mr. Pinkney." She put on her most professional mien. "Shall we settle that?"

"Oh, there's no hurry." He waved away her concern and sat back in his chair. "Your newspaper is the talk of the town. It's very well done. Very well done."

His repeating drove her crazy. She considered replying, "Thank you, thank you." Instead she told him, "I've hired some good help—Mr. Bradigan and Josh Dawkins. Without them I'm afraid I couldn't have gotten the first issue out nearly as fast as I did."

"How often do you plan to publish?"

"Twice a week."

"Ahh . . . industrious. Very industrious." He leaned close enough that she caught whiffs of his breath. It smelled like cloves, and she found herself wondering if he'd popped one into his mouth since she'd entered the bank.

"I thought perhaps we could set down the wording of your ad while I'm here."

"Of course! Of course!" he said eagerly. While they did business he smiled so broadly, attended her so ingratiatingly, that she felt claustrophobic. She brought up the subject of the building three more times, but he refused to name a price. Though he had a clerk to do so, he personally fetched her gold dust from the safe, and touched her hand while returning her pouch. She scarcely controlled the urge to recoil, but thanked him politely and bid him good day.

"One moment, Miss Merritt," he said, detaining her with a grip on her elbow. She knew instinctively what was coming and scrabbled through her mind for a graceful refusal.

"I wondered if some evening you'd do me the honor of allowing me to buy you supper."

But I'm looking down on the top of your bald, pink head.

"I do thank you, Mr. Pinkney, but I have so much to do these days, getting the business set up and acquainting myself with the town. Why, I still don't have a decent place to live."

"Perhaps I could do something about that, too."

"Oh no. I wouldn't want any more favors. My fellow townspeople might begin to resent me when the waiting lists are so long."

"I own a lot of property in this town, Miss Merritt. Where would you like to live? I'm certain something can be arranged."

And all I have to do is go to dinner with you. And let you fondle my hand and breathe cloves on my chin (the level where his mouth reached).

"Thank you again, Mr. Pinkney, but I'll wait my turn. The hotel really isn't so bad."

He smiled and extended his hand for a shake. She gave hers reluctantly and he held it in his damp palm. "The offer still stands. Supper anytime you're free."

Leaving the bank, the light dawned. He was bribing her! Free rent and a place to live, and all she had to do was submit to his attentions. Her face grew red and her temperature boiled. Why, he was no better than Campbell! He only disguised his proposition behind a façade of graciousness.

She had no delusions about herself and her pulchritude. She was a plain woman with too long a nose, overly tall, with more intelligence than most men wanted in a female companion. But she was—after all—female. No other qualifications were necessary in a town with the dearth of distaff that Deadwood suffered. It would have made some women feel heady. Sarah felt insulted. If a woman shortage was the only reason the men in this town wanted her, they could all go lick!

She returned to the newspaper office in a lather and had scarcely caught her breath when the door opened and the marshal walked in.

She knew in a moment that he had read the editorial.

She faced him squarely as he propelled himself across the room with clunking steps that said he'd as soon plaster the walls with her as speak to her.

"Your license," he said, without preliminaries, dropping it on a table where she'd begun arranging her wood engraving cuts.

"Thank you."

"See that you keep it posted on your wall."

"I will."

The two words hadn't cleared her lips before he was halfway back to the door, slamming it behind himself. No "Good day, Miss Merritt," no greeting for Patrick or Josh, just *clunk, clunk, hang this, clunk, clunk, bang!*

Sarah, Josh and Patrick were still exchanging surprised glances when the door opened and Campbell stormed in again. Standing two feet inside the entrance, he jabbed a finger at Sarah and said, "You owe me for a hat, lady!"

On his way out he slammed the door so hard the clock door drifted open.

"He must've read your editorial," Patrick said.

"Good!" she said, and threw down a woodblock with enough force to send two others jumping out of the case. With steps as aggravated as Campbell's she strode past the clock, closed its door, continued to her desk, collected what she needed and whisked toward the door.

"I have some errands to do. I'll be back in a couple of hours."

She was *sick and tired* of the men in this town!

At Tatum's Store she marched in and found herself ogled by a half-dozen more of them as she advanced toward the hats along the right. The store owner approached. He resembled a beaver, with prominent teeth, a rather receding, flat nose and thick hair that grew very low on his brow and was slicked straight back with pomade. His smile was broad and ingratiating.

"Miss Merritt?"

"Yes."

"I'm Andrew Tatum. Much obliged for the newspaper."

"You're welcome, Mr. Tatum. I hope you enjoyed it."

"Most certainly did and we're happy to have you in town."

"Thank you."

"Are you interested in a hat?"

"Yes, I am."

"I'm sorry to say we don't carry hats for ladies."

"No, not for myself. It's for a man."

"A man's hat?" he repeated, surprised.

"That's right."

"What color?"

"Black . . . no, brown." She'd be damned if she'd buy him the color he preferred.

"What size?"

"Size?" She hadn't given size a thought. Something for a bullhead, she supposed, considering the man's insufferable attitude.

"It's for Marshal Campbell." Six pairs of ears pointed her direction from all around the store.

"Ahhhh . . ." Tatum elongated the sound and rubbed the underside of his nose. "I'd guess Noah wears about a seven and a half."

"Fine."

"Now this one . . ." He took one off a block and donned it on his knuckles, pointing out its features with his free hand. "This one's called The Boss of the Plains, and there isn't a man alive wouldn't be proud to own this hat. It came clear from Philadelphia. It's a J. B. Stetson, made of one hundred percent nutria fur, with a silk band and lining. Crown is four and a half inches and the brim, four. But look here—it weighs only six ounces . . ." Holding it by the brim, he bounced it in both hands. "Yet it'll hold off the sun and the rain, and it's tough enough to be used as a whip if need be, or a pillow, or for watering your horse, or for fanning a campfire." Again, he demonstrated. "I believe Noah would be more than happy with this hat."

"Fine. I'll take it." Everyone in the store was gawping by now. Sarah wished Tatum would pipe down and get to his gold scale.

"Don't you want to know how much?" he inquired, loud enough to be heard by J. B. Stetson himself, clear out in Philadelphia.

"How much?"

"Twenty dollars."

Twenty dollars! She swallowed her surprise and went with Tatum to the scale, where he weighed out the full ounce of gold while speculative murmurings began among his other customers. When the purchase was complete, she inquired, "Can you deliver it, Mr. Tatum?"

Tatum appeared nonplussed. "Well, I guess I can, though I suspect Noah is in his office right now, and it's only a few doors down."

"Thank you so much. I'd appreciate it if you would do that for me. Tomorrow will be time enough."

"And what should I say about who's sending it to him?"

"Tell him Miss Merritt always pays her debts."

"You bet I will, Miss Merritt. You bet I will."

Leaving Tatum's store, she was certain she was blushing, which left her displeased with herself. She wished she were a man. Only those of the spear side could hope for any degree of anonymity in this male-dominated town. Not only was she a woman, but a newspaper publisher as well, and both virtues magnified her visibility. She had no doubt the news would spread faster than spilled water that the editor of the *Chronicle* had bought a new hat for the marshal, who had locked her in an abandoned mine the day before. Certainly there would be speculation about why. Well, let them wonder! She herself knew why. Because she wanted the books cleared between them so he'd have nothing to come back at her with. Her debt to Noah Campbell was paid in full. No further byplay need pass between them ever again.

Her temper had scarcely dimmed by the time she reached Rose's. This time the door was locked and she had to knock. Flossie answered.

"What you want?"

"I want to see my sister."

Flossie took a long, disparaging look at Sarah's pinched mouth and proper clothes, then thumbed over her shoulder. "Out back."

Sarah went down the center hall, passed the kitchen and found Addie collecting dry underwear from a clothesline in a tiny square of space behind it. The area was enclosed by a crude bark fence and held some water barrels and a huge woodpile that rested against the rear of the building. Addie's hair was wet and she wore a faded green dressing robe. Sarah watched for a moment and went down four wooden steps before speaking.

"Hello, Addie."

Addie glanced back over her shoulder before resuming her work. "What do you want?" she asked crossly.

"I brought you a copy of my first newspaper."

"I heard about it."

"It looks much the same as Father's. The same type and layout. I thought it might bring back some happy memories for you."

Addie plucked the last garment and dropped it into a wicker basket. She propped the basket on her hip and brushed past Sarah on her way up the steps. "You can keep your memories and keep your paper."

"Addie, please, why are you so bitter?"

Addie paused in the doorway, looking down on Sarah. "I'm surprised you come around here, a hoity-toity newspaperwoman like you. Don't you care about your reputation?"

"It's your reputation I care about."

"So I heard. You've been writing editorials."

"One, yes. I want you to read it." Sarah held out the paper.

"Leave me alone," Addie said and went inside, closing the door behind her.

Sarah studied the entrance for some time, then glanced down at the copy of the *Chronicle* in her hands. This made two times in as many days that she'd been told to keep her newspaper. She released a sigh and her shoulders sagged. What was she fighting for? For a sister who wanted to remain a harlot? For a dumpy, dirty town she didn't even like? To be accepted as a decent woman by a bunch of men who didn't have the faintest notion how to treat a lady?

She was sorry she'd come here. Sorry she'd found Addie. Sorry she'd left St. Louis. Disillusioned and very, very tired, Sarah re-entered the brothel, left the newspaper on one of the tables in the reception room and quietly went away.

CHAPTER 6

NOAH Campbell had read Sarah's editorial, all right. Read it and wanted to go over to that newspaper office of hers and run her through her own press a few times. The damned woman was a pain in the ass . . . and the eye and the lip and the ear, for that matter. One was black and blue, one was swollen and the other had a hole in it, all because of Sarah Merritt. To top it off, she wasn't content to get him mauled in the street, now she was mauling him in print. A hundred and fifty men probably went through *one* of those whorehouses in a night and she singled out *him*, Noah Campbell, the marshal of Deadwood, to hold up as an example of tarnished virtue!

For two cents he'd use her rag to light a fire in his office stove, but he'd be in trouble with his mother if he did. If Carrie Campbell found out the town had its own newspaper and Noah went out there without a copy—look out! And he *was* going out to the Spearfish, probably tomorrow.

Meanwhile, Noah had to find someone to fill in for him while he was gone. It was only an eighteen-mile drive, but he'd decided to stay overnight and get in a visit with his family while he was there.

On the morning following his starring role in Sarah Merritt's muck column, he was interviewing young Freeman Block with an eye to deputizing him when Andy Tatum came into his office wearing one hat and carrying another.

"Noah . . . Freeman," Andy greeted. "Mighty pretty weather we've been having, isn't it?"

"Sure is," Noah replied. "So pretty I'm fixing to take a ride out to the Spearfish and leave Freeman here in charge."

Freeman grinned and pointed at the brown Stetson. "You worried there's going to be a hat shortage, Andy?"

Andy chortled and needlessly brushed at the crown of the hat with his knuckles. "No. This is a delivery for Noah. From the new lady in town." Andy extended the hat.

Noah went stone-still. His expression turned dyspeptic.

"For you," Andy said. "Take it."

Noah leaned forward in his desk chair and reluctantly took the hat. "Do I understand you correctly? It's from that Merritt woman?"

"That's right. She said to tell you she always pays her debts."

Noah looked at it as if it might bite him.

"It's a damned good hat, too." Andy tugged up his pants.

"I can see that."

"Twenty dollars' worth."

Freeman whistled.

Andy was enjoying himself. "She didn't bat an eye when I told her how much it cost. Well, aren't you going to try it on?"

Noah settled the hat on his head very gingerly, using two hands.

"It fits," Freeman noted.

"Looks good, too," Andy said.

"Spiffy," Freeman added. "I wish I had some woman giving *me* hats."

"Aw, now, just a minute. There's no love lost between that bean pole and me."

Freeman's expression turned to one of lascivious speculation. "Any woman ever give *you* a hat, Andy?"

"Nope. The most any woman ever give *me* was a bad case of the crabs. Course, Noah ain't gonna have any of those from now on since he's gonna be staying away from the badlands."

While Freeman and Andy hooted and slapped their thighs, Noah glowered. "Now listen, you two, don't you go spreading any rumors about Sarah Merritt and me. Why, we can hardly be in the same room together without a pair of whips."

"Spreading any rumors! Hell, there were half a dozen men in my store when she walked in and picked out that hat and said plain as the sky for me to deliver it to you. Who's spreading rumors? My guess is she's got an eye for you, Noah. I'd put money on it. Why, hell, how many men do you figure there are up and down these gulches? Ten thousand? Twenty? And about two dozen women, which gives that little newslady a few to pick from. So who does she buy a new hat for? Noah Campbell, that's who."

"Must be his shiny tin badge," Freeman put in, smirking.

Noah took the hat off and flung it on the desk. "Now, Freeman, goddammit, watch yourself!"

Andy winked at Freeman. "I think it's that hairy mustache, myself. Some women like those things, you know. Me, I never could see why a man would want to hang a scrub mop beneath his nose, but it takes all kinds."

Freeman considered the marshal's upper lip with mock seriousness. "You think it's the mustache, huh? I heard a rumor about something that happened up at Rose's the first night that newspaper gal came to town and—"

Noah jumped to his feet and pointed at the door. "Freeman, goddammit! Do you want the job as deputy or not? 'Cause I can find plenty who do!"

"I sure do, Noah. I sure do." Freeman puckered, still chuckling silently.

"Then shut the hell up!"

"Sure thing, boss."

"And, Andy, I don't give a damn what your customers heard at the store. That woman and me get along like hot grease and water."

"As you say, Marshal. I'll do my best to stifle the rumors."

When the two were gone, Noah stomped around his office, kicked a chair and glared at the hat, still lying on his desk. If it were any other woman, in any other occupation, with any other kind of temperament, he might be interested. Lord knew it was lonely enough out here. But not that tall, gangly four-eyes, with her forked tongue and her pointed editorials! He'd continue at Rose's, thank you. But he'd wear the hat. Why shouldn't he? He'd earned it, by God.

He picked it up, creased the crown to his liking and plunked it on his head. On the floor in the corner lay a saddlebag. From it he took a small mirror and checked his reflection. Looked good. Looked damned good, if he did say so himself. His eyes dropped from the hat to his black eye, down his very Scottish nose to his bushy mustache, which he smoothed with his free hand.

All right, so what the hell was wrong with mustaches!

The next day Noah rented an American Beauty runabout with tufted, sprung seats and plenty of legroom—the most comfortable buggy available at Flecek's livery barn. In it he and True Blevins set out for the Spearfish Valley.

They'd ridden for some time, talked about the wonderful fall weather, the peace treaty the Indians had finally signed, the high market value of animal feed in the gulches and the relative merit of chewing tobacco. True helped himself to a fresh twist and offered some to Noah.

"No, thanks."

They rode on companiably, enjoying the balmy day, the blue sky, the peace. Their route followed Deadwood Creek northeast out of the gulch, then swung northwest, following the outer rim of the Hills through tranquil pine-and-spruce-covered mountains where quick streams flowed over shiny brown rocks. Beside these, peach-leaved willows flourished. Wild currants and serviceberries gleamed ripe in the autumn sun with black-billed magpies flying among them in sudden flashes of white.

After a long stretch of silence, Noah said thoughtfully, "Hey, True?"

"What?"

"What do you think about mustaches?"

"Mustaches?"

"Yeah."

"Hell, I got one, ain't I? What do you think I think of 'em!"

"No, I mean, do you think women like them?"

"Women! What brought this on?"

"Aw, hell, forget it."

True spit over the side of the buggy, then wiped his soup strainer.

"You got something stuck in your craw? Like that newspaperwoman maybe?"

"Ha."

"I told you to look out for her."

"She's the last female I'd cotton to. Why, hell, did you read that editorial she put in her paper? She might as well have come right out and said it was the marshal of Deadwood she ran into up at Rose's her first night in town."

"What do you care? Ain't a single man in the gulch don't use the badlands."

"Yeah."

"Me, I was plannin' on gettin' a little myself soon as I had my train unloaded, but after Doc got done puncturin' me a little bigger I wasn't sure my system could stand it."

They rode awhile longer, then True asked, "So what about her sister, the one named Eve—you done it with her?"

"Who hasn't?"

"Man, them two don't look atall alike, do they? That Eve, she's soft where a woman's got to be soft. And her face ain't too bad either."

Noah tossed a partial grin True's way. True had something there.

"I've been thinking . . ." Dropping the thought, Noah remained silent for so long True had to ask, "About what?"

"Oh, I don't know. Women. You know—the other kind. You ever done it with one that you cared about?"

True stretched his legs out and caught one wrist on the backrest behind Noah. He studied the ridge ahead and got a faraway look in his blue eyes.

"Yeah, I sure did. I was eighteen at the time. Had me a little gal that wanted to marry me in the worst way—Francie was her name. I was hauling freight for the Army then between Kansas and Utah, while they were trying to subdue those stubborn Mormons. She was one of them, a Mormon. I swear, for a while there, I was thinking about taking up the religion."

"What happened?"

"Her family had already promised her to one of her own. When she married him he already had two other wives. I swear, Noah, I never got over that. Hell, she loved me. She *said* she loved me. And I loved her, too, then she went and did a thing like that, married a man as old as Methuselah who already had more than his share of wives. I tell you, it soured me on *honest* women forever."

"How old are you now, True?"

"Forty."

"And you never met another one you cared for?"

"Nope, and I didn't want to neither."

"What about kids? You ever want kids?"

"A man like me's got no business wanting kids . . . never in one place, hauling freight and cussing at oxen. Hell, what would I do with a family? Nothing but a hobble on a man's leg."

If Noah detected a wistful note in True's words he refrained from saying so.

Shortly before ten A.M. they entered the Spearfish Valley. A natural amphitheater, it stretched out below them like an amethyst in a ring of jade. No wonder the Indians fought to prevent the white men from obtaining a foothold here. Not only was it beautiful, but fertile, with fast-running streams of pure cold water fed by melted snows and crystal springs. These streams coursed down from rockbound canyons in roaring torrents flecked with foam, a living, leaping source of health, wealth and happiness.

Noah's father, Kirk Campbell, had taken one look and decided the Spearfish Valley was destined to become the cradle of agriculture of western Dakota. Not for him the quick, fickle wealth of a mining claim, but the surer source of permanent prosperity to be found in a well-tilled farm.

Upon his arrival in the Black Hills in early May, Kirk had visited the valley's first white settler, James Butcher, who had already been forced by the hostile Indians from his original cabin and had built his second dwelling three miles east, near the spot where False Bottom Creek left the hills. Later in May, a large party of additional settlers arrived from Bozeman, Montana. Seasoned mountaineers, they were inured to hardship and Indian wars, fully capable of whipping any number of Indians daring to attack them. Along with them, Kirk Campbell settled in the Spearfish Valley. Immediately they had begun operations for securing ranches and water rights. They built a common stockade where they stored their provisions and ammunition and into which they drove their livestock at the close of each day. Through the summer Indian raids had continued sporadically, but the settlers—fully mindful of the shortage of arable, flat lands in this mountainous region, and of the insatiable demand for stock feed due to the influx of prospectors—posted guards and set about seeding their outlying fields.

Those fields lay ripe now at the turn of September into October, checkering the vista below with a range of hues from wheat gold to corn green. In the distance stock grazed—the great Montana herd—its population swelled by additional horses brought out from town each day to eat their fill at contract price. Drovers on horseback rode the perimeter of the herd, with one eye on the animals and one on the spine of the hills for any sign of Indians. In the patchwork fields the reapers worked, plying their scythes, followed by the shockers, leaving behind squares of tan earth tied by darker knots of brown—the shocks—like yarn in a crazy quilt.

Scattered across the valley were the farms themselves with the faint fuzz of failing fires drifting from the cabin chimneys, smudging the vast blue welkin above. Modest-sized outbuildings dotted the distance and from these, cart paths led like webbing toward the common stockade, which appeared to be made of toothpicks in the distance.

Down among the reapers Noah drove his rig, along the pummeled route the herd took each day, emerging from the foothills into the flat gold of an oats field where men raised their arms in greeting and women with their hair bound in kerchiefs paused to shade their eyes.

"Hello, Zach!" he called once. "Hello, Mrs. Cottrell!"

True waved, too, with his good arm.

"Looks like Mrs. Cottrell is pregnant," Noah remarked.

"Sure does."

They rode on until they came to the field south of the Campbell place, where the family was putting up hay—Kirk, his wife, Carrie, and Noah's younger brother, Arden. They were working with their backs to the approaching buggy, Kirk and Arden advancing side by side with their scythes swinging while Carrie followed with a curved wooden hay rake.

The three stopped working to watch the buggy approach.

"Anybody need a helping hand?" Noah called.

"Noah! . . . and True! Hello!"

They all came forward, smiling, dropping their tools and removing their gloves. "Well, this is a surprise." Noah's mother reached him first and rubbed her kerchief back off her hair before swabbing her face with it. "Holy Mother of God, what happened to you?"

Noah touched his eye. "I tangled with a woman."

Arden affectionately whapped Noah across the arm with his leather gloves. "Who was she, Calamity Jane?"

Kirk shook his son's hand, surveying the battle damage—"I'd like to see the woman that gave you this shiner." Next he glanced at True's slung arm. "The same one get you?"

True laughed and scratched his eyebrow with the edge of a horny index finger. "Not quite."

Kirk Campbell was a tower of a man, with hands as big as bear traps and a grip to match. He sported a bushy orange beard, bushy orange eyebrows and a faceful of fiery freckles to boot. His eyes, amidst all that color, shone bright as the bluebells of his homeland.

Carrie, on the other hand, was dark-haired and gray-eyed, though her skin took the sun much better than her husband's and had burnished over the summer. She was pudgy and pretty and only as tall as her sons' shoulders.

"A woman, huh?" Carrie repeated.

"It's a long story, Ma, but I brought True out here to recuperate for a week or so. Think you could feed him and keep him tied down?"

"Just watch me."

Noah put his mother in the buggy and sent her back to the house with True while he took her place with the hay rake. There was a measure of contentment to be found in working behind his father and brother, stepping off the lengths of the field to the rhythmic *shhhppp* of their scythes, to the greeny smell of fallen hay, scooping it into a windrow with the rake tines vibrating beneath his hands. For a day or two he enjoyed it. But always it became confining and he longed for the commerce and company of town.

"So, have you decided to come back to farming after all?" his father asked.

"Just for today."

It had been a disappointment to Kirk Campbell when his older son had decided to take the job in town instead of settling in the valley with the rest of the family.

"I suppose you know the Indians signed the treaty, Pa."

"Yup. News reached us."

"But you still have lookouts posted."

"We do, but we haven't had a raid since midsummer. Hardly ever see them on the ridges anymore. My guess is it's a lot less risky living out here these days than it is living in town. By the looks of you anyway. I'd sure like to hear what you did to get that purple eye."

So Noah told the story.

His father and brother exchanged inquisitive glances. Kirk asked, "How old is she?"

Arden asked, "What does she look like?"

At sunset, around the kitchen table, his mother asked, "Is she married?"

True answered, "Nope," and stabbed himself another piece of bread.

"Did you bring us one of her newspapers?"

Noah said, "I did, but if I let you read it I don't want any guff out of any of you."

When Carrie had read it she pronounced, "This is a smart woman and an honest one. You could do worse."

Noah nearly choked on his mutton stew.

"For Chrissakes, Ma!"

"You know I don't abide cussing at the table. You're not getting any younger, you know. How long do you think a single woman will last before somebody else snaps her up?"

"They can have her!"

"That's how your father felt about me the first time he saw me. I laughed at his red hair and freckles and told him he looked like a frying pan that had been left out in the rain. Six years later we were married."

"Ma, I told you, this woman is like a bad case of hives. She's making my life miserable."

"The next time you come out here bring her along. If *you* don't want her maybe your brother would be interested in her."

"I'm not bringing her out here! I don't even like the woman!"

"All right then, I'll go take a look at her next time we come to town."

"Don't you dare!"

"Why not? I want some grandchildren before I die."

Noah rolled his eyes. "Jesus!" he muttered.

"Didn't I say no cussing at the table?"

Arden said, "Ma's right. If you don't want her I just *might.*"

"What's the matter with you! You talk as if she's the last pork chop on the platter and all you have to do is reach over and stab her with your fork."

"Well, I could use a wife. I want a farm of my own," Arden replied. "And now that the Indian Treaty is signed, a woman would be more anxious to live out here."

"Then you'd better move to town and get in line, because half the men in Deadwood are eyeballing her everywhere she goes. But I wouldn't get my hopes up if I were you. The way she's running that printing press I doubt that she's the kind who'd want to be a farmer's wife. Besides, she's older than you."

"I thought you said you don't know how old she is."

"I don't. I'm just guessing."

"Twenty-five, you said."

"Thereabouts, yes."

"Well, I'm only twenty-one."

"That's what I said! She's older than you."

"So what?"

This was the damnedest conversation Noah'd ever heard! What did he care if his mother came into town and looked over Sarah Merritt, or if Arden came and poked her with his fork? Let them do what the hell they wanted! He, on the other hand, would stay out of the woman's way.

Which he did until three days later, the first Monday of October, when the first city council meeting—as prescribed by their new organizational policies—was scheduled to be held at seven P.M. in Jack Langrishe's theater.

Since the theater troupe would begin a performance at nine, the council members met promptly at six fifty-five in hopes of clearing up all business in the two hours allotted.

Noah was standing in the center aisle between the rows of chairs, with his arms crossed, waiting for the proceedings to begin, listening to a conversation between George Farnum and a group of others. The subject, as usual, was the Indian Treaty and the recent news that Chiefs

Sitting Bull and Crazy Horse refused to comply with it. "Spotted Tail promised the commissioners that he would be answerable for Crazy Horse making peace, but he says Sitting Bull has a bad heart and that no one could answer for him."

"But the treaty's already signed. The Black Hills belong to the United States now."

"That won't stop Sitting Bull. We took his last sacred lands."

"Then it's our duty to impress upon the money centers of the East the value of the gold coming out of these hills. Let them put pressure on the federal government and demand military protection for the Hills. I for one still worry about—"

Noah glanced idly down the aisle and lost the drift of the conversation.

Sarah Merritt was advancing toward the group, her notebook pressed to her ribs.

When their eyes met, his arms uncrossed and her footsteps faltered. Her gaze shifted briefly to his new Stetson as she continued toward the knot of men. "Excuse me, gentlemen," she said, passing within inches of Noah's chest on her way toward the front of the auditorium.

She took a seat in the second row next to a miner whose name he couldn't remember. The miner looked up and leaped to his feet as she nodded to him, then the man resumed his chair and sat gawking at her profile. Noah watched the back of her head as she opened her notebook, got out a pen and ink, donned her spectacles and sat still as a stork, waiting. She was dressed in the same fusty brown suit as always. Her hair was pinched into a tiny knot that stuck out no farther than a nose on the back of her head. A tight, prissy hairdo for a tight, prissy woman. Glancing around the theater, he noted with acerbity the majority of the men ogling her as if she were a single mouse in a roomful of cats.

When the proceedings commenced, he took his place at a table up front with the mayor, the aldermen and the town clerk, Craven Lee, who also acted as ex-officio treasurer. George Farnum called the meeting to order and business began. Craven reported the election results, including the establishment of this very council and the town ordinances. Next came his treasury report, then Noah stood to deliver his report on what new licenses had been issued, including that to Sarah Merritt for the operation of the town's first newspaper. He avoided looking at her while reading his chicken-scratching, glancing her way only briefly as he resumed his seat. She sat correctly, spectacles downcast, taking notes.

After that, Noah sprawled back in his chair with his shoulders slanted and one forearm on the tabletop, trying to ignore her.

An issue was raised by the floor: the possibility of converting valuable cross streets into city lots. It was voted down.

A chimney rule was voted in: all future chimneys built within the city limits of Deadwood, South Deadwood and Elizabethtown were to have walls no less than four inches thick of brick or stone, completely imbedded in lime mortar and plastered on the inside with a smooth coat of the same.

A burning rule took effect: no shavings, hay or other combustible matter were to be set afire in any street, alley or thoroughfare nearer than twenty feet from any building, unless by direct permission in writing from the town council.

A dispute arose over the fixing of license rates. The lawyers and butchers in town protested that theirs were too high and should be lowered, and that those of the lucrative saloons should be raised. The rates remained unchanged.

Farnum asked if there was any more business.

Sarah Merritt stood up, removing her spectacles. "Mr. Mayor, if you please . . ."

"Miss Merritt," Farnum allowed.

Sarah's blue eyes were bright with conviction as she began to speak. "During the week I've been here I've noticed several situations that bear rectifying. The first—and in my estimation, the most important—is the lack of a school. I've taken it upon myself to begin a census of the families in the gulch, and by my count there are twenty-two children of school age residing in the area. That is indubitably enough that their education should be of primary concern to all of us. Most of them were severed from institutions of formal education in the cities they left behind. Some of them are being tutored by their mothers, but not all the mothers are literate, which throws the burden—I say, responsibility—back on us, the general, taxpaying populace of this town. Add to those the six children still too young for school, plus the Robinsons' infant, the first one born here on the Fourth of July, over whose birth I'm given to understand there was much rejoicing—and you can see the present need for a school. The future bears consideration as well. The signing of the Indian Treaty has already prompted safe passage of the first stagecoach into Deadwood. It, and soon the telegraph, combined with the news about the Peace Treaty, will bring even greater numbers of families here. I propose that by next spring, when that influx regenerates, we should have a teacher hired and a school established.

"Secondly, there's the matter of the animal offal in the streets. Not only is it unsightly and odoriferous, it poses a health hazard. We all know where cholera comes from, don't we? Our standards of sanitation are sorely in need of improvement. This town should hire a street cleaner and hire him now.

"Thirdly—though admittedly of minor importance—we might consider putting up streetlamps and combining the jobs of street cleaner and lamplighter into one.

"Fourthly comes the issue of boardwalks. Obviously no thought was put into their uniformity. Some of the businesses have them and some don't. Main Street is aesthetically repugnant, to say nothing of inconvenient. To traverse it one is forced to either progress like a jackrabbit beside the businesses or resort to slogging through the offal down its center. In a town so dominated by males, this is no surprise. However, gentlemen, if you want to encourage ladies—with their heel-length hems—to live here, I suggest you consider remedying this situation. To this effect, I propose passing an ordinance that not only makes boardwalks mandatory, but standardizes their height.

"Next I approach the obvious need for a suitable jail. The lockup you currently use is appalling. You have blacksmiths in this town. Put them to use building bars and appropriate whatever funds are necessary for the construction of a decent jail. Even a criminal deserves light and air.

"Lastly—and little thought is necessary for all of us to agree on this—we need a church. I understand your feeling that it will be difficult to woo another minister out here after the unfortunate slaying of Preacher Smith in August, but it is imperative that we try, and that when and if we get one, we have land and means set aside for the building of a church. We might consider constructing one building to temporarily serve as both church and school.

"That's all for now, gentlemen. I thank you for listening."

Miss Sarah Merritt calmly took her seat, hooked her glasses behind her ears and resumed her note-taking, presumably covering the issues she had just raised. The members of the city council exchanged glances, dumbfounded by such articulate rhetoric coming from the only female in the room. In the gallery, necks were stretched so men could get a better view of the woman up front. The miner next to Sarah puffed up with reflected importance, just sitting next to her. Noah took a good gander at her himself, as amazed as the rest of his constituents.

George Farnum broke the spell by chuckling and rubbing the back of his neck. "Well now, Miss Merritt, that's quite a bit of fat to chew."

She raised her eyes. "Yes, it is, Mr. Mayor."

"And we've got only so much money to work with."

"But we live in the richest pocket of land in America. I've heard that when news arrived here about the Peace Treaty being signed, miners rejoiced by scattering gold dust promiscuously in the very streets."

"That's true, but most of them are single men without families. They'd undoubtedly raise objections to being tithed for the building of a school. The land alone is going to come dear."

"Ask one of your wealthier property owners to donate it, then organize a school raising. Better yet, I'll organize the school raising. It will be easy for me since I have the newspaper at my disposal, and since I've already done the school census and know which families would be most likely to donate their time and muscle for the benefit of their children."

"That's very generous of you. And the land—do you have a solution as to where to get the land?"

"I've only been a resident of Deadwood for one week. No, I don't. But I know education is paramount. It *should* not and *can*not be delayed."

It was decided the issues would be thrown open for public discussion at the next town meeting, and that the board would announce this in the *Chronicle*. Also, it was voted that the minutes of each town meeting be reported in the *Chronicle* in the issue immediately following such meetings.

When the council meeting adjourned, Sarah became surrounded by men. They swarmed around her like flies around a raw steak. Miners and business owners; clean, dirty, old, young, the more-favored and the less: none, it seemed, were unsusceptible to the fact that she was dressed in skirts. The crowd included Teddy Ruckner, Dutch Van Aark, Doc Turley, Ben Winters, who owned the hotel where she resided, Andy Tatum and Elias Pinkney, who nudged his way through the press and appropriated her hand with an unmistakable air of possession.

Noah observed with a rancorous eye, then left his chair up front and made his way down the crowded aisle. As he eased through the knot of men around Sarah she looked up. Their eyes met. He gave a curt nod, she returned it and he moved on.

To Noah's intense dismay he found himself thinking of her in bed that night, the way he'd last seen her, surrounded by all those men, who fawned over her like besotted pups. Men could be such fools when faced with a woman shortage. Why, hell, she was about as curvy as a twelve-year-old boy, and she wasn't even pretty. Her face was too long and her nose too thin. Those spectacles made her appear bookish, and there was something distinctly off-putting about looking a woman in the eyes at the same height as your own.

She had good eyes, though. When she took those glasses off and set those bright blue eyes on you, you felt it clear to your toenails.

And Ma had one thing right. Sarah Merritt was bright. And gutsy to boot. How many women would attend a city council meeting, much less stand up before a roomful of aldermen and bombard them with criticism on their town, then offer suggestions for its improvement? Certainly the editor of any town newspaper had the power and the means to become a leader. But for a woman to do so . . .

Her temerity startled him.

The following morning dawned gloomy and cold. Noah awakened, peered at the window and drew the covers up tightly beneath his chin. He heard the clang of the iron range below as Mrs. Roundtree built a fire. From an adjacent room came the sound of snoring and he stayed a while longer in his warm cocoon.

Now why in the sam hell was he thinking of Sarah Merritt again?

He put her from his mind, sat up and stretched, donned his trousers and boots and made the trip outside. Back in his room, he washed and shaved with icy water—so icy that it drew his belly nearly to his backbone. He wet his hair, parted it on the side and combed it back uselessly. It seemed to have a will of its own. By the time it dried it would be sprigging up all around his hatline.

The smell of frying meat and boiling coffee drifted up from below and the house grew warmer. Footsteps sounded in the hall and down the stairs. Noah donned a red flannel shirt, a black leather vest, pinned on his star, left his gunbelt hanging on the back of a chair, and went down to breakfast.

Two steps into the dining room he came to a dead halt.

Sarah Merritt was seated at the table, taking a bite out of a biscuit.

Their eyes collided and her hand lowered. Slowly. Around her the other boarders stopped eating. She stared at Noah for several seconds, swallowed, then wiped her lips with a napkin.

"Well . . ." He continued toward the table. "This is a surprise. Good morning, everyone."

"Good morning," they chorused—all but Sarah Merritt. He seated himself in his usual chair, directly across from hers, and reached for an oval platter of meat. Only then did Sarah echo, quietly, "Good morning."

Mrs. Roundtree swept in from the kitchen—a buxom, red-faced

woman with a mole the size of a watermelon seed on her right cheek. She set a bowl of fried potatoes on the table. "I believe you two know each other."

"Yes," Noah replied. "We've met."

Sarah found her voice. "You live here?"

"Ever since Loretta opened for business."

Loretta filled Noah's cup from a blue granite coffeepot. "Miss Merritt moved in yesterday."

"What happened to McCooley?" Noah asked, glancing up while the coffee gurgled into his cup. Yesterday morning a tinsmith named McCooley had been sitting in Sarah's chair eating his breakfast.

"Got lonesome for his family and went back to Arkansas. I thought it'd be nice to have some female company around this place, so I told Miss Merritt she could have the room."

Noah got himself busy spreading jam on a biscuit, cutting his meat.

Tom Taft, at Noah's left, said, "We were just talking about the play at the Langrishe. Miss Merritt says it's good."

"You stayed for it?" Noah asked her, making an effort for propriety's sake at being civil.

She picked up his lead and answered, civilly, too, "Yes. I thought I would write a review of it for my next edition of the paper, let the outside world know we do have a touch of culture here in Deadwood. Jack Langrishe's troupe is, after all, one of the most renowned and respected in America. I found *Flies in the Weed* very well done. Have you seen it, Mr. Campbell?"

"Yes, I have." He glanced up and found her face as red as his own felt.

"What did you think of it?"

"I liked it, too."

"Well, at last we find something upon which we can agree."

Their eyes met again while he chewed and swallowed a mouthful of food.

"Maybe more than one thing," he mused.

"Have we agreed on something else?"

"The points you raised last night at the city council meeting. I couldn't agree more. Thank you for putting in a word about the need for a jail."

"There's no need to thank me. It's the truth."

"You were very convincing."

"I should be, don't you think? I have firsthand knowledge." She cocked her left eyebrow.

"I wouldn't be at all surprised to see you get every improvement you asked for."

"It's been true throughout history that wherever men go first, they reface. Then the women come along and refine."

Once again he was impressed by her eloquence.

"You really intend to act as organizer for a school raising?"

"Absolutely. I thought I'd begin by writing an editorial about the need for a schoolhouse, and for land to build it on. If nothing turns up, I have an idea of whom to solicit for a land donation."

"Busy, busy," he said wryly, lifting his coffee cup.

"But without the board approving the funds to pay a teacher it will all be useless."

"I'd guess a teacher's salary would be—what? Five dollars a day and found?"

"Seven. We'd want a good one."

"Seven I should think we could manage. Fines alone bring in good revenue, plus licenses."

"Yes, I know about both from personal experience."

To Noah's surprise a faint glow of mischief shone in Sarah Merritt's eyes. Without her glasses, they glinted like polished sapphires. The meal continued while they talked of the other reforms—the street cleaner, lamps and lamplighter, the boardwalks. By the time breakfast ended, Noah realized they had dominated the conversation to the exclusion of the other men at the table. Pushing back his chair, he admitted with some amazement that he'd conversed with Sarah Merritt for a full thirty minutes and had come very close to enjoying every one of them.

CHAPTER 7

SARAH'S second issue of the *Chronicle* expanded to two pages. The first included the headlines: EDITOR OF *CHRONICLE* JAILED AND FINED; COMPLETE LAW LIBRARY EXPECTED IN DEADWOOD SOON; CAPITAL NEEDED TO BUILD STAMP MILLS; PROSPECT GOOD ON BEAVER, BEAR, SAND CREEKS; WILD GAME SCARCE AS BUFFALO, ELK, DEER RETREAT WESTWARD; BREWERY OPEN IN ELIZABETHTOWN; *DUTCH LOVERS* OPENING AT BELLA UNION THEATER; LANGRISHE TROUPE'S *FLIES IN THE WEED* CRISPLY AMUSING.

Elias Pinkney's ad ran on the second page along with Sarah's report on the city council meeting and an editorial about the need for a school. In it she suggested that if even a small portion of the gold funneling into the brothels of the badlands was channeled instead into a church/school fund, the building could be up in no time. She requested that all children be officially registered at the newspaper office so an accurate census could be obtained.

The *Chronicle* office got busier. Merchants came in to place ads. Mothers came in to register children. Miners came in to report their prospect. Everyone came to buy copies of the paper itself.

October made an angry entrance. One unseasonably bitter, snowy day early in the month, Sarah was leaving the building as a rider on a piebald horse drew abreast of her steps. The stranger drew rein and sat trembling, teetering low over the horse's neck.

"A doctor . . . ma'am . . . I need a doctor."

"We have seven of them. Up the street—Rathburn and Allen have tents on your left. Bangs and Dawson are in log buildings on your right, farther up. Henry Kice is in a tent around the corner on your right." She didn't bother naming the other two, who'd take more time to reach. "Can you make it, sir?" He appeared on the verge of tumbling from his mount.

"Thank you," he mumbled and, bobbing over his saddlehorn, urged his horse on.

She watched him turn right toward Henry Kice's.

Later that day she went to Kice's herself, wondering if the stranger had suffered a gunshot wound, and if so, under what circumstances. A stagecoach robbery perhaps?

Henry Kice said, "No, he's just a gambler from Cheyenne, name of Cramed. Got a bad case of lung congestion complicated by poison ivy. Undoubtedly the sudden change of weather caught him on horseback between Cheyenne and here and he caught a dilly of a cold. I ordered him to bed. I think he checked into the Custer Hotel."

Three days later Cramed's cold and poison ivy were both worse. A week after that, five additional cases of "poison ivy" were reported in town, three of them by residents of the Custer.

Sarah's headline asked, IS POISON IVY CONTAGIOUS?

Then Cramed died.

Sarah decided it was time somebody took some action. She stopped in the marshal's office one morning after Josh came to work and reported that his sister Lettie had fallen ill overnight. Campbell was at the rear of his office, speaking with a burly, bearded man Sarah recognized as Frank Gilpin, a local blacksmith. (It appeared the town was about to get a jail.)

Campbell looked over his shoulder when Sarah closed the door. He and Gilpin turned. Gilpin smiled and doffed his misshapen cap. Campbell came forward.

"Scouting for news this morning?" he asked.

"Could I talk to you when you're free, Marshal?"

"Of course. You know Frank Gilpin?"

Gilpin joined them, bringing the smell of body odor and a jovial if disjointed greeting.

"The young lady writes the newspaper, yes. Hello, so good to see you. We read about the jail, what you write, and Noah has me here. We see how many bars he needs and if these stingy miners got enough gold to pay for them, yes?"

She smiled and nodded, unsure of what she was concurring with.

"I go, leave you two to talk. Noah, you tell me yes or no, I make the

bars in three, four days." Gilpin added something in a foreign language—presumably a farewell—and left.

"So you'll get your jail soon?" Sarah remarked.

"Hopefully after the November town meeting. Just finding out what
it'll cost. Is that what brought you in here?"

"No. Another matter entirely. Tell me, Marshal, what do you know
about smallpox?"

"Smallpox?" He frowned. "Why?"

"Because I'm going to write an editorial and I don't want to start
any panics the law would frown upon. One run-in with you was
enough."

"The poison ivy?" he asked.

"Exactly. Lettie Dawkins just broke out, plus five others, and Henry
Kice is asking us to believe it's poison ivy. Rathburn, meanwhile, is
claiming one of the other cases is the great pox."

"Syphilis?"

She nodded. "Could it be that Kice made the wrong diagnosis and
is afraid to say so?"

"And Rathburn too?"

They considered silently awhile.

"What are the chances of two of them being wrong?" Campbell
asked.

"I don't know. I only know poison ivy isn't contagious, and a young
girl like Lettie wouldn't have syphilis. So what is it?"

"You think we have the start of an epidemic?"

"I've done some questioning. All the cases have started the same—
three days of fever followed by a generalized eruption. One death
already."

"Smallpox . . ." Campbell breathed and ran a hand over his curly hair.

"It might not be, but suppose it is. The entire gulch would already
have been exposed."

"What do you suggest?"

"That every qualified doctor in the diggings be called upon to consult
together and present a determination about the nature of the disease.
If the consensus is smallpox, we must send for vaccine points immediately, by Pony Express, and build a pesthouse for the afflicted. Also we
must arrange for some sort of isolation shelters for those who've already
been exposed but haven't broken out yet."

"Where would we get the money?"

"The funds would have to be solicited from the citizens, and anyone
who is financially able to contribute but declines would have his name

published in the newspaper. I'll need your permission, of course, before I do such a thing."

"What is the incubation period of smallpox?"

"Ten to sixteen days."

"How long ago did Cramed come to town?"

"Thirteen days."

"Have you talked to anyone else about this?"

"No."

"George Farnum should know." Campbell broke for the coat pegs on the wall. "I'll tell him and call on the doctors immediately. Don't print anything until one of us gets back to you."

It was after five P.M. when Campbell entered the *Chronicle* office with a drawn look about his mouth. Patrick was picking through the wood engravings, searching for a border design, and Josh was sweeping around the woodbox at the rear. Sarah turned at the sound of the door opening and left her chair immediately. She met Campbell some distance from the others where they could speak without being heard.

"It's virulent smallpox," he said in an undertone.

A skitter of apprehension zipped through her. She removed her spectacles, pushed a thumb and forefinger against her closed eyes and whispered, "Lord, have mercy."

"I've sent a rider to the telegraph crew. The lines are up about halfway between here from Hill City so the message will go out yet tonight. If there are vaccine points in Cheyenne we'll be in luck. If not . . ." He shrugged. "We'll just have to wait and see."

"We'll need quarantine cards."

"Can you print them?"

"Of course. I'll have Patrick typeset them right away. And some kind of notice to call the miners in for inoculation as soon as the points arrive. What about the infirmary?"

"George has called an emergency meeting of the council for tonight. He asked if you'd attend."

"Absolutely."

"Eight o'clock at the Number Ten Saloon. Both the Langrishe and the Bella Union have early shows scheduled."

"I'll be there."

"Thanks." He took one step away and stopped. "Oh, and keep Josh here tonight."

"I'd already thought of that."

For a moment their gazes held, grave with responsibility and worry. In that instant Sarah felt an accord with Campbell, tied as they were by this momentous discovery. She thought he was going to offer something reassuring. Instead he said, "I'll see you later," and strode toward the door.

Patrick and Josh had quit working, sensing something amiss.

"What's wrong?" Josh asked.

"I'll need you both a while longer tonight."

"What is it?" Patrick said.

"It's very bad news, I'm afraid. The doctors have determined that we have smallpox in the gulch."

"Smallpox . . ." Josh repeated. He glanced toward home, back at Sarah. "You mean Lettie?"

"I'm afraid so, Josh."

He hit for the coat tree, but she caught his shoulder. "No, Josh. You'll stay here tonight."

"I gotta go home. If Lettie's sick she—"

"No. The safest place for you is away from there. I'll speak to Mrs. Roundtree and see if you can sleep on the settee in her parlor until the vaccine points arrive. The marshal has sent for them. Besides, I'll need you tonight . . ." She looked to Bradigan. "You too, Patrick. We'll need to print quarantine cards and notices about the inoculations. You'll stay, won't you?"

Patrick simply bowed.

"But my mother . . ." Josh said worriedly.

"I'll let her know. Now let's get busy."

When Sarah left the newspaper office the press was running. She went to Emma's and spoke to her from the ground below the kitchen window. Emma's face was wreathed with worry for her stricken daughter. Sarah could not help picturing Lettie, whose whole life lay before her, the girl's beautiful face with its flawless skin, suddenly vulnerable to scars, at the very least.

The two women lingered after the most important messages had been imparted, each wishing to go to the other and exchange a hug of comfort. Instead they stood separated by the height of a building.

"She'll be all right, Emma. I know she will." With her head tipped back, Sarah sent her friend a look of commiseration.

"Say a prayer, Sarah," Emma said plaintively.

"I will. And I'll take good care of Josh."

With a lump in her throat Sarah walked away.

At eight o'clock the emergency meeting convened in the Number Ten Saloon. Word had spread and the saloon was filled. All the members of the town council were present as well as the seven doctors from Deadwood and two others from the adjacent camps of Lead and Elizabethtown, which fell under the jurisdiction of the Deadwood City Council. Businessmen and interested parties had shown up also.

Before the meeting adjourned, the council had officially set up the Board of Health of the City of Deadwood, and they were given jurisdiction over all decisions regarding the control and treatment of the smallpox epidemic. Both Sarah and Noah agreed to sit on the board along with doctors from all three towns, the mayor and two leading businessmen. Before they left the saloon the groundwork was laid for the battle ahead.

A pesthouse would be built in Spruce Gulch, where all the afflicted would be taken. (Reaching this decision took three of the four hours' meeting time while various factions argued about where the pesthouse should be, nobody wanting it in *their* vicinity.) The lumber for it would be appropriated from the sawmills, which would be given official notice by the marshal of the board's priority status. All miners, merchants and businessmen able to contribute funds for the building of the shelter would be ordered to do so, contributions to be made to the town treasurer, shirkers to be openly listed in the *Deadwood Chronicle*. Volunteers would be sought to put up the building as well as quickly constructed shelters of brush and hide for the internment of the exposed. Volunteers would also be sought to nurse the sick. Dawkins' Bakery and the Custer Hotel would be placed under quarantine until the board lifted it. The brothels of Deadwood would be closed (this to be enforced by the marshal) until all their residents could receive the vaccine and the general quarantine was lifted. A special issue of the *Chronicle* was to be printed the following day to announce these decisions.

By the time the meeting adjourned it was past midnight. Noah and Sarah, both weary, headed for Mrs. Roundtree's together. The town was oddly quiet, even the saloons and gambling houses, as if in respectful acknowledgment of the disastrous news. The theaters had closed and their lanterns had been extinguished. The hitching rails were nearly empty. The sky wore a milky blanket of clouds that held out all starshine and moonlight. Main Street wore a crust of frost on its rutted wagontracks. Beneath, it was soft from the day's commerce. A wind chased down the ravine, bringing the distant call and answer of two owls, and off to their right the creek rustled.

They climbed the path to Mrs. Roundtree's with heavy footsteps, up the crude zigzagging steps to one landing, then another, and finally to the front door. Noah opened it and let Sarah enter before him. In the parlor a small oil lamp burned. Josh was asleep on the settee, half on his belly, with one leg cocked. A brown blanket had slipped toward the floor.

They studied him awhile in silence, reminded again that his loved ones were some of those most threatened.

"Poor Josh," Sarah said softly.

"Yeah. Who knows what'll happen."

"Don't say that, Noah." She bent to pull the blanket over the boy's shoulders. "I've come to love his family, especially Emma."

When she turned she found him watching her with a strange look on his shadowed face. She had called him Noah without realizing it. The look fled and he said, "Don't worry. They'll be fine."

"They're such good people."

"Yes, they are."

Another silence while their antipathy slipped another cog.

"You go up first," he said. "I'll turn off the lantern."

She was halfway up the stairs when the light went out behind her. In the blackness she faltered, reached out for the wall and ran her hand along it for guidance. She heard his footsteps behind her, tiptoeing on the creaky wooden steps.

She stopped. Behind her, so did he.

"Mr. Campbell?" she whispered.

"Yes?"

"Do you pray?"

Silence . . . then, "Sometimes."

Silence again before she whispered, "Tonight would be a good time."

The thought settled around them. Somewhere the house cracked and she continued up the stairs with him at her heels. Her door came first, on the left. She located the knob and turned it, then herself . . . to face him.

"Good night," she whispered.

It was as black as the earth around a tree root. She had a sense of Noah Campbell close enough to touch, were she to reach out. In the absolute lightlessness she caught the smell of leather from his vest and a hint of coal smoke from the extinguished lantern.

"Good night," he whispered. "See you in the morning."

The last thing she heard was his hand rubbing along the wall, guiding him to his door, which opened and closed.

The whorehouse looked different in broad daylight. Noah had never been here in the morning before. When Flossie let him in, the light from the open door flashed across the dim parlor, then disappeared, leaving them in gloom. He followed Flossie through the room, through the smell of last night's cigar smoke and whiskey, past the nude who smiled down from the murky shadows, past the bathing room with its strong stink of sulfur and saturated wood, to a room on the left where Rose Hossiter was sprawled on a dingy settee, snoring.

Flossie passed a cluttered desk and snapped up a green windowshade. Sun exploded into the room.

"What the hell . . ." Rose shielded her eyes and rolled like a walrus, trying to see behind her. "What the goddamn hell you doin', Flossie!" She scooped up a whiskey glass from the floor and flung it at the Indian woman. It crashed against the desk. "Get out!"

"Marshal's here," the Indian woman said and left the room.

Rose's unfocused eyes found the man at the door. "Marshal . . ." She struggled to rise. Her elbow caught the sheeny pink fabric of her robe and dragged it down, exposing one fleshy breast. She scraped it into place with a rubbery movement. The kohl she'd applied last night had taken a journey down her face. Her brassy hair listed in a scraggly knot behind one ear. She dished it to her skull with two pathetic pats but it sagged again and a hairpin bounced to her shoulder. Her mouth formed a wavery line as she smiled.

"Little early in the morning, isn't it?"

"Sorry to wake you, Rose."

She yawned and the smell of her fetid breath filtered across the room. "What time is it?"

"Ten-thirty."

She grunted and sat up, dropping her wide, bare feet to the floor. "Middle of the night," she said and bent forward toward an oval table. Her robe gaped to her waist as she reached for a skinny cigar and lit it with a stick match. Smoke poured from her nostrils and mouth as she sat back and said, "Well . . . haven't seen you around here in a while."

He made no reply.

"Some problem, Marshal?"

" 'Fraid so. I'm going to have to shut you down for a while."

"Shut me d——!" In the middle of the word she started hacking. The sound cracked in her throat twice. She had a disgusting way of sticking her tongue out when she coughed. Finally she got control.

"What do you mean, shut me down?"

"You and all the others along here. We have five cases of smallpox in town."

Rose got to her feet, closing her robe. "What the hell do I care about smallpox?"

"With the business you run, you'd better care."

"Now, listen, Marshal, you know we put our customers through a carbolic bath. Probably keep 'em from getting the damn pox."

"You know as well as I do that won't kill smallpox."

"Aw, come on, Marshal, have a heart."

"Can't," he said. "The town council made the rule and I've got to enforce it. I've got to quarantine you, Rose."

"For how long?"

"Couple of weeks, probably."

"A couple of weeks! And what we supposed to live on for a couple of weeks?"

"Now, Rose, I've been in here enough to know how much gold comes through that door each night. You could shut down for a couple of months and not feel it."

She studied him awhile, put down her cigar in an ashtray and sidled across the room to him. "Tell you what, Marshal." She took him by his lapels. "I'll make you a real sweet deal. You shut the others down and hang your quarantine sign out front, but leave my back door open. I'll cut you in for ten percent of the take for as long as I'm open exclusively."

He removed her hands from his jacket.

"I can't do that, Rose. We're trying to prevent an epidemic here."

She advanced again, one hand on a hip. "I'll throw in anything on the menu, no charge—anything you want and as much of it as you want for the duration. How about that?"

"Rose . . ." He held up both palms.

"Who's your pick? Eve? You always took a shine to Eve."

"I don't want Eve. I don't—"

"One of the Frenchies then. How about Ember? Ember ever had her mouth on you, Marshal?"

"I don't want any of them."

"I'd come out of retirement myself. Haven't been with a man for a while but I haven't forgotten what you fellas like. I could do you good, Marshal." She reached for his crotch.

He caught her wrist in a steel grip. His stomach lurched.

"No deals, Rose. Tell your girls as of now you're shut down."

"You're a handsome man, Noah . . ." She reached to caress his face with her free hand. His head jerked back. Their eyes locked while Rose's hand froze, halfway to its destination. She pulled free of his grip and yanked her bodice in place. Her expression turned contemptuous. "All right—get out of here, you sonofabitch, and take your fucking star with you."

She spun and retrieved her cigar. When he left the room she was blowing smoke toward the ceiling.

Outside, he sucked the clean air and felt as though he needed a carbolic bath himself. All the while he nailed the quarantine sign to her door his mind kept returning to that room and the sight of her rolling up from sleep looking like a bad case of winterkill; her callousness and dissipation, the stench of her, her pathetic attempt to appear seductive, her soulless eyes when he'd recoiled.

He shuddered once, as if she'd reached him.

That night at supper he was already seated when Sarah Merritt entered the dining room. She took her place across from Noah. She said hello to everyone else, finally to him . . . quick, quiet, with scarcely an encounter of eyes. Her face was clean. Her hair was wet on the sides, drawn back into its tidy, tiny twist. On either side of a center part a shallow natural wave nudged her forehead. Her blouse was gray with a white standup collar and sleeves with puffy tops and tight white cuffs.

Looking at her seemed to remove the sullied feeling he'd worn since morning.

The vaccine points came in by Pony Express from Sidney, Nebraska, in time to ward off a full-scale epidemic. Nevertheless, Sarah and Noah had two of the hardest weeks of their lives. She, with a paper to run, also acted as organizer for the inoculation clinic and the volunteer nurses. He, with the law to maintain, acted as organizer for the volunteer carpenters and tried to keep the whorehouses under quarantine. Two more people died—a miner known as Bean Belly Kelly and a Kentuckian named Yarnell whose occupation remained uncertain. They were buried in Mt. Moriah Cemetery near Preacher Smith and Bill Hickok.

Sarah felt obliged to attend their funerals. Without a preacher in town, it fell to the general public to give the men a proper send-off with a decent show of mourners. On the afternoon of Yarnell's burial, however, she was working at the pesthouse herself and missed the ceremony. She went up later with a crepe-paper rose to pay her respects.

It was peaceful as she climbed the steep incline to the cemetery that hung on the mountainside southeast of town. The earth was snowy and the smell of the pines keen. Their trunks—rusty red and scaly—stood straight as compass needles in the windless, overcast day. A bluejay scolded and left a bough bobbing. A porcupine waddled up the path before her. A squirrel, alerted, stopped munching a pinecone and waited as she passed.

She reached the top of the incline and stopped.

There were the gravestones, and sitting beside one, with his head hanging and a whiskey bottle wavering on one knee, was a man. He was dressed in dirty buckskin. His blond hair hung in unkempt ribbons, the same dull mushroom color as the fringes on his jacket. It covered his face while he sat in sodden slumber, one leg outstretched, the other forming a triangle against the earth. The snow beneath him had melted as if he'd been there for some time.

Sarah approached silently. Passed him. Read the grave marker— William Butler Hickok—and proceeded to the fresh mound beyond, where she laid her paper rose. After a moment of reverence she returned the way she'd come, circling wide to leave the drunk undisturbed. But a twig snapped as she passed and he lifted his head.

The drunk was a woman.

The bottle teetered on her knee as she stared at Sarah.

"Guess I fell asleep," she mumbled.

"I'm sorry I disturbed you."

"S'all right. I was jss . . ." Her words trailed away and she stared blearily at Sarah's skirt. In time she lifted her chin and asked, "You know me?"

"You're Miss Cannary."

"S'right."

"You know what they call me?"

"Calamity."

"S'right." She sat awhile, weaving, then remembered her manners. "Want a drink?" She lifted the bottle.

"No, thank you."

"I'll have one myself then." A strand of hair got caught between her lips and the bottle. She strained the liquor through it, then smeared the whiskey off her lips with the back of a hand.

"You come fer the funeral?"

"No."

"You know 'im?" She gestured with the bottle toward Yarnell's grave.

"No."

"Me neither. I come to see Bill." She leaned forward from the waist and peered at Sarah. "You know Bill?"

"No, I'm sorry, I didn't."

She pointed with the mouth of the bottle at the stone behind her. "This here's Bill." She pivoted around, dragging her legs in the mud to drape a hand on Hickok's headstone. "Say h'lo to the lady, Bill. A real lady, not a whore like me."

Sarah stood transfixed, feeling like an intruder.

Jane leaned her face against the stone, closed her eyes and gave a great sigh. "He left me. Promised to marry me but he never did. Hell, I could ride and shoot as good as him 'n' skin mules 'n' drink any man under the table . . . but it wasn't good enough for him . . ." Tears seeped from her eyes and she curled herself to the gravestone. "Why'd you leave me, Bill . . . God, why din't you face that door . . . you always faced the door. . . ." Her pitiful weeping moved Sarah. She went to the woman and knelt, taking her arms.

"Miss Cannary, please . . . you'd better get up. Let me help you."

Jane drew her head up heavily, sniffed, and scraped the edge of her hand beneath her nose.

" 'Ass all right. I'm jss an old drunk. Leave me alone."

"You've been sitting on the ground. You're all wet. Please, let me help you up."

Jane lifted bleary eyes. "What you wanna help me for?"

Because the sight of you breaks my heart, sitting here grieving against your lover's headstone.

"It's time to go down now. You need dry clothes."

Sarah helped Jane to her feet and held her upright until she caught her balance. When she stood erect, Sarah gently took the bottle from her hands. "Here, let's leave that."

"Yeah, leave it fer Bill . . . he liked his whiskey neat."

Sarah hid the bottle behind Hickok's headstone and returned to take Jane's arm. As they started down the hill Jane waved back over her shoulder and said, "See y' around, Bill. Save me a place."

The downhill grade was steep. Sometimes Jane stumbled and Sarah would reach out to steady her. On Main Street they paused before the newspaper office.

"I have to go in here," Sarah said. "Do you have a place to go?"

"Yeah . . . I got me a place . . ." Jane gestured up the gulch as she stood weaving.

"Wait here," Sarah said. "Will you wait?"

Jane nodded as if her chin were weighted.

Sarah went into the *Chronicle* office and came back out with a packet containing some gold dust.

"Go take a hot bath," she said, handing it to Jane. "Then get yourself a good meal. Will you do that?"

Jane nodded and stumbled up the street. Sarah hurriedly returned to the *Chronicle* office, unwilling to watch Jane to learn if she used the gold for a bath and supper or a saloon.

* * *

The following day news reached Sarah that Calamity Jane showed up at the pesthouse, clean and sober, and worked there helping the sick until well past dark. From then until the quarantine was lifted the story was the same—Calamity Jane, who dressed in buckskins, rode like an Indian, swore a blue streak and drank like a man, proved herself a woman of kind and generous nature by giving the tenderest of care to the sick and afflicted.

Though Sarah occasionally encountered her, Jane would never speak. She would nod, and her eyes would linger warmly, but her silence seemed to say, you're a lady, I'll keep my distance.

A headline appeared in the *Deadwood Chronicle* when they knew the smallpox had been licked. MARTHA JANE CANNARY SELFLESSLY HELPS THE SICK.

CHAPTER 8

T HE lifting of the quarantine brought great joy to Deadwood. The brothels reopened, relieving some of the pressures that had led to increased belligerence among the men. Noah was called upon to break up fewer saloon fights. True Blevins returned from the Spearfish, collected his oxen and headed toward Cheyenne. The Dawkins family was reunited, grateful to have Josh back beneath their roof, even more grateful that Lettie had survived her ordeal with smallpox, though it appeared her face would bear several scars. Sarah returned to being a full-time newspaper publisher, and Calamity Jane returned to the saloons.

The telegraph brought word that Rutherford B. Hayes and William A. Wheeler had been elected president and vice-president, and it sent word that the quarantine of Deadwood had been lifted. Traffic resumed, bringing a marked increase in freight, the ox trains carrying in a stout supply of winter stores for the remote area before the big snows fell.

The women of Deadwood were particularly thrilled when a headline in the *Chronicle* announced the first mercantile items for them: bolts of cloth, spools of ribbon and even shoes of a smaller size. The article went on to note that future generations might diary the domestication of the town by the change in its incoming freight: seeds for spring, along with a barrel of tulip bulbs, which created a stir. Sarah's plaster arrived—much more than she had ordered, brought by two brothers named Hintson, a pair of plasterers with the perspicacity to realize that the first plastered building would signal a chain reaction and their business would flourish. There came a selection of framed pictures and broad-loom rugs to complement those first white rooms, factory-made furniture, and a single umbrella of a color other than black. It was pistaschio green with white stripes, and stopped every woman who passed the window of Tatum's Store.

But of all the freight that arrived, none was looked upon as a more certain sign of domestication than the load of forty housecats. They arrived in crates aboard a spring wagon, brought in by a speculator from Cheyenne who, within twenty-four hours of his arrival, sold the entire load at the preposterous price of $25 per head.

Though Sarah had no opportunity to announce the arrival of the felines before they were snapped up, she did, however, manage to buy one of them herself. It was a short-haired white female with one blue eye and one green. From the moment she picked it up—a placid, full-grown, overtly affectionate creature—she fell in love with it. The cat squinted, nuzzled and bumped the bottom of Sarah's chin with the top of its head, inviting attention. Sarah scratched its neck and it began purring.

"Hi, puss," she murmured. "You look just like old Ruler." Ruler was the cat she and Addie had grown up with, so named because they had all agreed he'd ruled the roost. "You like that scratching, huh?"

Much as she would have loved to keep the cat herself, she took it to the office only temporarily, where it immediately stopped the presses. Josh and Patrick left their work to take turns holding and scratching the new arrival, examining its colorful eyes, then turning it loose to nose around the perimeter of the room, where it explored the base of the press and sniffed the oily ink containers. Eventually it jumped up on Sarah's desk chair, licked its shoulders a few times, curled its paws to the inside and rounded up like a plumped pillow.

Josh was entranced.

"We can *use* a mouser around here. What're you going to name it?"

"I'm not. I'm going to give it to my sister."

"Aww . . . really?"

"Really. She always loved cats, and I've noticed there are other pets around that place. There's even a green parrot."

"Gosh! Really?" Josh's eyes grew excited. "I'd like to see that!"

"No you don't, young man. I told you once before, you stay away from there. But you know cats. This one won't take any time at all before she'll have a family of her own, and I intend to tell Addie that we want the pick of the litter. You're right. We could use a hunter around here to keep the mice from eating the newsprint."

She set out for Addie's late that afternoon. It was a gray, glowering day with snow threatening again. Above the surrounding rock walls fat-cheeked clouds seemed to whistle and spit gusts of wind down the ravine. It lifted Sarah's coat hem and sent shivers up her spine as she hurried along with the cat tucked below her chin, inside her woolen coat, with only its white face protruding. Though at their November meeting the town council had approved the building of a jail and a church, they had voted down standardizing the boardwalks, so it was up and down, up and down, as Sarah walked along the shelter of the building walls. Head-down, she was climbing the steps at the end of a section of walk when she bumped smack into a body going the opposite direction.

"Whoa! Careful there!" Two gloved hands closed over her coat sleeves, and she looked up into a face with a familiar auburn mustache. He was wearing his new brown Stetson and a sheepskin jacket that made him appear half again his normal girth.

"Marshal, I'm sorry. I wasn't looking where I was going."

He released her and grinned down at the cat. "What've you got there?" He reached out one thick-gloved finger that dwarfed the cat's head.

"I'm one of the lucky ones. I managed to get one."

"So I see." He attempted to scratch the cat's chin, but the animal was frantic and wide-eyed, squeezed as it was inside the coat.

"Look," Sarah told Noah, lifting the creature's head. "She's got one green eye and one blue eye. Isn't that odd?"

They inspected the cat for some moments. "Sometimes cats with two different-colored eyes are deaf," Noah told her.

"Really?"

"Mm-hmm. I remember one when I was a kid, belonged to an old man named Sandusky who had a candle shop. He used to kick the cat out of his way when it didn't hear him coming. Always made me want to kick old Sandusky back. So where you going, kitty?" he asked the cat.

"I'm taking her to Addie."

Standing close on the windy boardwalk, they finally allowed their eyes to meet. Sarah had one hand folded around the cat's head to keep it from leaping, while Noah's gloved finger remained at its nose.

"That's nice of you. I imagine you'd like it for yourself."

"We always had cats when we were children, and I think Addie misses them. She keeps a stuffed cat on the bed in her private room."

Looking into Noah Campbell's gray eyes, Sarah wondered if he still frequented Rose's, particularly if he still saw Addie. The idea of his doing so created a queer lump in her chest. It came so suddenly she hadn't time to reason why.

Her attention returned to the cat. "This one is the same color as our old pet, Ruler."

"She'll like that."

"I hope so. I hope she'll *accept* it. She still won't talk to me civilly, or ingratiate herself to me in any way, yet I think she's terribly lonely."

Noah had never imagined the prostitutes being lonely. They were brash and forward and lived in their cloister with each other for company, days, and no letup to the incoming company, nights. But of course they must be lonely. How blind of him not to realize it until Sarah Merritt pointed it out.

Before he could remark, she went on. "I'm her only sister, and in spite of her fallen state, we could be friends again if only she'd let me. It hurts very much, being shut out when all I want to do is help."

Noah studied the part in Sarah's hair, what little bit showed in front of the woolen scarf tied around her head; he studied her smooth forehead, her thick eyelashes and pretty blue eyes, her downturned face as she concentrated on the cat. She was so absolutely untarnished. By contrast, he recalled Rose the morning she'd tried to seduce him, with her hair sagging and her gown gaping, and her general look of dissipation. He hadn't been back to any of the brothels since that day, hadn't even wanted to go.

"Maybe she's ashamed of having you see her there."

"She doesn't act ashamed. She acts brazen."

"I'm sorry. I can't explain it. But I think she'll love the cat."

Two men came by. Sarah and Noah stepped aside to let them pass. When they were alone again, she returned her attention to the cat, resumed her scratching. "Mr. Campbell . . .?" It was on the tip of her tongue to pose a question beyond all impertinence. It had been on her mind for some time to ask him if Addie had ever spoken to him about home, if she'd given any clue to what had driven her away. In the end Sarah could not muster the courage to inquire about anything that had passed between her sister and this man while they were customer and courtesan.

"Oh, nothing," she said. "I guess I'll have to figure out Addie for myself." Sarah looked up and snapped out of her pensive mood. "I see the hat fits." It was the first time since she'd given it to him that it had been mentioned. He never wore it to the table at the boardinghouse, but she hadn't seen him anywhere else without it. The rich brown felt was almost the same color as his auburn hair, which quirked up below the hatband at his temples. By now she was quite familiar with it.

"Yes, it does. It's a dandy hat—thank you." He felt silly for not having said that a month ago, but a month ago they weren't speaking.

"And your eye is all healed."

"Oh that . . ." He waved a hand in disregard.

"And your hearing? Was it bothered?"

He cupped an ear and shouted, "What?"

They both laughed, then fell still and a little amazed, watching the change in each others' eyes before their gazes parted.

"Well," she said, increasingly ill at ease, "I'd better be on my way. It's cold out here."

"Yes . . . see you tonight at supper." He touched his hat brim and they moved off in opposite directions.

Twenty feet up the boardwalk, Noah gave in to the impulse to turn around and look back at her. He stopped, turned and found her doing exactly the same thing—standing on the boardwalk looking back at him with the cat tucked beneath her chin.

For several seconds they stared. And grew conscious and self-conscious by turns.

Then, simultaneously, they spun and hurried off, wishing they had not turned around in the first place.

Sarah had not seen Addie since the outbreak of smallpox. She hoped that the ensuing weeks might have mollified Addie and her reception might be warmer. Standing in the hall outside Addie's room, Sarah unbuttoned her coat, perched the cat on one arm and knocked.

Addie called, "Who is it?"

"It's Sarah."

After a length of silence the door opened narrowly. "What do you want this time?" Addie was wearing the same dressing robe as the day she'd been collecting clothes from the line.

"I wanted to make sure you're all right."

"I am."

"I've brought you something."

Addie's eyes dropped to the cat and the hard lines of her face melted. "For me?" The door opened more.

"A fellow from Cheyenne brought a load of them in this afternoon and it was a mad scramble, but I managed to get one. Here . . ." Sarah held out the creature. "She's for you."

"Oh . . ." Addie reached out as if mesmerized.

"She rode here buttoned inside my coat, so she's probably a little skittish right now."

"Ohhh, look at you . . ." Addie cooed to the cat, taking it beneath its front legs and drawing it near her body. "You look just like old Ruler." She turned, taking the cat inside. Sarah followed uncertainly, remaining near the open door. Addie cuddled the cat, settling it on her arm and dropping her face down to rub its head until the cat grew cautious and leaped onto the bed.

Addie followed, sitting on the edge of the mattress, stretching out a hand to entice the creature to come close and allow itself to be petted. When it did, she gathered it onto her lap, set to work giving its throat a two-handed workover.

"You came all the way from Cheyenne? Hey, we're going to take good care of you and keep you away from that nasty old parrot."

All of her antipathy had vanished. She spoke to the animal affectionately, even maternally. Looking on, Sarah glowed within. To see Addie with her veneer of antagonism finally dissolved had been Sarah's dearest hope.

"What's its name?" Addie asked, still lavishing attention on the beast.

"It hasn't got one that I know of."

"Maybe I'll call it Ruler."

"I was hoping you would." It was the first memento of the past Addie had allowed. Sarah inched into the room and stood near the foot of the bed a good distance from her sister. Though she wanted to sit down beside Addie, Sarah resisted the urge. Though she wanted to flop onto her stomach and lie side by side with Addie, admiring the cat, she refrained. She was wise enough to realize she could not force a return of affection; it would take time and nurturing to draw Addie from her indifference.

"It's a female, and I expect it'll have a litter someday. When it does, I wouldn't mind having one of her kittens to keep in the newspaper office."

For the first time since Sarah had presented her gift, Addie looked at her.

"You wanted Ruler for yourself, didn't you?"

"No. I bought her for you. But I took her over to the office to show the fellows, and Josh fell in love with her."

For a while their gazes held. The room seemed filled with tremulous feelings not unlike those preceding a first kiss—that moment of uncertainty and hope when two people poise on a brink that will forever change their sentimental climate.

"Who's Josh?" Addie finally inquired.

It was the first sign of interest Addie had shown in Sarah's doings. Encouraged by it, Sarah perched on the bed at the far end from her sister. Addie let her.

"Josh is a young boy who works for me. His parents own the bakery."

"And the other fellow is Pat Bradigan?"

"Yes. He's a tramp printer, but a good one."

Sarah was happy Addie didn't say, I know him. She called him Pat instead of Patrick—that was clue enough that he, too, had probably been one of Addie's customers.

"He drinks a lot, and someday I know he'll simply not show up for work and I'll never see him again, but meanwhile I don't know what I'd do without him."

Addie said, "I read your editorial."

"What did you think?"

"Rose didn't like it."

"I really don't care whether she did or not. I mean to close her down, and all the other houses in the badlands."

"And then what happens to me?"

"You'll be out of here, I hope."

Addie got to her feet, taking the cat with her. "Well, what if I don't want to be?"

"Please understand, Addie, there are things I must say, as a newspaperwoman. Father taught me that."

"Father, Father—I wish you'd stop talking about him!"

Studying Addie's back, Sarah sensed their thin reconciliation crumbling. She rose. "I think I'd better go now and preserve what little headway we've made today. Take good care of Ruler."

Addie stubbornly said nothing.

Sarah moved toward the door.

Suddenly Addie spun. "Hey, Sarah?"

Sarah stopped and met her sister's eyes.

"Thanks."

Sarah smiled, lifted a hand in farewell and left.

Outside, the late afternoon weather was abominable. It had begun to sleet. The sides of the gulch were obliterated by the downfall, which seemed to isolate any pocket of life afoot. The occasional lamplight falling from windows shimmered and fragmented across the glazed boardwalks. From inside the saloons the sounds were muted, and Sarah felt sorry for the animals left to stand in the elements with icicles forming on their manes and tails. She gripped her collar shut and stalked along with her head down. Her emotions were in a state of flux and she needed someone to talk to about both Addie and the marshal. It had been an unnerving afternoon. Patrick could close up the office for the day so she need not return there, and she had no desire to face Noah Campbell across a supper table. So she headed instead for Emma's, hoping for a supper invitation.

She found her friend, as expected, preparing the meal for her family in the warm, redolent kitchen above the bakery. Lettie answered her knock and smiled when she saw it was Sarah.

"Hello, Miss Merritt."

"Hello, Lettie, how are you?"

"Better." But Lettie hung her head.

Sarah tilted Lettie's chin up and spoke looking square into her striking brown eyes. "You are a beautiful girl, Lettie. Never forget that. Beauty is a thing that starts deep in the depths of one's soul and shines forth with an unmistakable glow from the eyes and the smile. You still have that glow, believe me. I, for one, would sign indenture papers if I could have your pretty face."

Lettie blushed—a healthy sign, Sarah thought. "I've interrupted your game. I'm sorry. Hello, Geneva."

Lettie rejoined Geneva at the kitchen table, where a game of rummy was in progress.

Geneva smiled and Sarah said, "Hello, Emma. May I come in?"

"What are you doing out on a nasty afternoon like this?" At the stove, Emma turned over a chop in a skillet, sending up a sizzle and a mouthwatering smell.

"I just came from visiting Addie."

"Girls, put your cards away now and go fetch your father. Tell him supper's just about ready." When they were gone, Emma inquired, "So how are things with your sister?"

"Thawing." Sarah began unbuttoning her coat without invitation.

"Well, hallelujah."

"Save your rejoicing. I haven't melted her yet."

"Sit down. Tell me what happened today."

"I bought her a cat."

"*You paid twenty-five dollars for one of those cats!*"

"It was worth it to see the look on Addie's face. It's the first time I've seen even a glimpse of the old Addie. She said she's going to name it Ruler, like the cat we had when we were children. Do you know, Emma, that's the first reference to our life back in St. Louis that hasn't soured her and made her grow hateful? And just before I left she thanked me."

"Sounds to me like you're getting through to her."

"Maybe . . . though we did have words about my stand on the brothels, which seemed to put us back on shaky footing. She's so distant, Emma. So guarded, as if showing any emotions toward me would belittle her in some way. I simply can't understand it."

Emma lifted a cover, sending up a cloud of steam. She tested a potato with a two-pronged fork. "I'm afraid I can't shed any light on it either."

"Marshal Campbell says maybe she's ashamed to have me see her there."

"Oh?" Replacing the cover, Emma glanced at Sarah and raised one eyebrow. "You've been *talking* to the marshal?"

"We've been talking for some time."

"Not voluntarily."

"We ran into each other on the street this afternoon."

"You mean you actually carried on a civilized conversation?"

"Quite a civilized one, as a matter of fact."

"It must have been, if you could bring up such a touchy subject as your sister." Emma went to a bureau and found a flowered tablecloth.

"What do you think of him, Emma?" Sarah inquired pensively.

"He's got a hard job." Emma flared the tablecloth and let it settle on the table. "Seems to come from decent folks. He's a fair man, I already told you that. What do you think of him?"

"I think he's stubborn—still he was very cooperative during the epidemic. I think he respects the work I do, but almost against his will. I think he believes women are much more suited to Addie's profession than to mine."

"Here"—Emma handed Sarah a stack of plates—"set the table, would you? Something happen between you two you aren't telling me about?"

Sarah spread the cloth and began setting the plates around. There was one extra, as she'd hoped.

"Nothing, really."

"Then why all the cogitating?"

"No reason. We've gotten a little less contentious since we worked together on the health board. Today we just talked about the cat and laughed a little bit."

"And then?"

"And then when I was walking away . . . oh, it's nothing."

Emma dropped a cluster of silverware on the table. "What? Spit it out."

"Well, like I said, we were walking away from each other and I just turned around to look at him for some reason, and he was standing there on the boardwalk staring back at me."

With her hands on her hips Emma studied the younger woman, who was carefully placing each fork and knife on the table. "That's not nothing. That's an interested man."

"Oh Emma, don't be silly. I've irritated him since the first day I came into town."

"You wouldn't be the first couple in history who started out hating each other."

"We're not a couple. If anything we're adversaries."

"Not since the smallpox fight. You just said so yourself."

The women's gazes held, Emma's matter-of-fact, Sarah's troubled. "Emma, I'm very confused about him." At that moment Josh came stomping in. "I'm home, Ma. Oh hi, Sarah."

"Hello, Josh," Sarah replied, regretfully dropping the subject of Noah Campbell. "Is everything all right at the office?"

"Yup. All closed up."

"Sarah's staying for supper. Get your hands washed," his mother ordered, "the others will be here in a minute."

The family gathered and there was no more time for private talk. After supper Sarah helped with the dishes, but the children remained in the kitchen until seven o'clock when she left for home, affording no further opportunity for her and Emma to pick up the threads of their earlier conversation.

Still, Noah Campbell remained on her mind as she walked home. Why had he been looking back at her? He was an unlikable, outspoken man of loose morals who had made it plain she'd better step wide around him. She was a woman of uncompromising morals who would never, never overlook a man's prurient bent. Why had she been looking back at him? Granted, they'd swallowed their antipathy out of necessity while they'd joined forces to fight the smallpox. But the fight was won; it was back to business as usual, and that business meant the two of them on opposite sides over the issue of closing the brothels.

The wind was still howling and the sleet had turned to snow. The night sky was inky but for the sheets of white that came down sideways. Sarah passed the newspaper office and tried the front door from force of habit. It was locked as it should be so she continued toward home. She took a side street and climbed the foot trail up the side of the gulch to Mrs. Roundtree's. She was ascending the steep steps to the front door when a voice from above startled her.

"Well, you're back."

"Marshal, what are you doing out here?" She stopped two steps below him, looking up. How distracting to encounter him after he'd been so strong on her mind.

"Smoking."

Smoking was, however, allowed inside the house; the parlor was provided with giant free-standing ashtrays. Furthermore, he'd never felt the need to do his smoking—what little of it he did—outside before. She got the distinct impression he'd been waiting for her.

"You missed supper," he said.

"Yes, I ate with the Dawkins."

"How is Lettie?"

"Self-conscious of her scars."

"That'll pass."

"Perhaps. Perhaps not." Sarah knew from personal experience that self-consciousness over one's shortcomings in the beauty department did not pass. For some reason she'd been dwelling on hers often lately.

He took a drag of the cigarette, and the wind tore the smoke from his mouth as he flicked the butt away. He peered off into the distance, as if the weather were of capital interest to him.

"Nasty night," he remarked.

She took the plunge. "You weren't worried about me, were you?"

"It's my job to worry about the residents of Deadwood."

"Well, I'm all right, so you can go back inside."

She climbed the last two steps and reached for the doorknob. Before she could turn it he asked, "So how did your sister like the cat?"

"She loved it. She's going to name it Ruler."

"Well . . . that should make you happy."

"Yes." They stood close in the windy, black night with the sound of her skirts luffing against his ankle and the fine shards of snow ricocheting off his hat brim and her forehead. She held her coat closed at the throat and he had stuffed both hands into his jacket pockets. If there was an embryonic attraction between them, it pleased neither of them.

"Well, good night, Mr. Campbell," she bid finally.

"Good night, Miss Merritt."

In her room she lit a lantern and built a fire in her tiny six-plate iron stove. Standing before it, with her palms extended, she wondered about him. Had he, indeed, been waiting for her? Could Emma be right about his being interested? Surely not. Then why had he turned to study her on the boardwalk? All right, supposing he was interested, what was her own reaction? This afternoon on the boardwalk, when she'd run into him there had been a moment—a brief moment, granted—of exhilaration when their eyes had met. He had been as surprised as she, and while he'd stood there gripping her arms she had looked into his gray eyes with their spiky auburn lashes and found them unduly attractive. His face no longer put her off. His freckles had faded over the autumn, and his cheeks had looked ruddy from the wind. Funny, she had even grown accustomed to his mustache. And his nose—well, his nose was Scottish, and very appropriate for a man named Campbell.

So, what of your feelings for him, Sarah?

She had, her entire life long, been a thinker; it was natural for her to dissect and rationalize rather than admit offhand that her feelings for him might possibly be changing. The truth was, she did not *want* her feelings for him to change. It could lead to nothing but an awkward situation, given that he'd been Addie's lover and probably still was.

The room warmed. She removed her coat and hung it on the wall pegs but found herself restless, pacing the confines of her sleeping space, thinking of Addie, wondering things about Addie and Noah Campbell that she had no right to wonder. She imagined Addie with her fingers in Noah's hair. He had the most beautiful head of hair she'd ever seen on a man, with enough natural curl to spring up and twine around a woman's fingers. Sarah had never in her life had her fingers in a man's hair.

She withdrew from her reverie and went to the mirror to take down her own hair. She brushed it vigorously, donned her nightwear and found a small hand mirror. In it she studied her Elizabethan nose, covering the end of it to imagine what she'd look like if it were shorter. She studied her lips. Too thin, not plump and seductive like Addie's. Her eyes—they still pleased her, vivid, blue and sparkly when she need not wear her glasses, but the moment she put them on, she looked frumpish and lackluster.

She sighed, set aside her mirror in favor of pen and ink and tried working on an editorial about the need to preserve the last of the great buffalo herds which were now centered in the valley east of the Big Horns. But often she'd snap out of a lapse to find the ink dried on the pen nib instead of the paper, and a picture of Noah Campbell's hair in her mind.

At breakfast the following morning she was uncomfortably aware of him across the table. In spite of her previous night's rationalization, the fact remained she and Noah had been seeing each other with disturbing regularity for quite a few weeks already—two meals a day and in between—and she had memorized things about him that a sensible woman would not have noticed. She had come to recognize the stubborn refusal of his hair to remain obediently sleeked down, and the various hues—from mahogany to nutmeg—that it took on as it dried each morning during breakfast. She had grown familiar with the hatline that dented it even when his hat wasn't on, and the curls that sprang up below it, at the temples, like the tail feathers on a mallard.

She had come to appreciate the faint scent of his shaving soap which he brought down to breakfast with him, accompanied by the shine of his freshly bladed skin above and below his mustache. She was familiar with all his shirts—he wore a clean one each morning under his black leather vest—the red flannel he'd been wearing the first morning; a green plaid with a collar badly in need of turning; two blue cambrics— one with a neatly sewn patch on the right elbow, the other newer; a tan one that looked terrible with his ruddy complexion; and the white one he wore on Sundays.

She knew his mealtime preferences: coffee black, salt and pepper over his entire plate before he even tasted it, a second helping of fried potatoes with his morning eggs; no cabbage, rutabagas or turnips— these he disliked—but any other vegetable offered; a huge puddle of gravy if it was on the table, two additional cups of coffee during the course of the meal, and a cigarette afterward instead of a sweet.

She knew his mannerisms, too. He always nodded to the men as he said good morning. Never nodded when he said it to her. When he was listening most intently, he rested a forefinger along his upper lip. When he said something humorous he often tugged at his right earlobe. He seemed comfortable using a napkin while some of the men used their cuffs.

Leaving the dining room when breakfast was finished, Sarah realized, to her dismay, that she had memorized none such things about Mrs. Roundtree's other boarders.

He had grown familiar with her, too. She wore mostly shades of brown—skirts, shirtwaists and jackets—and pinned her pendant watch in precisely the same spot upon her left breast each morning. She carried her dirty laundry downtown on Monday mornings and back home on Tuesday afternoons. She was a creature of utter punctuality, leaving her bedroom at precisely the stroke of seven-thirty each morning, appearing at supper on the dot of six. Ironically, she cared little for the food itself but ate only because she must, leaving food abandoned when her mind was preoccupied with a story. He recognized her preoccupation by the way she took little part in the mealtime conversation and the way she stared at the sugar bowl. Sometimes she'd have to be called twice before realizing she was being spoken to, though in print, she never missed a detail that was newsworthy, be it obvious or incidental. She was acute at picking out and printing items that would have seemed banal to the average ear, but beneath her skilled hand became articles of pertinence to both Deadwood residents and the country beyond the hills. The middle finger of her right hand was misshapen from overusing a pen, and most times it bore a faint black crescent of ingrained ink. She had arresting blue eyes that won a second glance from him whenever he encountered her without her glasses. She was a woman without artifice—no kohl on her eyes, no carmine on her lips—but he thought if she were ever to show up at the table wearing these, he would be outraged. Her coiffure scarcely changed from day to day except when the bump at the back was slightly off-center, as if she'd secured it without benefit of a mirror. Her nails were clipped short and she owned a single pair of unbecoming shoes, as far as he could tell—lace-up, brown, blucher-style boots that saw her through mud, snow, sleet, and the dung on the street, about which she continued to badger in each issue of her newspaper. He suspected, if the town had a church, the same shoes would appear there with her Sunday clothes. One fact he was aware of above all others: ever since the day they'd spoken on the boardwalk she had stopped looking him directly in the eye when she spoke to him. Instead, she fixed her attention on the star on his chest.

Sarah Merritt's and Noah Campbell's jobs put them into contact with one another on a regular basis. In collecting news, she consulted him for items about arrests and the law. In making his rounds, he walked into businesses at random—hers included.

Whenever they met she greeted him formally as "Marshal Campbell," and he did likewise, calling her "Miss Merritt."

If, as the days passed, they encountered each other more often, they credited it to necessity and nothing more.

A week after their encounter on the boardwalk, Sarah and her staff were working in the newspaper office when a short, pudgy woman entered. She was brown as an old saddle and had dark hair with a few streaks of gray curving away from a center part. Her gray eyes were direct, if not quite piercing, and she zeroed in on Sarah as if the others were not present.

"So you're her!" the woman said in a voice that rang through the room like a dinner triangle.

Sarah rose from her desk, removed her cuff guards and left them behind.

"I'm Sarah Merritt," she said.

The woman stuck out a hand. "I'm Noah Campbell's mother, Carrie."

Sarah saw the resemblance immediately—the gray eyes, the tiny knob that ended the nose, the high, round cheekbones.

"Hello, Mrs. Campbell." She shook the woman's hand.

"He told us about you. About this place, too. Thought I'd come and have a look-see for myself. Howdy." She nodded to Patrick and Josh without pausing to allow introductions, all the while giving the premises a blatant assessment. "By the sound of it you're a regular go-getter. Noah admires that."

"He does?" Sarah was doing her best to hide her surprise.

"I says to him, Noah, why don't you bring her out here sometime, but you know how sons are. Once they leave home you've got the triple dickens trying to get them back themselves, much less bring any of their friends."

Friends? This woman thought Sarah was Noah's friend?

"So I says, all right, I'll just go into that newspaper office myself and say hello. My other son, Arden, he'll probably be in here sometime today, too. Kirk, now—he's my man—he's got better things to do, since we don't come into town too often, but Arden and me, we were just plain curious since Noah he talked so much about you when he was out last time."

He did? Sarah was conscious of Patrick listening, all the while he manned the press, and Josh, too, as he did the inking.

"Sounds like you're a bright lady, running this newspaper like you do. Me, I have a struggle just to read, let alone write, but Noah, he brought us out a copy of your paper, and though I had to muddle through it, I have to admit it was downright exciting to read what's going on in the rest of the country, as well as here in town."

"You live out in the Spearfish Valley, I believe?"

"That's right."

"Would you mind answering a few questions about it?"

"Why . . ." Carrie Campbell's eyebrows rose. "Why, no, though I don't know what I'd have to say that you'd be interested in."

"The Spearfish was the last stronghold of the Indians. The rest of the country is watching it carefully to see if the Indians uphold their part of the treaty."

The ensuing interview reiterated to Carrie Campbell how bright Sarah Merritt really was. Her questions touched upon the quality of this year's harvest, which particular crops had been grown, the number of bushels yielded per acre, the current price of stock feed, the overall weather conditions including rainy days versus sunny during the past growing season, the number of families residing in the Spearfish, their ethnic background, their geographic background and what if any social events took place there.

When all of Sarah's questions had been answered, Carrie watched the younger woman remove her oval spectacles and lay them aside, wondering what the deuce her boy Noah was waiting for. The girl wasn't much to look at, but she was smarter than a few men Carrie could name. Furthermore, she'd come all the way out here and opened up this business, hadn't she? That took spunk. And though she was skinny, she looked healthy enough to bear a few grandchildren, and probably bright ones at that!

"When the piece is written, I'll be sure to send a copy out with Noah," Sarah offered.

"Yes, I wish you would, unless of course you'd care to bring it out yourself, maybe stay for dinner along with Noah."

"Thank you, Mrs. Campbell, but I'm afraid I'm very busy keeping the paper running. I gather all the news myself, you see, and write the articles, too, besides selling ads and attending whatever local functions and meetings need to be covered. I have very little time to myself, I'm sorry to say."

"Sure . . . well . . . it's been a pleasure meeting you." Carrie extended her hand again. "You take care of yourself now."

"Thank you. You do the same."

When she was gone, Sarah felt Patrick's eyes following her around the office. She avoided them. He got out his flask, took a nip and went back to work.

At ten minutes to twelve someone else entered the newspaper office. He was dark-haired and cute and several years younger than Sarah.

"Hi," he said, removing his hat. "Are you Sarah Merritt?"

She suspected who he was even before she answered. "Yes, I am."

"I'm Arden Campbell, Noah's brother. I came to ask if I could take you out to dinner."

She stood staring at him for five seconds, stupefied, then burst out laughing.

He laughed, too, then asked, "Well, could I?"

"Mr. Campbell, I don't even know you."

"Well, I know that. That's why I asked you out to dinner, so we could *get* to know each other. I'm harmless, and a lot more friendly than my brother. I'm twenty-one and I like pretty women and I haven't had the pleasure of one's company since we moved out here, and we both have to eat a noon meal, so why not do it together?"

"I don't think that's a good idea, Mr. Campbell."

"Why? Has Noah got dibs on you?"

"No." She felt herself begin to blush.

"Has somebody else?"

"No."

"Then why not?" He lifted his left arm and sniffed beneath it. "I smell bad or something?"

Again she laughed. "Mr. Campbell—"

"Call me Arden."

"Arden, there aren't a lot of women in this town. I think we would start a lot of gossip if I ate lunch with you."

"Why, shee-oot, who's afraid of gossip! Come on . . ." He took her by an arm. "If they say Arden Campbell's out sparking the new woman in town I'll spit in their eye and say damned right."

She found herself being hauled toward the door, and resisted. "But I don't know you, I said!"

"You're going to! Now get your coat, or your pocketbook or whatever you need, because you're going to dinner with me whether you like it or not."

It was quite a meal. He dragged her down the street to Ruckner's and deposited her in a chair and glued his eyes to her, removing them only long enough to cut his elk roast. He jabbered like a magpie and made her laugh so often she had to keep covering her mouth with her napkin to keep food from flying out. He volubly greeted every man who entered the place, calling out, "You've met Sarah Merritt, haven't you?" He said he was a Christian, and looking for a wife, and intended to be farming his own place inside of two years, and have a family inside of three, if he had to send for a mail-order bride to do it, which he hoped he would not have to do. He said he could sing like a nightingale, fight like a terrier, dance like a highlander and cook flapjacks better than his ma. He told her one day he'd like to whip some up for her. He claimed he found life too serious to be serious about, and thought the best way to get through it was to laugh whenever you could. He told her he was tough, and honest, and hardworking and lovable—just that he'd never been around a woman long enough to prove it. He *told* her he was coming into town Saturday night to take her to the play at the Langrishe, and gave her no option to refuse. He'd pick her up at seven, he said, leaving her, somewhat overwhelmed, at the door of the newspaper office.

CHAPTER 9

NOAH heard the news before Arden came into his office.

"Hey, big brother!" Arden greeted with a wide smile.

"Big brother, my foot! What the hell's the idea of taking Sarah Merritt out for dinner?"

"I told you I was going to."

"And I told you to keep away from her."

"I asked her if you had dibs on her and she said no."

"You did *what!*" Noah came up out of his chair.

"I asked her if you had dibs on her and she said no. I asked her if anybody else did and she said no again, so I'm courting her."

"Courting her! Why, you just met her two hours ago!"

"We got along real well in those two hours, though. I had her laughing fit to kill. I'm taking her to the Langrishe Saturday night."

"The hell you are!"

"I don't know what you're getting so upset about. *You* don't want her."

Noah didn't, so he dropped back into his chair. "Does Ma know?"

"Not yet, but she'll be happy. She went over and checked Sarah out, too."

Noah clutched his head. "Judas priest."

"Ma invited her out to the house for a meal sometime. I wouldn't be surprised if she comes."

"What about Pa? I suppose he went to gawk at her, too."

"Pa's in the saloon getting happy. He'll be patting Ma's butt while she's fixing supper tonight." Arden laughed. "You see him yet?"

"Yeah, I talked to him and Ma both, earlier." After a pause he said, "Listen, about that woman—forget what I said, and whatever you do, don't tell her I said it!"

"Don't worry. I've got better things to do with Sarah Merritt than talk about you."

For the remainder of the day Noah stewed over the turn of events. He remembered Arden's grin when he'd said he had better things to do. Exactly *what* better things? Hell, the brat was only twenty-one! But recalling himself at twenty-one, Noah scowled. Unless he missed his guess, Sarah Merritt was one hundred eighty degrees from her sister in the worldliness department. She wouldn't be accustomed to fending off randy young whelps with hubris the size of a barn loft and precociousness to match.

At suppertime that night Noah stood inside his bedroom with his hand on the doorknob and his watch in his palm. At the dot of six he heard a door open down the hall, opened his own and snapped his watch shut.

"Well . . . hello," he said, feigning surprise as he overtook Sarah Merritt from two doors down.

"Hello."

"You had quite a day."

"Yes, I did."

"By the sound of it, you met my whole family." He loitered in the center of the hall, forestalling her progress toward the stairs until he'd said what he was disinclined to say before the big-eared audience around the supper table.

"Not quite. I didn't meet your father. The other two were charming though."

"Obviously."

"So you heard about my going to dinner with Arden."

"The whole town heard about it."

"Well . . . he's a persuasive young man."

"Obviously."

"I imagine you know that he's taking me to the theater, too."

"Do you think that's a good idea?"

"The bill has changed. Mr. Langrishe's troop is performing *Only a Farmer's Daughter,* which I must see anyway in order to review it. I may as well take the opportunity with your brother."

My brother who's only twenty-one and keeps you laughing fit to kill? The thought was irksome because Noah was much more suited to her age and he'd never seen her laughing fit to kill. That once on the boardwalk she had let go briefly, but usually she remained serious, almost contained, around him.

What could he say?

"That makes sense," he replied. With a flourish toward the stairs he said, "Shall we go down? I think I smell onions."

For the remainder of the week he continued to stew.

On Saturday evening he retired to Mrs. Roundtree's parlor immediately after supper and parked himself there with the only reading material he could find, a copy of the Montgomery Ward Catalog for Fall and Winter of 1875–76. He really should be uptown. Saturday night and Sunday, when the miners all came to town for liquor, baths and whoring, were the rowdiest days of the week in Deadwood. Many Saturdays Noah skipped his supper or gobbled it and ran back on duty, for he'd discovered that his mere presence on Main Street put qualms in the way of most belligerent fist-slingers. So it might look fishy, him sitting here in the parlor when he'd normally be uptown, but he sat nonetheless, scanning all the tempting bargains as if he cared one iota.

Spring beds for $2.75.

Farm wagons for $50.

72 dozen buttons for 35c.

The haberdasher, Mr. Mullins, sat for a while with him, then went away. Tom Taft stuck his head in and said, "Staying home tonight, eh, Marshal?" Taft continued out the front door. In the kitchen, Mrs. Roundtree clattered dishes.

Shortly before seven, Sarah Merritt came downstairs and entered the parlor.

"Hello again," she said quietly, taking a seat on a maroon horsehair settee.

Noah looked up and said nothing. She had used some contraption to make her hair look like chain, all quirked up and kinked in peculiar squiggles around her face. Low at the rear, it was clumped loosely with a few wormy-looking strands crawling down her neck. She wore the same brown coat he'd seen dozens of times, but where it fell open he saw a bluish, striped skirt he'd never seen before. And damned if she didn't smell like lavender!

"Ordering buttons, are you, Mr. Campbell?" she inquired, tilting toward him to eye the open catalog. He slapped it shut and tossed it aside.

"So you're going to review the play."

"Exactly."

He linked his hands over his vest and drew doughnuts with his thumbs.

She had never seen this precise pursed expression on his face before, like that of a headmaster facing a naughty student. It made his mustache beetle out in the most unattractive fashion.

"Is there some reason you object to my going to the play with your brother, Mr. Campbell?"

"Object? Me?" Wide-eyed, he tipped his thumbs toward his chest. "Why would I object?"

"I don't know. That's what puzzles me, yet earlier this week you asked me if I thought it was a good idea, and tonight, here you are, waiting in the parlor like some grousing father. *Have* you some objection?"

"Hell no!" He shot from the chair, flapping both arms heavenward. "I have no objection at all. I was just sitting here letting my supper settle before I went back to work." He plucked his jacket and hat from a tree in the corner and clapped the latter on his head while opening the door. "I've got enough drunks to tussle with that I don't need to do it with you!"

He met Arden coming up the path, wearing a smile as wide as a miner's pickax, smelling sweet enough to corrode metal at fifteen paces.

"Hey-a, big brother, what's n——"

"H'lo, Arden."

"Hey, wait a minute!"

"It's Saturday night. They'll be raising hell in town." Noah stalked on downhill at a bone-jarring clip.

"Well, cripes, can't you even stop to say hello?"

"Nope. I've got work to do!"

"But Ma sent these shirts she mended!"

"Just put them in my room. Mrs. Roundtree won't mind. And tell Ma thanks!"

Continuing down the hill, with the smell of Sarah's lavender water and Arden's bay rum lingering in his nostrils, Noah thought, *I hope the two of 'em choke each other!*

Entering the parlor, Arden Campbell seemed to bombard the room. There was no description for him as apt as *cute*. He had a face shaped like an apple, with round, boyish cheeks and the faintest notch in the chin. His black sparky eyelashes gave his deep blue eyes a look of perpetual excitement. His mouth looked as though it had been sucking on a very sweet peppermint stick for a long, long time: lips slightly puffed, pink and shiny, wearing the expression of a man very pleased with the world.

When he smiled—and he smiled most the time—one could imagine that he'd taken in some effervescent substance that filled and vivified him. He had the ability to focus all his radiance in one direction—for the present on Sarah—and gave the impression nothing else of importance was happening within at least a hundred miles.

His comeliness quite startled Sarah.

"Hello, Sarah! I thought tonight would never come!" he bellowed. "Gosh, you look pretty! Let's go!" Without wasting time on polite parlor talk he commandeered her hand, linked it through his arm and took her from the house. Luckily she was wearing her coat or he might have herded her off without it, he was so eager.

The night was brisk and clear, but she had little chance to appreciate it. He walked as he did everything else, at the clip of a buck deer at rutting season. She had to quick-step to keep up with him.

"So how have you been? How's the paper doing? What have you heard about the play?"

"Fine. Wonderful. Nothing yet—Mr. Campbell, would you please slow down!"

He did so with a laugh, but it lasted only a dozen steps before he was towing her again at his enthusiastic stride.

At the Langrishe, he led her right up front to the third row, bellowing out hellos that drew additional attention their way. He solicitously helped her with her coat, draped it over her shoulders, then sat forward in his seat without using the backrest, as if preparing to spring from it. During the performance he hooted uproariously at the humor, and at the end of each act not only clapped but stuck two fingers in his mouth and whistled, nearly puncturing Sarah's right eardrum.

When the play was over he tucked Sarah's hand in the crook of his arm while walking her home.

"Did you like it?" he asked.

"No, I'm afraid I didn't."

"You *didn't!*"

"The way I saw it, it poked fun at the rural community, and I intend to say so when I review it."

"I'm more rural than you, and I didn't feel like they were poking fun at me."

"We all have a right to our own opinions. I could see you enjoyed the show very much, and that's fine, but consider the humorous lines again—don't you think they portrayed farmers as slow-witted dolts?"

He considered a while and answered, "Maybe in some ways, but a person has to be able to laugh at himself."

"At himself, yes. But should he draw the line when others do so at his expense?"

They had a lively discussion on the subject, and by the time they reached the path leading to Mrs. Roundtree's house he was holding her hand. At the foot of the stairs leading up to the house he tugged her to a halt. "Wait." He captured her other hand and tipped his head back. His palms were hard and smooth as boot soles. "We've got some great stars tonight. Stars this great deserve to be admired, wouldn't you say?"

She gave them her attention. "Do you know what George Eliot calls stars? Golden fruit upon a tree all out of reach." She lowered her chin and met his eyes. "Eloquence has always touched me."

He gazed at her. "You're the smartest girl I ever met."

"I'm not a girl, Arden. I'm twenty-five years old. Most women my age are married with families already."

"You want to be?" He grinned.

"Not particularly. I just meant to point out the difference in our ages."

He transferred his hands to her neck and began rubbing it through her coat collar. "Let's see if it makes any difference."

Her heart did a little dance of curiosity as he tipped his head and kissed her. The pressure of his mouth was warm, moist and brief. It turned her cheeks warm. She had never smelled bay rum at such close range, nor had her lips wet by any tongue but her own. It was a startling but grand sensation.

He drew back and said, very close to her mouth, "Nobody ever done that to you before?"

"A time or two."

"How old were you?"

"Eleven, I believe."

He laughed, landing a puff of moist breath on her nose. "And truthful, too."

"I must go in, Arden."

"Not so fast. One more."

What a one more. He used both arms, both hands and opened his lips wider than before. With his tongue he encouraged her to do the same. Bedeviling sensations skittered everywhere through Sarah. When he turned her loose he said, *"That's* how it's done. Now what do you think?"

She was surprised to find herself slightly breathless as she answered,

"I think I'd better say goodnight and thank you for a lovely evening."

"Can I see you next Saturday night again?"

"I don't think it would be a good idea to make a regular thing of it."

"Why? You didn't like the kissing?"

"The kissing was interesting. I enjoyed it."

"Interesting! Is that all?"

"Actually, no. It was a lot more than interesting."

"Well, then . . ." Had he been a rooster his neck feathers would have been ruffled.

"Good night, Arden. Let's not rush things."

He attempted to waylay her for one more kiss, but she turned him around and waited until he'd retreated down the path. She climbed ten steps, turned at a landing and climbed another thirteen before reaching the final landing where she came up short.

"What are *you* doing out here?"

"Having a last smoke before bed." In the deep shadow of the house with its unpainted exterior, Marshal Campbell blent into the dark, propping his spine and the sole of one boot against the wall behind him. He drew on his cigarette and made a bright red dot in the blackness.

"Shouldn't you be making your rounds?"

"Quiet tonight. Town's starting to settle down since we got our ordinances."

"Marshal, let's get one thing clear. I resent your spying on me."

He blew out some smoke and chuckled once so quietly it scarcely carried to her.

"I'm twenty-five years old!" she said, piqued. "Quite old enough to take care of myself, and I can spend my evenings with whom I *choose!*"

"You're absolutely right," he answered levelly, still leaning indolently against the wall. "Good night, Miss Merritt."

She left him as he was, smoking alone, and went to her room to lie and evaluate kissing his brother. It had been, she decided, a thoroughly pleasant distraction.

Given the amount of attention Sarah's presence had generated since her arrival in Deadwood, even she had been surprised that no other male than Arden Campbell had dredged up the nerve to come calling on her. His doing so, however, seemed to release a ground swell. On the Sunday following her date with him no fewer than three suitors appeared at Mrs. Roundtree's asking to see her.

The first was a total stranger—middle-aged, thick-waisted, with heavy-lidded eyes and a face like a bumpy gourd—who introduced himself as Cordry Peckham and said he was a wealthy man; he'd struck a rich vein early in the summer on Iron Creek and would be pleased to buy her the best the town had to offer of whatever she'd like if she would only come for a ride with him in his buggy.

She thanked Mr. Peckham but told him it would be unacceptable for her to ride out with a man she'd never before met.

The second was Elias Pinkney, who looked up into her face and turned the color of his name and got great sweat dapples on his bald head as he invited her to his home for supper. He had a thirteen-stop organ, he said, which she would be welcome to play, and a stereoscopic viewer with a large collection of photos of such wonders as Niagara Falls, Covent Garden and the Taj Mahal. He owned, too, a lap harp, a priceless chess set carved of Indian ivory, a respectable collection of books, any of which she was welcome to borrow, and a wonderful curiosity called a kaleidoscope which must be seen to be believed. She would, he believed, find a number of entertainments if she'd accept his invitation.

She thanked Elias as graciously as possible, feeling a measure of pity for the poor sap, and subdued the urge to find a handkerchief and dry his dripping pate.

The third caller was Teddy Ruckner, who invited her to his restaurant for supper that evening. He had, he said, been hoarding a roast of beef, which he would prepare along with the vegetables of her choice and warm bread pudding (which he already knew was one of her favorite desserts). Teddy seemed like a sensible young man. He had always appealed to her; they were more suitable in age; she ate most of her noon dinners at his place and thought he would be pleasant company. Also, she thought it prudent on her part to demonstrate to Arden Campbell that her evening with him was not to be construed as any sort of assignation. Furthermore, real beef sounded heavenly.

She accepted Teddy's invitation.

They passed a most enjoyable evening. He cooked the beef with bay leaf, onion and sherry, and served it with rich, dark gravy and a bevy of vegetables. As she'd guessed, he was an engaging fellow. Not only did he make a special effort to please her with the meal (he had closed his eating saloon to all but them and had produced a coral-colored tea cloth, matching napkins and a candle for their table), but they passed three thoroughly enjoyable hours discussing a variety of topics: *Only a Farmer's Daughter,* which he, too, had seen the previous night; the unpalatable habit of snuff-chewers expectorating in the street; his origins (he had left an aging mother and father behind with a married sister in Ohio to come here and make his pot of gold); her origins; the rumor that someone was planning to build the first much-needed stamp mill for the reduction of ore in the gulch; the domestic economy of blowing out a candle by holding it above you, thereby preventing the wick from smoldering down as it does when blown from above. He claimed the latter and demonstrated to his companion, ending their meal with a laugh when he proved himself correct.

When he walked her home he made no attempt to hold her hand, but at the foot of her steps he stopped and asked, "Would you mind if I kissed you, Sarah?"

She had suffered a dearth of male attention throughout her growing-up years, and thought she deserved this superabundance of it. Furthermore, she was curious to know whether her reaction would be as agreeable as it was to Arden's kiss.

Teddy, however, was much less impulsive than Arden. His kiss was executed without the use of his tongue. It was more of a gentle settling of his mouth over hers, and a small parting nibble. She found herself faintly disappointed.

"Good night," he said quietly when it ended. "I've enjoyed it."

"I have, too. Thank you, Teddy."

Much to Sarah's relief, Marshal Campbell had taken her at her word and stopped his spying. She encountered him nowhere on her way through the house.

At breakfast the following day they exchanged forced good mornings, establishing a status of edgy neutrality.

Later, she arrived at the newspaper office to find Patrick Bradigan already there working.

"Good morning, Patrick, are you turning over a new leaf?" she teased. "It's only eight o'clock."

"Y' might say that, miss, yes."

He didn't look exactly well, she realized upon closer scrutiny. His eyes were abnormally bright and his color high. "Patrick, aren't you feeling well? You look terribly flushed this morning."

"I'm feelin' fine. Well, perhaps a wee bit murky."

"Why, Patrick, what is it? If you're ill you certainly needn't have come to work." She approached him and touched his forehead. "You should be resting if—"

"I'm not ailin' with the smallpox, so y' needn't fret yourself on that score." He caught her wrist and held it, rising from his chair. No whiskey tainted his breath, but his eyes were bloodshot.

"Then what is it?"

"Ah, well . . ." A sheepish half-grin tilted his lips. " 'Tis the daft wishes of a lovestruck man." He took her hand in his and studied it. "I thought perhaps I'd best be askin' y' now before one o' those other young swains pops the question and y' decide to jump the stone with him. I was wonderin', pretty colleen, if you'd do me the honor of becomin' me wife."

Her lips dropped open in surprise. "Why, Patrick . . ."

"I know this is sudden, but hear me out. I've turned over a new leaf. You see, I haven't tipped the barley bottle once today. No, don't pull your hand away." He gripped it tighter. "From the minute I laid down me gold t' pay your first night's lodging I says to meself, Patrick me boy, there's the girl of your dreams. And when you turned out to be in me own trade, I says to meself, faith and begorra, the match was made in heaven!"

"Oh Patrick—"

He took her head and kissed her, halting her words.

She stood still as a newel post and allowed it. None of the pleasant amplification of Arden's kiss followed, only disenchantment accompanied by a wish to have it over. His mouth was wetter and more desperate than either Arden's or Teddy's and she could feel the trembling in his hands.

When he drew back, still holding her head, he vowed, "I can give up the drink, you'll see."

"Of course you can, with or without me."

"Then say yes."

She drew back, forcing him to drop his hands. "I'm not Catholic, Patrick."

"What does it matter clear out here? We'll likely be married by the circuit judge when he comes through, and later by a man of the cloth, whatever cloth comes first."

"I'm sorry, Patrick," she told him softly, "but I don't love you."

"Don't love me! But how could y' not love me when I can set type at two thousand ems a minute and print a page in forty-five seconds?" He grinned boyishly.

"Patrick, please," she pleaded quietly. "Don't make this more difficult for either one of us. I don't want to lose you as an employee, but I cannot marry you."

She watched his need for a drink escalate as he stood soberly before her, chagrined and trying not to show it, heartbroken and attempting to laugh it off.

"Ah, well . . ." With a wave of the hand he turned aside. "What you lose on the swings, y' gain on the roundabouts. I won't have t' buy a house then, and a wagonload o' furniture, will I? I wasn't just sure how I'd manage that." He returned to work, but within minutes she noted him sipping from his flask, and by midmorning he wore the effulgent glow of an Irish sunset.

When Josh came in he sensed the tension and asked, "What's wrong?"

"Nothing," Sarah replied.

There was, of course, something wrong between Sarah and Patrick from that morning on. The equanimity they'd shared over their work was strained as never before. However, she silently thanked Patrick for one consideration: he had pronounced himself in the privacy of the office so nobody else need ever know, for as the week progressed, the male attention continued and Sarah began to feel more than ever like a prize specimen under a bell jar. Men came into the newspaper office and offered her everything from their mothers' lockets to shares in their gold mines. In return they sought her company at dinner, supper, plays, the gambling tables, picnics (It was November, for heaven's sake!), and more than likely at breakfast, too, if any could be so lucky. She turned them all down, for she had business to do.

On Saturday, Arden Campbell showed up with the pistaschio and white striped umbrella and presented it to her with his full-moon smile.

"I can't accept this, Arden."

"Why not?"

"Well . . . because."

"Because people might know it's from me and think you're my girl?"

"Yes, as a matter of fact. Besides, it's the middle of winter. What would I do with it?"

"Save it till spring. Now, I'm taking you out to dinner tonight and I won't take no for an answer."

"Yes, you will."

"No, I won't. I paid a half an ounce of gold for that bumbershoot. You owe me."

She laughed and snapped the umbrella open, gave it a twirl and watched the stripes blur. "Arden, you're incorrigible."

"Damned right. Now shut that thing up and let's go."

She went with him and had a lovely time. He made her laugh as no other man she'd ever known. He teased—something new for her—and brought out a humorous side she'd never known she possessed. And at the end of the night, he kissed her again and turned her stomach to frogs' eggs, and dazzled her with his tongue, and tried to touch her breasts and nearly convinced her to let him.

*   *   *

She went, the next afternoon, to Addie's where her initial reception was halting but became more genuine as the two shared some affection-ate exchanges about Ruler, scratching her and letting her act as the bridge between them. In time Addie sat cross-legged near the pillows on her bed where Ruler gamboled with a string of red glass beads. Sarah sat at the foot. It was a dingy afternoon and a small lamp was lit—the perfect setting, Sarah thought, for two sisters to exchange confidences and thereby begin rebuilding trust.

"I seem to have an admirer," Sarah began.

"The way I hear it, you seem to have a whole townful."

"Well, one in particular."

"Who?"

"The marshal's brother, Arden Campbell."

"Ohhh . . . the cute one."

"Yes, he is, isn't he? But he's four years younger than I. Do you think that matters?"

"You're asking me?" Addie exclaimed. "Why?"

"Because you've always seemed to know about these things. Even when we were young you knew how to act around boys. I was busy helping Daddy publish a newspaper when I should have been learning the fundamentals of . . . well, of, of dalliance."

"Dalliance?" The prudish word caught Addie and brought out a laugh. "For a woman who always seems to be able to pull a thousand words out of a hat to suit any occasion, you had some trouble saying that one, didn't you?"

"Don't laugh at me, Addie. I'm four years older than you but I'm ten years behind in matters of concupiscence."

"It doesn't strike you as unfitting that you should be asking me when you know what I am? What I do?"

"I'm asking you to forget for a while what you do and not let it come between us. I don't know any other way for us to become sisters again. Besides, I need your advice."

Addie stopped sidewinding the beads, and the cat took up swatting at a fold in her dressing robe. For moments neither sister spoke, though their gazes remained earnestly locked.

"So what do you want to know?"

"Three men have kissed me recently. Should I have let them?"

"I don't see why not."

"Because one is my employee, one is not anyone I'm particularly attracted to, and the other one is four years younger than me and altogether too attractive for his own good."

"What did you think of it?"

"It was an interesting comparison."

"It'll be more than interesting once the right one kisses you."

"How do I know the right one hasn't?"

Addie looked very wise. "Because when the right ones does, he'll make you feel like you're a thimbleful of fondant, and you're going to wish you were, and that he'd lick the last drop from you or die trying."

"It was a little like that with Arden, but Arden is too young and much too eager to suit me. He wants everything to happen last week. Teddy Ruckner isn't that way at all. We simply had a good time together. We talked about so many things, and he fixed me the most delicious supper, then walked me home. But his kiss was rather flat and disappointing. Then there was Patrick . . . that one was embarrassing and we've both been self-conscious ever since. But what I wonder, Addie, is this—is it fair to a man to accept his invitations for dinner and plays when you're accepting the invitations of others as well?"

"Of course. If they want to spend their money on you, let them. But just remember one thing: if you want them to marry you, keep your bloomers buttoned."

The newspaper was growing. Sarah was putting out four sheets twice a week, the current edition announcing that the office of the *Deadwood Chronicle* was the first plastered building in Deadwood; an exceedingly rich quartz lode had been discovered on Black Tail Gulch and the owners were making grub by pounding the ore in mortars and afterward panning out the precious metals for lack of quartz mills and arrastras. At Claim #3 above discovery on Deadwood Gulch, Pierce & Co. was taking out an average of $400 per day, while the cold weather had put a stop to surface mining on many of the creeks until next spring. The telegraph was completed to within twenty-five miles this side of Custer City, and by next week the poles would be set as far as Deadwood. A party was planned at the Grand Central when the long-awaited wires reached the city. The Black Hills Country would soon have a reliable map, as Mr. George Henkel, well-known civil engineer, had been engaged all summer upon a survey and would soon have his maps completed. A two-hundred-dollar reward for the arrest of road agents operating on the Cheyenne & Black Hills Stage road was offered by Wyoming Governor Thayer and a number of county commissioners. No new cases of smallpox had been reported. Land for a combined church/school building had been donated to the city by Elias Pinkney, the amount of money to be appropriated for construction of the building to be put to a vote of the general public on December 4. An ad for a schoolteacher for next term would be placed in larger city newspapers as soon as the telegraph reached Deadwood.

Sarah was reading over the proof sheets of the edition on a cold afternoon in late November. A fire burned in the potbellied stove at the rear of the office, which was so much brighter with the lanterns reflecting off its new white walls. At a worktable Patrick was teaching Josh the rudiments of setting type as they composed the program for the Bella Union's next play. The room was pleasant with the smell of printer's ink and burning pine. The sound of the male voices murmured on while now and then the soft clatter of wood sounded as they selected furniture or maple engravings for their project.

The door opened and Sarah turned in her swivel chair.

A man had entered and stood smiling broadly at her. He was dressed in a beaver bowler and a dark plaid woolen greatcoat with attached cape. She removed her spectacles to see him more clearly.

"Hello, Sarah."

"Robert!"

Her heart did a doubletake as she bolted from the chair and met him in a fond embrace halfway across the room. In all the years she'd known Robert Baysinger they had never touched more than hands in a formal greeting, but his unexpected arrival chased propriety from both their minds. "What in the *world* are you doing here?" she asked, quite crushed in his arms.

"I received your letter."

He released all but her hands, gripping them firmly as they stood back to study one another.

"Oh Robert, it's so good to see you." From the first time he'd come to their house as a very young boy, she had thrilled at the sight of him. But he'd had eyes for no girl but Addie.

"It's good to see you, too. You look very well."

"So do you." She had never seen him in such rich clothes before. He had grown a beard and mustache—those old dislikes which on most men looked shoddy. On Robert they look distinguished, and immediately she loved them. "How I've longed for a glimpse of someone from back home, and here you are, stepping into my office as if you'd only crossed the street."

"Believe me, I crossed more than a street." They laughed and he released her hands reluctantly. "Is there somewhere we can talk privately?"

"Oh goodness . . ." She thought fast. "Yes, at Mrs. Roundtree's, where I live. There shouldn't be anyone in the parlor at this time of day.

But first come and meet some friends of mine." She led the way toward
the others, who'd been watching with unconcealed interest. "Patrick
Bradigan and Josh Dawkins, I'd like to introduce an old friend, Robert
Baysinger, who's just arrived from St. Louis."

During handshakes Sarah explained, "Patrick is my typesetter and
Josh is our apprentice." The three exchanged pleasantries while Sarah
fetched her coat and tied an unadorned brown wool bonnet on her
head. "I'll be gone for a while. Lock up if I'm not back before closing
time."

With her hand tucked securely in the crook of Robert's arm, the two
of them made their way to Mrs. Roundtree's.

"You gave me such a surprise, Robert."

"Undoubtedly. But not unpleasant, I hope."

"Of course not. How have you been?"

"Heartsore. Wondering if what I'm doing is the right thing."

"You've come here to see Addie of course."

"Of course. I made the decision as soon as I received your letter, but
it took some time to get arrangements made."

"She's not the same, you know."

"Perhaps not, but I find I cannot live in peace until I make an attempt
to get her out of that sordid life she's fallen into. Call me a fool—I
know, I am—but I've never been able to forget her. So I persuaded a
group of investors to back me and I've come to the hills to build a stamp
mill."

"A stamp mill! Oh Robert, you'll be rich in no time."

He laughed. "I dearly hope so."

"We need one so badly here."

"Which you implied in your letter. That's what put the idea in my
head."

"What do you know about it?"

"Not a lot, but I'm learning. I've been to Denver and bought the
stamps themselves and learned what I could there. It's a relatively simple
procedure, and I'll be relying on the experienced miners to help me set
it up."

They had reached Mrs. Roundtree's. In the parlor, Robert politely
helped Sarah remove her coat.

"Thank you," she said, slipping from it, watching as he hung it on
the tree along with his own. It had been a long time since a man had
performed this courtesy for her. Robert did it with the naturalness of
a true gentleman. He had been her ideal and still was. How ever could
Addie have run away from him?

He waited until she sat before doing so himself on an adjacent chair.

"Now tell me about Addie," he said.

"Oh Robert . . ." She sighed, her expression doleful. "You mustn't expect to see the same woman or to be welcomed with any degree of warmth. She's become very hard, remote most of the time, wearing a sort of shield to ward off any sort of closeness to other human beings."

"She's still that way with you?"

"I've made some progress. I bought her a cat—it looks just like old Ruler. You remember Ruler, don't you?"

"Yes, of course I do."

"That seemed to break the ice infinitesimally. I've been allowed to sit in her room and visit with her briefly, but she refuses to come and visit me at either my newspaper office or here. I've never run into her on the street, and she won't talk about the past. So if you intend to change her, you have a big job ahead of you."

"Thank you for the warning. I'll move with the utmost caution."

She felt pity for him, for his undying devotion to a woman who did not deserve it and who would undoubtedly hurt him far more deeply than even she, Sarah, had been hurt.

"Oh Robert," she said, leaning forward in her chair and reaching a hand to cover one of his. "It's so very good to see you again."

He turned his hand over, gave hers a squeeze and said, "That goes both ways." After several beats of fond silence they sat back. "So tell me all about you, your newspaper, the people here and all that gold. The reports continue to astound the rest of the country."

They had a long, friendly visit, lasting until nearly suppertime, when the other boarders started clumping in.

"Where are you staying?" she inquired as he rose to leave.

"At the Grand Central Hotel."

She rose and stood facing him. "I understand some of its rooms are getting plastered. Maybe you'll be lucky and get one."

The door opened and Noah Campbell stepped into the room, dressed for the weather in his thick sheepskin jacket and Stetson. As he closed the door his eyes, unsmiling, scanned Sarah . . . Robert . . . returned to Sarah for no longer than it takes a flint to spark. He nodded curtly and hit for the stairs.

"Just a minute, Marshal," she called.

He turned back and stopped several paces from them, his boots planted wide, his hat still on.

"This is Robert Baysinger, who's just arrived from St. Louis." Sarah added for Robert's benefit, "Noah Campbell, our marshal. He lodges here, too."

"Baysinger."

"Marshal."

The men shook hands. Robert smiled. Noah did not.

"Mr. Baysinger intends to open up a stamp mill here."

"Good luck," Campbell said and withdrew abruptly enough to appear unpardonably rude.

"Your marshal doesn't seem to like me," Robert ventured when Noah's bootsteps sounded in the upstairs hall.

"Think nothing of it. He doesn't seem to like anybody. I think he has a dyspeptic stomach."

They chuckled softly in parting and Robert touched his cheek to hers.

"I'll be seeing you soon."

"You know where to find me."

"Wish me luck with Addie."

"Good luck."

At supper Noah remained aloof. He talked with the others, joked and laughed, but whenever he glanced Sarah's way his face turned passive. Afterward she went upstairs to fetch her coat and returned to her office to finish the proofreading she had abandoned earlier.

There were still coals in the stove, and the clock kept her company with its soft, metronomic *tuk, tuk, tuk.* She had been reading at her desk for fifteen minutes when the door opened and Noah Campbell entered.

She removed her spectacles, swiveled her chair and remained sitting. "Yes, Marshal, is there something I can do for you?"

"I'm just making my rounds."

She sat back, holding her eyeglasses upon her knee by their wire bows. "I'm sure you could see through the windows nothing is amiss here."

"You don't usually come down here after supper."

"Am I required to get your permission before doing so?"

"No."

"Then I shan't." She turned back to work, waiting for him to leave. Behind her all remained quiet while the clock continued its message.

Out of the blue, Campbell inquired, "Where's Baysinger?"

Again she swung to face him. Again she removed her spectacles, made a triangle of them and tapped her knee. "You were very rude to him, you know."

"Who is he?"

"An old friend."

Campbell's mouth took on the shape of one who is trying to bite a poppy seed in half with his incisors. After staring at her for several seconds he shifted his weight to the opposite foot and said, "You're getting to have quite a few of those, aren't you?"

"Must I get permission for *that?*"

"Don't get impertinent, Sarah, you know what I mean!"

To the best of her recollection it was the first time he'd used her given name.

"I'm afraid I *don't* know what you mean. Would you care to elucidate?"

"People talk, you know! It won't take long and they'll be saying you're cut from the same bolt as your sister if you keep on the way you have been."

"Keep on doing *what?*"

"Spending time with every Tom, Dick and Harry who comes along, that's what!"

"Are you lecturing me on my morals, Mr. Campbell?"

"Well, somebody's got to! Baysinger makes four men you've spent time with in the past two weeks! What do you think that looks like, for God's sake?"

"Are you forgetting where you were the first time I met you?"

"That has nothing to do with this!" He jabbed a finger at the floor.

"Oh, doesn't it! You frequent the local whorehouse, but I cannot even meet self-respecting men in public places without getting evangelized! If our situations were reversed, would you appreciate being lectured to by me?"

He glowered at her for some time before throwing up his hands. "I don't know why I bother wasting my breath."

"Neither do I. In the future, why don't you just save it? Now if you'll excuse me, Marshal, I have work to do."

She presented her back while he stood for several seconds glaring at it. Then his footsteps clunked toward the door and he slammed it with unnecessary vehemence, leaving her to stare at the cubbyholes of her desk with her heart tripping fast in confusion.

CHAPTER 10

UP at Rose's it was dinnertime for the first shift. Cook had made chicken and dumplings this noon. The aroma drifted upstairs and made Addie's mouth water. Garbed in her dressing gown, she picked up Ruler and left the room. "Come with me, missy, and I'll get you some gravy." There wasn't much good to say about *the life,* but the food was one of them. They ate like royalty. Had the freshest foods available, and their own cow boarded at a livery (after all, they *needed* the butter!) and all the milk, cream, sugar and mashed potatoes and pies and cakes it took to keep a covey of confined females happy. Glorianne was a good cook and didn't skimp on anything.

In the kitchen doorway Addie met Ember, one of the Frenchies.

Addie's expression grew vengeful. "What're *you* doing down here? You're not allowed in here with us!" She passed the woman shoulder-first, making sure not even her cat's hair brushed Ember's arm.

"Don't get your tits in an uproar, Eve baby. I just came down to fill my butter bowl."

"Fill it on your own dinnertime!"

"You don't own the kitchen, bitch!"

"If I did you wouldn't be working here at all!"

They had their social stratum which segregated them at mealtime: the Frenchies, who specialized in oral sex, ate after the straights, who disdained what the Frenchies did upstairs. The ill feelings between the two groups spawned verbal sniping at the best of times, killings at the worst.

In the last house where Addie had worked, a straight girl named Laurel had put ground glass in the douche of a Frenchie named Clover.

Addie had friends here, though—good friends. Jewel, Heather and Larayne were already at the table when she entered the kitchen with the cat on her arm. Flossie was there, too, but Flossie never said anything, only ate without bending over and left the room with a belch.

"I'd watch that cat around Ember," Heather warned. "She's jealous 'cause you got it."

"She touches this cat and she's a one-nipple whore."

Everyone but Flossie laughed, then they spooned up. On the floor beside the table, Ruler was treated to her own helping of chicken and dumplings, and gravy made of pure cream, while around the table four overweight women ate their fill, followed by enormous servings of thick chocolate cake with butterscotch-nut filling, topped with whipped cream. Prompting them all to eat more, more, more was Glorianne, an immense white woman who played no favorites, so was loved by all. Glorianne was the mother some of them had never known, the grandmother some of them remembered and the provider of the greatest solace in their sordid lives: food. They ate this way every noon, gorging. At suppertime, just before the customers started arriving, they didn't eat much at all.

"Girls, you done me proud," Glorianne approved as she waddled around the table refilling their coffee cups.

Flossie got up, burped her way to the door and left without a word.

"Have you ever seen Flossie smile?" Larayne inquired of the others.

"Never," Jewel answered.

"A couple of times when she scratched Ruler she looked like she was threatening to," Addie said. "but I guess it was just gas bubbles after all."

Larayne reached down and picked up Ruler. Holding her near her face she said, "I wish I had a cat."

Jewel said, "I wish I had a man."

"How many you want?" put in Addie. "At six o'clock they'll be pouring through the doors."

It was a hackneyed joke with many variations. They had laughed at it a hundred times. Dutifully, they laughed once more.

Scratching the cat, Larayne grew wistful. "Someday one of those miners is gonna walk in here with his pockets bulging and—"

"Oh—his *pockets* are going to be bulging." Jewel's interruption got the requisite laugh from Addie and Heather.

"—and he's going to say to me, Larayne honey, let's go buy us a farm down in Missouri and raise some cows and some babies and some chickens and listen to the mourning doves coo while we sit on the porch in the evening."

The group had grown quiet. The cat's purring filled the room.

"That what you want? A farm in Missouri?" Jewel asked. "Me, I'd take a big city—Denver, maybe. My man would run a bank or a jewelry store maybe, and we'd live in one of them grand houses with the porches and roofs like a witch's hat, and there'd be a carriage house out back where the help would live, and on Sundays we'd drive along the thoroughfare like I heard the gentry do."

"Would you have kids?"

"Mmm . . . one or two maybe."

"How 'bout you, Heather? Where would you live?"

"I'd live where you could see the ocean, and my man and me we'd saddle horses and ride in the surf. We'd have a lot of flowers around the house, and sometimes when my back was tired he'd rub it and that's all he'd want . . . just to do that for me without asking anything in return."

They thought about it awhile . . . a man who asked nothing in return. A man who'd deliver them out of this life into one of marital love. It was the fantasy that propelled them from day to day.

"How about you, Addie?"

Addie's expression grew brittle as hard-crack taffy. "You and your men. That's all you think about—well, you're wasting your time. Nobody's going to come in here and carry you off, and if they did, you'd be sorry anyway. There's not one of them worth daydreaming for."

No matter how often they indulged in fantasies, they could not lure Addie. She alone remained cynical.

At that moment Rose bustled in, dressed in a red wrapper. "Time to pack it upstairs, girls, and let the others eat."

They gave her the usual grumblings. "We're still drinking our coffee . . . let 'em wait . . . you're a hard woman, Rose . . ." Nevertheless, they vacated the room, taking the cat and their cups with them.

Addie spent the afternoon ironing her cotton underclothes. She stitched up some popped seams in her gowns and corsets, mixed up a new batch of hair dye and made three poor charcoal sketches of the cat in various poses. At five o'clock she lit her lamp, debated about hairdos—Oriental or French?—heated the hair tongs, arranged her hair in a high pompadour, trimmed it with a feathered aigrette, floured her chest, vermilioned her lips, kohled her eyes and lashed herself into a corset that barely covered her nipples. Beneath it she wore cotton bloomers; over it, the black robe with scarlet poppies, and on her feet, scarlet satin slippers—the girls who wore red shoes turned the most tricks, without fail.

The talk about husbands had, as usual, brought a backlash of depression. As she checked her reflection in the mirror, Addie's mouth was tight, her eyes lifeless.

There was time to go downstairs and have a piece of cake: Glorianne's healing chocolate cake with butterscotch nut filling.

In the kitchen she cut a piece and stood beside the woodbox, eating it. Larayne came in, drank a dipperful of water and found an oatmeal cookie.

Rose bustled in, trussed in a sapphire-blue surah dress, its twills worn flat from overuse.

"Fella out there askin' for you, Eve. Better get out there."

"Oh damn. Who is it?"

"Never saw him before."

"I'm having a piece of cake."

"Can't keep the customers waiting."

Addie slammed down her plate. On her way toward the door Rose gripped her arm. "Put away the egg timer for this one, Eve. Judging by the way he's dressed, he's worth a lot more than a dollar a minute. You peek his poke first, understand?"

"Yes, ma'am," Addie answered. In this business there were no such things as set fees. For the familiar men who breezed in and out in a matter of minutes, the egg timer was used, but when a new man showed up, a girl was expected to visit first and use her seductive wiles to get an idea of the fellow's worth, then sap him to the limit. Sometimes if a man had no money, his gold watch would do, or whatever of value he happened to have. Once Addie had entertained a trick for a bag of dried beans.

This one, Rose had said, looked rich.

Addie saw him first from behind. He was standing in the murky lounge reading their "menu" when she entered and caught a glimpse of him through the hand railing of the stairway.

Though no one at Rose's called her Addie, there were times since Sarah had shown up in town that she thought of herself by that name: Addie as she'd been before age twelve, holding Ruler, feeding the cat beside her chair, in the company of her friends, she was as close to Addie as she'd ever be again. But the moment she began moving toward the man in the parlor she became Eve.

She loosened the belt on her dressing gown.

Strolled with rocking hips.

Lowered her eyelids.

Opened her lips.

Spoke in a smoky contralto.

"Hello, sugar. You lookin' for little Eve-ey?"

He turned . . . slowly removed a bowler from his head. "Hello, Addie," he said quietly.

Her smile collapsed. Her heart plunged and the blood dropped from her face. The last time she had seen him he was nineteen. Five years had transformed him into an adult with thick side whiskers, a fuller face and a neck to match. He was taller, too, and his caped greatcoat gave the impression of substantial width and acquired wealth. He wore kid gloves and held the expensive beaver hat.

"Robert?" she whispered.

He hid his dismay well. She was nearly unrecognizable, fleshy and half-dressed, with brittle hair and kohl on her eyes. At fifteen she'd been shy and girlish, at sixteen she'd disguised her young breasts behind dresses with large half-moon yokes bordered by ruffles. Now she had breasts the size of cantaloupes, exposed nearly to the tips, the skin as coarse and loose as bread dough.

He smiled sadly. "Yes, it's me."

"What are you doing here?" she asked, closing her dressing gown with one hand. His eyes followed, then dropped politely to the hat in his hands.

"Sarah wrote to me when she found you. I asked her to." Not until her clothes were adjusted did he raise his eyes. Her face had grown red with chagrin.

"You shouldn't have come here."

"Perhaps not. Sarah said the same thing. I found, however, that I could not seem to get on with my life until I had settled this matter of you in my mind."

"Forget me."

"I wish I could," he whispered earnestly. "Don't you think I wish I could?"

"I'm nothing. Less than nothing," she claimed flatly.

"Don't say that."

"Why not? It's true."

"No," he said simply.

For a moment they exchanged gazes, silent and confused.

"It's true," she repeated.

"You were the center of all my hopes and dreams. You were sweet and innocent and caring."

"Well, I'm not anymore!" she snapped. "Now, why don't you just get out of here?"

"I'm not the one who should get out of here, Addie. You are."

"What is this, a conspiracy? First Sarah comes poking her nose into my life, now you! Well, I don't need either one of you! I'm a prostitute, and a damned good one! I earn more money in one week than she'll earn with that goddamned newspaper press in a year, and I don't have to work half as hard to do it! I eat like a queen and lay on my back and get paid for it. How many people do you know that have a life so soft?"

He stood a while before replying quietly, "So coarse, Addie. Are you trying to show me your worst side to scare me off?"

She gazed at him as if he were a sliver on the board wall behind him. "I've got paying customers to get ready for. You'll have to excuse me." She turned toward the stairs.

"You're not getting rid of me that easily. I'll be back."

She climbed the steps without a backward glance, rocking her hips, holding her head high.

"Do you hear me, Addie? I'll be back!"

In her room she closed the door and flattened her spine and palms against it. Her chest ached. Her eyes stung. She squeezed them shut, riveting herself against the door, breathing as if someone had just broadsided her.

He came here to find me!

There wasn't a prostitute in the universe who didn't have dreams like the girls had been voicing this noon: a man coming to take them out of the trade. No matter how tough they talked, how they hated men, how they disdained men every chance they got, they all wanted to be rescued by one and transformed by his love into a woman of virtue. And Addie was no different.

Oh Robert, I didn't want you to see me like this, here in this place where I've become soulless. I've had to—don't you see?—to survive. Now here you come to rake up guilt and confusion and wants that a woman like me doesn't deserve.

She relived the shock of seeing him downstairs. He had been reading the list of aberrations performed in this place on any man who requested them. Did he think she did all that? What the Frenchies did? In spite of it, he had removed his hat. Oh, he had removed his hat. Still pressing the door, she opened her eyes to the blurred rafters. How long had it been since any man had removed his hat in her presence unless it was to sail it out of the way from the middle of a bed? She saw again the shock Robert had almost been able to hide at the sight of her scarcely covered breasts. She saw his cheeks growing florid as he dropped his gaze, and the hurt in his eyes at her purposely coarse language.

Don't come back, Robert, please. I wasn't worthy of you then and I'm not now. It will only hurt you more if you make me tell you why.

Downstairs the piano player struck up "Clementine." Addie had heard it so many times it made her ears jangle. Thrusting herself away from the door, she bolted across the room to her mirror, swiped at the smears of wet kohl dripping down her face and poured water from her pitcher into her bowl. When she had washed her face she applied fresh kohl to her upper and lower eyelids, painted her mouth with carmine paste; glued a black velvet mole on the high inner side of her left breast; atomized her neck, cleavage and thighs with orange blossom cologne; checked the results in the mirror and went to the room next door.

There, she lit a lantern, put a clean flannel pad on top of the counterpane, wound the clock on the table beside it, stationed it beside the egg timer, glanced at the butter bowl to make sure it was amply filled, moved it over to within easy reach of the bed, filled the pitcher and bowl from the tin in the hall, splashed two inches of water into the china chamberpot beside the door, replaced the pitcher and bowl on the wash table and smoothed her corset over her round stomach.

She glanced over the room and discovered Ruler had followed her. She picked up the cat and said, "Come on. You don't belong in here." With the care she displayed for no other living creature, she gently put the cat back in her private room, curled its tail around it on the bed, kissed its face and left it there where it could not witness the degrading side of her life.

Downstairs the men were waiting. One named Johnny Singleton brightened and hurried to the foot of the steps as she descended.

"Hello, Johnny-boy. You're back."

"You betcha, Eve-ey. To see my favorite."

With practiced ease she led him to believe she liked him, felt seduced by him and would rather be with him than with any other man on earth. She teased him in the proper tone, dredged up laughter when it was required, inquired in a seductive whisper if he'd had his carbolic bath, took him upstairs to the room she had prepared, turned over the egg timer, performed the rite with enough false relish to make him feel bullish and virile, collected seven dollars in gold dust when it was over, gave him a goodbye kiss, closed the door behind him, squatted over the china pot to give herself a quick finger douche, washed her hands, dumped the basin in the slop jar in the hall and replaced the pad on the bed with a clean one.

Downstairs, she deposited the gold in the drop box near the kitchen door, made an x and two l's on a paper (x equaling five dollars, l equaling one dollar), signed her name and deposited it, too, then went back to the parlor to smoke a cigar and wait for her next trick.

By four A.M. she had performed the ritual twenty-two times. Beside the bed the butter bowl was nearly empty. In a wooden hamper lay twenty-two soiled flannel pads. In the box downstairs was $236 she had put there.

But Adelaide had had no part in it. Eve had done it all, had lain beneath man after man in the dreary room where the bedding was never turned down. Had laughed and coaxed and joked and stroked. Had drawn from them guttural sounds matching others that could be heard through the thin walls. Had satisfied their needs while pretending she was slicing peaches for a family of four; picking colorful flowers in a dooryard while dressed in white organdy; following a collie out to meet a man walking up a lane, a man who looked very much like Robert; ridden in the surf behind him on a galloping horse . . . whatever fantasy it took to escape the room and the man . . . all the fantasies she refused to divulge when the others daydreamed aloud.

And when all twenty-two had expunged themselves within her body, when she had cleansed herself one last time with a potash douche to kill their seeds and had bathed the smell of their secretions from her skin, she slipped into her own room and coiled herself around the warm, purring cat who demanded nothing of her, who neither used, accused, abused nor asked questions.

Ruler . . . warm, purring sweet Ruler . . . don't ever leave me . . .

The following day Addie roused toward noon, her thoughts indistinct. There was something she was going to do today. She tried to grasp it, but the images that drifted through her mind appeared smudged, as if viewed through a fingerprint.

Her eyes flew open. Oh yes—Sarah. She was going to set Sarah straight today.

Shortly after two o'clock that afternoon Sarah was helping a customer, Josh was gone on an errand, and Patrick had his hands full, cleaning type with a turpentine rag when the door opened and Addie stepped into the *Chronicle* office.

Sarah glanced up and smiled. "I'll be with you in a minute."

Addie waited near the door, wearing a navy blue brimmed hat with a veil drawn down to the chin and tied at the back, partially concealing her face.

Sarah accepted a nickel for a copy of the paper, bid good day to the customer and followed him toward the door. He eyed Addie warily as he passed her, giving Sarah the distinct impression he knew her but was reluctant to admit it in broad daylight in a respectable place of business. Neither did Addie glance his way but waited, stiff as a dagger.

When the door had closed behind him, Sarah gave Addie a second glad smile.

"Addie, I'm so happy you've come!"

"Well, don't be!" Addie snapped. "It's the first and last time I'll set foot in here."

Taken aback, Sarah felt her smile wilt. "What's wrong?"

"You sent for Robert!"

"No."

"Don't lie to me. He's been to see me and he told me you wrote to him."

Across the room, Patrick—bless his soul—kept his back turned, put his rag away, released the quoins from a chase and began to put type away. The sound of metallic clicks created a welcome sound in the otherwise silent room while the two sisters faced each other.

"Yes, I wrote to him because he asked me to. But the truth is, I advised him not to come."

"Well, he has, and it's all because of your meddling."

"Addie, he simply asked me to let him know if you were all right. He was worried about you."

"Seems everybody is lately—him, you—I'm getting more visitors than an Irish wake! Well, I'm not some freak show you can come and stare at whenever you want, so stay away! I don't know what you came nosing around for in the first place. I don't need him and I don't need you. You're not going to reform me, if that's what you have in mind, so you can give up that idea. I said it to him and I'll say it to you—I have a soft life and I don't have to lift a finger to have it. Just stay away—do you hear me—just stay away!"

Addie whirled, yanked open the door and slammed it as she left.

Behind her, Sarah remained rooted, bewildered and hurt, her mouth small, her cheeks burning. She felt the insidious sting of tears build behind her nose and knew in a moment her eyes would be brimming. Patrick had stopped putting away type and stood watching her with a long face, his work forgotten.

She walked primly to the hat tree beside her desk. If she met Patrick's eyes she would embarrass them both. She kept her own downcast while methodically donning her coat and plain brown bonnet.

"I hope you can manage alone for a while, Patrick," she said quietly.

"Sure," he replied with equal quiet. "You just go."

She went. Retreated. Hid. In her room at Mrs. Roundtree's where she sat on a hard chair beside the window and let her tears flow at last. She cried silently, motionlessly, her hands lay listlessly in her lap, the teardrops plopping between them and making dark circles on her brindle-colored skirt.

Addie, Addie, why? I only want to be your friend. I need a friend, too, don't you see? We share bonds that cannot be broken, no matter how you try. The same mother, father, memories. On this entire earth we are the only blood relatives to one another. Does that count for nothing?

How consuming, the loneliness of the discarded. To reach out in love and have that love flung back hurt as nothing Sarah had experienced before. She felt an aloneness as deep as that of the orphaned, or the aged who have outlived their offspring. Sitting at her window, depleted, motionless, she felt as if the tears rolling quietly down her cheeks drew from her, her last reserves of strength. With a great sigh she rose and stretched across the bed to escape in sleep.

The window had darkened to the blue of early gloaming when Sarah awakened. Someone was knocking.

"Yes?" she called. "Who is it?"

"It's Mrs. Roundtree. Are you all right in there?"

Sarah sat up unsteadily. "I'm fine."

"Supper's been on the table for ten minutes already. Aren't you coming down?"

She made a muddled mental search for a time reference—What day? What hour? Why am I in my dress?—and answered, "I'll be right there." She dragged herself to the edge of the bed and waited for reality to return. Her head hurt. Her entire body felt shaky. Her pulsebeats seemed to be magnified until they jiggled the bed. Horrible feeling, coming out of a deep sleep that way and groping for crisp edges.

As those edges returned she stood, moved about in the gloom, touching her tender eyelids, straightening her hair, wetting the sides with a comb, brushing at her skirt, tugging at her sleeves. When she'd put herself in reasonable order she descended into the light below. Entering the dining room, she felt each man turn and look.

"You all right, Miss Merritt?" Mr. Mullins asked. She had come to be regarded as an ingenue over whose welfare all the men presided.

"I'm fine, really. Go on with your meal."

She took her chair across from Noah Campbell and saw his hands stall over his food as he studied her wrinkled shirtwaist and puffy eyes. Without speaking, he reached for a platter of fried fish and extended it her way. "Thank you," she said, avoiding his eyes. The others resumed their mealtime chatter. Noah Campbell took no part in it but watched Sarah surreptitiously as she nibbled at the food on her plate, leaving much of it untouched.

"Why, you haven't eaten enough to keep a sparrow alive," Mrs. Roundtree chided as she collected plates.

"I'm sorry. It's very good, really, but I just don't seem to have an appetite tonight."

"There's blackberry sauce for dessert."

"No, none for me," Sarah replied. "If you'll excuse me, I have some writing to do." She rose and left the room.

The marshal watched her go, guilt-stricken for having brought this on with his outburst last night in her newspaper office. He hesitated less than five seconds before hastily rising, sending his chair scraping back. "No sauce for me either. Good meal though, Mrs. Roundtree."

He took the stairs two at a time and reached the upper hall just as Sarah's door was closing.

"Miss Merritt," he called, "could I talk to you?"

She reopened the door and stood waiting, the room behind her black, only one lantern shedding dim light from its wall bracket two doors down.

"Yes, Marshal?"

He stopped before her, hatless, gunless, the star on his black leather vest catching the light. "I'll be going out again to give the town the once-over. If you need Doc Turley I can send him up."

"Mr. Campbell, I'm not certain I can handle all this concern from you. Have you taken it upon yourself to become my personal guardian angel?"

"I got a little heavy-handed with you last night. I'm sorry."

"Yes, you did."

"I'm trying to apologize," he said.

She looked square into his eyes and saw the potential of a good man. "Apology accepted."

Eye to eye, they stood and felt their misgivings beginning to slip, uneasy as they so often were when this happened. Foes . . . friends . . . antagonistic . . . sympathetic. It seemed they could not find an even emotional keel with one another.

"Now, about Doc Turley . . ."

She gingerly touched her eyelids. "Do I look like I need him?"

"Well, something's wrong, I can tell."

"I've been crying," she admitted point-blank. "I don't do it very often, I can assure you."

His eyes settled on hers and stayed. "Was it about your sister?"

Sarah nodded.

"There was scuttlebutt in town that she came out of Rose's and went to see you today."

"Yes, at the newspaper office. It was about Robert Baysinger. By now you probably know who he is."

"No, I don't."

"We all grew up together in St. Louis. He was Adelaide's first suitor when she was sixteen years old."

"Adelaide's?"

"Yes. When I left there Robert asked me to write him and let him know if I found Addie, and how she was. I did that after I arrived in Deadwood, never suspecting that Robert was planning to come here himself. When he showed up yesterday no one was more surprised than I. Except, perhaps, Addie."

"I can imagine."

"I don't know what passed between them, but he went to see her at Rose's, and she came to me today accusing me of bringing him here to try to reform her."

"Did you?"

"No. I told you, I had no idea he was even coming. He simply arrived unannounced."

"At Rose's, too, I take it."

"Exactly."

Noah crossed his arms and leaned a shoulder against the doorframe. "What does he want from her?"

"I don't know, but she's so angry at me and I don't understand why."

"Ask her."

"I have. It's as if she doesn't hear me. For a while I thought I was making some progress. I didn't push her, but I didn't let her forget I was here. I went to visit her regularly and thought if I just let her know I cared, that I was here for her to rely on if she needed anything, it would effect a slow healing of whatever it was that had come between us." She paused thoughtfully before continuing. "For a while it seemed to be working. Especially after I gave her the cat. She actually let me sit on the foot of her bed. She named the cat after . . . oh, I already told you that, didn't I? Well, I took it as a good sign. The first memory of our childhood she allowed, you see. But today . . ." Sarah's expression became dejected and she leaned against the opposite doorframe. "I'm afraid I just don't know what to do anymore."

They stood facing each other, their enmity forgotten for the moment. After some silent reflection Noah said, on a sigh, "Ahh, sisters and brothers . . ." He gave a mirthless chuckle. "We're reared being told to love them, but sometimes it's hard, isn't it?"

Tom Taft and Andrew Mullins came upstairs and excused themselves as they went by the couple at the near end of the hall. Noah removed his shoulder from the doorway to give them room to pass, then resumed his pose.

"Addie and I have always been so different," Sarah continued, as if the interruption hadn't taken place.

"So have Arden and I."

"You and I are the older ones. We're supposed to set a good example, but even when we do they don't always follow it, do they?"

"Not at all."

They spent some time pondering before Sarah went on. "When we were girls I always worked and Addie never did. Our father made me learn the newspapering trade while she was never required to do anything. I couldn't understand why he babied her so, why she didn't have to at least run errands for him. Now I see that I was the lucky one. She told me this afternoon that she has no intention of reforming, because she has a soft life with no work."

"She said that?"

Sarah nodded.

He left the doorframe, settling his weight on both feet. "At the risk of treading on forbidden ground, I don't think the life of those women in the badlands is soft. The men who go there aren't always gentlemen. I know becauses I've been called up there more than once to arrest some of the customers."

"For . . . for hurting the girls, you mean?"

He leveled his gaze on her without replying.

"Answer me, Marshal."

He did so reluctantly. "It happens, whether you want to believe it or not."

Sarah closed her eyes and rubbed her forehead. She looked at Campbell again and asked, "Then why won't she leave it?"

"Maybe she feels caught. Where would she go? What would she do?"

"I'm here. She could help me with the newspaper."

"No offense, Sarah, but your sister isn't exactly . . . well, let's say she'd have to go some to get as bright as you."

"I could teach her."

"Maybe you could, but how much would she earn?"

"Enough to live decently."

"I don't think she ever could live decently, not in the sense that you mean, not in the town where she knows all the men the way she does. The women would shut her out."

"What women? There are only twenty of us here and I think they'd give her a chance out of respect for me if I asked them to."

"There'll be more coming and you know it. Besides, I think you overestimate the extent of the 'good women's' forbearance."

"I suppose you're right. So what should I do . . . ." With a hand on her heart, Sarah thrust her head forward. ". . . let her live there and do what she does and pretend she's not my sister?"

"I don't know. Sometimes we just have to let people make their own mistakes. It's the same with Arden. He never thinks things through, just charges headlong when he gets an idea before he takes time to think it through. I try to tell him, Arden, if you're going to survive in this world you'd better take time to think about the consequences of your actions *before* you move."

"Does he ever listen to you?"

Again the marshal relaxed against the doorframe. "No, hardly. When we were pups he'd be the one with all the reckless ideas—jump off the riverbank before you knew if there were rocks underneath, tease a wild badger before you knew how fast he could run. Arden would get hurt and I'd catch hell for it. Ma would get on me something awful without waiting for me to explain. But he's one of those guys—hell, you just can't hold 'em down."

"So I noticed." They exchanged a long, placid look.

"I never asked before, but how did the two of you get along?"

"The way you'd expect. He ran two steps ahead of me all night long. I was much too breathless for comfort."

Noah thought about remarking that they'd been neck and neck when Arden escorted her to the bottom of the steps, but refrained. He studied her shadowed face, realizing that at some time during the past two months he had grown accustomed to her tallness, to her eyes being nearly on a plane with his, to her utilitarian mode of dress and her long thin face which no longer put him off. At some point in their acquaintanceship his respect for her had come to supersede these superficialities.

"He says he's going to ask you out to the place sometime. You going?"

She looked him straight in the eye. "Actually," she replied, "I'd rather go with you."

Her honesty caught him by surprise though he continued lounging against the doorframe with his weight on one hip.

"I think that could be arranged."

"Your mother intrigued me and I'd like to meet your father."

"They're good people."

"You're very lucky to still have them."

"Yes, I know."

They sent each other timid half-smiles and she realized that at some time since she'd lived here she had begun anticipating mealtimes with him across the table, she had ceased objecting to his unannounced appearances at the newspaper office, and had grown to feel secure because he was always sleeping down the hall.

After a moment he said, "We could go out some Monday. The town's usually quietest then."

"I'd like that."

He drew away from the wall. "Well . . . I'd better get my jacket and hat and go make my rounds. I could walk you up to the newspaper office if you're going back up there."

"I'm staying home tonight. I'm going to write in my room."

After a hesitation beat, he said, "Well, good night then."

"Good night."

He headed for the opposite end of the hall.

"Mr. Campbell?" she called after him.

He turned and paused directly beneath the lantern, which put rich rust highlights in his hair and mustache.

"Thank you for offering to get Dr. Turley."

He smiled, becoming a male reflection of his mother.

"Don't worry about your sister. She'll make out all right."

He turned and continued away while she quietly closed her door.

CHAPTER II

*T*HE following evening Mrs. Roundtree knocked on Sarah's door. "You have a caller, Sarah."

"Thank you. I'll be right down."

She capped her ink, looked in the mirror, patted her hair and went downstairs.

"Robert," she said with a glad smile. "I was hoping it would be you."

"I thought perhaps we might go out for a walk so we could talk privately." There were three men in the parlor.

"Of course. Let me get my coat and I'll be right back down."

The November night was clear and brisk. A quarter moon hung like a lopsided smile, trimming the edges of objects with a rim of silver. The shadows of the gulch walls were as black as printer's ink. He took her arm as they headed down the path and followed Deadwood Creek to the spot where it intersected with Whitetail Creek, then up the incline toward Lead.

"You saw Addie?" Sarah opened.

"Yes."

"And you got no further than I did."

"No."

"Depressing place, isn't it?"

"How can she live there? And do that?"

"I don't know. Did you see her room?"

"No. The lobby was bad enough."

"They refer to it as the parlor."

"Parlor . . . ha."

"My feelings exactly. My skin crawls each time I walk through it."

"There was a list on the wall."

"Yes, I've seen it."

No more was said on the subject. They walked along through the shadows.

"Are you sorry you came?" Sarah asked.

"Yes. And no. Seeing her for myself—the way you described her— was a shock. But with two of us working on her, maybe we'll be successful in making her leave that life. And I came for one other reason."

"To get rich."

"Yes."

"You always said you would."

"You remember how it was in my family . . . so many mouths at the table that my mother didn't even peel the rutabagas. The skins were too precious. Well, I made up my mind early that I'd never be like that. I wouldn't have to worry where the next meal was coming from, or the next stick of wood. I want to be rich so I never have to go through what my parents did. Does that sound avaricious, Sarah?"

"Not at all. And I'm sure you'll do it."

"I have a good head, and I've never been short of ideas. When you wrote about the need for the stamp mills I *knew*. I just *knew* it was the opportunity of a lifetime. If I could get financial backing to build one I'd see my dream come true, and I will. The men behind the stamp mill have placed great trust in me and I aim to see that trust pay off for them and for me."

"And what then, Robert?"

"What then?"

"If you could get Addie to leave Rose's, would you marry her?"

"I don't know. While I was traveling out here, I thought about it. I pictured myself taking her out of that brothel and making her into the sweet girl she used to be. I guess I fancied myself some kind of noble cavalier. But facing her as she is today, I really don't know."

"It would take a very special man to forget her past."

"To tell you the truth, Sarah, I'm not sure I ever could."

She thought, *If you cannot, I'll be here waiting. Perhaps one day you will finally notice.*

"But enough about me," Robert said, changing the mood. "What about you? Tell me everything that's happened since you've been here."

"Well, I haven't gotten rich, nor do I want to, but I'm happy running Father's press. I started with a single page and have already expanded to four. The paper is paying its way, and of course I print everything from the theater bills to 'wanted' posters, which also brings in good money. I've attracted many of the merchants to advertise in the *Chronicle,* and I have excellent help in Patrick and Josh. I don't know what I'd do without them."

"And what about your social life? Considering how few women there are in this town, I imagine the men sit up and take notice."

"Well, yes . . . actually. I've had offers to play a thirteen-stop organ and look at the Taj Mahal through a stereoscopic viewer."

They laughed, and Sarah went on. "I've been cooked a real roast beef dinner, which is hard to come by here, and I've been given a green and white striped umbrella in the middle of November by a man four years my junior who made me an offer of marriage—sort of."

"Sort of?"

"You'd have to know Arden to understand. But that's not all. I've also been arrested for causing a riot, thrown in jail for causing a man to get shot, threatened by the marshal who said he'd like to drag me down the street by my hair, and tried by a local grocer. It certainly hasn't been dull."

"Sarah, is that all true?" Robert stared at her agape. They had returned to town and stopped before the doorway of her shop.

"Every word."

"And you aren't going to enlighten me?" His eyes were wide with amazement.

"Of course, but it'll take awhile. Would you like to come inside where it's a little warmer?"

In the newspaper office she lit a wall lantern and put a stick of wood on the glowing coals. Robert sat on Patrick's tall stool and Sarah on her swivel desk chair. They talked for two hours.

Marshal Campbell saw the windows of the *Chronicle* office glowing and crossed the street on foot. His exchange with Sarah last night had been as close to pleasant as any so far. At breakfast today she'd been friendly, and at supper congenial. He'd just step into her office and say hello, let her know he was on the job, maybe pass a few minutes chatting. She was interesting to talk to, involved as she was in all the news of the town. She had opinions about everything, and though sometimes they weren't the same as his own, he'd come to appreciate the amount of thought she put into her views.

He reached her window, glanced inside and stepped back into the shadows.

She was there all right, but so was Baysinger, settled comfortably on a high stool while she—on her chair with one foot on an open desk drawer—rocked left and right as they talked. Their coats hung on the bentwood coat-tree as if they'd been there for some time. There was no evidence of interrupted work. The cover of Sarah's desk was rolled down. Her pen and ink were nowhere in sight.

Noah Campbell stood at the edge of the window light, coming to grips with a small pang of jealousy.

Jealousy? Where had that come from?

Baysinger said something, pointing to the plastered walls, and she laughed. He laughed, too, then she rose and went to the rear of the room where she opened the stove door. He followed and took over the job of sticking another piece of wood in the stove. With her back to the window, Sarah crossed her arms. Baysinger slipped the fingers of both hands into the rear waist of his trousers. They stood together that way, facing the stove, presumably talking.

Campbell watched until he grew tired of waiting for them to move, finally doing so himself, walking away without ever entering the *Chronicle* office.

Robert and Sarah had made a pact. Every day, without fail, each of them would visit Addie. No matter how bald her rejections, no matter how repugnant her domicile, they would pursue a campaign of invitations. To dinner. For a walk. To the newspaper office. For a ride. They would take her small gifts. They would—they vowed—break her down with love.

Meanwhile, the town of Deadwood reveled in the news that it was to have its first stamp mill. Robert Baysinger's name was spoken with near reverence even before Sarah put an article in the *Deadwood Chronicle* announcing his arrival and intent. Robert had brought the stamps themselves—there were forty of them—from Denver. Construction got underway immediately on a steep sidehill of Bear Butte Creek. A sturdy wooden structure was built to support the great steel shoes, which were driven by a steam engine. The shoes raised and lowered upon a sheet of mercury-coated copper, to which the smaller gold particles adhered while the larger ones rolled on down the hill to be collected below. The mill would do contract work, keeping 10% of all the gold that was stamped.

Robert had no trouble finding employees to build and work in his mill; not everyone in the gulches had "seen the elephant." There were many whom the color had eluded, or who had lost their diggings at the gambling tables, or whose claims had petered out.

Because he brought a service to the goldfields that had been much needed, while at the same time providing steady work for over two dozen employees, Robert became a prominent and well-liked man.

He settled into the Grand Central Hotel, returning to it without fail at four o'clock every afternoon to wash and shave, splash his face with bay rum, don a clean white shirt with a new linen collar, his gray and brown striped cassimere suit, his heavy caped coat and his freshly brushed bowler. As a finishing touch, he carried an ivory-headed walking stick each day when he set out for Rose's, making certain he arrived well in advance of the evening customers.

"Good afternoon," he would say politely to Flossie when she answered the door. "May I see Miss Merritt, please?"

Addie would come downstairs, often in a state of semidress. He would ignore her exposed skin and ask, looking straight into her cold eyes, "May I buy you a piece of pie, Addie?" or "Do you have a night off when I might take you to the theater, Addie?" or "Would you like to ride out with me to see the stamp mill, Addie?"

Addie would answer, "Only if you buy me off the floor."

He would reply politely, "No, not that way. Perhaps another day you'll feel like getting out." And he would hand her some token—a bright blue jay's feather he'd found by the mill, an abandoned bird's nest he'd plucked from a pine, an exceptionally pretty rock with pink stripes running through it, a humorous drawing from some old publication, a braided clump of dried sweetgrass he'd found out in the hills which could be burned to scent the air.

He never took her anything of monetary value, only offerings he thought of as "gifts of the heart."

She never refused them, but she never said thank you.

Sarah went, too, each day around noon when Addie was likely to be up and on her own time. She would offer news about Robert's enterprise—"The mill is going up fast," or about neutral subjects—"Everyone in town is talking about the telegraph coming." She would bring offerings, too: a fresh bun from Emma's bakery, the latest issue of her paper, an origami bird Patrick had folded from a sheet of newsprint, the raisin-filled cookie from last night's supper. She would keep her smile intact while Addie offered none, and at the end of the visit would remind her sister, "I have work for you anytime you want it, Addie, and a room at Mrs. Roundtree's we can share."

If the way to Addie's heart was by showing they cared, Sarah and Robert believed that one day their method would work.

On December 1, 1876, the telegraph line reached Deadwood from Fort Laramie, where it connected with Western Union. The town went crazy. It was a clear, mild winter day and everyone piled into the streets to watch the final wire being hung in midafternoon. When the connection was made, the man on the pole raised his arm and a deafening cheer rose. Sarah was standing below with Patrick, Josh, Byron and Emma. Hats flew in the air. The roar became immense. Byron picked up Emma and swung her off her feet. Someone did the same to Sarah and she hugged him hard and shouted in his ear, "Isn't it wonderful?" He set her down and kissed her hard on the mouth—a miner whose name she did not know—then they laughed and cheered with the rest of the town.

"Come on, Patrick, we must get to the telegraph office!" she shouted above the din.

They pressed through the crowd to the tiny office where the town's first telegraph operator, James Halley, was sitting at his spanking new desk with his finger on the brass telegraph key. It was too crowded inside for two more bodies, so Sarah tapped on the window and a man named Quinn Fortney raised it so Sarah could hear what was being said as the mayor of Deadwood sent a message to the mayor of Cheyenne.

"Shhh! Shhhh!" The signal hushed the crowd while those nearby heard the first *tap-t-t-tap* come back with a congratulatory message. When it was complete, James Halley came out onto the telegraph office steps and read it loud enough for those a block away to hear.

"Congratulations, Deadwood. Stop. Now a copper wire connects the fabulously rich goldfields of the Black Hills with the world at large. Stop. Expect great progress to follow. Stop. Congratulations. Stop. R. L. Bresnahem. Stop. Mayor of Cheyenne. Stop."

Another cheer rose. Men were hugging men. Patrick was hugging Sarah. Somewhere a banjo played. Men danced jigs. Patrick kissed Sarah, and she was too excited to consider objecting.

"Just think, Patrick!" she shouted joyously. "We can get news from all over America the same day it happens!"

"And you'll go to six pages, then eight, and me fingers'll be nubbins keepin' up with y'."

She laughed happily. "No, not for a while. Now let me go. I must get people's impressions during all this excitement."

She wove through the crowd asking the question, "What does the arrival of the telegraph mean to you?"

Dutch Van Aark said it meant he could place an order one day and have it arrive by stage three days later.

Dan Turley said it could mean saved lives, as in the instance of the smallpox outbreak they'd just had, when the disease could have been identified faster and the vaccine points ordered in one day instead of three.

Shorty Reese said it meant the miners would get the going rate for their gold dust.

Teddy Ruckner said it meant he could let his relatives in Ohio know he was all right without having to write letters.

Benjamin Winters said it meant he was throwing the biggest party the town had ever seen at his Grand Central Hotel starting *immediately!* He ended with a fist in the air, raising a roar of approval. He led the way toward his establishment with a surge of men following. "Hey, everybody, party at the Grand Central! Get that banjo player!"

In the midst of the crowd, Sarah turned and found Noah Campbell behind her.

"Marshal, isn't it wonderful?" Her smile was broad as a sickle blade.

"I hope so. We'll see if this crowd gets out of order before it's all over."

"Oh, they're just celebrating. It's the biggest day in Deadwood's history. Tell me, Marshal, for the *Deadwood Chronicle*—what does the coming of the telegraph mean to you?"

"Means I can get any news about stagecoach holdups while the trail's still hot. Maybe pick me up a couple of rewards, huh?" He grinned mischievously, which she'd never seen him do before. "But right now it means I'm going over to the Grand Central to join the celebration, whether it gets out of hand or not. How about you? Do you know how to celebrate or is that all you do is work?"

"Oh, I know how to celebrate. I'm actually quite good at it."

"Then let's go."

"I'd love to, but I must find Patrick and Josh first and tell them I'm closing the office for the day."

"Then you'll come over yourself?"

"Yes."

"*Without* your notebook and pen?"

"Well, I can't promise that."

"You can't dance with your inkpot open."

"How do you know I can dance at all?"

"You'd better be able to when you're a woman and there's a banjo playing in this town."

"We'll see," she said, and left him in the middle of the street with the crowd milling and the sound of the banjo moving his way.

Patrick and Josh were nowhere to be found, so she hung a sign on the office door, saying, CLOSED FOR THE DAY, and locked it behind her. The street was still clogged with people, all gay and excited, more than ready to regale until the wee hours.

On an impulse she detoured to Mrs. Roundtree's. If this was to be her first party in Deadwood she had no intention of spending it dressed in her puce-brown skirt and workday shirtwaist. Though it was nearly suppertime, the house was empty: even her landlady was somewhere in the crowd downtown, kicking up her heels.

In her room, Sarah washed, put rosewater beneath her arms, brushed down her hair and tucked it back behind her ears with a pair of shell side-combs, then, at her forehead, squiggled six strands with the curlings tongs. She hooked on a sturdy jean corset, topped it with two white petticoats, tied on her crinoline bustle for the first time since coming to Deadwood and dressed in her only good suit—a forest-green polonaise jacket over a rose and green striped nansook skirt with a square-pleated ruffle at the hem.

Before the mirror she neither simpered nor quailed, only gave herself a parting glance and went out to join the fun, leaving her pen and notebook at home.

Up at Rose's it was later than usual when Robert arrived. The piano player was plunking desultorily in the parlor, and Rose was playing solitaire at a table, with a burning cigar in the corner of her mouth. Though it was time for customers to be arriving, none were.

Addie came downstairs when summoned, and for once she was fully dressed, though the cerise garment left much of her chest unveiled.

Robert was waiting at the foot of the stairs. "Addie," he said, "have you—"

"My name is Eve."

"Not to me. Have you heard the news, Addie? The telegraph has arrived. Benjamin Winters is throwing a party at the Grand Central Hotel. Will you come with me?"

"Sure. But an outdate'll cost you plenty."

"This is a social invitation, not a business one."

"I don't accept social invitations."

"Make an exception for an old friend."

"Are you crazy?"

"Not at all. Will you come to the Grand Central with me for the evening?"

"I've got to work."

"No, you don't. There aren't any customers. They're all down at the Grand Central. Now, go upstairs and get rid of the raccoon eyes, and put on a decent dress and come with me."

A fleeting expression touched Addie's face, making it momentarily vulnerable. Her eyes met his and stayed. He sensed her resolve weakening, and saw a first crack form in her veneer of heartlessness. Then Rose dropped her cards and pushed back her chair. Sauntering over to Robert with the smoking cigar crooked in her finger and a hand on her hip, she said, "You're suckin' wind, mister. Eve told you she's working, and she is. Where would I be if I let my girls walk out of here with cheap-skates like you who expect their attentions for free. I'm running a business here, Baysinger. Either dig out your gold dust or leave."

His glance encountered Rose. It struck him that although the girls were not locked here physically, she held them with a grip more restraining than any steel lock. She fed them a daily diet of self-recrimination and intimidation cleverly disguised as tact. *We keep off the streets because nobody wants to see us there.* She kept her girls off the streets so they wouldn't get a taste of what they were missing.

Coming to this conclusion, Robert let his glance slide away from Rose as if she were an insect in his soup.

"Addie?"

"Do as she says."

"All right. But you must have *some* time to yourself. You need to get out of here, Addie. You can't live your entire life shut inside this building. Think about it, and I'll be back."

He extended his hand and she took it. Under the guise of a handshake he transferred to her palm something small and soft.

"I liked your hair much better when it was the color of cornsilk. Goodbye, Addie. I'll see you again soon."

When he was gone she returned upstairs. Alone in her room she opened the small square of tissue and found within it a lock of hair he had snipped from her head many years ago. She touched it—soft, golden, slightly curled—and reminiscence flooded back. She had been what—fourteen? Fifteen? He had come one evening in spring to play dominoes, and had brought her a red tulip he'd stolen from his mother's garden. She had told him, "I don't have anything to give you in return."

"I know something," he'd said.

"What?"

"A lock of your hair."

He had taken the scissors himself and snipped it from the nape of her neck while they had chuckled secretly and, afterward, had kissed and forgotten all about playing dominoes.

In her room on the second floor of Rose's, Addie touched her nape and recalled the exquisiteness of his youthful admiration. She looked into her mirror and reality returned in the form of the coarse black pelt hanging square-cut below her ears. Rose had said, dye it. Too many blondes this far north. You want to make money as a blonde, you go south where most of the women are black-haired. You want to make money up north, you go black.

Studying her reflection in the mirror, Addie wondered what it would be like to return to blonde after all these years.

The Grand Central was mobbed when Sarah arrived. Someone had hung bunting on the front porch rail and decked the inner hall with pine boughs. In the lobby the furniture had been pushed back against the walls, and three pails of sand had been used to anchor fake telegraph poles connected by ropes which were also festooned with garlands of evergreen. The banjo had been joined by a fiddle, and the dancing had begun, with every available woman pressed into service. Emma was there, as well as her daughters, and Mrs. Roundtree, and the butcher's wife, Clare Gladding, and Calamity Jane, in buckskin. Those men who could neither resist the music nor find a female partner danced with each other. A portion of the dining room had been cleared for dancing also and the two musicians roamed through the crowd, spreading the music as they went. Against one wall a long table held an array of food. Before Sarah could see what it held, she found herself swept up by Teddy Ruckner, who appropriated her without asking and danced her into a two-step to the tune of "Turkey in the Straw."

"Teddy, slow down!" she exclaimed, laughing.

"Not tonight! Tonight we go full-tilt!"

"I'm not used to this!"

"You will be! These men are going to dance the soles off your shoes."

Their execution of the two-step was graceless but gusty. Whirling and stomping in Teddy's arms, Sarah caught a glimpse of Noah Campbell, eating a sandwich and watching her. People came between them and she lost sight of him. The dance left her and Teddy laughing and winded. When it ended, Sarah was snapped up by Craven Lee, and after him,

Shorty Reese. When the third song ended she found a queue of others waiting to partner her.

"Gentlemen, I need a break . . . please."

They regretfully backed off and allowed her to escape toward the food table. Reaching it, she murmured, "Oh, my stars!" She had not seen such an array of food since leaving the East. Sliced roasts of wild game and a mountain of buns, whole baked fish, their eye sockets filled with cranberries, fricasseed rabbits and roasted chickens. Breaded parsnips, dark and light breads, hot rice cakes, a bevy of hot vegetables and every pickled thing imaginable from herring to tomatoes to watermelon. There were macaroon cakes, brandied peaches, apple fritters and an English walnut cake.

And in the center of the table—presided over by Ben Winters himself—a washtub half-full of pale amber liquid. Ben was adding brown sugar to the tub when Sarah drew up at the table to admire the spread.

"Miss Merritt—help yourself. Plenty to eat, and this here's a little posset for ladies and gentlemen alike."

"Posset, Mr. Winters?" She smiled knowingly. "If it's posset, where's the milk?" Sarah knew perfectly well the genteel lady's drink was made with milk.

Winters grinned and stirred the mixture with a long-handled spoon. "Oh, all right, call it a peach cordial then. Or call it a rum punch. But have some. It's not every day our town gets a telegraph. Running that newspaper, you've got more reason than most to celebrate."

"If it's all the same to you, Mr. Winters, I'll start with a little food. It looks wonderful." While she selected tidbits from the table, Sarah saw rum, brandy, nutmeg and water go into the tub. Nevertheless, she accepted a cup of the punch when Ben handed it to her and sipped it in an effort to cool off. It *was* slightly peachy in flavor and quite delicious.

She was lifting the cup for a second drink when someone clasped her elbows from behind.

"Sarah! I found you!"

She looked over shoulder. "Arden, how did you hear the news?"

"Gustafson rode out to the Spearfish this morning and said the connection with Western Union should be made by tonight. Guess we missed the grand event, but we sure found the party! Let's dance, Sarah!"

He stole her plate and punch cup and abandoned it on a table, hauling her amidst the dancers with his usual impatience. "Arden, you might ask a girl instead of telling her," she chided when he had her bobbing fit to shake her bones from their sockets.

"You came, didn't you?"

"Arden Campbell, I'm not sure I like your cocky attitude."

"Like it or not, I've got you now and I'm *keeping* you." He hauled her close and executed two galloping turns while her cheekbone bumped his jaw and from across the crowd his brother and mother watched. Oh, gracious, his mother was here! Probably his father, too, if the red-bearded man between them was the family member she hadn't met.

"Arden, let me loose," she insisted and got her wish, but by the time the dance ended, she felt as if she'd been through Robert's stamp mill.

"Come on, meet my father."

Again she had no choice. She was hauled off so abruptly her teeth clacked. Arden brought her to a halt before the trio of Campbells.

"Pa, this is Sarah. Sarah, meet my father, Kirk Campbell."

They shook hands while she tried not to stare at his freckles and red beard. She'd never seen a face so big and orange or had her hand gripped by one any larger.

"Hello, Mr. Campbell."

"So you're the one my boys been talking about. And Carrie, too."

"Hello, Mrs. Campbell," Sarah added while Noah stood by with his arms crossed over his chest, offering nothing.

"This is some shindig, isn't it?" Carrie Campbell said. "I said to Noah, it's a good thing you've got that jail because you'll probably have some drunks to throw into it tonight."

A delicate subject, Noah's jail. It brought a dead end.

"That newspaper of yours looks mighty good," put in Kirk. "I imagine this new telegraph will be a good thing for you."

"Yes, sir, it will be."

They talked about the telegraph, and the food, and the expected growth of the town, come spring. All the while, Noah stood silently while Arden shifted from one foot to the other and finally demanded, "You can talk about all that later. Now we've got to dance. Come on, Sarah!"

Once more she was unceremoniously hauled to do his bidding. Over Arden's shoulder her eyes caught Noah's and she thought, *Please rescue me.* But at that moment someone tapped him on the shoulder and apparently asked him to follow, for he turned and went into the crowd at the far end of the lobby. When the song finally ended she glanced across the crowd and saw Noah heading her way, but before he reached her, Robert appeared.

"Miss Campbell," he asked, very properly, "may I have the next dance."

"Of course, Robert. I don't believe you've met Arden Campbell."
When the two men had exchanged cordialities she danced off at a much
more sedate pace with Robert. Arden watched dolefully and she'd lost
sight of Noah.

"Well, Robert, I haven't seen you for a few days."

"I've been very busy at the mill."

"And I at the paper."

"Are you making any progress with Addie?"

"None. Are you?"

"I think I might have cracked through to her tonight." After that
their talk centered on Addie, and his mill and the telegraph, of course.
They danced three dances, then retired to the punch bowl and Sarah
had her second cup of the "peach cordial."

The party grew livelier and Sarah got slightly giggly. She danced, it
seemed, a good twenty-five dances, with everyone in the place except
Noah Campbell. Every time it seemed he was heading her way, someone interrupted. Once a gunshot rang out and he was called upon to
make an arrest and was gone for some time, locking the merry-doer in
jail as Carrie had predicted.

When he returned it was after midnight and she was near the door,
taking her coat from a rack. He walked up behind her.

"Are you leaving?" he asked.

She turned, smiling disjointedly, her cheeks abnormally flushed. "I
do believe, Marshal, that I've had too much to drink."

"So have a lot of others. I'd better walk you home."

She leaned close to his ear and whispered, "Thank goodness. I wasn't
sure how to get rid of Arden."

She was having some difficulty finding her sleeve with her arm, so he
helped. Arden approached, breathless after hunting up his own jacket.
"Noah . . . I'm walking Sarah home."

"I'll take care of that," Noah informed him.

"Now, wait a minute!"

"Ma and Pa are looking for you. I think they're ready to start for
home."

"Good night, Arden," Sarah added as Noah took her elbow and
ushered her out the door.

"But Sarah . . ."

"Good night, Arden," Noah added, closing the door between them.

"I think I must apologize, Marshal."

"For what?"

"Tippling. It isn't very ladylike to be caught in this condition."

"You had a good time, didn't you?"

"Oh, I did. All except for your brother. He dances like popcorn!"

Noah laughed while she hurried two steps ahead, swung about and lifted one foot straight at him. "Look! Do I have any soles left on them?"

"Some."

"Well, that's a miracle. It's hard work being one of only twenty women in a town like this."

They walked side by side without touching. She was actually quite steady on her feet.

"You were a good sport. The men loved it."

"I thought we were going to dance, you and I."

"You were quite busy."

"Didn't you dance with *any* body?"

"I was quite busy, too."

"I'll bet you don't know how. That's it, isn't it?"

"You guessed it. I'm worse than Arden."

She laughed, then pressed her palms to her cheeks. "Goodness, my cheeks are so warm."

"Rum does that to a person."

"Ben Winters told me it was posset."

"You didn't believe him, did you?"

"No. I saw him put the liquor in. I just decided to have a good time, like everybody else."

"You'll probably have a headache in the morning."

"Oh dear."

"It helps to drink a little coffee. Maybe we could find some in Mrs. Roundtree's kitchen."

They were climbing the long steps to her house by this time. From behind and below, the faint noise of celebration could still be heard. Noah opened the door and they entered the dark parlor.

"Just a minute," he said. She stood in the dark, unbuttoning her coat while he found a match and lit a lantern. "Come on," he said, picking it up, leading the way to the kitchen.

He set the lantern on the table among a collection of wooden bowls, a lard crock, and a saltcellar. The fire in the stove had long since gone out and the room was chilly. He hefted a coffeepot and gave it a swirl. "There's something in here." He stepped into the dark pantry and reappeared pouring the cold coffee into a heavy white mug.

She sat at the table. "Aren't you having any?"

"I'm not drunk."

"Oh, that's right." She smiled, accepting the cup as he stepped over and handed it to her, then returned the pot to the cold iron range. He angled a chair away from the table, sat down to her right, dropping an elbow on the table edge and crossing an ankle over a knee. He was dressed in his thick sheepskin jacket—unbuttoned—and the hat she'd given him.

"Your father is the orangest man I've ever seen."

Noah burst out laughing.

Sarah covered her lips with a finger. "Shhh! You'll wake up the whole house."

"Orangest?"

"Or should that be orangiest?"

They'd begun whispering.

"My mother says when she first met him she told him he looked like a frying pan that had been left out in the rain."

She giggled, suppressing the sound behind her fingers, then took a gulp of cold coffee.

"Oh yuk . . . this stuff is terrible."

"Drink it anyway."

She grimaced and followed orders, then shuddered and wiped her mouth with the back of one hand.

"You'll live through it," he said, grinning.

The room grew quiet. Their eyes met. Hers dropped.

"I like your hair that way . . . loose."

Her blue eyes lifted, wide and somewhat surprised. Self-consciously she hitched a wisp of hair back behind one ear.

"I've got awful hair."

"No, you don't."

"Addie's the one with the pretty hair. You should see it when it's blond. You never saw anything so shiny or bright."

He sat calmly studying her, an elbow on the table, his fingers twined loosely before him, his silence a gentle rebuff for her belittling herself in favor of her sister. Another lull fell and she groped for a topic of conversation.

"You have a nice family," she said, no longer whispering, speaking very softly. "I envy you."

"Thank you."

Again came quiet. She filled it. "The cold air and the coffee helped. I feel much steadier."

"Sarah, could I ask you something?"

"Yes?"

"What are you to Baysinger?"

"A friend."

"That's all?"

"Yes. I told you that before."

"The two of you are together a lot."

"Yes. We talk easily, and both of us are interested in Addie's welfare. Why do you ask?"

"Because I'm considering doing something." He got up from his chair, took her empty cup and deposited it in the empty dishpan beside the water pail. He crossed his arms and ankles and leaned his backside against the dry sink, regarding her from across the room. "I've actually been considering it for some time, but I thought it was only fair to warn you before I did it."

"Did what?"

"Kissed you."

Her jaw went slack and her eyes forgot how to blink. She couldn't think of one darned thing to say.

"Would that be all right?" Noah Campbell asked.

"I guess so."

He boosted off the dry sink and came across the wooden floor, stopping beside her with a shuffle of his boots. Leaning one hand on the back of her chair and one on the tabletop, he bent forward and tipped his head so the brim of his Stetson would miss her head. He kissed her once, quite dryly and briefly on the lips, so dryly and briefly neither of them bothered to close their eyes. He straightened his elbows and and their eyes met. "I thought I should ask first," he said. "Knowing how you felt about me in the past."

"Yes. That's all right. It's . . . uh . . ." She cleared her throat. She was not a woman given to stammering. "How long have you been thinking about it?"

"Since the day you took the cat to Eve."

"Oh."

"Well . . ." He straightened fully and began buttoning his jacket. "It's late."

"Yes. I should get to bed."

"And I should get back uptown and make sure the night ends peaceably."

He picked up the lantern and waited for her to rise and move before him through the kitchen doorway into the dining room to the foot of the stairs.

"Good night, Sarah," he said, without a smile.

"Good night, Noah."

"See if the lantern is on up there."

She climbed to the landing and saw that the hall lantern had been left burning on its bracket.

"Yes, it is."

"Good. See you in the morning."

He went out and she went up and sat on the edge of her bed in somewhat of a daze. What did it mean when a man considered kissing a woman all that time and finally did it with as much thought as if he were taking a test. Or giving one?

CHAPTER 12

IN the morning Sarah was relieved to find the marshal did not appear at breakfast. She'd heard him come in near four o'clock and imagined he, as well as several others of the meal's absentees, was still asleep.

Sarah seated herself gingerly at the breakfast table and accepted a cup of coffee but declined eggs and toast. Her head buzzed and her neck ached. Food sounded repulsive. Not only had she been imprudent at the punch bowl, she hadn't slept any more than Noah Campbell. Instead, she'd lain awake thinking about that kiss.

It hadn't been particularly romantic, but she supposed Noah Campbell wasn't a particularly romantic man. Still, for a prosaic kiss, it certainly had lingering power.

She thought about it a good half dozen times that day—while she and Patrick laid out an extra issue of the *Chronicle* announcing the arrival of the telegraph and telling about the celebration at the Grand Central; while she ate an enormous dinner at Teddy Ruckner's and reminisced with Teddy about what a good time last night had been, and declined his invitation to the Bella Union for that evening; while she limped back to the newspaper office on her poor tired feet and tried to keep from nodding off at her desk during the afternoon; while she waited for the marshal to pop into the newspaper office and he didn't.

They met at suppertime.

Sarah had changed to a clean shirtwaist, combed her hair and used a touch of rosewater at her throat. She was dismayed to find Noah acted as if the kiss had never happened. He was friendly, but no friendlier than to the men. They all talked about last night's party, but his eyes never once passed her any ulterior message, nor did he speak to her any more directly than to the others.

She supposed she'd failed the test.

Christmas was approaching. Jack Langrishe came into the *Chronicle* office one day three weeks before the holiday. He was a dapper man with a dark goatee and mustache, and always wore a square-crowned black silk hat.

"Good morning, Miss Merritt." His voice held the rich tenor of distant thunder, and his elocution was flawless.

"Mr. Langrishe, how nice to see you. You've come for the new theater programs. They're all ready."

"Not specifically. I've come about Christmas."

"Christmas?"

"I decided to approach you first because you've been the most out-spoken citizen of Deadwood regarding our lack of a church and a minister."

"Have I offended you, Mr. Langrishe?"

"Not at all. Quite the opposite. I feel as you do, that this town needs both. Since we have neither, and since the holiday is upon us, I propose to offer my theater for a Christmas Eve program and pageant which might stand in lieu of an official church service."

Sarah smiled. "What a marvelous idea. How generous of you to offer your facilities once again."

"I want to include the children."

"Of course."

"And as many adults as we can charm into taking part."

"I believe we'll have more luck with the children." She chuckled.

"Undoubtedly."

"Still, their mothers are more than eager to see anything organized for their benefit. We might entice some of them onto the stage."

"I hope so, and fathers, too. We'll use the theater troupe, of course, but I'd like to see the other members of this town become an integral part of the production."

"How can I help?"

Jack Langrishe touched a corner of his mustache and inquired, "Can you sing, Miss Merritt?"

She laughed self deprecatingly. "Not as well as I can write."

"I need someone to organize the children and direct their musical renditions."

"I can try."

"I *knew* you'd come through!" He emphasized with a fist.

"We'll need to announce it in the paper."

"Yes, that was going to be my next request."

"I'll have Patrick lay out the announcement right away."

Jack Langrishe was a magician. He charmed not only Sarah into directing the children's choir, but Elias Pinkney into crating his thirteen-stop organ down to the theater to join the piano already there, and a blacksmith named Tom Poinsett into constructing eight large triangles out of drill steel. He found a xylophone musician named Ned Judd to practice playing several numbers on the triangles, and talked Mrs. J. N. Robinson, the mother of the only infant in town, into playing the part of the Madonna and allowing her baby to represent baby Jesus. (As luck would have it, the Robinson child was a boy.) From the Langrishe troupe's supply of costumes came angels' gowns, shepherds' crooks, kings' crowns and more.

It was Sarah's idea to use the occasion to appeal for money for the construction of the church/school building, and to incorporate its collection into the pageant. (What better time to ask men to open their purses than when their ears are filled with the sounds of children's voices, their heads are full of memories of home and their hearts are brimming with holiday charity?) Though the gulch had no frankincense and myrrh, it had more than its share of real gold. They would collect it in a replica of a gold casket which Jack found among his theater props, and the three "kings" would offer it to the infant "Jesus" as part of the pageant itself.

Word spread that Jack Langrishe and Sarah Merritt had some lavish plans for the Christmas production, and sixteen children showed up to be in the choir. So many adults came that Jack actually had to audition and select from among them.

Rehearsals were held in the early evenings to allow Jack time to prepare his troupe for their regular nine o'clock performances of the current play, *Othello*.

On the evening of the first practice, Sarah excused herself from the supper table early. Noah Campbell glanced up and said nothing. The second evening he said, "Rehearsal again?"

"Yes," she replied and hurried away.

The third evening he stopped by the theater shortly before eight o'clock. By now the building had a wooden roof and two cast-iron stoves. The door squeaked as he entered. He inched it shut behind him, closed the latch soundlessly, removed his hat and stood at the rear to listen. Sarah was up front, her back to the door, directing the small fry of the town as they sang "Oh, Come, Little Children." She wore a dark green skirt and white shirtwaist with a string tie gathering it into a ruffle on her spine. Her hair was done in a tidy chignon. She stood very straight, directing with tiny movements of her arms, occasionally nodding her head to encourage the children not to lag. Their voices—a mixture of clear and off-key—carried through the room and touched a soft spot in Noah's heart.

> *Oh, come, little children*
> *Oh, come, one and all*
> *Draw near to the cradle*
> *In Bethlehem's stall*

They sang the verse while Noah's eyes remained on Sarah's back. He imagined her mouthing the words, bright-eyed and enthusiastic for the children's benefit. The verse ended, her arms stilled, and she said, "Very good. Smaller children, stay where you are. Older ones, circle to the outside and get the candles. No whispering now while Mr. Langrishe reads the verse."

They all followed orders—for the purpose of rehearsal, small wooden spindles were being used for candles. While these were being distributed, Jack Langrishe read the Christmas passage from the Bible in his resounding voice, and townspeople drifted onto the stage—uncostumed tonight, but clearly playing the parts of Mary, Joseph, the shepherds and wise men. Mrs. Robinson laid an empty rolled-up blanket in a wooden cradle and stood looking down at it. On the opposite side of the cradle stood Craven Lee, equally pious. Three men left a rear row of chairs and moved up the aisle; the last, Dan Turley, placed a small gold box at the foot of the cradle. A chime sounded, slowly, three times (one of the steel triangles), and Sarah raised her hands. As the last reverberation faded, she gave the children the downbeat for "Silent Night." They sang one verse alone, then she turned as if to direct the audience to join the second verse, singing herself.

She saw Noah and missed some words.

He nodded and her cheeks took on a slight flush before she resumed singing. He took a deep breath and joined in.

> *Shepherds quake at the siiiight . . .*

He sang full-out, experiencing an unexpected accord with Sarah Merritt as he did. It was the strangest thing he'd ever done with a woman, but it felt good. Mighty good.

Christ the saviour is born
Christ the saviour is born . . .

The song trailed into silence and their gazes dovetailed for a moment before Sarah turned to attend the children. Jack Langrishe's voice returned. Noah remained at the rear of the theater, watching the woman in green and white, jarred by the realization that he was, in all likelihood, falling in love with her. She touched a blond head, bent and whispered an order in a child's ear. For a moment he imagined the child was his and hers: she was good with the children, he could see that. She was educated and bright and brave and moral. What a mother she'd make!

What a mother?
Whoa there, Noah, you're getting a little ahead of yourself.

He'd kissed her once, and sung a Christmas song with her and already he was imagining her as the mother of his children? That was Arden's fancy, always talking about having a wife and a family, not Noah's! The idea of being so abruptly swayed to that way of thinking brought him a backwash of denial tinged by panic.

Nevertheless, he waited until the rehearsal ended, following Sarah Merritt with his eyes, dissecting his newfound feelings. She raised both palms in the air, calling for attention. "Children, you sounded like angels from heaven. You may go home now, and the next time we'll practice with our costumes and the lighted candles."

She came down the aisle, retrieving her coat and a small bonnet from a chair near the rear. He smiled and waited for her.

"Good evening, Marshal."

"Hello, Sarah. Here, I'll help you with that."

"You have a very fine voice," she said, slipping into her coat while he held it for her.

"So do you."

"So if we cannot dance together, at least we can sing," she said, smiling, closing the button at her throat. He handed her the bonnet, watching as she tied it beneath her chin. How amazing: he had difficulty tearing his gaze away from the curve of her throat and jaw while she tied the ribbons. She finished and began drawing on gloves, suddenly lifting her head and flashing him a full smile that seemed to catch him beneath the ribs. He struggled to recall exactly when she'd begun to change in his eyes, when her tallness had become elegance, her plainness purity and her ordinary face his ideal.

"I've come to walk you home."

"All right. But I need to stop by the newspaper office on the way."

"Fine."

Outside it was cold and windy. He wanted to take her arm but refrained. What had come over him? He'd done tens of things more personal with tens of women in his day, yet he was wary of taking her arm.

"The children need wings. I'm going to see what I can do with some newsprint and flour paste. Didn't they sound wonderful?"

"Angelic. They certainly like you."

"I like them, too. I've never worked with children before. It's a surprise how responsive they can be."

At the newspaper office she lit a lamp. He waited while she gathered a roll of paper, then helped her tie it with string.

"I wish I could think of some way to make the wings glitter," she said.

"Mica," he suggested.

"Mica . . . why, of course, that's it!" she exclaimed.

"A mortar and pestle would break it up fine enough, and if you sprinkled it on while the flour paste was wet it should stick."

"What a wonderful idea!"

"If you want I'll go out and find you some."

"Would you really?"

"Sure. I won't have time tomorrow, but I'll do it the next day. I'll even break it up for you."

"Oh Noah, thank you." Her blue eyes sparkled with genuine gratitude.

He smiled and nodded, pleased with himself and with the glow created by her approval.

"Ready?" he asked, picking up the roll of paper and reaching toward the lantern.

"Ready."

He lowered the wick and followed her to the door.

As she opened it, he said, "Sarah, wait a minute."

She paused and turned, pulling on her gloves. "What is it?"

With his free hand he pressed the door closed, sealing them inside the dark, quiet newspaper office.

"Just this . . ." he said, tipping his head and moving toward her. His hat brim bumped her bonnet. They chuckled while he backed off and removed his Stetson. "Could I try that again?"

She answered quietly, "Please do."

His second aim was perfect, and their mouths joined lightly, remained so while the pendulum clock ticked away ten . . . fifteen . . . twenty unhurried seconds. With his hat in one hand and the roll of newsprint in the other, he had no means of holding her. She might easily have slipped away after a brief touch of their lips, but remained near, tilting her face in compliance. In the dark, their sense of touch became magnified. Soft became softer. Warm became warmer. His breath fanned her cheek, hers fanned his. They waited, in counterpoint, to see what the other would do. He opened his lips and touched her with his tongue and she met it with her own. They sampled each other, still somewhat surprised, with their mouths slightly open. The kiss ended as cobwebs break, with a reluctant drifting apart.

The clock ticked several times before Noah spoke.

"Something happened tonight when I was singing with you."

"It was such a surprise when you did it."

"It was a surprise to me, too. I've done a lot of things with women, but that was the first time I ever sang with one. Did you know you blushed when you turned around and saw me standing there?"

"Did I?"

"Yes, you did. And that's when it happened."

"What?"

"The same thing that's happening now."

"What's happening now?"

"My heart is racing."

"Is it really?"

"Isn't yours?"

"Yes . . . but I thought . . ."

"What?"

"I thought the first time you kissed me, I failed a test."

"What test?"

"I thought you were testing me . . . to see if you liked it, and you didn't."

"You were wrong, Sarah."

"I would not have known it. After that kiss, you looked at me no differently than you looked at the men."

"I was trying to do what was proper."

"I'm not sure this will ever be proper—you and I."

"Why?"

"Because of my sister."

"Your sister means nothing to me."

They remained close, acclimating to honesty and the reaction they set off in one another.

"Sarah, would it be all right if I set down these things I'm holding?"

"If you want to."

He squatted and set them on the floor. Rising, he took her by the upper arms and they listened to the faint, fast fall of one another's breathing. He drew her to his breast and found her mouth once more and kissed her as neither of them had believed would ever happen, with a lush embrace and a thorough blending of tongues. He spread a hand upon the back of her scratchy woolen coat while she did likewise on the back of his rough sheepskin jacket. Buffered by the two garments, they indulged in the time-honored intimacy that rattled them with disbelief.

They parted as reluctantly as before, still somewhat stunned.

"Noah, this feels so strange."

"I know."

"It doesn't feel as if it could be you and me."

Standing close in the dark, they thought about it awhile—their rocky beginning and how they had disliked one another, now this.

She surprised him by requesting, "Could we do it again, Noah?"

"Why, Sarah Merritt," he said with a smile in his voice. "You surprise me."

In the darkness he took her head in both hands, and she found her mouth fully inundated, and her senses captivated by the smell of his shaving scent, which had been wooing her across the breakfast table all these weeks. His mustache was soft, his tongue even softer as it touched her, wet and warm, within. She returned his kiss in full while his embrace grew powerful enough to lift her onto tiptoe.

When her heels once more touched the floor, both of them were slightly breathless.

"I think we'd better go home now," Sarah whispered.

"Of course. It's late." He retrieved his hat and the paper roll and followed her out of the building, waiting while she locked the door. They found curiously little to say to one another on their way up the hill. At Mrs. Roundtree's she climbed the steps ahead of him and paused at the top, a woman uncertain of how such things proceeded. Were doorstep kisses expected now?

"I'll go out and find the mica on Thursday," Noah said, halting her with words instead.

"Thank you . . . yes, the children will love it."

"I'll bring it by your office."

"All right."

She reached for the doorknob but he detained her with a touch on her sleeve.

"Sarah, I'm not very good at saying things, but . . ." He released her arm and shifted his weight from one foot to the other. "It was a good feeling, singing 'Silent Night' with you tonight."

"Yes, it was. You have a beautiful voice, Noah. Perhaps when we get our church you'll be in the choir."

"If you direct it, maybe I will."

It was brighter beneath the starry night sky, bright enough for him to make out her face, though his remained hidden by the shadow of his hat brim. She gave a short smile and said, "Well, I'd better go in."

"And I'd better make one more round." He handed her the paper roll.

"Good night, Noah."

"Good night, Sarah."

"See you at breakfast."

She prepared for bed slowly, perplexed by her changing sentiments for him. When she'd donned her nightgown she wrapped herself in a shawl and got out her journal in an effort to sort out her feelings.

> *I have been kissed, truly kissed, by a man who has carnal knowledge of my sister, a man I once avidly hated. I am the only eligible young woman in this town, and I've been trying to be very honest with myself about whether that is the reason for his attentions, but I think not. I believe our feelings for one another are genuinely changing, but to what end I must ask myself now. The women in my family have set a precedent—first my mother, and now Addie. Have I the inborn predisposition to be like them? Does he think I am easy game? I should not like to think so, yet how can the doubt not crop up, considering that I met him the first time in the entry to a brothel? Is this the kind of man I should encourage? What would Father advise? Supposing Noah Campbell's intentions are honorable, let us even suppose he falls in love with me and proposes marriage. How awkward it would be to lay with him and realize my sister had come before me. . . .*

In the morning she was still confused. Facing him across the breakfast table, she was torn by the wish to meet his eyes and the equally strong one to avoid them. Thankfully, he treated her no differently than at any other breakfast. They lived, after all, in the same boardinghouse, on the same floor, with only two doors between them. By unspoken agreement they observed the same polite conventions they'd shown one another all along. It was the same at supper that evening, and during the following day's breakfast.

The afternoon of the second day, however, he brought her the ground mica, as promised. Patrick was working at a table near the front of the office when Noah came in and went directly to Sarah at her desk and handed her a drawstring bag.

"Here's your mica," he said, looking pleased and a trifle expectant.

"Thank you." Sarah was surprised to find a tightness around her heart as she accepted it. She glanced at Patrick, easily within earshot, then said to Noah, "I've been experimenting with the wings. Would you like to see them?"

"Sure."

She led him to the rear of the office, where three various shaped wings of paste-laden newsprint were drying over barrels. They stopped with their backs to Patrick.

"I like this one," Noah said. "If angels really do have wings, I bet they'd look like this."

"With mica on them they'll be even more seraphic. Thank you again for getting it."

"It was no trouble. Are you making them all?"

"No, Emma volunteered to be in charge of the costumes. I'm only making the prototype."

A lull fell. He could tell by her downcast face she'd had some sort of change of heart since the last time they'd been in this office together.

"Noah, I've been thinking . . ." she said quietly, toying with the drawstring bag.

"What?"

"About you . . . and Addie." She looked square into his eyes. She had not removed her spectacles, and with them appeared vulnerable.

"There's no point in you and I . . . well . . ." She gestured with one hand and returned her attention to the bag. "It's pointless, that's all."

"Sarah, I haven't—"

From behind them Patrick called, "Sarah, would y' be wantin' me to use a cut of a horse and sleigh on this ad for Tatum?"

"Yes, that would be fine," she replied, raising her voice; then more softly, "I really must get back to work. Thank you again, Marshal."

He studied her somberly for five seconds—so it was back to Marshal again.

"All right, Sarah, if that's the way you want it." Not a muscle moved on his face as he stared at her, then touched his hat brim and left.

He bowed to her wishes between then and Christmas, making mealtime tense as they sat in their customary chairs across from one another.

They became adept at passing platters without meeting glances; at joining in the mealtime conversations without exchanging any but the most unavoidable words with each other; at leaving the table at separate times so they need not walk up the stairs together.

One morning, while it was still dark outside and she'd just rolled from her warm bed, she opened her door and encounted him heading for the same place as she. They froze, each of them disheveled from sleep, with their outerwear thrown on carelessly. The top of his underwear showed behind his sheepskin jacket. She held her coat closed over her nightgown. His whiskers were shady, his hair stood on end. There were sandmen in her eyes, and her hair looked untamed.

"Morning," he said.

"Morning."

Still neither of them moved. Or smiled. Or breathed.

Finally, he found his voice. "You go first. I can wait." He turned and hurried back to his room.

On Christmas Eve afternoon it snowed. Sarah made a trip to the bathhouse, spread rosewater on her skin and donned her best bustled suit with the polonaise jacket. At home she crimped her hair, added a rat to the back, left tendrils trail at the hairline and pinned her locket at the throat of her high-collared white blouse. Before the small mirror she paused, lifted a wrist to her nose and thought of Noah Campbell, probably down the hall changing clothes at this very minute.

I miss him.

She picked up the gift she had made for Addie—a delicate tussie-mussie made of dried flowers tied in a punchwork doily by a lavender grosgrain ribbon. She studied the gift sadly, wondering about the two of them, together up at Rose's. *And how many others, Noah?*

She sighed, stared out the window where the snowflakes fell like goosedown. The sky was lavender, like the ribbon she held. Each time she thought of Noah and Addie it was like touching an old bruise. When had he last seen her? Did he go there regularly? Did he kiss Addie in the same lingering way he had kissed her?

If she, Sarah, were to allow the kisses to go on, would he expect, in time, to do with her the other things he had done with Addie?

Despondently she donned her coat.

Outside, the gulch wore an ermine cape. Miners were arriving already from the hills, leaving their mules at the hitching rails and entering the eateries. Many of them greeted her by name.

At Rose's the parlor was deserted. Sarah went straight up to Addie's room and knocked. Addie was holding Ruler when she opened the door. The sight of her with only the cat for company created a lonely prospect on Christmas Eve.

"Merry Christmas, Addie," Sarah said. "May I come in for a minute?"

Addie stepped back, silent.

"I brought this for you."

Addie looked down at the gift. "I don't have anything for you."

"I don't need anything. Here . . . take it."

Addie let the cat go and reached for the nosegay. Her face was sad and downcast. "You never let up on me, do you?"

"It's Christmas. I wanted to give you something."

Addie stared at the tussie-mussie and said nothing.

"I know that you've heard about the Christmas program we're putting on at the Langrishe tonight. I'm directing the children's choir and I'd like very much for you to come."

"I can't."

"Of course you can. You simply put on a coat and hat and walk down to the theater with me."

"And let them throw stones at me?"

"No one will throw stones."

"You live in a dream world, Sarah. I couldn't go back to a normal life even if I wanted to."

"So you won't even try?"

"No."

Disappointed, Sarah studied Addie. "Have you seen Robert?"

"Nearly every day. He won't let up on me either."

"So accept one of his invitations. Become his friend again."

"He lives in a dream world, too."

"Addie . . . ?"

Of all the times she'd visited Addie, Sarah had never seen her sister as approachable as now. There was a question she deeply wanted to ask. If she did so at this moment she would get the truth, she was sure. *Addie, does the marshal still come here to see you?* Her mouth opened to ask it, but the words lodged in her throat.

In the end, afraid of the answer, she could not ask.

"Nothing . . . I hope you like the tussie-mussie. I must get on to the theater. The children will be arriving soon."

Addie's expression grew more forlorn.

"Merry Christmas."

"You too."

They stood separated by a mere four feet, each longing for something the other could not give. Suddenly Sarah rushed forward and caught Addie in a hug, their cheeks joined.

"Oh Addie, will we ever be sisters again?"

For a moment Addie hugged her back.

"You'd better not count on it."

"Please come tonight."

"I can't, but good luck with your program," she said.

Sarah spun from the room before she could cry. Sixteen children were counting on her to be exhilarated and smiling. She could not let them down.

The Langrishe was filled with men in an appropriately subdued mood for the first religious observance ever held in Deadwood. The stage was trimmed with pine boughs. The cradle was lined with straw. The children were scrubbed and eager. The mothers were nervous. The pageant members were in costume.

The marshall was not there.

Sarah's disappointment outweighed anything so far as she peeked from behind the curtain, searching the crowd for his familiar mustache and gray eyes. She saw Robert, and Teddy Ruckner, Mrs. Roundtree, Mr. Mullins, Mr. Taft and dozens of others she recognized. But not Noah. In spite of her misgivings, it was he of whom she'd thought as this night approached, he for whom she wanted the children to perform well, he whose eyes she would seek when she turned to face the audience and direct them in the last song. She supposed he had gone out to the Spearfish to spend the holiday with his family.

The program began with a rousing rendition of "Adeste Fideles," sung by all, accompanied by Elias Pinkney on the thirteen-stop organ and the xylophone musician, Mr. Judd, on the eight triangles. There followed an original reading by Jack Langrishe, leading into a series of vignettes of Christmases in other lands. Sarah sat to one side of the stage with her angel choir, watching the door. The reading of the Christmas story had just begun when it opened and Noah came in.

Sarah's heart gave a leap.

His eyes scanned the stage, found her and stopped.

Hello.

Hello.

Their silent communion was unmistakable. For the first time that night she caught the spirit of the season.

The children sang well. The Robinson baby fussed very little. Everyone loved the chimes. Jack Langrishe's voice was dynamic and his costumes rich with authenticity. The miners filled the king's casket with so much gold dust a second container had to be employed.

And when Sarah turned to direct the last verse of "Silent Night," she and Noah sang to each other.

The thunder of applause at the program's end set forth a round of jubilant hugging onstage and handshaking among the audience. Above the heads that separated them the eyes of Sarah and Noah found each other time and again. Robert located her, gave her a crushing hug and a grand smile, but he had come to seem less extraordinary to Sarah than she'd once thought. Over his shoulder she watched Noah. There were punch and cookies for the adults, and for the children sacks of popcorn and hard candy. The crowd, made up mostly of single men separated from their families, was reluctant to break up and end the evening, so began a round of informal caroling accompanied by the organ. In the midst of the celebration costumes had to be collected and clothes changed backstage. Reluctantly Sarah went off to gather angel wings and find Jack Langrishe to ask about a place to store them till next year, fearing all the while that when she returned to the theater floor Noah would be gone. He was still there, however, and they began working their way toward each other. A cluster of Norwegian men struck up a carol in their native language. A roulette wheel clicked: someone had rigged it up with gifts for the children substituting for numbers. Amidst the singing and the clicking and the sound of happy voices, Sarah and Noah met.

For a while they only looked at each other without smiling.

Finally he said, "It was a wonderful program."

"Thank you."

"The children sounded as good as they looked."

"Everyone loved their wings, thanks to you."

They tried for timid smiles and found them. The Norwegians ended their song, which sparked another by a group of Swedes, louder than the previous one, so loud it drowned out everything else.

"I thought you weren't coming," she said.

"What?" He dipped his ear near her mouth. She caught a whiff of something sweet from his skin.

"I said I thought you weren't coming. You were late."

"I had to wait in line at the bathhouse."

"Oh."

"Everybody in the gulch must've taken a bath tonight."

"I got mine early enough that I missed the crowd."

"Good for you."

A lapse fell while they tried to think of some reasonable subject of conversation to give them an excuse to remain together.

"I don't see your family here," she said.

"No, they didn't come. I'm going out there in the morning."

"You're lucky. A lot of these men are missing their families tonight, I think."

"Sarah?"

She waited, with her eyes lost in his.

"I was wondering if you'd want to come with me."

"I'm sorry. I've made other plans."

Their silence lasted several seconds while they read the disappointment in each other's eyes. "Well, maybe some other time."

Finally he thought to ask, "Could I get you some punch?"

"Yes, I'd love some."

He went away and returned bearing two cups filled with red liquid, handing her one.

He raised his. "Merry Christmas."

"Merry Christmas."

The rims of the cups clinked. After he drank he glanced over the crowd while drying the bottom fringe of his mustache with the edge of an index finger. He caught her watching him and she looked away.

He leaned close enough to be heard. "Looks like you'll get your church and school building after all."

"I hope so."

"How much do you think they collected?"

"I couldn't even guess."

Emma appeared with her brood. "Time we were getting home. Have you seen Byron?"

"He's over there." Sarah pointed.

"Go get your father, Josh. Tell him we're ready to go. Marshal, Merry Christmas."

"Same to you."

"Sarah, we'll see you tomorrow then."

"Yes."

"Dinner will be ready at four."

"I'll be there."

When they'd gone off, Noah said, "You're spending tomorrow with them?"

"Yes. You didn't believe me, did you?"

He shrugged and looked down at his cup.

She kept thinking about missing the chance to go out to the Spearfish with him. When she spoke, her voice held passionate disappointment. "Why didn't you ask me earlier?"

"I wasn't sure you'd want to."

"But you could have asked, Noah."

"You haven't called me Noah since the night I kissed you."

"I've been very mixed up."

His unsmiling eyes took hers and kept them. "You don't make it easy on a man, Sarah."

"I know," she replied meekly. "I'm sorry."

He seemed to consider awhile, then he set down his cup, and his face took on a look of remoteness. "Well, I have to get an early start in the morning."

"Yes, I suppose you do." She set hers down, too, while he glanced off across the room and made no move to leave, obviously troubled.

They both spoke at once.

"Sarah—"

"Noah—"

In the silence that followed, with their eyes locked, she took courage.

"Could we walk home together?" she asked.

"Where's your coat?"

"In one of the dressing rooms backstage."

"Did you wear a hat?"

"No."

"Stay here," he said, leaving her. She waited despondently while he disappeared, thinking this was one of the more difficult struggles with which she'd ever dealt, developing feelings for a man she felt obligated to shy away from. The missed opportunity to spend Christmas with him and his family crushed her, took all the joy out of her plans for tomorrow. He knew her well enough to recognize her coat in a jumble; it seemed significant that they'd spent that much time becoming friends. So what did she want of him? Of herself? Alas, she did not know.

He returned with her coat, held it while she slipped it on, then guided her toward the door, both of them wishing and being wished Merry Christmas several times on their way.

Outside others were walking home. At the hitching rails the blankets and saddles on the animals were covered with snow. Two mules plodded up the street bearing riders who called out holiday greetings in the dark.

Sarah and Noah replied in unison, Noah raising one hand. In silence they traversed the boardwalks—up one set of steps, down another, across a street, up steps again. Occasionally their elbows brushed but they did not speak. At a corner they turned onto a side street and began climbing the steep hill.

Suddenly, in the still night, a musical note sounded, stopping their footsteps.

"What was that?"

It came again and they lifted their faces to the night sky.

"The chimes," she breathed.

From somewhere up high above the gulch the notes struck and reverberated, bouncing from wall to wall, down the chasm, shimmering up their spines.

"It must be Ned Judd. He's playing 'Adeste Fideles,'" Sarah whispered.

They stood in place and listened as each note echoed and re-echoed. The night came alive with music that seemed to have an almost celestial splendor as it resounded through the wondrous acoustical chamber around them. It filled their ears and seemed to skitter out the tops of their heads while, enraptured, they held still.

When the song ended, Noah said, "Where do you suppose he is?"

"On one of the ledges. He must have carried the triangles up there. What a Christmas gift for us all."

Another song began. "Away in a Manger."

Noah found one of Sarah's hands and tucked it tightly beneath his elbow. They turned and continued toward home, bound once again by music. On the top landing at Mrs. Roundtree's, she and some of her boarders stood with their faces lifted, listening too, as the carol seemed to emanate from the rocks, the pines, the very heavens themselves. Noah discreetly released Sarah's hand and they climbed the stairs and joined the others, elevating their faces, too.

The song ended and a mutual sigh rose, like that following a burst of fireworks.

"For a Christmas that started out to be the loneliest one a lot of us has ever faced, it sure turned into something special," Mrs. Roundtree said.

A murmur of voices concurred.

"Thanks to Mr. Poinsett's triangles."

"And Mr. Judd's playing."

They mingled awhile, remarking on the pageant, the children's choir, the angel's wings, complimenting Sarah on her part. The heavenly concert continued, but in time they tired and drifted inside, bidding one another goodnight as they shuffled upstairs, moving like a slow tide, each to his own door. In the sluggish current of night-going, Sarah lost Noah without a private farewell—a disappointment—surrounded as they were by others.

In her room she undressed in the dark, hung up her outerwear and donned a thick flannel nightgown. She removed the pins and rat from her hair, took her brush and a warm blanket, opened the window and sat before it on a wooden rocker. Two songs played. Three. She brushed her hair slowly to their rhythmic bonging, unwilling to submit to sleep until the last note had been savored. The winter air threaded inside. In time she drew her feet up and hooked her heels on the chair seat, tipped her head back and listened to the soulful sound of the carols ricocheting through Deadwood Gulch.

In his room down the hall, Noah Campbell, too, opened his window. He lit a lamp, removed his jacket, boots and shirt, sat down in his stocking feet, trousers and long underwear, and rolled a cigarette. He lit it from the lamp flame and watched the smoke linger at the window opening before it drifted back inside. He smoked two cigarettes, listening to the lovely, lonely chimes, before his fingers grew cold.

He extinguished the lamp, pulled the rocking chair near the bed, resumed his seat and propped his calves on the mattress, covering his front with a blanket. Thinking. Thinking. Of Sarah Merritt and himself singing face to face across a crowded theater, of Sarah Merritt and himself trying to avoid each other's eyes across the breakfast table, of Sarah Merritt and himself kissing in her newspaper office with a great deal of uncertainty, then afterward pretending it had never happened.

He rose, stretched, stood before the open window, rubbing the back of his neck.

If she were one of the girls up at Rose's he'd know how to approach her. But she wasn't a woman with whom a man trifled.

He stood for some time considering before he crossed to his door, opened it silently and shut it just as silently behind himself. In stocking feet he ventured down the hall and paused before her door.

He tapped quietly and waited.

Momentarily her door opened a crack. Her room was dark, leaving her only a suspicion in the blackness.

"Yes?" she whispered.

"It's Noah."

"Noah . . . what do you want?"

"I can't sleep. Can you?"

She paused warily before answering, "No."

"What were you doing?"

"Sitting by the open window, listening to the chimes."

"Me too."

The implication sneaked through the crack in the door even before he said, "We could listen to them together."

No reply.

"Could I come in, Sarah?"

"No, I'm dressed for bed."

"Put on a robe."

"Noah, I don't think—"

"Please."

She remained motionless for a long time before stepping back. He touched the door and it swung freely. He stepped into her room and closed the door without a click. By the faint light of the new-fallen snow he could see she had backed off several feet and stood clutching a blanket around her shoulders.

"You shouldn't be here," she told him.

"No."

"What if somebody heard you?"

"Everybody's asleep, and I'm stocking-footed."

He took a step toward her and she fled to her chair, drawing her knees up tightly to her chest and wrapping them with the blanket. He went to her bed and sat down in the deeper shadows while the midnight snow turned the side of her face and hair and blanket into a pale wash.

For a while they listened to the triangles playing "O Sanctissima."

At length he spoke out of the dark. "Sarah, I don't know where to go with you," he said, as if the admission were the accumulation of all his thoughts during his vigil down the hall. "Do you know?"

"I don't know what you mean."

"Yes, you do. I've kissed you twice and both times we've enjoyed it, but the next day we look at each other and get spooked."

"You too?"

"Yes, me too."

"I'm sorry. I . . ." She had no idea how to reply.

"I think about you a lot, yet I'm scared to death of you. It's the damnedest thing I've ever been through."

"You? Scared of me?"

"You're a very intimidating woman."

"I didn't know that," she whispered, chagrined.

"Well, you are. You're better than most men at what you do, and you're one hell of an organizer and a reformer and a choir director and an editor and . . ." He paused.

"And?"

"And I want to know what you think of me."

Her reply came in a quiet, fearful voice after long moments of silence. "I'm afraid of you, too." He made no reply, so she continued. "And I think of you, too, more than I believe is advisable. You see, you're not at all the sort of man I thought I'd . . ." She stopped.

"You thought you'd what?"

"Be attracted to." There, she'd said it. She supposed her cheeks must be glowing in the dark.

"What sort am I?"

She regretted having to say it. "The sort who visits brothels."

"I haven't been back to Rose's since the first night you came to town."

"But the fact remains you've been there . . . with my sister."

"Sarah, I'm very sorry about that, but I can't change it."

"And I can't change how I feel about it. It will always be there between us."

"I said I haven't been back and it's the truth. Ask your sister."

"My sister is lost to me because of your kind."

"No! I'm not the reason she is what she is!"

"Hold your voice down."

Softer, he repeated, "I'm not the reason she's a prostitute."

"Then what is? If only I understood it."

She dropped her head to her knees and for a while only the sound of the chimes filled the room. When he touched the back of her hair she started and threw back her head. She hadn't heard him move to the front of her chair.

"You must leave," she whispered, panicked.

"Yes," he agreed, "I must leave. I have known your sister in the biblical sense, so I must leave. Anything you or I might feel for each other should be shunted aside because of something that happened before we ever met, is that right?"

"Yes." Her eyes were wide, her heart hammering.

He gripped her arms and drew her to her feet. "That's bullshit, Sarah, and you know it." His head lowered and their mouths joined—his opened, hers closed. He waited, but she would not relent and allow herself to kiss him back. In time he lifted his head.

"I'm in no hurry," he whispered. "Take your time deciding."

He returned to his preoccupation with her lips, wetting them languidly with his tongue, undeterred by her tightly crossed arms and her refusal to comply. He was very adept, very patient, very convincing.

She trembled and tightened her grip on the blanket.

Lifting his head, he remained close, kneading her shoulders through the thick wrap of wool while her wide eyes fixed upon his: light pricks of contact in the darkness.

He slipped his hands through the break in the blanket and found her hips, rested his hands on their notches and drew her against him. Like the pause between lightning and thunder, he allowed a hesitation before tilting his head for another kiss.

She took part primly, with her arms wedged against his chest, her body canted back at the waist. After a stretch of persuasion which bore no results, he retreated and they stood facing each other in the half-embrace.

"You want to enjoy it, don't you?" He lifted his hand to stroke the hair from her temple, and she shivered. "Let yourself . . ." In slowest motion he kissed her eyelids, her cheek, earlobe, the underside of her jaw, stealing her wariness, setting her heart a-hurry. He kissed her mouth once more, spreading the flavor of smoke upon her tongue, bringing the texture of silk where his mustache rode her skin. His hands slipped behind her, low, where her nightgown lay full and loose, made faint movements that sent it whispering across her skin like a curtain across a sill. He spread his hands wide and brought her flush against him.

With a despairing cry she conceded, flowing to him like a breaker to a shore, throwing her arms up and veiling them both with the blanket. Their warm, full lengths joined and he held her in place without moving, their hearts beating crazily.

She had not known simply standing so against another could make mockery of all one believed. Again a sound formed in her throat, trapped, fearful. From outside came the dying peal of the last chime. It seemed to ring within her body and shimmer outward to all the surfaces he embraced.

She freed her mouth. "Noah . . ." Her eyes had closed. "This is wrong."

"This is human nature," he said. "It's how men and women find out what they think of each other."

"No . . . you must go," she said feebly.

"Poor Sarah . . ." he whispered. "So confused." He went on kissing her neck, where the faint taste of rosewater remained . . . descending until his breath warmed a path through the coarse flannel of her night-gown to her right breast.

"Stop!" she whispered, straining away, pushing on his shoulders. "Please . . . I cannot. Please . . ." She lost her grip on the blanket. It slipped to the floor as she wedged her arms between them, took fistfuls of his underwear and pushed him away. Tears were raining down her cheeks. "I'm not like Addie! I will not be like her! And my mother . . . my mother, too. Please, Noah, stop!"

He went motionless, his hands still touching her, but without insistence.

"Please, Noah . . . " she whispered once more.

He stepped back, beleaguered by guilt. "I'm sorry, Sarah." She stood with her arms crossed like a bandolier, protecting her breasts.

"Please go."

"I will, but I want your promise that you won't think less of yourself. It's all my fault, I should have gone back to my room when you told me. Sarah, I didn't know about your mother."

She turned away to the window, hugging herself—no chimes now, the magic all gone.

Apologetically, he retrieved her blanket from the floor, took it to her and draped it across her back, leaving his hands curved over her shoulders.

"I want you to know something, Sarah. I'm as surprised and bewildered about what's happening between us as you are. I don't think either one of us planned to have any feelings for each other. As a matter of fact, I think we're both fighting it. But I'm honest enough to admit that I didn't just walk into your room tonight because I was randy. There's more to it than that. I've come to admire you for dozens of reasons—you're bright, and hardworking, and plucky, and you fight for what you believe in. Churches, schools, boardwalks, stopping an epidemic of smallpox, even closing the brothels. I know you're going to doubt my honesty once I leave you, but it's true. Even when I was locking you up in that mine I thought you were one of the spunkiest human beings I'd ever met. Spunky and fearless. Since then you've shown me I was right. And lately I've been enjoying other things about you—the way you are with the children, how hard you worked on the pageant—all right, so laugh at me—but even singing 'Silent Night' with you changed something between us. All that came first before tonight. Sarah . . . please look at me." He forced her to turn and face him. "What happened here is nothing to cry about."

Her tears continued nonetheless. "What we did is not allowable. It cheapens what we feel."

"I'm sorry you feel that way."

"I do."

"In that case I promise it will never happen again." His hands dropped from her shoulders and he stepped back.

"Well . . . I'll go now."

With his head hanging, he moved toward the door. She felt bereft and wanted to reach out toward him and say she was sorry too, but she couldn't, because she was right and he was wrong to have come in here and forced the issue. Good, honorable men didn't.

At the door, he turned. "Merry Christmas, Sarah. I hope I didn't ruin it for you."

"I enjoyed the chimes," she said sadly.

He studied her silhouette against the dim window light, opened the door and soundlessly disappeared.

CHAPTER 13

At midnight on Christmas Eve, Rose Hossiter's brothel was crowded with lonely miners who sought company to relieve their Christmas desolation. Kithless, they had watched the Christmas pageant and thought of home—of mothers, fathers, siblings, sweethearts and friends left behind in the cities as large as Boston, Munich and Dublin; or in rural communities with names too obscure to bring the light of recognition to a listener's eye. They thought of familiar hearths and mothers' bread and their old pet dogs, maybe long since dead. Some of them thought of the children they'd abandoned and the wives they'd send for, come spring.

Some were drunk.

Some were tearful.

All were lonesome.

The triangle bells of Tom Poinsett were the greatest boon to the flesh business since the discovery of gold itself. While they played, the tide of lonesome males, fresh from giving gold dust to the infant Jesus, brought the remainder of it to be exchanged for any soft, warm, sympathetic breast upon which they might lay their sorrowful heads and forget their homesickness.

Robert Baysinger was among these.

Remaining at the theater until the lanterns were being extinguished, he had watched Sarah leave with the marshal; the Robinsons leave with their baby; the Dawkins with their family; even Mrs. Roundtree with a group of her lodgers. As the theater emptied, Robert's solitariness closed in. Who was there for him in this town, save one for whose company he must pay? Damn the woman for her continued aloofness. He should disdain her, but found himself unable. He had, after all, come here largely because of her.

Forlornly he donned his coat and hat, took up his cane and went from the hall into the street, where the sound of the chimes lifted his face to the sky and seemed to widen the spaces between his bones. He stopped a minute, pulling on his capeskin gloves, letting the hymn shimmer through him. At home there had been church spires with bells that tolled the hour. Sometimes, as a child, they would awaken him in the mornings.

Three in a bed they'd slept—he, Walt and Franklin. Seemed like there were never enough beds, nor food, nor money. Sometimes not even enough love. Perhaps he was wrong about that: maybe the shortness had not been of love itself, but of the time to show it.

When he remembered his parents, he pictured them overworked and weary. It seemed they'd never had time to relax. His father labored fourteen hours a day in an effort to scrape together enough money to provide for his outsized family, which seemed to increase by one head per year. Ten hours a day Edward Baysinger worked as a trunkmaker at Arndson's Leather Factory; evenings, in a tiny shop behind their house, he fashioned wooden stocks for brushes on a foot-powered wood lathe. Sometimes he sharpened knives and shears. Sometimes he repaired chair rungs. Sometimes he bought and sold bone. Always he collected fat and tallow which his wife, Genevieve, brewed into yellow lye soap and sold to supplement the family's income, which never seemed adequate.

Whatever the secondary labor, the boys were always expected to help. They carted wood; sold wood shavings for kindling; fashioned bone handles for toothbrushes; begged waste fats door to door; peddled soap door to door, and as each one grew old enough, went to work in Arndson's Leather Factory. The only job the boys escaped was stirring and cutting the soap, which fell to the two girls of the family, who also helped their mother with the never-ending laundry and cooking for the tribe of thirteen.

By the time Robert was twelve he knew he wanted something better for himself than the endless toil and struggle he witnessed in his parents. His mother looked haggard and shriveled by the time she was thirty. His father's disposition became grumpier and more cynical in relationship to his growing responsibilities.

Though school was considered a luxury by Genevieve and Edward Baysinger, their son Robert fought for the right to continue his studies at the age when the others went into the factory. It was at school he met the Merritt girls. And later, when he was old enough to go begging grease and fat from the back doors of kitchens for his mother's soap pot, he knocked one day upon a strange door and to his surprise, it was answered by Adelaide Merritt.

"Why, Robert!" she had said. "Hello!"

He was chagrined to have to ask one of his schoolmates for the runoff from their frying pans, but Adelaide was sweet and friendly. She took him inside to a wondrously uncrowded kitchen where an uncorseted, buxom woman named Mrs. Smith found a good-sized tin of leftover grease and offered it along with fresh apple cakes and cold milk. These Robert shared with Addie Merritt at a grand round table covered with a crocheted cloth and decorated with a bouquet of daisies and fresh, red, pungent basil, which the housekeeper said kept the spiders and ants from visiting her kitchen.

From the first Robert was taken with all that space for only four people. Space, order, fastidiousness and quiet. Such marvelous quiet. Where he lived total quiet prevailed only in the deepest hours of the night, and even then the place was likely to rumble with snoring from one quarter or another. Around Addie's table were only four chairs instead of thirteen. On the range was one teakettle instead of three. In a cookie jar on the sideboard was an entire *batch* of snickerdoodles of which he was invited to partake at will after he finished his apple cake. In his entire life he'd never known such plenty, for at the Baysinger house cookies were rare and never lasted long enough to be stored in a jar.

And Addie's house was so clean! The floor had no footmarks, the windows no handprints, the curtains were starched and the rag rug at the kitchen door looked as though no one had ever stepped on it. In the parlor the antimacassars were perfectly centered on the sofa, the reading materials were stacked in bookshelves and folded in magazine racks; Mr. Merritt's pipes and tobaccos were neatly housed in a smoking stand, and there was space enough for a fern wider than the spread of a man's two arms. The room also held the ultimate luxury: a spinet. Robert tried to imagine his parents ever accumulating enough extra money to afford a spinet. The idea was preposterous.

Beside the piano stood a high chest of twenty skinny drawers containing sheet music. Addie selected some and played for him—a mazurka, "Für Elise" and "Londonderry Air"—sitting straight as a gopher with her fingers curled precisely over the keys. Her blond hair was looped up from her ears into a plaid moiré ribbon from which it flowed down her back in gentle curves. She was wearing a blue dress with a white lace collar. His eyes were equally taken by the girl, the room and the spinet. A large white cat came padding in and preened himself against Addie's ankles. She stopped playing to scoop him up and introduce him as Ruler before handing him to Robert and resuming her song.

Everything about that evening remained indelibly in Robert's memory. Addie's quiet reserve—so much greater than that of most girls her age that it made her seem older than her nine years; the obvious quality of every furnishing in the house; the tranquillity which prevailed. Even when Mrs. Smith came into the parlor and announced that it was late and time for Robert to leave and for Addie to retire, Addie accepted the order with grace far above her years.

She saw him to the front door, took Ruler from his arms and invited him to come back anytime. Without compunction, as if the difference in their ages and class did not exist, she said, "I'll let you know when Mrs. Smith has another batch of grease saved up and you can come and collect it."

Though Addie turned a blind eye to the differences in their class, Robert was stung afresh as he walked away. No, his parents would never have a spinet, nor luxuries of any kind, but from that first evening Robert spent in the Merritt house he vowed he would have them aplenty.

The next time he went there Sarah was at home. At fourteen, she was one year older than Robert and so much better acquainted, since on alternate years they had shared the same teacher and classroom—their school was arranged with two grades per room. Sarah was a brain. She won every spelling bee ever held, partook in every essay contest (often winning first prize), finished all her schoolwork in the time allotted, so carried books home only by choice. She often helped the children of the younger classes with their arithmetic, and when the teacher left the room was appointed monitor.

At home she spent all her time reading, or writing in a composition book, which she carried with her at all times. She had to be encouraged to play a duet on the spinet with Addie, doing so finally with a humph and a sigh as if put upon. Once she joined the music, however, she seemed a good sport (though she was not as natural on the piano as Addie), and after that, when Robert visited, the three of them formed a trio of friendship that made his visits there even more anticipated.

Addie—he discovered—was moody. At times she would be morose and withdrawn, taking all of Sarah's and Robert's best efforts at clowning to draw her from her glumness and make her laugh. They went on

picnics together in the summer, Mrs. Smith providing them with entic-
ing delicacies packed in a wicker basket with a linen liner: cucumber and
minced ham sandwiches, cheese straws, raspberry tarts and a delectable
specialty called chutree, made of vinegared, sugared and spiced straw-
berries, favored particularly by Robert, who (while the girls turned up
their noses) spread the chutree on Mrs. Smith's crusty white bread and
thought it the finest treat one could hope to eat.

In winter they skated on Stepman's millpond, where large groups of
young people met and built fires and drank hot peach punch spiced with
cinnamon sticks. Many evenings Robert and Addie studied together
while Sarah wrote in her journal. Often Sarah and Robert both helped
Addie, who was much slower to learn and never quite understood many
of the advanced mathematics problems they solved for her, nor how to
properly parse a sentence, nor the reason for learning any of these
things.

Their father was seldom home. When he was, the trio of young
people would leave him to whatever room he chose—parlor or
kitchen—moving to the opposite room to carry on whatever activities
they were pursuing. Sarah introduced Robert to Isaac Merritt the first
time.

"Father, this is our friend Robert Baysinger. He's come to study.
We're helping Addie with her numbers."

"Robert," the older man had said, offering a handshake. He was an
impressive man with straight, tall stature and a clean-shaven face, wearing a three-piece business suit trimmed by a linked gold watch fob.
"Welcome. It's always seemed to me that Sarah never invited enough
young people to the house. I'm glad to see she's made a new friend."

His assumption that Robert was there primarily as Sarah's friend went
uncorrected, for at the time he was as much her friend as Addie's.
Anything else would have been improper, given Addie's age. Yet the
undercurrent of attraction between the younger two was already beginning to bloom.

Addie bloomed, too. Robert watched it happen, remaining the soul
of propriety while her thinness took on the first gentle turns of puberty
and the fuller curves beyond. Her hair touched her waist, curling at the
tips like white wine hitting the bottom of a glass. Her face lost its
childish appeal to the greater one of adult beauty. But as she grew older
she seemed to distance herself from him and Sarah. More often she
retreated into the puzzling realm of reticence and cheerlessness. She
played the spinet with a look of disassociation—by now she was playing
Mendelssohn—breaking into occasional passages when she displayed a

nearly vitriolic passion. The first time it happened Robert became frightened and touched her shoulders to stop her. "Addie, what is it that's bothering you?"

She withdrew her hands from the keyboard as if it had suddenly burned her and tucked them into the folds of her skirt.

"Nothing." The word emerged toneless.

Sarah was seated by the gas lamp, wearing her spectacles, writing in her composition book. Mrs. Smith was in the kitchen, stitching beside the stove. Robert rubbed Addie's shoulders.

"I think I'll leave now. Walk me to the door," he requested.

Addie rose from the piano stool, lifeless but correct.

"Good night, Sarah," Robert called.

She looked up. "Oh . . . good night."

In the shadows of the front entry where the stairwell emptied down from above, he buttoned his jacket while Addie waited with that same remote look on her face, her eyes fixed upon the carved work on the umbrella stand.

"Addie," he told her, "perhaps I shouldn't come anymore."

Her ennui vanished. "Oh no, Robert!" Her eyes widened in distress. "Whatever would I do without you!" Without warning, she threw her arms around his neck and gripped him quite desperately. "Dear Robert, you're the best thing in my life, don't you see?" Her breath came fast, almost terrified. He closed his arms across her back and held her for the first time ever. She was fifteen at the time, he eighteen, and miserable with unexpressed love. He had at some time during their friendship decided he could not openly court her until she reached age sixteen. By then he might even have prospects and could ask her to marry. Meanwhile, he resisted the flare of desire and kept his hands on her back.

"Sometimes you don't seem to remember I'm in the room."

"I do . . . oh I do. Come again on Thursday the way you always do. Please, Robert, say you will."

"Of course I will. But I want to make you happy, and more often lately, I don't know how."

"You do, Robert. Please believe me."

Heroically, he put her from him. How beautiful her eyes and mouth, even when dismayed. In the deep shadows where they stood she gazed at him with undisguised affection and true fear at the thought of losing him.

"You do make me happy. I should die if I were to lose you."

He thought he should die if he could not kiss her.

"Addie," he whispered, touching her face with both hands, holding it with exquisite tenderness. He lowered his head and she stretched to meet his first kiss as if she, too, had suffered waiting for it. He felt her mouth tremble beneath his, though he stood carefully disjoined from her body, bending to reach her. Tens of times he had resisted this impulse and the greater one that followed. He embraced her fully, opened his mouth, and to his delight, she responded ardently.

With an effort he ended the kiss and stepped back.

Even in the subdued light he could tell she blushed.

"I think you should go now, Robert."

He tried to lift her chin, but she pulled it sharply aside and said, "Don't!"

"But Addie—"

"Don't, I said." She wouldn't lift her head. "We must not do this anymore."

Five months passed before they kissed again. They did so on a bitter cold January night out beside the woodpile where they'd made excuses to go. She had thrown on an unbuttoned coat; he had followed in his shirtsleeves. She had bent forward to begin stacking logs on her arm when he gripped her elbow and said, "Addie . . ."

She straightened, swinging about, meeting his eyes with a mixture of alarm and innocent craving. There wasn't a doubt in the world what was on both their minds.

He took the stovewood from her arms, piece by piece, and tossed it onto the pile.

"No," she whispered. "Robert . . . no . . .," wedging the butt of one hand against his chest as he gripped her arms in a manner indicating he'd brook no refusal.

"I kissed more girls before I was thirteen than in all the years since. Because of you, Addie . . . because I was waiting for you. Ever since the first day I came into your house and you played the piano for me I've been waiting for you to grow up. Well, you're almost there, so don't say no, Addie."

The kiss began as a struggle and ended in submission.

As with the first time, their years of repression came to bear upon them, lending their juncture a desperation.

He cupped her head.

She gripped his shirt.

He opened his mouth.

She opened hers.

He opened her coat and stepped against her.

But he denied himself the places he would touch, clasping her against his tumescent body with only the consolation of freeing two buttons between her shoulder blades, slipping his hand inside against her warm back, circling her waist with the opposite arm, kissing her mouth passionately.

She stopped it, tearing away, averting her face, the top of her head to his chest. They were both panting.

He kneaded her shoulders while rebellion built in his throat.

"Don't do that, Addie. You did that last time. Why should you feel ashamed?"

She swung her head remorsefully. He struggled to understand her disproportionate remorse. He struggled with anger that boiled up out of nowhere because he could not understand her, nor stop loving her.

"Addie, I've kissed you, nothing more. What's wrong with that?"

"Nothing." She was crying . . . silently . . . all by herself . . . crying with her sweet-smelling hair against his chest while he was left to wonder and soothe.

"Has your father warned you against this? Is that it?"

She made negative motions with her head.

"Are you afraid I'll go further? Addie, I wouldn't, not unless you wanted to, too."

The head wagging continued.

"Are you afraid we'll be discovered, or that Sarah might know, or be jealous, or what? What is it, Addie? You wouldn't cry like this over just a kiss."

She pulled back and dried her eyes as if she'd gathered a reserve of implacability from deep within. "You take the wood in, Robert, will you please? Tell Sarah I'm not feeling well and that I went upstairs to bed."

"Addie, wait . . ."

She'd already put space between them, walking backward toward the side of the house and the front door.

"It's not you, Robert, it's me. Please believe me, you've done nothing wrong."

"Addie, I promise I won't kiss you that way again . . . please, don't go in . . . Addie, I'm sorry . . . I love you . . . Addie? . . . Addie, please stay."

She had reached the corner of the house and paused, still facing him, her dark coat like a bloodspill on the dead, snowless grass. "You'd better not love me, Robert. You'll be sorry if you do."

He took a step toward her and she ran around the corner while he gave up the chase before it began, wilting with frustration, arms hanging loosely, head lolling back while he closed his eyes. He didn't understand her. How could he when she refused to confide the source of her fears? Perhaps she feared a total physical relinquishment and its probable outcome. What woman would not, considering the disgrace of pregnancy without wedlock? He was eighteen already and she only fifteen, not a woman at all, but a nubile young girl, afraid of her own budding sexuality. She kissed like a woman who loved it, yearned like a woman who wanted more, but backed off like the girl she was.

Nevertheless, he'd promised to respect her wishes. So why had she admonished him against loving her?

The probability struck him as if the woodpile had collapsed on his head.

She was dying! Most certainly that was it. His precious Addie was ill with some fatal disease for which no cure was known. Why else her gloomy introspection and her lapses at the piano while she played with despair in every note? Why else her bursts into impassioned fortissimos as if at the unfairness of fate? Why else her withdrawal from his kisses when he knew she had feelings for him? And her withdrawal even from Sarah, whom he knew Addie loved unquestionably?

If Sarah wondered why Addie returned to the house via the front door that night, and Robert not at all, she tactfully refrained from asking.

Robert went home without his jacket, sick with worry and shivering from chill in the fifteen-degree January night.

The following morning after Mr. Merritt had left for his office he knocked on the back door. Mrs. Smith answered.

"Why, Robert, whatever are you doing out there without a coat in this weather?"

He offered no explanation. "Would you get it for me, Mrs. Smith? I left it on the hall tree."

"Well, of course, but . . . land sakes, come inside. You look like you're freezing to death."

When Mrs. Smith returned with the garment, he inquired, "Is Addie all right this morning?"

"Addie? Why, I think so. She's off to school as usual. Why do you ask?"

If Addie was dying of some invisible disease, Mrs. Smith certainly acted blasé about it.

"Don't tell her I said anything, will you? We had an argument last night, that's all."

"Mum's the word," she promised with an affectionate glint in her eye. Mrs. Smith had always been their ally and had held a soft spot in her heart for Robert from the first night he'd come asking for grease. Since then he had fought his family for the right to attend school, had completed twelve grades and taken a job in a bank down on Market Street, where he was clerking for good wages, saving them and meeting the moneymakers of St. Louis. From them he was learning more than any college could have taught him about how the rich get richer. Though he had only one jacket to his name, he knew Mrs. Smith respected his frugality and the reason for it. She believed, as he did, that one day he would make his mark on the world.

When his jacket was buttoned, he lingered, silently composing and recomposing a question about Addie's health. In the end, with a lump in his throat, he blurted it out.

"Mrs. Smith, is Addie dying?"

Mrs. Smith's jaw dropped. Her double chin hung like forgotten bread dough over the edge of a pan.

"Dying?"

"Something's wrong with her—something serious. I know!"

"Goodness gracious, *I* don't know," Mrs. Smith whispered.

"She scarcely speaks to Sarah and me, and sometimes she gets terribly silent and stares at us like she's on a ship that's drifting away into a fog. Last night she . . . please, Mrs. Smith, forgive me for being blunt, but I kissed her and she cried for no reason at all and said that if I were to fall in love with her I'd be sorry. Since I'm reasonably sure she loves me too, and since I have every intention of marrying her someday, I can't think of why I might be sorry unless she were to die."

Mrs. Smith plopped into a chair, pinching her lower lip, and stared at some kitchen corner.

"Oh dear me, I've known something was amiss, too, but I never considered this."

Robert sat on the opposite side of the table, tense in the face of Mrs. Smith's commensurate worry.

She looked up. "Did you ask her? What did she say?"

"No, I was afraid to. That's why I came to you."

"I simply don't know. If there is something wrong with her, neither she nor Mr. Merritt have confided in me. I think, perhaps, he's the one we should ask."

"Together?"

"Why not? We're both worried about her, aren't we?"

They did so that afternoon while the girls were still in school. Robert asked for an hour off work and they met at the newspaper office, clasping hands and exchanging grave glances before entering together.

Isaac Merritt sat in a cubicle of glass and mahogany, his name in gold leaf on the window of the door. When he saw the unlikely duo approaching, he rose and rushed forward with anxiousness bending him toward them.

"Mrs. Smith, Robert, what is it? Has something happened to the girls?" Twin lines dented the plane between his eyebrows.

"Nothing immediate," Mrs. Smith replied, "though young Robert has come to me with some concerns and we thought it best to speak to you about it."

Baffled, Merritt looked from one to the other and belatedly offered, "Most certainly. Come in." They all sat but Robert, who stood beside Mrs. Smith's chair, facing Addie's father behind the desk.

"Please," the older man said, "don't keep me in suspense. If one of my daughters is in some trouble, I want to know about it."

"It's not exactly trouble, sir, it's . . ." Mrs. Smith began, then groped in her sleeve for a handkerchief and pressed it to her mouth as her chin began to tremble. "It's . . ." Mrs. Smith broke into weeping.

"Well, good God, out with it!" Merritt exploded, overwrought with concern.

Robert spoke up.

"We were hoping that you could tell us, sir, what's wrong with Addie."

"Wrong with her?"

"Yes, sir. Some things she's said lately, and her increasing despondency led us to believe she might be ill. Perhaps gravely so."

"What has she *said?"* Merritt's voice hissed. Inexplicably, his anger seemed to flare.

Robert hesitated, swallowed. He glanced to Mrs. Smith for guidance.

"Go on, tell him. He's a fair man."

"She said, sir, that if I were to fall in love with her I'd be sorry, but I'm afraid it's already too late. I *am* in love with your daughter and I would very much like to marry her when she comes of age. I had intended to wait until she was sixteen to declare myself, but this . . . this curious condition seems to have taken hold of her and I thought, since I have reason to believe Addie loves me, too, there must be something very serious wrong with her to make her say such a thing. The only thing I could think of was some dread disease."

Isaac Merritt's face had grown red. His lips were compressed.

"What do you know about this, Mrs. Smith?"

"Only that she hasn't been acting herself lately. She is a sad young lady, and—"

"I'm speaking of this man and my daughter!" Merritt snapped. "I've left her in your care and you've obviously allowed her to indulge in improper tête-à-têtes with a man three years her senior when she is nothing but a girl barely out of pinafores!"

Mrs. Smith stared at her employer in surprise.

"Why, Mr. Merritt, whatever . . . why, you know Robert. He's been the girls' friend for years."

Merritt rapped his knuckles on the desktop. "I thought he was Sarah's friend, not Addie's!"

"He's that, too, sir. He's both of their friends."

"But while Sarah is of marriageable age, you've allowed him to spend time privately with Addie, who is not!"

Mrs. Smith got spunky. "With the deepest respect, too, I'll be bound, which he's earned from me who knows him nearly as well as I know your own daughters. Why, he's come here to speak to you honestly about his feelings, which took a good deal of courage, considering he thought—and I did too—that Addie might possibly be ill, very ill, maybe even dying. For you to attack him this way when he was sick with worry is not like you, sir."

Merritt calmed himself and replied quietly, "You're right, Mrs. Smith. Robert, I'm sorry. There is nothing physically wrong with Addie. If she'd seen a physician, even without my knowledge, I'd surely have known, for wouldn't I have received a bill? She has, I'm afraid, inherited her mother's temperament—moony and distracted by turns, which made my wife very difficult to live with, and makes Addie much the same. Though I appreciate your concern, take it from me, it is ill-founded."

Both Robert and Mrs. Smith relaxed.

"Ooo, sir, I'm happy to hear it," she said, passing a hand over her forehead.

"I apologize, too, for implying that you've done less than a good job with the girls. Your care for them has been impeccable, better perhaps than their own mother could have provided, had she stayed."

"Why, thank you, sir."

"I believe, though, that we must allow for Addie's moods. She isn't the intelligent girl her sister is nor has she the wit and personality to attract friends easily. She's always preferred to be alone, and loners must be granted their curious shifts of temperament, must they not? She is a young girl standing on the threshold of womanhood. Let's give her time to step into it gracefully without badgering her to cheer up, shall we? She'll do so in all due time, I'm sure."

"Perhaps you're right, sir." Mrs. Smith crossed herself. "I'll say a novena for her, that's what I'll do."

"Thank you, Mrs. Smith. Now if you wouldn't mind excusing us for a moment, I'd like to talk to young Robert alone."

"Of course." She worked herself out of her chair with no small effort. Over the years she'd grown rounder. "I've got some marketing to do, and since Robert's going back to the bank from here, I'll bid you both good afternoon."

When she was gone, Isaac Merritt waved a hand toward her chair. "Sit down, Robert."

Robert did so.

Merritt sat, too, joined his hands, steepled his fingers and tapped them against his lips. He studied Robert silently for some time, then let his joined hands drop to his lap.

"So you love Addie, do you?" He sounded remarkably calm, considering his earlier vehemence.

"Yes, sir, I do."

"And you want to marry her."

"When the time is right."

"Ah, yes . . ." Merritt reached for a humidor and extracted a cigar. "When the time is right." He snipped the end. "And when is that?"

"As soon as her schooling is done, I thought, although I'd always intended to let my intentions be known when she was sixteen."

"Next year."

"Yessir."

"And you'll be nineteen then, is that right?"

"Yessir."

Merritt lit his cigar and blew smoke toward the ceiling. Leaning back in his chair, he said, "I thought it best not to expound upon the subject while Mrs. Smith was here, but you're old enough for a man-to-man talk." He leaned forward, bracing his elbows on the desk, studying the cigar while rolling it between his fingers. "I've been eighteen myself, Robert. I know the"—he thought a moment—"the impatience a man feels at that age." He looked up. "Like a ripe watermelon waiting to be dropped, eh?"

Robert blushed but his gaze held steady. "In spite of what you may think, sir, Addie and I have never been alone together by design, and when we are there've been no improprieties between us."

"Of course not. But you've kissed her, I suppose."

"Yessir, but nothing more."

"Of course not, only the struggle with yourselves."

Robert could not in all honesty deny it.

"I would imagine that a girl of fifteen is of an age to be kissed—in my day they were. But think, Robert, of the exigencies it places upon her. You are eighteen already . . . a man. Old enough to be married, should you choose; to have a family, a home of your own, the freedoms of the marital state. You've begun treating Addie as a woman, yet she knows she is not one. So is it not believable that she should react as she has? With periods of despondency and gloom? She feels guilty, believing she is holding you back. And in spite of your declarations of honor, in spite of your good intent, and in spite of the fact that I believe you, the best thing for both you and Addie might be for you to see her less until she's reached the age where she *can* marry."

Though Robert felt downhearted he admitted he'd had the same thoughts himself at times.

"Two years isn't so long," Merritt went on. "I understand you're learning under the big boys over at the bank. In two years you'll know nearly as much as they. Undoubtedly you'll be saving your money and investing it under their tutelage. I'll be the first to admit I wouldn't mind having a daughter married to an up-and-coming banker who will—I have every reason to believe—be a prosperous leader of his community one day. Mrs. Smith's faith in you is not ungrounded. I've asked around about you and what I've learned is most impressive. I was, however, as I said earlier, under the impression that it was Sarah who'd caught your eye. Forgive me for admitting I'm disappointed that it isn't. With her plain looks and her bookishness, Sarah will have some difficulty finding a husband. But since it's Addie, perhaps you and I could reach an understanding.

"During these next two years, you tend to learning all they can teach you at the bank. Make a good solid start for yourself, invest your money—I'll even advise you on that if you wish—but ease away from Addie. See her occasionally, of course, but offer logical excuses for having less time to devote to her. And when she's seventeen I'll be more than happy to give my blessings at your wedding."

Robert felt relieved in a dampened way. Two years of avoiding Addie; how could he do it when he'd seen her almost daily for years?

"I have your permission then, to propose when she's sixteen?"

"You have it."

"Thank you, sir."

Robert rose and extended his hand. Merritt shook it solidly.

"You won't be sorry," Robert promised. "I'll work damned hard during the next two years to give Addie the kind of home she deserves."

"I'm sure you will. And I'll be keeping my eye on you, whether you're aware of it or not."

Robert smiled and released his future father-in-law's hand.

"You just watch me. I'm going to be as rich as you someday."

Isaac Merritt laughed as the younger man headed for the door.

"Oh, one more thing, Robert." Robert paused and turned. "I see no reason to trouble Addie by telling her of this conversation. We must, after all, allow her to do her own choosing when the time comes."

"Certainly, sir."

"Good luck to you, Robert."

"And to you, too, sir. Thank you."

There had followed the most miserable six months of Robert's life, avoiding Addie—and thereby, Sarah, too—giving up their friendship while offering plausible excuses for his absences. He lived with the fear that Addie would lose her feelings for him. Once he spoke to Sarah about it, inviting her out for a walk and confessing his loneliness and confusion, and his hurt over Addie's earlier withdrawal. He told Sarah he was working to secure his future and hinted it was Addie's future, too, but he was bound by his promise to Isaac Merritt to keep his intentions secret.

Were there other boys at school who'd caught her attention? No, none Addie spoke of, Sarah assured him. Had she confessed to Sarah that her feelings for him had waned? No, Sarah had replied. Does she speak of me at all? he'd asked with longing in his eyes. Sarah had simply refrained from answering, returning his look with one of shared dismay.

Addie's birthday fell in June. Two weeks beforehand he sent her a note, asking for the pleasure of her company on the Sunday preceding it. They would picnic at the Botanical Gardens.

He rented a rig for the first time ever and picked her up with great pomp and ceremony. He had bought for the occasion a vested linen suit the hue of oatmeal and wore a choking, high collar under a painstakingly knotted tie. She wore an airy dress of lavender dotted Swiss, a wide-brimmed straw bonnet, and carried a white lace parasol. From the moment they regarded one another at the door they recognized a mutual somberness, a sorrow-wasted state bordering on melancholy which accompanied them to the carriage. He helped her embark and she held her skirts aside as he seated himself beside her.

"Would you like the bonnet up?" he asked.

"No, my parasol is fine."

He flicked the whip and the bay trotted off briskly, its hooves making the only sound as the two of them rode side by side in silence.

"How have you been?" he asked, and she replied, "Fine."

They had dressed in finest regalia—his first costly summerweight suit, which had set him back dearly; her first grown-up bonnet and the dress with its rustling petticoats such as full-grown women wore. They had breached some indefinable line between callowness and majority that had nothing to do with age, but having breached it they found it execrably silencing.

At the gardens he helped her alight and took up their picnic food, tied in his mother's dish towel: though he'd outlayed cash on a fine suit which would enhance his image at the bank, he would not get rich spending money on wicker baskets.

"I thought we would try the arbor seat just beyond the orangery. Have you been there?"

"Yes. My father has brought us here many times."

They walked together in the sun, along gravel paths between shoulder-high delphiniums the color of sky, past velvety purple petunias that turned the air to nectar, between a pair of magnificent copper beech trees as wide as houses with great drooping arms of shade, into the sun again along a rose path and through an ornate glass orangery where lacy palm trees thrived in the humid warmth; back into the cool between high boxwood hedges and through a topiary arch that brought them to a circular green enclosure surrounded by more square-edged boxwood hedge. Within it beds of white petunias, brilliant red celosia and purple ageratum formed a starburst design. In its center, painted white and draped with thick emerald grapevines, waited the double-benched arbor seat.

Reaching it had taken ten minutes of walking while neither Robert nor Adelaide spoke a word.

She stepped up onto the painted floor and took a seat; her skirts covered the width of the wooden bench, leaving Robert little choice but to seat himself opposite.

He waited for some sign, and with his eyes called her, but she looked up at the leaf-screen overhead and remarked, "It's cool here."

Her remoteness hurt. He didn't know how to perforate it, to force her to bend or mend or end this indifference she had espoused.

"It's been a long time since we were on a picnic."

"Yes, it has."

He untied the dish towel. "It's not as fancy as Mrs. Smith's, but it's what I could manage. Corn gems, currant preserves, cheese and ham." He piled a selection on a cloth napkin and offered it.

"Thank you." She arranged the napkin on her crackling skirt, toying with it distractedly, bringing points up like mountains surrounding a valley. She studied the food instead of him, but showed no interest in eating anything. He chewed some cheese, which seemed to lodge in his throat, then gave up the effort.

"You aren't eating," he said.

She rested a hand on her ribs and flashed him a glance. "I'm sorry. I'm not really very hungry."

"Neither am I."

He set aside their napkins and sat watching her gaze at the gardens sparkling in the sun. He bent forward, bracing his forearms on his knees.

"Happy birthday, Addie," he said quietly.

Her attention shifted to him and stayed. For a moment he saw undisguised yearning in her eyes and the same affliction that had narrowed his throat, but she quickly hid it, dropping her gaze.

"I'm sorry I'm not more cheerful. I know you meant this to be a festive occasion. You've gone to all this trouble, and I . . . I . . ."

Her eyes could no longer refrain from resting upon his. They returned, illuminated with regret and hurt he could not comprehend.

"What's the matter, Addie?"

"I've missed you."

"You don't act like you've missed me."

"I've missed you, Robert, so very much."

"May I come and sit beside you?"

"Yes." She lifted her skirts, and when he sat, they covered most of his trouser leg. His knee pressed her thigh within the voluminous petticoats as he took her hand.

"I love you, Addie."

She closed her eyes and dropped her chin, though not before he caught a glimpse of tears.

"I love you too," she said to her lap.

He touched the crest of her cheek. "Why does that make you cry?"

"I don't kn–know." She had begun to sob quietly, her shoulders curled forward. Her sorrow reached within him and seized him about the heart.

"Please, Addie . . . don't cry . . ." He took her in his arms but the embrace was awkward, complicated by her wide hat. "Addie, darling . . . shh . . ." He had never before used the endearment; it resounded in his own head and gave his stomach a clenched feeling. "There's no more reason to cry, because everything is perfect. I've asked your father permission to marry you and he's said yes."

She drew back, her wide eyes streaming. "He did?"

"Yes, a year from now when you've finished school." He reached up and removed her hat. The pin clung to her topknot of curls and disheveled them, trailing one strand, like a drop of honey, down the side of her neck.

His news released a fresh flow of tears. He felt helpless in the face of them, groping for the proper means to end them, certain it was not within his power. Nevertheless, he took her face in one hand and drew her to his side, where his hammering heart at last pressed against her arm. "What is it, Addie? You're breaking my heart and I don't know what to do for you anymore. Don't you want to marry me?"

"I can't . . . you must not ask m–me."

"But I am asking. One year from now, tell me you'll marry me."

She pushed back and said, "No."

His fear became brittle, intense. He reacted instinctively, gripping her arms and forcing her into his embrace, kissing her with furor, need, and an unholy terror unleashed by the possibility of living without her when he had known since he was thirteen that he would marry her one day. Her resistance vanished and the kiss became a terrible thing, a heavy-hearted trade-off of uncertainty and desire, a lament, an exquisite end of their vernal longings, with her arms about his neck and their mouths wide. He flattened her breast with one hand and she whimpered against his tongue.

"Addie, let's go where we can be alone."

"No . . ."

"Please . . ." He kissed her again, openly caressing both her breasts through the crisp dotted swiss and layers of softer underclothes.

"Robert, stop. We're in the middle of the public gardens."

He knew where they were: he had chosen it to preclude the possibility of just such a scene.

"Come with me, Addie, please." His voice was hoarse.

"Where?" Hers was thin.

"I know a place. I delivered plant stakes here once for my father."

"No."

"How can you say no when you feel yes?"

"We can't."

"Please . . . where we can see each other. I want to see you, Addie."

Voices drifted to them from beyond the boxwood hedge, and footsteps sounded on the gravel, coming their way. Robert released Addie, keeping her stirred with an intense gaze while reaching for her hat.

"Put it on. Let's go."

Protected from view by Robert and a partial cascade of grapevines, she adjusted two hairpins and rammed a pin through the straw hat. He handed her her parasol, took her elbow and left via the only path, exchanging inane greeting with the intruders. Beyond the boxwood border he took her hand and led her at a rush through floral lanes to a break in the greenery where they were forced to dip low and remove Addie's hat to make their way through. Beyond lay a cart path in a patch of uncultivated woods, leading to a white shed with crossbucked doors. Before it stood a pony cart filled with the heads of flowers plucked by the gardeners from the plants the previous day.

Robert tried the doors. They were unlocked, but inside, the shed was crowded with gardening tools, buckets, lath and trellis wire, leaving a little patch of floor, and it strewn with garden soil.

"Damn." Robert swept a glance over the woods around them. He struck off toward the front of the pony cart, hauling Addie along behind him, stepping over the wagon traces, which rested on the ground, tilting the cart forward and spilling its load in an array of wilting color. Down upon it he took her, already kissing and embracing her as they fell to the resilient floral cushion.

"Robert," she managed, "your new suit . . ."

"I don't care." The stains of rose petals and marigolds and larkspur had already soiled his elbows during the fall.

"But someone will come."

"It's Sunday. The gardeners are all at home."

He kissed her as Adam had kissed Eve before she found the apple tree, then rolled her to her back and leaned over her, studying her face in the dappled shade, framed by fading flowers and wilting greenery that gave up a spicy redolence.

"Oh Addie, you're so pretty."

He sat up and stripped off his jacket, tossed it aside and took her in his arms, rolling to his back with her atop him. Many long, wet kisses later, when his knee had forced her skirts high between her legs, and their mouths were swollen, they paused for breath.

"Addie, I love you so much," he breathed.

With their gazes locked, he rolled her to her back.

"Robert," she whispered, "my new dress . . ."

A petal fell from his hair onto her face, where it remained as he spoke. "Let's take it off too." Her green eyes fixed upon his and she swallowed as if with great difficulty.

He struggled to his knees, drawing her after him by one hand, the petal from her cheek drifting to her skirt. When she sat, he got behind her, freed a long row of buttons and turned her dress down to her waist. Beneath it she wore a white cambric shift gathered at a scooped neckline. He kissed the slope of her bare shoulder, then moved around to face her on his knees. Her shift was held together by a white center bow. It disappeared at his tug, the ribbons falling to the depression between her breasts. He put his face there and pressed her back down, kissed her breasts first through white cambric, and saw them naked for the first time as she lay upon the wilting flowers of yesterday.

"Robert, we can't," she whispered breathlessly when they'd kissed again with their legs plaited.

He continued his seduction, wooing and weakening her with touches and kisses while the spent blossoms lifted their haylike scent into the cool green woods. Her murmurs and flushes and closed eyelids spoke of acquiescence until he brushed her skirts up and touched her beneath them.

She uttered a cry and pushed his hand away, but he persisted. She was wearing stockings and garters and one bright tear in the corner of each closed eye. Her jaw was clenched.

As his hand found its destination she cried out and recoiled, scrambling away from him as if in revulsion.

"Stay away from me!" She was on all fours, sliding down the tilted wagon, taking dead flowers with her. Her eyes were wild and rabid.

"Addie, where are you going?" He sat up.

"Stay away!"

"I'm sorry, Addie." He reached out one hand in appeal. "I thought you wanted to."

"No!" She lurched back, posed on all fours, like a dog, her eyes dark and terrified.

"I won't hurt you. I promise I won't touch you again. Dear God, Addie, I love you."

"You don't love me!" she screamed. *"How could you love me and want to do that to me!"*

Her voice rang through the clearing, carrying to the public gardens, he was sure. People would come running if she continued.

"Addie, what's wrong with you?"

He could see she was in a state of irrationality as she struggled to her feet and stood hunkered forward, like a Neanderthal brandishing a spear, while attempting to draw her shift into place with her other hand.

His throat was tight with fear. "Let me help you with your dress. I won't touch you anyplace else, I promise." He moved toward her warily, but she backed up and yelped, "No! Stay away, I said!" tripping on her dress, soiling the hem and stumbling.

He stood by helplessly while she began babbling, scrabbling her bodice into place, her eyes searching the ground as if confused about the litter of dead flowers. ". . . all these roses . . . must get home . . . shouldn't have come here . . . birthday . . . Sarah will know . . ." She scuttled backward some distance before turning and running with her clothing still disheveled.

"Addie, your hat! Your umbrella!" He grabbed them and jogged after her. "Addie, wait!"

The last he saw of her was her stained dress, opened up the back as she lifted her skirts and ran as if red lava were at her heels.

The following morning she was gone.

CHAPTER 14

AND now it was Christmas Eve, five and a half years later. All that time he had carried guilt and confusion as well as the memories of their unresolved love. He needed resolution; absolution, maybe—he was not sure.

He sat in the parlor at Rose's, in a stuffy room with thick velvet curtains, a round black iron stove and a good two dozen lonely men. He alone, among them, seemed sober. The cigar smoke hung like fog. The beer-soaked floorboards emitted a malty smell. He imagined he detected, too, the odor of human secretions and felt befouled by his surroundings.

The menu on the wall seemed to leer at him; he turned his head to look at something else. A brassy-haired bawd was petting the buttocks of a man with a large boil on the back of his neck. The old harlot who ran the place was smoking a cigar and squinting at him through the haze. Robert shuddered and studied his knees. Another whore came down the stairs. The harlot came to him and said, "Ember is free now. How 'bout her?"

"No, thank you. I'll wait for Eve," he replied, the name strange on his tongue.

"You're sure about that bath now, honey? We don't want our girls catching nothing."

"I'm sure. I took one this afternoon."

He waited a total of forty minutes, wondering what Addie's customer would look like when he came down, imagining sordid pictures of

Addie ministering to someone who resembled the thickset miner with the boil on his neck.

He watched every man who came downstairs, guessing which one was Addie's. He guessed right—she descended minutes after a tall, scraggly fellow with skin the color of a mushroom who came down running his thumbs under his suspender straps. Addie disappeared into the hall momentarily as every girl did after every descent—presumably depositing her earnings under the gimlet gaze of her employer. Returning to the parlor, Addie was signaled over by Rose, who spoke while nodding in Robert's direction. Addie's head snapped around even before Rose finished speaking.

Across the smoky, stuffy room tension immediately stretched between the two of them like a turnbuckle. He nodded, sitting straight on a hard chair with his hat and cane on his knees.

She stared at him, her expression unreadable, before beginning to thread her way across the room.

His palms got sweaty. Surely his chest would implode. He thought, *I'm not at all sure I can do this, not to her and not to me.*

She wore an open kimono, sheeny and black, with large orchid flowers; stockings, garters and black slippers with high heels. Her underwear showed in the break down the middle.

"Hello, Robert."

"Hello, Addie."

"Rose doesn't like it when you call me that."

He cleared his throat and said, "Eve," and after an interim, "Merry Christmas."

"Sure. What can I do for you?"

He knew nothing of whorehouse protocol. Was he expected to pick a selection from the menu here and now?

"I'd like to go upstairs."

"I'm working, Robert."

"Yes, I know."

Ten seconds of electric silence, then, "I can't do any favors for old friends."

"I don't expect any. I'll pay whatever is required."

She studied him with a deliberately flat expression, then turned away. "Get one of the other girls." He caught her arm and swung her around.

"No! You!" His expression was grim, his grip indurate. "It's time we had this over with!"

"This is a mistake, Robert."

"Maybe so, but only one in a long line of many. Where do I pay?"

The madam and a huge, menacing Indian woman were already moving toward them. He dropped Addie's arm and the pair fell back.

"Upstairs," Addie answered. "Follow me."

In the midst of the crowd Rose halted Addie with a pudgy, beringed hand. "Don't forget now, Eve—no special considerations for old boyfriends. He pays like all the rest."

"Don't worry, Rose. I wouldn't dream of cheating you." And to Robert, "Come on."

Her hair was cropped straight across the forehead and bottom, Oriental fashion. He watched it refuse to sway as he followed her upstairs and through a door on the left. Inside, his eyes took a quick flight around the room—the pad on the bed, the egg timer beside it, the butter bowl, the gold scale, the clock, the pot beside the door: an airless, windowless cubicle where he was one in a progression of thousands.

Addie said, "I'll take your coat." She hung it on a tree in the corner and laid his hat and cane on a hard, armless wooden chair that had probably been used for more than a hatrack. He resisted the urge to pluck it off and hang it on the tree, too.

She returned to the door and closed it, lounging back upon it, watching his eyes search for locks.

"No locks here, honey," she said in a cornsilk voice. "But don't worry. Nobody will come in unless I scream." The implication chilled him. He wondered how many times she had, and how badly she'd been hurt before anyone reached the door.

"I have a request, Addie."

"Eve."

"Eve," he repeated. "Please don't call me honey."

"Sure." She still lounged against the door. "Anything else?"

"No."

An immense silence passed while she stood against the door and he tried to pretend she was a stranger.

"This your first time in a place like this?" Addie inquired.

"Yes."

"We're required to ask—did you take a bath?"

"Yes, this afternoon."

"Good. This we're not required to ask—is it your first time?"

A moment, then, quietly, "No."

She boosted away from the door and said on a gust of breath, "Well, then . . . about the business."

He reached in his pocket for his pouch of gold dust, but she came to him and pressed his hand to detain it. "Not so fast. We can talk a minute first." She circled him, running her hands over his trunk, making broad swipes that crossed his watch fob from above to below and back again. He clenched his stomach and held it taut.

"If you collect the money first, then fine. I'll do like everyone else."

"Just relax, Robert . . . relax. We'll get to that in a minute. We need to talk about what you want."

He wanted her to stop rubbing him the way she rubbed every other man who entered this room. He wanted her to grow back her beautiful blond hair and put on a decent dress that covered her. He wanted to scrub the filth off her face and take her to a church somewhere and kneel beside her and put this sordid room behind them forever.

"What do you want, Robert, hmm? This is the way it's done. You tell me what you want and I'll tell you how long it takes and that way neither one of us gets surprised in the end. How does that sound, hmm?"

"Fine." He dropped his hand from his gold pouch pocket.

"We can do it quick and slick. See the egg timer? It's a dollar a minute that way."

Sweet savior, an egg timer. How many men could churn through here in intervals that short? Without time for even a pretense of affection?

"Otherwise we can do the trip. Most men like the trip. It's got just about everything and it'll take about forty minutes. Tell me what forty minutes of heaven is worth to you, Robert. We'll start out nice and slow . . ." She reached down his trousers and stroked him indolently, and to Robert's chagrin he was turgid. He grabbed her by both elbows and held her away. "Please, Addie . . . Eve. I'll pay whatever you ask, just don't . . . don't . . ." Don't be so facile and practiced. "Could we just get on with it in a straightforward manner?"

"Sure." She backed off and dropped the seductive act, exchanging it for cool detachment. "Let's say twenty dollars. In advance."

Twenty dollars, twenty minutes or thereabouts. Could he get her to talk in twenty minutes? He'd been unable to do so in the weeks that he'd been here. What purpose would it serve if he put them both through this and she shed no light on that time five years ago?

She accepted his gold pouch and weighed out a full ounce, returned the pouch to him and waited while he stood uncertainly.

"Would you like to kiss me, Robert?" she asked.

He swallowed and answered honestly, "No."

"Would you like me to kiss you?"

"I'd like to talk, Addie. Could we just talk?"

"Of course." She took his hand and led him to the bed. They sat on the edge and she pulled one knee up on the mattress, turning to face him. "But I won't talk about the thing you came here to talk about. Anything else, but not that. Are you lonesome, Robert, because it's Christmas? Is that it?"

The words he wanted to say were trapped in his throat.

"You miss your family?" Her voice seemed genuine with caring for the first time since his arrival in Deadwood.

"No. I never was close to them. Well, maybe my brother Franklin."

"I never met him. I never met any of them."

"I wanted you to."

"Well, sometimes things just don't turn out." She reached out and stroked his lapels. "You've done very well for yourself, haven't you, Robert. You're rich, just the way you always wanted to be."

"I wanted to be rich for you, too, didn't you know that? It's why I was away from you so much during that time when—"

She covered his lips with a finger. "Shh . . . nothing about that."

He gripped her hand and held it against his breast. "Why?" he asked passionately.

She shook her head slowly, breaking into tiny pieces inside, Eve and Addie warring with one another. She had survived the minutes since spotting him in the parlor by reverting to Eve, by hardening herself to all human emotion. She could get through this if she kept Addie locked up and out of sight. Vulnerable, aching Addie, who was weeping inside her right now, who wanted to cover herself and hide in Robert's arms and beg his forgiveness, beg him to excuse her from this unspeakable act that would reduce them both beyond redemption.

"Why, Addie?" Robert repeated. "I deserve to know after all this time. I've been through seven hells believing it was my foolish advances that forced you to run, but I've never fully understood the rest of it. You were young, I know, and I was old enough to realize you weren't ready, but why did you desert your family? Do you know how your father suffered? How Sarah did?"

"I did too," she said poignantly.

"Then why? Why this?" He passed a hand through the air of the sleazy room.

"Because it's the only thing a woman knows."

"No. Don't tell me that because I won't believe it! You were a virgin that day we were in that cart of flowers. I know it just as surely as I know tonight that you're not. You were terrified of what nearly happened between us. That's why none of this fits!"

Addie begged, *Tell him.*

Eve said, *Get it over with.*

Her expression glazed over. She glanced at the clock beside the bed. "Robert, I have to start timing you from the minute the door closed. We've already used up fifteen minutes. You've got fifteen more to go. Are you sure you want to spend it talking?"

Any sentimentality she'd shown had vanished; there would be no further answers, he could tell.

He rose from the bed and began loosening his tie: two brusque yanks while the skin on his facial structure seemed stretched so tightly the bones showed through. His mouth was rigid, his eyes dispassionate.

"All right, let's get on with it."

He removed his jacket, hung it on the coat-tree. Then the watch fob. The vest. The suspenders. His shoes and socks, sitting on the bed as if he were the only person in the room. His shirt, standing with his back to her. His trousers. Down to his wool union suit.

He turned to face her. "Well, are you going to sit there all night on my twenty dollars?" She hadn't moved a muscle. Her eyes were wide like that day on the flower cart.

"Well?" he snapped.

Don't, Robert, please. "Sometimes the men like to undress us."

"I have no desire to undress you. Do it yourself," he ordered.

His union suit was opened to his navel. He dropped his arms to his sides and waited, little understanding why he wanted to humiliate her. Perhaps because he himself was humiliated to be here, to be engaging in this depravity which with each passing moment was approaching the time of least grace.

"I'm waiting, Eve," he ordered.

She rose and stood before him, as straight as St. Joan's stake, her eyes fixed unwaveringly upon his. She removed her kimono, tossed it to the bed. Slipped off her satin shoes. Garters. Stockings. The corset: its hooks came free in a series of lunges which he followed with his eyes, breast to belly. It dropped to the floor. She opened her chemise and dropped it, too. Beneath it the skin was crosshatched in a pattern of wrinkled cotton. His eyes perused the wrinkles, lifted to her naked breasts, lingered, then rose to her face while she worked the button at the waist of her pantaloons. One glinting tear had formed in each of her eyes, hovering at the outer corner like dew at the tip of a leaf.

His throat filled. Inside him, something rended.

"No, Addie, not this way," he whispered, stepping forward and hiding her against himself, pinning her arms at her sides. "I cannot do it this way." His eyes were closed, his eyelashes wet. "Not for gold. Not with you hating me and me hating myself. Forgive me, Addie."

She let herself be held and hidden, standing limply in his arms while Addie crept out of isolation and tapped at the door of a hurting heart.

"Aw, Addie, what have we come to?" He caught the back of her head in an open hand and held her while they cried together silently, too close to see faces, too shaken to speak. A door closed down the hall. Someone laughed. Downstairs the parrot squawked. The clock beside the bed ticked off two costly minutes . . . three . . . still they remained, her hair meshed with his beard, two of her bare toes stacked upon his big one.

"Put your clothes back on, Addie," he whispered hoarsely, moving as if to release her.

"Wait." She clung, hiding still. "I have to tell somebody. I can't live with it any longer."

He resumed the pressure of his arms around her shoulders and waited. Her throat was caught on his shoulder. He felt her swallow.

"It was my f–father," she whispered at last, with her fists closed in the scratchy woolen underwear on his back. "He used to c–come into my b–bed at night. He used to make me d–do all these things with him."

The splash of shock caught him like scalding water. His stomach took up some slack he had not known was there. Denial sprang to mind— *somehow you've misunderstood, Robert.*

"Your father?" he whispered.

She nodded, bumping his shoulder, holding her sobs inside so they palpitated against his stomach.

His hand went to her head and pulled it more tightly to his neck. Could he have made of himself a complete circle to shield her from every side, he would have done so.

"From the time my mother left."

"Oh Addie . . ." He had not known pity could reach such immense proportions.

"I used to sl–sleep with Sarah, and then Mother left and I st–started wetting the bed so Father put me in a room of my own and that's when it st–started. He used to tell me that if he rubbed me down there I w–wouldn't wet the bed anymore. It was very lonely without Mother and at f–first I liked having him climb in with m–me and h–holding me."

Robert's tears fell on Addie's hair while the two of them remained sealed together like blades of wet grass.

"You were just a child."

"It was long before I knew you. Long before I fell in love with you." Her words were distorted against his collarbone.

"He forced himself on you? Totally?"

"Not at first. That began when I was twelve."

"Twelve . . ." *Twelve . . . sweet heavens, twelve.* He had known her at twelve. He had watched her play the spinet with that haunted solitariness that kept drawing her away. She had owned a green plaid dress with a white pilgrim collar that hung down nearly to the points of her budding breasts. He had sometimes sneaked glances at them while her eyes were on the music. Remembering, he felt guilty for even so small an infraction.

"Just at the time you began to mature."

"Yes," she whispered.

"About the time I began noticing you growing up, too."

She remained silent.

"It got worse then, because of that, didn't it?"

Still she said nothing.

"Didn't it, Addie?"

"It wasn't your fault. You didn't know."

The world behind Robert's eyelids was blood red with agony. "Oh Addie, I'm sorry."

"You weren't the cause. It had begun long before you."

"Why didn't you tell someone . . . Mrs. Smith, Sarah . . ."

"He warned me nobody would believe me. I would be laughed at and pointed at. What we did was forbidden. I knew it by that time, and they might even take him away, he said, and then Sarah and I would have nobody to take care of us. I believed him and I was afraid to tell Mrs. Smith. And how could I tell Sarah? She would never have believed me. Father was her hero."

Some hero. Robert's shock began congealing into anger at the bestiality inflicted by Isaac Merritt upon a child of utter innocence, too young and indoctrinated with fear to have means of combating it.

"And all that time, while you were growing away from me, I thought it was something I was doing. At one point I believed you were dying of some deadly disease, you had changed so much and seemed so frail with worry. Did he ever tell you I spoke to him about it?"

She drew back to see his face. "You did?"

His hands remained curled around her shoulders. He spoke directly to her eyes. "He told me it was the differences in our ages, yours and mine, and that you undoubtedly felt pressure to allow my advances when all the time he was the one preying upon you."

"Oh Robert . . ." She rested her hands on his chest. "I could see the heartache I was causing you and Sarah, and so many times I ached to confess to you."

"Not confess!" he insisted. "Never confess. To confess implies guilt when you were guilty of nothing." Robert's rage thickened.

"But you loved me and I was unlovable and unworthy."

"That's what he wanted you to think. Did he pump you full of those ideas too?" He could read the truth in her face, could imagine how Merritt had manipulated her by fear and debasement, infiltrating her mind with whatever lies it took to keep her quiet and submissive. Robert's rage came full force and brought with it a passionate fury. He swept Addie's robe from the bed onto her shoulders. "Get dressed, Addie. You don't ever have to disrobe for a man again. Your ordeal is over." As if to a third party, Robert cursed while donning his trousers. "God damn him to hell. What *fools* we were, all of us! Why, I played right into his hands. I went to him asking permission to marry you when you were seventeen and he said yes. After that you drifted farther and farther away. I see it now. It all fits."

Addie had donned her robe. He gripped her hands so hard her fingers overlapped. His eyes blazed as he spoke. "Do you know what I would give to have him alive for one hour? I would cut off his testicles and stuff them in his mouth like a roast pig!"

"Oh Robert . . ." She could think of nothing else to say.

"What does it take to get you out of here for the night?"

"Robert, you can't—"

"What does it take!" he repeated more demandingly.

"You have to buy me off the floor."

"To the tune of what?"

"Two hundred dollars."

He gave her his gold pouch. "Measure it out."

"Two hundred dollars? Robert, that's silly."

"I'm a damned rich man. Measure it out."

"But Rose will—"

"We'll fight with Rose later." He was hurriedly donning the remainder of his clothes. "It's Christmas Eve, Addie. I'm not leaving you in this whorehouse on Christmas Eve, and if I have it my way you won't be back at all, so weigh the gold!"

When his clothes were in order she was still facing the bureau with the gold pouch held limply in one hand. From behind her shoulder he took the pouch and told her quietly, "I'm sorry I shouted at you, Addie. Here, I'll finish that while you get dressed. Pack only what you need for decency sake. I want you to take nothing away from this place."

He suddenly realized she was standing with her back to him, crying quietly. He turned her to face him. "Addie, don't cry. The time for crying is over."

"But Robert, what can I do? I've lived behind these doors so long . . . you don't understand."

How many times could a man's heart break? "You're afraid?" he said gently. She had since the age of three never lived a normal life. Walking out with him would be an act of normalcy, but more—of courage. "My poor, poor girl, of course you're afraid. But I'll be there with you. Now come . . . get dressed. Do you have street clothes?"

She nodded forlornly.

"Where are they?"

"In my room next door."

"We'll get them."

He carried the remainder of her garments and they closed the door on the wretched room he vowed she would never enter again. In the dark next door he said, "Where's the lamp?"

"Straight ahead."

When he lit it a white cat lifted its head off the bed and squinted at him over its left shoulder.

"Can I take Ruler?" she asked.

"Absolutely. He's the only good thing in this place."

"And my tussie-mussie from Sarah?"

"Of course."

Her clothing hung on pegs, little of it suitable for polite company. He chose the plainest dress he could find and waited with his back to her as she put it on. When he turned, she was waiting, her makeup run, blurring her face like an impressionist's painting. He wet a cloth in a nearby basin and held her chin while gently washing away the diluted kohl from her eyes and the carmine from her lips.

"You won't need this anymore either, Adelaide Merritt," he vowed softly, and when he was done, stood before her studying her familiar green eyes, which were swollen from crying. "How I've longed to see the Addie I remember. Little by little we'll bring her back."

"But Robert—"

He silenced her with a touch on the lips. "I don't have all the answers, Addie, not yet, but how can we find them if we don't start searching?"

Downstairs she deposited the two hundred dollars in gold dust in a drop box in the hall, and told Rose as she passed, "Robert is buying me off the floor."

"Twenty-four hours and not a minute more, you hear me, Eve?" Rose called after her, then added, louder, "Where are you taking that cat?"

With Ruler in her arms and Robert at her side, Addie walked into the cold Christmas air.

Above them, "O Sanctissima" was ringing through the gulch.

"Could it be a sign?" Robert asked, lifting his face as they strode in long, matched steps.

"Heaven doesn't send signs for prostitutes," Addie replied.

"Don't be too sure," Robert replied, slipping his hand around her elbow.

At his hotel the desk was abandoned. A note, tacked to the pigeon-holes, said, GONE HOME FOR CHRISTMAS. Robert stepped behind the desk and selected a key.

"Who says there's no room at the inn?" He smiled as he returned to Addie and touched her back, directing her toward the stairs. On the second floor he opened a door, went inside and lit a lantern. The room was plain but plastered, and there was a curtain of sorts on the window. He opened the door of a round iron stove and knelt before it.

"But Robert, we haven't paid for this room."

"I'll catch up with Sam in the morning or whenever he gets back."

She stood uncertainly near the open doorway as he rose and turned. "I have to go out back for some wood. You'll find a tin in the hall with water, if it isn't frozen. It should be empty enough for you to lift by this time of the day. Get the whole thing and bring it to the stove, will you, Addie? I'll be right back."

She released Ruler, who explored the room. Robert returned in minutes with an armload of wood, knelt and built a fire, closed the squeaky stove door and adjusted the grate. He rose once more, brushing off his hands as he faced her.

"When you've finished your bath, knock on the wall. We can talk then if you like."

"Thank you, Robert."

He smiled. "I'll bring you a nightshirt, just a minute."

She listened to his footsteps fade and return. He re-entered and handed her a folded nightshirt. It was blue and white striped flannel. The stripes quavered as she looked down at them through fresh tears and repeated, "Thank you, Robert."

He stepped nearer and lifted her chin with a knuckle. "Knock," he whispered, and left her, closing the door behind him.

The room had a rocking chair. She dropped to it and doubled forward, burying her face in the blue flannel stripes. She sat a long time, motionless, acclimating to freedom, wondering what Robert's intentions were, if any. The water began to sizzle and she rose with a sense of wonder to stir it with her finger. The only bathing vessel present was the bowl beneath the pitcher. She made do with it, and afterward hung her towels carefully and stood beside the radiant stove, warming her skin, feeling fear bake out of her. She dressed in the nightshirt. It felt like crawling into Robert's skin, where everything was normal and secure and you had a sense of purpose. She brushed her hair and recalled how he disliked it black, so reclaimed her damp towel and bound it turban-fashion around her head before quietly tapping on the wall.

She heard his door open and close, and his footsteps approaching. Her door opened and he said, "Your room is warmer than mine. May I come in?"

"Of course."

He stepped inside and closed the door without compunction. He was dressed in his black woolen trousers, white shirt and suspenders. High-topped shoes, too. He took her hand and led her near the lantern. "Well, look at you . . ." He took her head in both his hands and placed her clean-scrubbed face in the direct yellow glow. He studied her minutely, a faint smile on his lips. "It's really Addie Merritt after all. How do you feel?"

"Much better. Amazed. Adrift. Afraid."

He dropped his arms. "Would you rather be alone, Addie?"

"No, I . . . it's Christmas Eve and who wants to be alone on Christmas Eve? I would like to talk, Robert, really I would, but it wouldn't be good for you if word got out that you'd been in my room with me. Up at Rose's is one thing, but here . . . this is a respectable establishment, I'm sure."

"Addie." He took her hand and led her to the bed. "You need to start concerning yourself with things that really matter."

He cocked her pillows against the headboard, ordered "Sit," and when she did, "Move over." Atop the coverings he took his place beside her, put both arms around her and snuggled her against his side. He stretched out his legs, crossed his ankles and said, "Listen . . . the bells have stopped."

They both listened.

A coal sang a sizzling note in the stove.

Across the hall someone was snoring.

Ruler vaulted up onto the bed and picked his way onto Robert's lap, settled himself square atop his fly buttons and curled up like a jelly roll.

Robert and Addie laughed.

"Well, I guess that settles that," he remarked.

She laughed again and ended with a sigh. "Oh Robert, I don't know where to begin."

Somehow they found the place. She began with her disillusionment when her mother ran away, the feeling after that of being different from other children who still had mothers. Those years of lonely longing, after Mrs. Smith came, when Sarah and she would stand at the window looking down Lampley Street, still believing their mother would return. Her childish chagrin when she began wetting the bed, and her fear when Sarah's complaints about it prompted Addie's move to a room of her own where the loneliness took on space and intensity. Her relief the first time her father had slipped in, in the dark to comfort her. The hazy area between puerile ignorance of what was truly happening and the dawning of revulsion followed by sexual guilt. The clearer recollections of begging to sleep with Sarah, who most often argued, "But you kick and take the covers and talk in your sleep. Go sleep in your own room." Begging for a lock on her bedroom door while her father declared before both Sarah and Mrs. Smith that the way to cure Adelaide's problems was not through locking out bogeymen but by leaving the door open and realizing there were none. Going to bed before her father got home, lying rigid with eyelids trembling, pretending to be asleep in hopes he'd pass right by her room and go to his own. Studying hard in hopes she'd become smarter and would be taken under Father's publisher's wing as Sarah had been, and so please him that he would reward her by leaving her alone in the bedroom. Learning to hate her physical beauty, which she blamed for the perverted attention it sparked.

And the advent of Robert himself into her life.

Her immediate gravity toward him. Her relief when Isaac had allowed Robert's visits. Her occasional jealousy of Sarah, who, with her intelligence more matched to Robert's, could offer him so much more by way of stimulating discussion and even humorous exchanges. Then puberty and the onset of Isaac's forced intercourse. The added shame it brought. The arrival of her incontestable love for Robert, confounded by guilt at her lack of virginity and fear that even if and when they either married or became lovers he would discover her unchaste state and hate her for it.

"I felt so helpless," she said. "He would tell me that if I ever told anybody no man would want me, and I believed him."

"Of course you did. He stripped away all your feelings of self-worth."

"I felt like I was wearing a coat of shame, and no matter where I went everyone could see it, especially you."

"I never guessed, never."

"When I told you tonight, you were shocked, weren't you?"

"I felt like I'd been poleaxed."

"So imagine my fear of your guessing it when I was only fifteen or sixteen years old. You would have been revolted, just the way my father said."

"Maybe I would have. Who's to say now?"

"Every time after you kissed me, I went to my room and cried."

"And that day in the flower cart . . ."

"I thought you'd be able to tell I wasn't a virgin if we did anything. I was so afraid of losing you."

"So you ran away and I was the one who lost you."

"I thought I didn't have a choice. I couldn't stay with him any longer, and I couldn't go to you."

"You left two very confused and worried people behind—three counting Mrs. Smith."

"I'm sorry I had to do that."

"Where did you go? First off, I mean."

"I started in Kansas City, but one of the girls there got pregnant and gave the baby out for adoption, and that sort of ruined everything for all of us so I moved on to Cheyenne for a change of scenery. There one of the girls put ground glass in one of the other girl's douches—there was a lot of jealousy over the good-paying customers. The girl nearly died. She was my friend—or as close as you can get in the business. So anyway, after that I came up here when the gold rush started. But the houses were all the same. I really only exchanged one prison for another. The difference was I hated men and could get even with hundreds of them for what one had done to me." They lay in silence awhile before she finished, "You should know, Robert, I still hate men."

He accepted her remark without comment, even though she was still beneath his arm with her head on his shoulder and her hand on his chest. He supposed she had a right.

In time he asked quietly, "Does Sarah know about Isaac?"

"No."

"Do you intend to tell her?"

She rolled away from him. "What good would it do?"

He pulled her back where she'd been. "It would help her understand, just like it did me."

Addie sat up and hugged her knees. "But it would hurt her."

"Yes, it would hurt her."

Silence settled, a long, trying silence. She broke it as if Robert had argued.

"But I'd be so ashamed to tell her."

"Then he's still got a hold on you, even though he's dead."

She dropped her forehead to her knees and said, muffled, "I know . . . I know."

He had planted the seed; let it bear fruit or not, as it would.

"Come . . . lie back, Addie. You don't have to decide tonight."

She returned to the lee of his arm, lying silent and thoughtful. He lay as before with his ankles crossed, but gave her arm a squeeze. She sighed and stared across his chest at the doorframe, where lamplight and shadow created a sharp edge of gold and gray. Her eyelids grew heavy and blinked . . . grew heavier . . . blinked again and remained closed. Shortly, his followed suit.

She awakened to find the room sunny and smelling of an oil-fed wick that had run out of fuel, the bedding flipped from the outsides toward the middle and Robert sleeping with his back to her.

She yawned and tried to stretch without waking him.

Robert made minuscule waking movements, eventually looked back over his shoulder and said, " 'Morning."

"Closer to noon, I think."

He rolled to his back and yawned, great big, stretching with his hands behind his head, making the mattress tremble. When his mouth closed he turned his head, grinned at her and said, "Let's go give Sarah a Christmas surprise."

She smiled and said, "All right, let's."

CHAPTER 15

CHRISTMAS began for Sarah with a bittersweet cast, her first without her father; without Addie, too. Though she was looking forward to dinner with the Dawkins family, they were not her own. Furthermore, the day seemed to stretch interminably toward four P.M., the time of her invitation. Meanwhile, Mrs. Roundtree's felt forlorn, filled with men missing loved ones back home, crowding the parlor until it became stuffy, reminiscing about pung rides or lutefisk or oyster stuffing, depending upon the geographic location or nationality from which they'd hailed.

To her credit, Mrs. Roundtree did her best to offer a festive air. There was the tree in the parlor and a special late-morning breakfast of ham and potato pancakes, herbed eggs and assorted sweetbreads with a rare delicacy: real butter. Mealtime, however, lacked attraction due to Noah Campbell's absence.

Sarah had awakened thinking of him, of something Addie had once said about certain men making a woman feel like a thimbleful of fondant. Last night in her room she had for the first time begun understanding the treachery of such feelings. Kissing him, breast to breast, she had felt the hollow hand of temptation reaching to be filled. For those few minutes—seconds?—she had felt voluptuous. He had said inviting such feelings was natural, but there were Commandments against such situations. Now she understood why.

He remained in her thoughts, vivid and imposing, the key to her day's brightness or eclipse. She supposed, much to her dismay, that she loved

him. In her childish fantasies she had imagined that falling in love was
like being lifted by seraphs to a supreme plane where roses trailed forever
at one's feet and the soul so radiated joy that it lit the space around it.
Instead, it resembled falling off a horse—a stumble, a roll, and reproach
with herself for having chosen poorly and tumbled when she might as
easily have drawn a Pegasus and flown.

No, this was not flying. This was picking one's way through the
morass of cans and cannots, do's and don'ts, must and must nots that
had been fixed in her conscience years ago by a good Christian father
who took her to church every Sunday and so respected that church's
laws that he clung to his marriage vows until death, even in the face of
his wife's desertion.

She wished Isaac were here now. How comforting it would feel to
sit in the same room and confide in him, "Father, I'm so confused."

Instead, she went to her room and penned a letter to Mrs. Smith.

> Deadwood, Dakota Territory
> Christmas Day, 1876
> Dear Mrs. Smith,
>
> The blessed holiday is here, spreading its beneficence on Dead-
> wood Gulch.

She went on to describe the pageant, then wrote:

> It has been exciting to be a part of the growth of Deadwood.
> The *Chronicle* not only succeeds, it thrives. I'm up to six pages now
> and having no trouble filling them with the freshest news: the
> telegraph, you see, has arrived at last. When Mr. Hayes and Mr.
> Wheeler take their oaths of office next month, I will be reporting
> their inaugural addresses at the same time the rest of the nation
> reads them. Imagine that.
>
> Addie is well. I see her daily, though we don't live together. I
> am still residing at Mrs. Roundtree's boardinghouse, though I
> believe it's time I purchase a house of my own since I know I'll be
> staying in Deadwood indefinitely.

Now where had that come from? She didn't recall consciously making
such a decision, but once the words were on paper she reread them and
found the idea splendid. A home of her own with furnishings of her
choice and more than a mere parlor to move about in, where she wasn't

engulfed by men or crowded into a lonely cubicle. She spent time imagining it, and afterward, her day felt brighter.

I'm afraid I must abbreviate this, for I am invited to the home of friends—the Dawkins—for Christmas dinner. Dear Mrs. Smith, I hope this finds you hale and hearty. You linger on my mind often with the fondest of regard. Please do write back soon to let us know you are as wholesome and happy as we remember you.

Your loving,
Sarah

Upon rereading the letter Sarah found the description of the Christmas program suitable for publication with minor revisions and some additions. She made these, recopied it for Patrick, and was proofreading the final draft when a knock sounded at the door.

She opened it to find Mrs. Roundtree in the hall, looking as if all her sphincters were cinched.

"Visitors for you downstairs."

"Visitors?" Sarah was surprised.

"I'd as lief they wouldn't come here again," the landlady added sourly. "You might tell them that. Not him, just her. Mind you, I run a respectable place here."

"Who is it, Mrs. Roundtree?"

"Mr. Baysinger and one of them from up at the badlands, judging from the look of her, and marching into my parlor as bold as brass. What are my men going to think!"

Sarah's heart began pounding. "Tell them I'll be right down."

"I don't speak to her sort, thank you, and if you want to you'll have to do it somewheres else besides in my house."

"Very well," Sarah snapped, flushing with indignation at the woman's captiousness. "I shall do exactly that. Thank you for your *charitable* attitude, Mrs. Roundtree, especially in this season of love!"

Mrs. Roundtree swung away in a self-righteous huff. Sarah snagged her coat and hat and clattered down the stairs with excitement brimming in her throat.

Robert and Addie stood just inside the parlor door, flanked by a roomful of gawking men with faces red as scalded pigs. Robert looked wonderfully at ease, maintaining a light hold on Addie's elbow. Addie fixed her stare on Sarah's descending form as if petrified to swing her eyes aside.

Sarah walked directly to her, extending both hands, smiling so hard her molars showed. "Addie, darling . . . merry Christmas." She squeezed Addie's hands and suggested, "Let's go," as if a plan had been previously made.

Outside, beneath the two o'clock sun, Sarah gave her sister an immense hug. "Oh Addie, you've come at last. Now my happiness is complete." After a moment she turned to do the same to their longtime friend. "And Robert . . . you've brought her. I always knew I loved you and now I know why. Thank you from the bottom of my heart."

"I thought you two sisters should be together for the holiday."

"Absolutely. And with you here, too, our gathering is complete."

Addie said, "Your landlady didn't like me in her parlor."

"My landlady has a worm up her posterior—you'll forgive my vulgarism, especially today, but her superciliousness galls me!"

"Sarah!" Addie said in amazement.

Robert laughed heartily while Sarah secured her outerwear.

Addie was still too shocked to linger over the snub. "I've never heard you talk like that in my whole life!"

"Hadn't you heard?" Sarah tugged on her gloves, leading the way down the endless stairs to the path below. "I'm a firebrand. You have to be to run a newspaper that's worth anything at all. What have you planned for the day?"

"Nothing. We just came to see you," Robert replied, following both women.

"Wonderful. I can offer you a cup of coffee at the newspaper office."

"Fine," he said.

Sarah sensed that somehow Robert had talked Addie out of Rose's, but that Addie had capitulated reluctantly. A keen thread of understanding ran between her and Robert: they would win Addie over by keeping her off-guard. At the bottom of the long steps each of them captured one of Addie's arms and they walked along linked three abreast.

"Addie stayed overnight at my hotel last night."

"You did!" Sarah came up short, bringing the others to a halt. "Does this mean you've left Rose's for good?"

Addie and Robert answered simultaneously.

"I don't know."

"Yes."

Robert spoke as they moved on. "I've told her I don't want her to go back there and I think she'd be willing if we came up with a plan."

Addie said, "And I've told Robert that he doesn't know how terrifying it is to face a world of people who cross to the other side of the street when they see you coming. Besides, I don't know anything else. What would I do?"

"You'd live with me."

"At Mrs. Roundtree's? Don't be absurd. You saw how she treated me."

"Not at Mrs. Roundtree's. We'll get a place of our own. Why, I was just thinking this morning that it's time I did that. I even wrote to Mrs. Smith and told her so."

Robert put in, "And I'd subsidize you in return for . . . oh, let's say darning my socks. How good are you at darning socks, Addie?"

Addie pinched back a smile. "I've never darned a sock in my life and you know it."

"That's right. Mrs. Smith did things like that, didn't she? Then cooking. How good are you at cooking? I'd pay you handsomely for a home-cooked meal now and then."

"I don't cook either."

They reached the newspaper office and went inside.

"If you'll light a fire, Robert, I'll go out to the pump and get some water. Addie, will you grind the coffee?"

"I just realized," Addie said forlornly, "I've never done that either."

Sarah said cheeringly, "Well, it's easy enough. Just put the beans in and crank. Maybe we'll make a domestic of you yet."

At a small rectangular table near the rear of the office Addie found the coffee grinder and the sack of coffee beans. "What do I catch them in?" she asked.

Whisking out the rear door, Sarah answered, "On a piece of paper will be fine." When she returned, Robert had the fire started and Addie was still grinding.

"How many?" she asked.

Sarah set the pot on the stove and said, "Oh, about a quarter of the amount you've already ground." The two sisters looked at each other and laughed. Abruptly Addie's face fell and she said, "I'm so ignorant. I just don't know anything."

Sarah went to Addie and clasped her cheeks lightly. "Just think of how exciting your life will be from now on—you'll learn something new every day. Robert and I will teach you, just as we did when we were children, and I think I know someone else who'll help, too."

"Who?"

"Stay here. I'll go ask her."

Sarah headed for the door.

"But Sarah, where—"

"Just wait here for me. Robert will show you how much coffee to put in that water and when I come back I'll expect a cup."

She went out without further enlightening them, straight to Emma's, where her knock was answered by Lettie, swathed in a cobbler's apron with a glow on her cheeks.

"Sarah, it's you already! Merry Christmas."

"The same to you, Lettie."

"Who is it, Lettie?" Emma called.

"It's Sarah already. Come in, Sarah."

Emma came to the door, wiping her hands on her apron. "You're a little early, Sarah, but if you don't mind we sure don't."

"I'm leaving again in a minute, and I'll come back at four, but I had to talk to you first."

"Sure, come on in."

The room smelled delicious, of garlic and onion and roasting meat. Of cinnamon and apples and the green tang of fresh-cut cabbage. At a worktable, Geneva wielded the grater. The windows were opaque with steam that collected in beads and painted clear stripes to the sill. Byron wandered in and said, "Well, if it isn't our children's choir director. Those young ones sounded good enough to be in one of Langrishe's stage shows."

"Oh Byron, you always say the nicest things. They *were* wonderful, weren't they?"

Josh followed his father into the room and announced, "Next year I want to sing in the choir, too."

"You'll be more than welcome." They rehashed last night's affair before Sarah spoke of the business at hand. "I'm glad you're here, all of you, because I've come with a very special request."

Emma said, "You just name it."

"I believe you all know Robert Baysinger, my childhood friend from St. Louis. He's finally convinced my sister to leave the brothel. They're at my newspaper office now, and if it's at all possible, I'd like to bring them here with me for Christmas dinner." Before anyone could speak, Sarah hurried on. "I know it's presumptuous of me to ask, especially considering how late it is, and the food is already prepared, but she was very badly snubbed at Mrs. Roundtree's this morning. I'd like to show her that there are people who'll still treat her decently, that's why I've come to you. But I'd only bring her if all of you are in agreement . . . and if there's enough food, of course."

Emma spoke for all. "What kind of Christians would we be to close our door in judgment? Of course you can bring her, and Mr. Baysinger too."

Sarah's shoulders slumped in relief. "Emma, you're a true friend—all

of you are. Thank you." Her eyes touched each of them in turn. "There
are some things you should know. We're still trying to convince Addie
not to go back, so her acceptance here will be especially encouraging.
She believes that nobody will treat her civilly, but after today she'll
realize that not everybody is like Mrs. Roundtree. Also, Emma, Robert
and I have been racking our brains trying to come up with some reasonable form of occupation for Addie. She's no good with words at all, or
I'd put her to work at the newspaper office. I've been thinking, if she
and I took up housing together she might simply act as our housekeeper, but she doesn't know anything about that either. Would you
help?"

Emma beamed, her cheeks red from kitchen heat. "You've come to
the right woman. These girls of mine can already cook durn near as
good as their mother. Bring her on and watch us make a new woman
out of her!"

"Oh Emma . . ." Sarah crooked an elbow around the good woman's
neck. "Perhaps I've never told you that I love you. All of you . . . Byron . . ." She hugged him and each of the others in turn. "Josh, Lettie,
'Neva. I simply don't know what I'd have done without you. You've
been the family I didn't have since I've lived here in Deadwood."

"Well, you've got one now, and we're going to do all we can to see
that you don't lose your sister again. Now go on back there and get
those two."

"Yes, ma'am," Sarah answered with her heart full. "You're sure there's
enough food?"

"Josh shot the goose. Josh, you think that honker will feed eight?"

"You bet!" Josh replied proudly. "He went a good fourteen, maybe
sixteen pounds."

As Sarah left, Emma was ordering, "Girls, grate a little more cabbage."

The newspaper office smelled like coffee when Sarah returned. Addie
and Robert had pulled up a pair of chairs near the stove and sat sipping
from Patrick's and Sarah's mugs. They turned as Sarah closed the door
and reached for her bonnet strings.

"You'll both be very happy with my news."

"What?"

"You're invited to my friends the Dawkins' for Christmas dinner."

Robert smiled.

Addie shrank.

"Oh no."

"What do you mean, oh no?"

"I'd rather go back to Rose's," she said into her cup.

Sarah briskly crossed the room and took her sister by the shoulders. "Listen to me, Addie. The Dawkins are good people. Emma and Byron have raised three wonderful children who've had a good example set by their parents. None of them will walk a wide berth around you. Granted, Mrs. Roundtree did, and I'm not saying others won't. But not Emma, and not her family. You have to start somewhere, Addie, and Christmas dinner with them is far from the worst occasion you could draw."

"You went there and asked them if I could come, didn't you?"

"Yes. You and Robert both."

"I don't want to trail along on your skirt tails."

"I do," Robert put in jovially. "For a homemade Christmas dinner in a real home, I don't mind how I get invited."

Addie looked unconvinced. "Addie, listen," Sarah reasoned, "Emma Dawkins knows a lot of people in this town. What she does is noticed by others. Most of the women see her nearly every day to buy bread from her. If she accepts you, chances are many of them will follow her lead. You must come."

"I can't."

Sarah grew stern, backing off with her hands on her hips. "Honestly, Addie, sometimes I grow so peeved with you! *And* with Father! If he hadn't spoiled you silly you might have had more gumption. All you ever had to do was pout a little bit and feel sorry for yourself and you got your way."

"I did not pout!"

"You're pouting now, just like a child."

"And I did not get my way!"

"You certainly did. While I was made to go to the newspaper office and work, you stayed home and dawdled."

"Well, maybe I wanted to go, too. Maybe I wasn't allowed!"

Robert sat silent and watchful.

"We'll argue about this later when Robert isn't here. For now I'd like you to give me just one good reason why you won't accept Emma's invitation."

Addie's chin got stubborn. "I thought I shouldn't go where there are children."

"Emma's children know what a brothel is. How could they live in this town and not? Why, I've been warning Josh not to deliver papers up there at the badlands since the first day I hired him. If Emma's not afraid they'll be jaded by your presence, why should you be?"

Addie had no retort. She stared at her sister, who went on authoritatively.

"And let's get one more thing settled—I won't have you at the Dawkins' unless you have every intention of never going back to Rose's again."

"But if I don't—"

"If you don't you and I will live together here at the newspaper office until we can find a house, which we'll start searching for the moment Craven Lee opens his door tomorrow morning. I have no intention of renting from a snob like Mrs. Roundtree, who shuns my sister with one hand and takes my gold with the other. She has a lot of nerve expecting me to. So we'll get some cots and sleep here until other arrangements can be made. That way Josh can sleep later in the mornings since he won't have to come in and light the fire to melt the ink. And I won't have to be running back and forth up that infernal set of steps, or traipsing out in the cold before the sun is even up in the morning. We'll eat at Teddy's until we can find a house, and when we do—well, I hope you'll learn how to cook, and if not, we'll live on a lot of fried eggs. Now what do you say?"

Addie considered silently for some time, glancing from Addie to Robert and back again.

"You mean we'll sleep here tonight?"

"No, not tonight. We'll have to think of something else for tonight. Not only you, but me. I refuse to sleep one more night at Mrs. Roundtree's after the way she treated you."

"What about Addie's room at the hotel?" Robert put in. "Couldn't the two of you share that for a night or two?" He understood that Sarah was determined to stick beside her sister to make sure she didn't backslide to Rose's.

Sarah replied, "We could if it's all right with Addie."

Addie said doubtfully, "I guess it would be all right. But I'd have to go back to Rose's to get the money she owes me from last night."

"Absolutely not!" Sarah yelped.

"But—"

"I won't have you taking one more penny from that hog ranch!"

"But she owes me a hundred dollars' worth of gold from Robert alone!"

Sarah's eyes widened and her cheeks took color. She shot a discomfited look at Robert.

"Oh, you mean . . ." She stumbled to a halt.

"I bought her off the floor," he admitted.

"For two hundred in gold," Addie added. "Why should Rose get all of that? She owes me half."

"All right, you go get it—but one hundred and not a flake more. And Robert will go with you."

"Absolutely," Robert put in.

Now that the decision was made, Sarah could see Addie quailing. "Rose will be very angry," the younger woman said.

"That's why he should go along. I want to make sure you come back out of there once you go in. I don't trust that big hulking Indian woman or that bawdy madam. What do you think, Robert, should you go now before the evening traffic picks up over there? Then Addie would have it behind her and could enjoy her dinner without worrying about having to face Rose. And while you're over there, I can go back and collect a few things from Mrs. Roundtree's."

"Now is fine with me if Addie agrees."

"Addie?" Sarah leveled her sister with a straightforward gaze.

Addie looked slightly pale. "Now?"

Robert took her hands. "Sarah's right. Then you'll have it over with and you can think about your new tomorrows. Just think, Addie, a future with possibilities—all you have to do is hand Rose your walking papers. As for the money, I don't care about that. Leave it there if you want."

"But I earned it fair and square. And if you don't want it—well, it's the only thing I have to give to Sarah toward my keep."

"Very well, we'll take it and you do just that, give it to Sarah. But let's go now."

Beneath his direct gaze she turned docile and replied meekly, "All right, Robert, if that's what you want me to do."

The sun had retired behind the western rim of rock and pine as they walked toward the badlands. Main Street lay in shadow, nearly deserted. Somewhere a chickadee sang his repetetive two-note song and off in the distance a burro brayed.

As they neared their destination Robert felt Addie gripping his elbow tighter.

"Are you afraid?" he asked.

"Rose won't be able to find another girl so easily in the middle of the winter, and without girls she loses money."

"Has she ever threatened you?"

"No, not directly, but she's a hard woman. They're all hard women there, especially when they're angry."

"I'll stay with you all the time."

They walked awhile before she asked, "Are you afraid, Robert?"

"Yes, but I have conviction on my side."

Staring straight ahead, Addie told him, "I don't deserve your kindness, Robert, not after what I've done."

"Nonsense, Addie."

"They call us the fair and the frail, but you can't be frail to survive there, and if you're fair at first, that soon changes. Why are you doing this, Robert?"

"Because everyone deserves happiness, and I could see you weren't happy there. And for Sarah, and myself, too, because we couldn't bear the thought of the girl we used to know doing work like that."

"You must forget her, the girl you used to know. She doesn't exist anymore."

They'd reached Rose's. Robert turned to Addie.

"Maybe she does and you just don't know it. Let's go in and get this unpleasantness behind us."

Inside, the smell was awful—carbolic water, cigar smoke and liquor. Living in it day in and day out, Addie hadn't realized how cloying it was, but after a single day away, entering Rose's parlor, she covered her nose with a glove. There were three men sitting at a table, desultorily sipping drinks. Rose herself was with them, packed into a satin dress the color of a bottle fly's wings. She swung her head, fixed her pewter eyes on Addie and drawled, "Well, look who's back, and bringing her rich little daddy along with her." To Robert she said, "Just can't get enough, can you, sugar?"

Addie said, "Could I talk to you in your office, Rose?"

The madam's eyes took a slow walk down Robert's trousers and back up to his neatly trimmed beard. "Why, sure," she replied belatedly and pushed herself up from the table. To the trio at the table she said, "Be right back, boys, and I'll bring a new bottle."

Addie led the way toward the far end of the hall. Just short of her office door Rose turned and poked four fingers against Robert's chest. "No men allowed back here, sugar. It's private, you unnerstand."

Robert looked beyond Rose to Addie, who unobtrusively waggled her head. Addie entered Rose's office, asking over her shoulder, "How was the take last night?"

Rose followed, answering, "Big. Damn big. Best I ever done, matter of fact. Now today's another story, so far anyway. Everybody gettin' *Christian* on me, holing up and becoming do-gooders."

"I missed the divvying up this morning." Every morning Rose tabulated the previous night's take and gave each girl half of what she'd taken in. "I'll take mine now."

Rose went to her desk and opened a drawer. "Sure, Eve. You did all right. A hundred from that Jake alone. You must have something he likes." Rose tossed her a bag of gold dust.

Addie called, "Robert, would you come in here, please?"

Robert stepped around the doorway into the room.

Rose scowled. "Now just a minute! This is private, and no man puts foot in here unless I invite him!"

"Robert has come to escort me away. I'm leaving, Rose."

"Leaving? What does that mean—leaving?"

"For good."

Rose raised her big face and bellowed, "Ha! You might think so, Evie-honey, but you'll be back."

"I don't think so."

"You will be. Wait till those holier-than-thou women out there lift their skirts aside so they won't brush against you. Wait till the men who soaked their dinks in you treat you like you're invisible when they meet you on the street. Wait till one of them grabs you in an alley and thinks he'll get a little free. Wait till you run out of money and wish you could earn a dollar a minute without lifting a finger. You'll be back. Mark my words."

Addie's expression remained stolid. "I won't be taking any of my things. You can give them to the other girls."

"So you take up with him instead?" Rose shouted. "You think you won't still be a whore? Well, I got news for you, sister, you spread your legs for one or a hundred, it's all the same. Whether they give you gold or a place to live, you're still their whore! So go live with him then. Be his private whore! I don't care!"

"Goodbye, Rose."

"Don't you goodbye Rose me, you ungrateful bitch! You owe me!" Rose struck like a snake, grabbing Addie's hair. "Leaving me high and dry with an empty—"

Addie screamed.

"—bed and losing me money when I took you in and—"

Robert picked up a marble penholder and cracked Rose across the forearms.

"Mraaawk!" she squawked, releasing Addie. *"Flossie!"* she screamed, her face turning red as her hair. "Get the hell in here, Flossie!"

Robert said calmly, "We'll be going now." He put an arm around Addie's shoulders. "If you make any attempt to stop us, I'll break your arms—both of them. Tell your Indian woman the same goes for her. Tell her to let us pass."

Flossie had appeared in the doorway. Robert turned to her and ordered, "Step aside. Miss Merritt is leaving."

Flossie took one menacing step forward and Robert struck her with the marble penholder across the back of her left hand. She cried out and buckled halfway, couching the bruised hand against her thigh and moaning quietly.

"Excuse us, please," Robert said, reverting to his usual impeccable manners, herding Addie around Flossie.

"Stop them!" Rose shouted.

Flossie continued moaning and coddling her hand.

"I'll have the law on you, Baysinger! You can't barge in a person's home and assault them and think you can get away with it just because you own a goddamned stamp mill!"

Robert paused in the doorway and said to Rose. "I'd welcome the opportunity to recount before a circuit judge the scene that just happened here. Please do call Marshal Campbell. If he needs me he can find me at the home of Emma Dawkins having Christmas dinner. Merry Christmas, both of you."

In the parlor, the three men were sitting on the lips of their chairs, gaping at the hall. Robert set the hunk of marble on a table as he passed. "Good day, gentlemen. This belongs to Mrs. Hossiter. She'll be back to get it in a minute, I'm sure."

He and Addie were outside within three minutes of their arrival, the break made, the threats quelled. To Robert's amazement, they had strode no more than four steps when Addie folded and dropped, covering her face with both hands as she broke into intense weeping. He squatted beside her, curling a hand around her sleeve.

"Addie, what is it? Why are you crying?"

"I don't know . . . I don't kn-know . . ."

He drew her to her feet and put both arms around her, her face still covered with her gloved hands.

"Are you doing this against your will?"

"No . . ." she wailed.

"Do you want to stay?"

"No . . ." she wailed again.

"Then why are you crying?"

"Because . . . it's all I c-can do. They're my only fr-friends."

"I thought you said they were hard."

"They are, but they're my friends, t-too."

"I'm your friend. Sarah's your friend, and soon the Dawkins will be."

"I know . . . but I'm such a useless person. What good am I on this earth? I'll only be a burden to Sarah and to you."

"Shh. You mustn't talk that way. The burden was knowing you were in that place. Knowing you're making a clean break is lifting the burden, don't you see?"

She peered at him through streaming eyes. "Is it really, Robert?"

"Absolutely. And I never want to hear you say again what good are you on this earth. Whatever would it have been like for me if you hadn't been on it?"

"Oh Robert . . ." Behind her gloved hand her mouth trembled while a new waterfall of tears appeared. On the street before Rose's she flung both arms around his neck and repeated, "Oh Robert . . ." And after a moment, still sniveling, "Robert Baysinger, you'll make an honest woman of me yet."

He rested his hands on her waist and smiled, then pressed her away. "Would you like to stop at the hotel and wash your face before we go to the Dawkins'?"

She gave him a quavery smile, a nod, and he took her arm.

While Addie and Robert were checking her out of Rose's, Sarah was doing the same at Mrs. Roundtree's. Returning to the house, she packed a trunk, which she left, and a valise and bandbox, which she carried downstairs. She found her landlady in the kitchen, peeling apples into a crock bowl on her lap as she sat at a worktable.

"Good afternoon, Mrs. Roundtree," Sarah said from the doorway.

The woman looked up, her lips downdrawn. "I hope you told your sister not to come around here again."

Sarah replied brusquely, "I'll be vacating my room now, Mrs. Roundtree. I'm sure you'll have no trouble finding another renter. I'll send someone after my trunks first thing in the morning."

Mrs. Roundtree's mouth dropped open. "Well, there's no need to be hasty."

"My decision was made the moment you spurned my sister."

"What decent woman wouldn't after she's been soiling herself up there with the rest of those doves and taking money for it?"

Sarah pinned her with an audacious stare. "Charity, Mrs. Roundtree. Charity for those less fortunate than ourselves—I'd advise you to adopt it. My sister wants to reform, and I intend to do everything in my power to support her, beginning with my leaving here. While you're taking such a high-handed position, you might consider the intended spirit of this holiday. Is it *selective* love for mankind that Christmas stands for, or unbiased love for all?" Sarah tugged on one glove. "If in the future you should recognize yourself in one of my editorials, don't be surprised." She tugged on the other. "If anyone should ask, I'll be lodging at the Grand Central with my sister for a while. Good day, Mrs. Roundtree."

She left the house feeling the ardent zeal that so often drove her when she espoused a new cause.

The trio who arrived at the Dawkins' at four P.M. were in the formation that seemed to symbolize their relationship throughout their young lives—Addie in the middle, flanked by Robert and Sarah. Ever it would be, it seemed, the two stronger ones shoring up the weaker.

Emma, always the spokesman for her family, met them at the door and offered a handshake when introduced to Addie.

"Miss Adelaide," she said, "welcome. These are my children, Josh, Lettie and Geneva, and this is my man, Byron. We're awful pleased you could join us for supper. Mr. Baysinger . . ." She shook his hand. "You too. We're very fond of Sarah, and it just wouldn't do to leave her out of the holiday celebration. Your being her dear ones, well . . . shoot. This is right where you belong."

Emma's welcome assuaged the first of Addie's misgivings. Each family member followed with a welcome, the girls' shy, Josh's wide-eyed with curiosity, Byron's quiet but sincere.

They gathered at a table whose seating had been extended with planks between the chairs. Byron said a simple grace.

"Dear lord, we thank you for this food, these friends, and this wonderful Christmas season. Amen."

They ate a delicious meal of roast goose, mashed potatoes, apple dressing, cole slaw, candied yam pie and a bevy of breads and sweetmeats. Though Addie took little part in the conversation, she was neither excluded nor included to any greater degree than anyone else. The primary topic was last night's Christmas program and the impromptu triangle serenade that had taken the whole gulch by surprise.

Geneva said, "Mother let us leave the windows open and listen after we went to bed. Did you leave yours open, too, Sarah?"

"Yes, I did," Sarah answered, then grew pensive, remembering what had followed, wondering what it was like in the Spearfish Valley where he was, if he, too, was eating Christmas supper, when he would return, and if he was thinking of her at this moment.

Emma interrupted her reverie. She was speaking to Addie. "Your sister tells me you'd like to set up housekeeping but you don't know much about it. Well, that's all right. Most of us have a lot to learn when we do that. Anytime you want to learn to mix up a batch of bread, you just come on over to the bakery about five A.M. Heck, we might even put you to work!"

"Five A.M.?" Addie repeated dubiously.

"Shouldn't take you but three or four times and you'll get the knack."

"That's terribly early, isn't it?"

"Got to start that early to get the bread baked by nine."

"Thank you. I—I'll remember that when we find our house."

"No time like the present to get started, then by the time you find a place of your own you'll be as comfortable around the kitchen as these girls of mine."

"They bake bread?" Addie glanced in wonder at Lettie and Geneva.

"They don't need to with us owning the bakery. But they know how, and they know their way around a cookpot, too, don't you girls? Why, they made the cabbage salad and the sweet potato pie and helped with prett' near the whole meal. You're a little late getting started, but don't you worry, Miss Adelaide. We'll teach you what you need to know."

When they'd thanked the Dawkins and were heading to the hotel, Addie said despairingly, "Those young girls know more than I do."

"Well, of course they do," answered Sarah. "They've had a mother to teach them. Don't worry, though. If Emma says she can teach you, she can. And you won't have to learn everything overnight. Heavens, we don't even have our house yet."

At the hotel they parted in the hall. Robert gave them each a kiss on the cheek and said, "It's been a wonderful Christmas, thanks to you both. I won't be seeing you in the morning. I'll be going out to the mill early."

Addie watched him abjectly as he proceeded along the hall to his adjacent room. At his door he lifted a hand, sent them a smile and went inside.

Sarah watched and waited. After a long moment, Addie turned toward her. Sarah gave an understanding smile. "Without him, you're afraid again, I know. But I'm here for you, too, and you must not doubt that within yourself there is a strong, resilient person waiting to spring back and show the world her spirit. Come . . ." She held out a hand. "Let's go to bed, just as we used to when we were very small and afraid of the dark. Together."

Addie put her hand in Sarah's and they opened the door of room 11.

CHAPTER 16

*T*RUE Blevins happened to be in town, so Noah took him home to spend Christmas with his family. They rode out on horseback, since horses were faster and surer than a wagon at this time of year. They moved single file, in silence for the most part. The Spearfish Canyon was incredibly beautiful beneath its quilt of snow. Spearfish Creek, still open, whispered beneath thin-edged ice, then gurgled into the sunlight, breaking into a million reflected pinpoints of silver. Sometimes it disappeared underground to re-emerge later and become a surface stream again. Banks climbed from it, immense tumbles of great brown rocks amidst which an occasional mouth of a cave would appear, with animal tracks having worn away the snow at its door.

The pine-shrouded hills loomed up in silent majesty, the black-green branches of the ponderosas drooping like old shoulders clad in heavy ermine capes while overhead they hobnobbed with the very blue Black Hills sky. Here and there splashes of color appeared—a covey of red crossbills working among the conifer branches extracting seeds from pinecones; the brighter green of dog-haired pine growing in crowded, stunted clusters; the flash of a bluejay; the straight red pillars of the ponderosas themselves.

The silence was broken by the dull thump of the horses' hooves, the taunting of a crow, the chatter of the open water. A solitaire spiraled above the treetops singing its clear, musical warble. A doe came crashing through a thick stand of deerbrush in an old burn area, heeled sharply when surprised by the horses and bounded off the way she'd come.

True's mount whickered and sidestepped. Behind it, Noah's did too. True said, "Easy, girl," then moved on as before.

Noah did likewise, then relaxed in the saddle and took up thinking of Sarah Merritt again.

The woman had him in a tizzy. He should have dropped her to the bed last night and found out whether she was capable of melting or not. No, he shouldn't have. He'd done the right thing. But doing the right thing was so damned fustrating! So how the hell was a man expected to proceed with such a woman?

Sarah Merritt—her face came to him in vivid detail—*I don't know what to do about you.*

It struck him that for the first time in his life he wanted to court a woman and he didn't know how.

Court her?

The idea still terrified him.

He wanted to court a woman who was so excessively virtuous she could not allow herself to kiss a man without tearful recriminations? *He,* whose first sexual liaison had taken place at sixteen? *He,* who had since enjoyed women wherever he could find them? *He* wanted to marry a woman whose Puritanical virtue would in all likelihood lead to a lifetime of frugal caresses and dutiful subservience at bedtime?

It wasn't supposed to happen like this. If you fell in love with a woman she was supposed to get short-breathed and willful, like you. She was supposed to touch your face and your hair and your body like the soiled doves did, look into your face the way they did, only meaning it.

Instead, Sarah Merritt recoiled.

Yet she'd admitted she was attracted to him.

There was the puzzlement. If she was, and last night was an example of what he could hope to expect, where could it lead? Not every girl in Noah's past had been paid for. Some had been good, wholesome girls who favored him to the extent that denial became difficult. They were chaste girls like Sarah, yet they'd had what he considered a normal curiosity and appetite for seduction. If Sarah had acted like them— tempted rather than threatened—he'd be less confused, but she seemed to have the distorted idea that intimacy presumed wantonness, which was not true.

Nevertheless, he couldn't stop thinking about her. He pictured himself returning to the boardinghouse, knocking on her bedroom door and leaving it wide open while he said point-blank, *Sarah, I love you. Do you love me?*

The truth was he was deathly afraid she'd say no and he'd be decimated. Kissing a girl the way he'd kissed Sarah last night was supposed to give a man a clue to her feelings. Instead, the experience left him even more unsure and vulnerable than before, frightened because he was actually getting serious about the idea of marriage.

True slowed and waited until Noah came up on his left flank, then they walked their horses, side by side.

"You're quiet today," True remarked.

"Sorry."

"Actually, I don't need a man gabbin' my ear off to be comfortable with him."

"Guess I'm just tired. Those bells kept me awake last night."

"Me too. Sounded pretty though, didn't they?"

"Yup."

True turned and studied Noah lazily, as if waiting for Noah to say more. When he didn't, they rode on in silence. Soon they scaled a hogback and ahead of them stretched the Spearfish Valley with its hayfields lying like great white linens on a fallen clothesline. Chimney smoke rose in lazy plumes. Haystacks appeared like snow-covered hummocks in the unbroken expanse of white.

At his parents' house Carrie hugged them, Kirk took their jackets and Arden asked, "Have you seen Sarah? How is she? Is she seeing anyone?"

True's eyes nonchalantly passed to Noah, who ignored the question.

"Well, tell me!" Arden demanded.

Removing his hat, Noah replied, "Yes, fine, and I don't know."

"What do you mean, you don't know. You know everything that happens in that town. You make it your business to know!"

"I don't know."

"Well, that's a fine how-do-you-do!" Arden threw his hands in the air.

"Arden, for pity sake, quit nettling your brother," Carrie chided.

"I saw her at the Christmas program last night," Noah offered—a crumb in hopes of shutting Arden up. "She directed the children's choir."

"She did?" Obviously a crumb wasn't going to do the trick. "How'd she look? What was she wearing?"

"Hell, I don't know—True, how did she look?"

True said, "Like an angel."

"Damn! I knew we should've gone in and seen it. Didn't I tell you, Ma, we should go?"

"That's a long ride in there and back again the same day when Noah was coming out here anyway, and a person never knows about the weather at this time of year. Besides, I told you both, you and your pa, I didn't want to be in any hotel on Christmas Eve."

They had to recount every particular about the Christmas program. Noah left most of the telling to True, who went into surprising detail in describing Sarah's green jacket, her hair, even the angel costumes.

Noah turned to stare at True. What the hell was going on here? How did True remember all that? True's gaze rested on Arden throughout the recital, but from all he said Noah supposed True had seen him leaving with Sarah. If he did, he never mentioned it.

For Noah it was a flat day, in spite of True's presence, Carrie's home cooking and being with his family again. All the while he was in the valley, he kept wishing he were back in town. All the while he sat at his mother's table he kept wishing he were at Mrs. Roundtree's. All the while he faced Arden across it, he kept wishing he were facing Sarah instead.

Often he'd find himself taking no part in the conversation around him, remembering given moments during the last three months: the day Sarah had given him the Stetson and Andy Tatum had said, my guess is she's got an eye for you, Noah; the day he'd run into her on the boardwalk when she was taking the cat to her sister; the night he'd first kissed her in Mrs. Roundtree's kitchen.

They stayed overnight, he and True, and started for town at midmorning, beneath a sky turned turgid with gray-cheeked clouds that scudded and scowled, each one seeming to bear a face with a warning that their return trip would be colder than their trip up had been.

True again rode lead with Noah's gray gelding close on the mare's wind-whipped tail, closing rank even when Noah attempted to rein him back. In the deep canyons and creek-bottoms the wind eddied and whistled like a morning teakettle. It arched the tips of the pines. It lifted great sheets of snow from their branches and scattered them like puzzle pieces on the earth below. It plucked Noah's voice from his lips and hurled it at the back of True's head.

"Hey, True, you mind if I ask you something?"

True cranked his head ninety degrees to the right. His cheek bumped his upturned collar.

"Ask!" He had to shout to be heard above the wind.

"Remember that little Mormon girl you told me about, the one you wanted to marry?"

"Francie?"

"Yeah, Francie."

"What about her?"

"How did you know you loved her?"

Noah watched True bob up and down in the saddle. They were trotting on a fairly flat stretch of trail with a patch of paper birches on their right. True's hat was pulled low over his forehead. His wool collar nudged it from behind. Once again True turned his head to be heard.

"I knew 'cause making her happy in bed seemed less important than making her happy out of it."

Noah thought about that some. "You mean you took her to bed—a Mormon girl?"

"Nope. Never did. Wanted to, but I never did. I wouldn't've done that to her unless we were married."

They rode a while in silence, Noah feeling guilty for placing so much importance on Sarah Merritt's aversion to sex. All right, so that part shouldn't matter so much. If you were really in love the other things mattered more—respect, friendship, being able to talk to one another, enjoying a few of the same things, looking forward to being in the same room together.

"Hey, True?"

"Yeah?"

"Were you scared when you asked her to marry you?"

"Nope. I only got scared after I asked her and she said no—thinking about spending the rest of my life without her." The mare picked its way down a rocky incline and the gray gelding followed. True hollered back, "You get a little scared ever, thinking about spending the rest of your life without that little newspaper lady?"

"I figured you knew it was her."

"Doesn't take much guessing, watching the two of you in the same room. Like a pair of witching sticks above water."

"I didn't know it was so obvious."

"I saw you leave with her on Christmas Eve."

"I figured you did. Thanks for not telling Arden."

"Any fool could see she's not for Arden." True bobbed several more times before he shouted over his shoulder, "So you gonna ask her or not?"

"I've been thinking about it."

"Got that lump in your throat, do you? Like a cud caught sideways?"

"Yeah." The lump was there as Noah answered. He tried to swallow it but it stuck, even as he hollered at True's back. "She's scared of what happens in the bedroom, True. Real scared. Says she doesn't want to be like her sister."

True cocked himself sideways in the saddle and cranked his head clear around to cast a long glance back at his companion. The horses trotted along. Their manes lifted in the wind. Finally True faced front again.

"Now that's a problem," he called.

Back in town, Noah slowed his horse to a walk as he passed the office of the *Deadwood Chronicle*. Inside, the lanterns burned. He could see Bradigan and the Dawkins boy moving about, but not Sarah. Absurd, this overwhelming sense of disappointment, just because he'd expected to see her head beyond the gold leaf printing on the window when he passed by. He found himself looking in every window he passed, hoping to catch sight of her if only fleetingly.

He checked in at his office. Freeman Block, now a salaried deputy, reported that things had been quiet. No saloon fights, no trouble in the gambling halls, scarcely any traffic on the street yesterday.

Noah sent Freeman home and returned his horse to the livery barn, stopped by Farnum's store, bought six sticks of jerky and returned to his office to gnaw them and do paperwork.

The afternoon seemed to crawl. Sometimes he'd find himself staring at the street, wishing she'd walk by so he could make an excuse to go out and bump into her, talk a little bit, see her face and try to figure out if asking her to marry him was the right thing to do.

Sometimes he sat with his face in his hands, miserable for reasons too complex to unsnarl.

He left the office a good fifty minutes before suppertime, went up to Mrs. Roundtree's and took a sponge bath, combed his hair, shaved meticulously, trimmed the lower edge of his mustache with a scissor, splattered a little sandalwood vegetal on his cheeks and neck, put on clean clothes clear down to his hide and checked his pocket watch.

Ten minutes to supper.

He dropped the watch into his vest pocket, returned to the mirror and assessed his face. Funny-looking face—what would a woman see in it? Everything too round and high to turn a woman's head, plus that silly-looking dent in the end of his nose. Well, hell, it was the best he could do.

It felt like he'd been away from her for two months instead of two days. The five minutes before he left his room and clattered downstairs put grasshoppers in his stomach.

In the dining room the men all said hello, how had his trip out to the Spearfish been, how was his folks, was they getting snow up that way?

Mrs. Roundtree brought in a huge brown crock full of baked beans, a platter full of venison chops, a bowl full of pickled beets, a plate of sliced bread.

Noah glanced at Sarah's empty chair.

Mrs. Roundtree plunked into her own place at the head of the table and said, "There you are, gentlemen. Go to town."

Again Noah studied the chair where Sarah usually sat. So she was a little late. Unusual, but it *could* happen.

The venison platter came from Noah's left, went around the corner and took a long pass over Sarah's empty seat.

"Aren't we waiting for Miss Merritt tonight?" Noah asked.

"She moved out," Mrs. Roundtree replied tartly, looking down her nose as she stabbed a hunk of bread and passed it on. "Lock, stock and barrel."

"Moved out! When?"

"Last night. Sent the Dawkins boy after her trunks this morning."

"Where?"

"I didn't ask. Have some beets and pass them on."

"But why?"

Mrs. Roundtree leveled her disapproving gaze on Noah. "It's not my business to ask people why they come and go. You're holding up the proceedings, Mr. Campbell. Mr. Mullins is waiting for the beets."

Noah passed them on woodenly. She was gone! On the night when he'd pretty much decided to take her out for a walk and ask her to marry him, Sarah Merritt was gone. He figured he knew exactly why.

Supper tasted like fodder. He ate because he was expected to: to leave the table and run to find her would look most peculiar. All the men seemed to be casting him surreptitious glances, gauging his reaction to her absence. He avoided looking at her empty chair.

After supper he went upstairs to collect his gun and make his evening rounds. The *Chronicle* office was black. He stood a long time, looking in, feeling black himself. He could see the outline of his hat reflected in its windowglass, but could not make out his features.

You know perfectly well why she moved out of Mrs. Roundtree's, Campbell. She didn't want to deal with a rounder like you coming into her room in the dark of night and pestering her.

He pivoted and headed toward the next boardwalk, past the sound of a tinkling piano muffled by closed doors, past the laughter of men at the gaming tables, stopping beneath the overhanging roof of the boardwalk across from the Grand Central Hotel. She'd probably moved back there. If he stood here long enough she might come out. And he might cross the street and say, Hello, Sarah. Then what? Everything he imagined happening after that made him look like a lovesick fool, so he stomped into the Eureka Saloon, had a double belt of Four Feathers whiskey and went home to bed.

In the morning he awakened surly, remained surly through breakfast, and while he returned to his room for his gun, jacket and hat, and while he resolutely returned the Stetson to its peg on the hat tree, and while he plucked it off again and slammed it on his head, and muttered, "All right, I'll wear the sonofabitch."

They'd had snow overnight. He shoveled the boardwalk in front of his office, went inside and made a checklist of all the license taxes that needed collecting at the turn of the quarter, added wood to his stove, drank a cup of coffee that tasted like buffalo piss, stood staring out the window at the ruts in the street, sighed and gave up.

He needed to see her. Needed to spill what was on his mind. Needed to find out what was on hers. Needed to rid his gullet of this great lump of nothingness he'd felt since leaving her room on Christmas Eve.

There were four people in the newspaper office when he opened the door: Patrick Bradigan, running the handpress; Josh Dawkins, inking it with a brayer; Sarah's sister, Eve, folding newspapers at a long table on the side; and Sarah herself, wearing a leather apron, squatting over a bucket of turpentine, cleaning a hunk of metal with a brush. He passed the typesetter and apprentice, nodding to them. He passed Sarah's sister, saying quietly, "Hello, Eve." He gave them the barest edge of his attention. It was all for Sarah, who looked up and went very still when she saw him approach. She released the brush and rose, wiping her hands on a rag, her face smileless.

"Hello, Noah," she said.

He removed his brown Stetson, held it in both hands and asked, "Could I talk to you outside a minute, Sarah? It's personal."

"Of course," She set the rag aside and untied the leather thongs at her spine, took off the apron and donned a coat from the hat tree beside her desk.

She headed for the front door but Noah asked, "Could we go out back instead?"

Her gaze collided with his and slid away. "All right."

Her hair was pinned up in a neat coil, and the smell of turpentine followed her.

Outside the weather was much like yesterday, the wind picking up last night's snow and pelting it against her skirt and his trouser legs. She held the neck of her coat closed and turned to him as the wind whipped a strand of hair from its moorings into the corner of her mouth. She reached up and scraped it away, but it blew back immediately into her face.

He faced her with his hat pulled low, collar up, gloved hands joined before him like a ball and socket. He dropped them to his sides as he said, "I missed you at Mrs. Roundtree's last night."

She hesitated a beat before replying, "Yes, it was a rather sudden move. How was your Christmas?"

"It was . . . all right."

"And your family?"

"They're fine. Arden asked a thousand questions about you."

Her lips smiled, but her eyes remained fixed on Noah's as if she scarcely registered the remark.

"Aw, hell, Sarah, the truth is my Christmas was terrible. I kept wishing I was with you and I couldn't wait to get back, then when I did I found out you'd moved. You didn't have to do that, Sarah." He lifted one hand and let it fall. "I shouldn't have come into your room that night after you asked me not to, but I told you it wouldn't happen again, and I would have kept that promise."

"You think that's the reason I moved?"

"Well, isn't it?"

"No."

"Then what—"

"It's because of Addie. She's left Rose's for good."

"For good?"

"That's what she says."

"Well, that's . . . that's good news."

"At least we're hoping it's for good, Robert and I. He talked her out of there and brought her to see me, and we all had a delightful Christmas dinner at Emma's. But Mrs. Roundtree treated Addie abominably and told me if I wanted to visit with her I'd have to do it somewhere else from now on because she didn't want women like that in her house. So I got angry and . . . and I suppose a little bit retaliatory—after all, if a woman like Addie wants to reform and nobody will help her, what chance has she got? I gave Mrs. Roundtree the sharp side of my tongue and moved into a room at the Grand Central with Addie for the time being until we can buy a house of our own."

"A house of your own?"

"I've already talked to Craven and he thinks he may have one for us, but in the meantime, I'm so afraid Addie will go back that I won't let her out of my sight. That's why she's here folding papers. But as soon as we can find a house, Emma's going to teach her how to do house-keeping. That should keep her out of trouble."

He digested it all, watching the wind make flags of her hair, watching her scrape a strand of it away from her eye.

"I'm so relieved. I thought you were moving out to get away from me."

"No . . . not at all."

She met his eyes. For a while neither of them spoke.

"Can I tell you the truth, Sarah?"

She waited.

"I thought about you all the time I was gone, and I kept blaming myself over and over again, and telling myself that you're not like the women up at Rose's, and I should have known better than to go to your room. Sarah, I'm sorry for what I did . . . but on the other hand, I'm not, you see . . . hell, I don't even know how to say what I mean."

"I think you're doing quite well, Noah."

"Am I?" He looked rather miserable. "You're the one who's good with words. Sometimes when I try to say things to you they don't come out the way I intend them to."

"What you're trying to say is that you missed me."

"Yes . . . yes, I did."

"I missed you, too." The wind lifted a few strands of her hair straight up and settled some down across her forehead. "Christmas at Emma's was wonderful, but I kept wondering what the Spearfish Valley looked like, and where you were and what you were doing."

"Did you, Sarah?"

She nodded silently, looking square into his eyes.

The lump reappeared in his throat and breathing took a tremendous effort.

"This isn't the time or the place I'd planned to say this, not . . . not here in the alley by your woodpile. I thought I'd take you out walking up toward Mount Moriah some night when it was quiet and the owls were calling and . . . and . . ." He stumbled to a halt. Her blue eyes appeared silver, reflecting the leaden sky, waiting. "I think I love you, Sarah."

She seemed to lose her grip on her jacket front. Her lips parted and her eyes went wide and motionless. It took some time before she spoke in a voice airy with surprise.

"You do?"

"And I think we should get married."

She stood dumbstruck while he presented his case. "I thought about it all through Christmas, and I believe it's the right thing to do. Now, I know what you're thinking, that I've been around the horn a few times, and I have, but that doesn't mean a man can't change. And as

for your sister, I swear to you, Sarah, from this day forward I'll treat
her like she was my own sister. I know it's asking a lot of you to forget what . . ." He gestured toward the world behind his shoulder. ". . .
well . . . what's gone on up at Rose's, but that was before I knew you,
and everything's changed since then."

"Noah, I don't know what to say."

He studied her face with his heart racing while she stood utterly still,
only her hair lifting and falling like loose cobwebs. "Well, for starters,
you might tell me if there's any possibility that you love me too."

Her cheeks got very red and she dropped her gaze. "I think there's
a very good possibility of that, Noah."

"But you've been fighting it, right?"

She tactfully refrained from replying.

"Well, so have I," he admitted. They stood a while with the wind
eddying around them, wondering where to go from here.

"It didn't happen anything like I expected it to." He reached out his
gloved hands and took her by the upper arms, remembered how she
disliked being touched and dropped his hands. He glanced at the woodpile, pushed a stick of firewood in line with those beneath it. Pushed
a few others. "You weren't what I expected. I wasn't what I expected—I
mean, the way I acted."

"How did you think it would be?"

He gave up his preoccupation with the wood and faced her. "I don't
know, but I didn't think I'd be walking around miserable like this all
the time."

"Well, if it's any consolation, I'm miserable, too."

His voice softened. "But then I see you and it feels like everything
falls into place."

"Yes," she replied, "for me, too."

Silence passed.

He smiled.

She smiled back.

"Well?" he said quietly.

"Well . . ." she replied.

Their uncertain smiles remained while at his side his gloved hand
worked a piece of bark, then dropped it and became still.

"I know what I promised in your room on Christmas Eve, Sarah, but
is there any chance you'd like to kiss me?"

A tender, half-sad smile touched her lips. "Oh Noah," she said quietly, and moved toward him.

He moved, too—a step from each and their heads tipped, their mouths joined. It felt like starting at the beginning, standing in the brisk winter wind, tasting each other with cold lips and warm tongues, while a wellspring of emotion flooded their breasts. Their embrace was chaste, by anyone's standards, with his hands on her sleeves and hers on his jacket front. When the kiss ended they drew back to study one another's eyes while wind whistled between them.

"So what do you think?" Noah said at last. "Would we be less miserable together?"

Her hands remained on his heavy jacket. "Could I have some time to think about it, Noah?"

His spirits fell. "How much time?"

"Until I can be sure Addie won't backslide. If I told her now that I want to marry you, she'd have the perfect excuse to go back to Rose's. She's very unsure of herself, you see. In there—strange as it seems—she felt secure. She was paying her own way and she was accepted. Nobody pointed fingers at her. Out here, none of those things are true."

"How long will it take?"

"I don't know. I must find us a house—I think I should do that and get her accustomed to fending for herself. She doesn't know anything, Noah, not how to cook or to wash clothes or how to handle herself in gracious company. She never had to learn. Who'll teach her if I don't?"

"And if you buy a house, what about us? Are you saying that's where you'd want us to live?"

"I don't know. I hadn't thought that far ahead. Where did you think we'd live?"

"I haven't thought that far ahead either, but it wouldn't work for all three of us to live in the same house."

"No, of course it wouldn't. But there's no rush, is there? Why, we don't even have a preacher yet."

He hadn't thought of that either.

"So what are you saying? Yes, you'll marry me, but after we get a minister and after Addie's settled into a house of her own?"

She opened her mouth to say *I guess so* when she thought of her newspaper.

"What about the *Chronicle*?"

"You can still run it, can't you?"

"Not if we have a house and a family."

"Would you want a house and a family?" he asked. He was really asking if she wanted a family.

"Why, of course. When you get married those things just happen."

"But would you *want* them? *My* house and *my* family?"

The idea was new. She needed some time to think about becoming a mother. She would be as green at it as Addie was at housekeeping, yet who was there to teach her?

"Noah, one hour ago we were both rebelling against the idea of falling in love with each other, now we're discussing details that . . . that . . . oh Noah, I don't have answers for everything. Not this quickly."

He stepped back, feeling rebuffed. "All right, we'll let it ride for a while. Would you like a locket or a pin or anything like that?"

A puzzled frown crinkled her eyebrows. "A locket or a pin?"

"To seal the engagement? There's enough gold in this town to make you whatever you want."

He wasn't so much different from his brother after all. He suddenly seemed in a hurry.

"You want to make it official? You're sure?"

"If you do."

"Very well . . . a locket or a pin."

"Which one?"

"You choose."

They remained awhile, feeling some of the joy dribble out of the moment. "But Noah . . ." She touched his sleeve. "I would have to hide it for a while, otherwise Addie might feel she was holding me back."

His disappointment grew. He'd always imagined betrothals occasions for great celebration. Hell, if it were up to him he'd be proud to have her print in her newspaper that Noah Campbell and Sarah Merritt were engaged to be married and would do so as soon as the town got a preacher.

Nevertheless, he had to admit, "Yes, that's probably a good idea. I need time to tell my family first, too. Arden is going to be upset."

"It's strange, isn't it, how this all started? You with my sister and me with your brother while you and I found each other intolerable?"

"Well, somehow things worked out, didn't they?"

The sound of a whinnying horse carried to them on the wind while they stood in the shelter of the building, close enough to touch, but refraining.

"I'll miss you at the boardinghouse," Noah said.

"I'll miss you, too," she replied.

Her blue eyes wore an expression of longing that set off a reaction in his heart; still he waited, tethered by self-imposed restraints, afraid to assume he had the right to kiss her, even as her espoused.

"I've wanted to tell you something for the longest time," she whispered.

"Te—" His voice broke and he cleared his throat. "Tell me."

"I think you have the most beautiful hair I've ever seen."

"Oh Sarah . . ." They moved as one, into a swift embrace, her arms around his neck, his around her back, kissing open-mouthed while impatience pressed upon them like a gale. She clung, fitting her tongue to his, and her body to his, and her will to his. The first kiss ended and he held her head, taking a journey across her face with his mouth, strewing it with tiny bites and kisses.

"Oh Noah," she whispered, her eyes closed, her head thrown back as he kissed her throat. "All my life I thought I would live alone. I thought I would never have this . . . that no man would ever ask me to be his wife. I was so afraid of being unloved."

"Shh . . . no . . . no . . ." he whispered. "There's so much good in you it makes others good, and you're pure and fine and bright and brave. And you have the most beautiful blue eyes I've ever seen."

She opened her eyes and encountered his at close range. "Really?"

"Really." He smiled, still holding her head in his gloved hands.

A sluice of joy struck her. She beamed, and kissed him once more in celebration . . . then in yearning.

When their mouths were wet and their propriety threatened, he drew back, breathing erratically, and put distance between them.

"You'd better go inside now, Miss Merritt, and I'd better go back to work."

"Must we?"

"Yes, we must. But Sarah?"

"Hm?"

He kissed her nose. "Please hurry and get your sister settled."

They exchanged an intimate look that said the wait would be long, regardless.

"I'll try," she answered, and bidding him a reluctant goodbye returned to the newspaper office wondering how the others could possibly miss the glow that must be radiating from her like a nimbus.

CHAPTER 17

CRAVEN Lee found them a house with miraculous speed, eliminating the need for Sarah and Addie to take up temporary lodging at the rear of the newspaper office. A man named Archibald Mimms had moved into the gulch the previous spring and built the house for his wife and family who were to follow. In the meantime his wife had taken ill and been unable to travel. Two days after Christmas Mimms received a telegram bearing the news that his wife had died back in Ohio, and he left on the stage the next day to return to his children. To Craven Lee, he said, "Sell it with everything in it. I ain't never coming back to this hellhole. If I hadn't left Ohio in the first place my wife would still be alive."

The house had two rooms up, two down, and was cubic and unglamorous. Mimms had furnished it with only enough to get by, though he had taken advantage of the plastering craze in hopes of pleasing his wife. The plastered walls cut down drafts and added brightness, but the place lacked any other charm. One bedroom and the parlor were totally bare. The only covered windows were the two in the bedroom Mimms had used; they were covered with sacking that had been nailed to the window frames. The kitchen had a sparse collection of tinware and dishes, an oak table and four chairs, a dry sink and a good Magee range.

Sarah took one look at the place and decided two women with a sizable chunk of inheritance money could certainly dress it up enough to make it homey. Mimms had the gold dust in his pocket before he left on the stage, and four days after Christmas Addie and Sarah were outfitting for domestic life. More accurately, Sarah was outfitting, for Addie refused to accompany her sister when she went uptown to make purchases.

"The men all know me," Addie said, standing in their room at the Grand Central Hotel.

"So what?"

"They act strange when they see me away from Rose's, like I've got two heads or something. And there might be women in the shops."

"Addie, you have as much right to be there as anyone else."

"No . . ." Addie shrugged sheepishly. "You go."

"But Addie, what good did it do to break free of Rose's if you make yourself a prisoner here?"

"I'm not a prisoner. I'll go . . . sometime soon, but not just yet."

Sarah felt disappointed, but realized she could not force her sister back into the mainstream of life overnight. "Very well, I'll go alone. May I get you anything?"

"Some yard goods for dresses. Robert made me leave all mine behind. And some thread and chalk and needles. And buttons, I guess."

"There's a tailor in town. Why don't you just go see him?"

"I'd like to try making them myself. I can't do much—I can't darn Robert's socks—but after all the samplers Mrs. Smith made us stitch, I think I can make a dress. But I want you to use my money, please, Sarah."

They'd already butted heads about buying the house with the inheritance money, which Addie claimed she didn't want, but there was no other answer, of course. Still, Sarah understood Addie's necessity to cling to some figment of pride. "All right, Addie, I'll try to pick out something you'd like. Something blue if Andrew has it." Addie had always loved blue.

"Blue would be nice."

Sarah waited while Addie fetched the money from beneath her pillow. Accepting it, she tried to think of it not as tainted lucre, but as a contribution toward Addie's solid future.

"I'll have arrangements made for everything to be delivered to the house later on this morning. You'll be there?"

"Yes."

It was almost a test for Addie to leave the hotel all by herself and walk the few blocks to their house: in the five days since she had left Rose's this would be the first time she was left totally alone.

Sarah had her hand on the doorknob when Addie said, "Oh Sarah, please . . . one more thing?"

Sarah turned.

"Could you bring something to bleach out this dye?" Self-consciously, Addie plucked at her coarse black hair. "Robert just hates it."

Sarah returned to Addie and embraced her, feeling hopeful and happier than she had since Addie ran away from home. "I'll bring back the whole apothecary!"

Before she was done, Sarah had to enlist the help of Josh and Patrick to rent a wagon at the livery and bring it around to Tatum's General Store, followed by Parker's Apothecary, the meat market, Emma's bakery and the Grand Central, where they collected Sarah's possessions.

Mimms' clapboard house was located about halfway up the hill toward Mt. Moriah on the side of the gulch that caught the afternoon and evening sun. Mornings, it would be shrouded in shadow until ten o'clock, but at two o'clock when Sarah and her entourage arrived, it was awash in sunlight, reflecting off the snow. Smoke lifted from the chimney, and inside, Addie was happily washing windows while Ruler nosed the water in the bucket.

Patrick and Josh greeted her with smiles, carrying in a carved maple bed. "Hello, Miss Addie."

"We've nearly cleaned out Tatum's!" Sarah announced, breezing in behind them, "to say nothing of the apothecary and Farnum's Store."

Sarah had bought a wagonful. For the kitchen, a rocking chair, washtubs, a copper boiler, a hand wringer, Pearline washing compound, castile soap, brushes, floor oil, a broom, a supply of rags from Henry Tanby and Skitch Johnson, a willowware set of nested baskets, a pie safe, a good iron spider, a spice mill, a granite roaster, a set of Marlin dinnerware, a bone-handled carving set, tinned steel tableware, a glass vinegar crewet, and for the wall, a tin matchbox with matching comb case painted with crowing chanticleers in bright reds and oranges on an écru background.

For the front room, a three-piece upholstered parlor suite, an oval piecrust table, two banquet lamps, a large Smyrna rug, a library table, and to drape it with, a tapestry table cover, complete with tinseling and tasseled edge.

For upstairs there was new furniture for Addie's room, plus pillows, blankets, linen sheeting, brass wall hooks, bedwarmers, a peerless enamel chamber pot and Scotch crash for toweling.

For Sarah's own bedroom (the one previously used by Mimms) a fine drop-front desk and a center-draught bracket lamp for the wall beside it.

As Addie watched it all being carried in, her eyes grew wide. "So much! Should you have bought so much, Sarah?"

"Father did very well in St. Louis. He would have wanted us to have a nice home here."

Addie's face became expressionless as she stooped down to brush the seat of the divan.

The men came through and said, "Well, that's it!"

"Thank you, Patrick and Josh," Sarah said.

"We'll get that wagon back to the livery."

When they were gone, Sarah said, "Addie, come see the sewing supplies I bought you."

For the only occupation in which her sister had expressed an interest or a hint of confidence, Sarah had admittedly overindulged. There were twenty yards of white goods, a length of woolen druggeting in ink blue, another in deep cranberry with tiny flecks of bone-gray, some plain homespun in two designs, tinted muslin, a small piece of beaver cloth cloaking, satin surah for lining, buttons, dress braids, hooks and eyes, ribbons, cording, elastic, dress reeds, lead dress weights, brass pins and an ebony sewing box containing eight spools of cotton, a thimble and a pincushion shaped like a strawberry.

When the packages lay strewn about the parlor, Addie seemed pleased and said, "Thank you, Sarah. I'll try to do Mrs. Smith proud."

"I've bought us each something special—something just for ourselves."

Addie rose, sweeping a hand over the collection. "This isn't special?"

"No, not really. This is mostly things we need, and they're not nearly as good as anything we had in St. Louis. I'm only sorry I couldn't buy you a spinet. But if the railroad ever comes through here, you can be assured I will. Meanwhile, I thought we should each have something very elegant and personal to remind us that we were brought up among good taste and fine things." Sarah held out a package. "For you."

Addie reached out reluctantly.

"Oh Sarah . . ."

"Sit down on our new divan and open it."

Addie perched gingerly on the dusty-rose divan and placed the parcel in her lap. From its wrapping of cotton wadding she withdrew matching glove- and handkerchief-boxes of fine, translucent opal glass. On their covers hand-painted florals were surrounded by raised, gilded rococo ornamentation. When Addie had run away from home she had left behind many such pretties, gifts from their father, or from Mrs. Smith, or from Sarah herself. The pieces were expensive and finely crafted. She ran her fingers around and around the gilded rim of one cover.

Watching her, Sarah said, "Two times now you've been forced to leave your personal belongings behind. These you'll have for keeps."

"Oh Sarah, they're beautiful."

Across the cluttered room, Sarah felt a wisp of maternal care just as she'd experienced many times after their mother left, in those days when she would try in any small way to make up for the loss. Addie truly wasn't very bright, but she had always loved bright things and had felt comforted by having them around her.

"Addie . . ." Sarah called quietly. Addie looked up from the handkerchief box. "I'm sorry I said what I did about you being spoiled and not having to work at the newspaper office when we were young. I loved it there, truly I did, just as I knew you didn't. And I was good at it, just as I knew you weren't. What I said was cruel and self-serving. Forgive me."

Addie set down the handkerchief box and replied, "It doesn't matter. It's all behind us now."

Abruptly shifting moods, Sarah said perkily, "Would you like to see what I got?"

Addie found her smile. "Not a glove or hanky box, I'm sure."

Sarah laughed. She had never been the glove-box type. From another roll of wadding she took a flint-crystal writing set with two silver-capped ink bottles and a pair of fine pens on an embossed silver base.

"For my new desk." She held it aloft.

"It's very pretty," Addie said. "But I'm glad I got my handkerchief boxes instead."

Again they laughed. With the good mood restored, Sarah put her writing set on the library table, pushing aside other items. Turning, she searched the parcels on the floor. "And I did stop by the apothecary as you asked." She found the correct bundle, dropped to her knees and began rooting through it while the inquisitive cat came to investigate the crackle of paper and paw at the tangle of string. "I'm not sure what will get rid of hair dye, so I brought everything . . ." Item by item, she set them on the floor. "Salts of lemon, oxalic acid, lye, Borax, salts of tartar, dry ammonia, carbonate of soda, Fuller's Earth Water, and if none of those work, something called Magic Annihilator, which Mr. Parker said truly does work miracles—if it doesn't rot your hair out of your skull."

"I can't wait! Will you help me, Sarah?"

"As soon as we get our house in order."

The two women set about unpacking the purchases, putting their furniture in place, making a home out of a house. They put dishes on Mimms' crude kitchen wall shelf, food in the pie safe, a blue and white checked cloth on the kitchen table. In the late afternoon they made a pot of coffee and spread lard on slabs of Emma's bread, cut cheese and shared their first repast. Afterward, they sat down with needles to hem sheeting for their beds, then made them up in tandem. They hung Sarah's new wall lantern, filled it and a table lamp for Addie with coal oil, set out their new ornaments and stood back to admire their rooms. On Sarah's new desk the pen set reflected the lamplight. On Addie's new bureau the glass boxes added a touch of femininity. Ruler had already curled up on Addie's bed.

She stood in the doorway, perusing the room, genuinely excited for the first time since leaving Rose's.

"A room of my own . . ."

From the opposite doorway Sarah added, "And a room of my own. Now I won't have to spend so many evenings at the newspaper office."

Addie remarked, "We need some rugs."

"We'll get them, and some curtains and maybe even some wallpaper when spring comes and the freight wagons start rolling again."

"And we'll plant some flowers around the kitchen door the way Mrs. Smith used to."

"Absolutely." Sarah took it as a good sign: Addie was planning a future.

Addie turned to Sarah and asked, "Now could we work on my hair?"

With evening fallen and the lamps lit, they hung sheeting over their kitchen windows, stripped Addie down to her shift and set about bleaching the dye out of her hair. First they tried plain glycerine soap; next, oxalic acid mixed with salts of lemon. The rinse water looked murky, but Addie's hair remained black as tar. Next they tried the Magic Annihilator. It smelled like it could rot the heads off nails but removed no more dye than the other solutions had. Finally they dissolved lye, Borax, salts of tartar and dry ammonia in hot water. It stung Addie's eyes and nearly stopped her breath, but the color began fading. Addie leaned over the dry sink while Sarah dipped cup after cup of the acrid mixture over her hair and massaged it through the strands.

"Addie, I think it's working!"

"Is it really?" Addie said, upside down.

"Look at the water!"

"I can't. If I open my eyes I'll go blind."

"The water's all black. Wait—I'm going to dump it and make another batch." Sarah took the basin and slung it in the yard. She mixed up a second batch of the fetid brew and watched it grow darker and darker with each trip through Addie's hair.

During the third batch she reported enthusiastically, "You're getting gray, Addie! And grayer and grayer!"

"Oh Sarah, hurry! I'm dying to see!"

Finally Sarah threw away the last basin of solution and rinsed Addie's hair with plain water, then with Fuller's Earth Water. She wrapped her sister's head with a length of their new toweling, jostled it around a few times and ordered, "All right, take a look."

When the towel fell away, Addie took up a hand mirror to examine the results. Her hair stood up in spikes—not exactly blond, but certainly not black. Rather midway between—the color of old nickel.

Looking forlorn, Addie plucked at the spikes as if stripping seeds from them.

"It's not blond."

"But it's lighter than it was."

"But I wanted it to be blond."

"Sit down, let me comb it."

Addie sat, looking in the mirror while Sarah attempted to draw a comb through the snarls. It took some doing. When the comb would finally cut through, Sarah opened the oven door and said, "Pull your chair back here." Addie moved her chair near the warmth, slumped low on the seat and closed her eyes while, in silence, Sarah combed her hair.

During those minutes of silence, while the older sister ministered to the younger, they recovered something of what they had lost as siblings. The room was cozy—lamplit, curtained, quiet. Some soot tumbled down the stovepipe in a rush of muffled ticks. The teakettle hummed softly. Upstairs, the cat slept.

"Sarah?" Addie said.

"Hm?"

"I've been thinking . . ."

"About what?"

"Robert."

"Mm . . ."

"He invited me to go out with him on New Year's Eve, first to supper and then to the Langrishe."

"And what did you say?"

"Nothing yet. But I don't want to go."

"Robert will be disappointed."

"I was thinking . . ."

Sarah continued combing. "You were thinking . . ."

"That maybe I could invite him here instead."

"Well, of course you can. You don't need my permission."

"I thought maybe I could invite him for supper, but I don't know how to cook."

"Certainly I'll help you, if that's what you're asking."

Addie boosted up and cranked around to look back at Sarah. "You will?"

"I'm not the world's most experienced in the kitchen, but I know a little from watching Mrs. Smith, and what we can't figure out we can ask Emma. Now, about that hair. The ends are snagged. Should I try trimming them?"

"Do you know how?"

"No better than you probably. No worse either."

"Should I trust you?" There was an actual gleam in Addie's eye.

"No," Sarah replied, grinning as she went to find the shears.

Addie submitted and Sarah went to work, dropping nickel-colored floss on the floor. When she was finished, Addie swept up the trimmings and stitched them into a small piece of cheesecloth. She coiled her hair around the rat, flattened it against the back of her head and with four deft stabs hairpinned it into place.

"There are some things, Addie, that you do a hundred times better than me. A remarkable improvement."

Addie looked pleased. "Do you think Robert will approve?"

"He'll love it. You look like a *hausfrau.*"

Addie checked the hand mirror once again. "I do, don't I? I never really liked the black either."

"It's late. I'm tired, how about you?"

They replenished the woodbox from the pile Mimms had left in the backyard, stoked the range, set the dampers and retired to their rooms upstairs. Ruler came into Sarah's room while she was getting ready for bed, did a turn around her ankles, checked out her bed and returned to Addie's room for the night, where—it was apparent—the feline would make her permanent nest.

When the lanterns were extinguished the two women settled into their rooms beneath their crisp, new sheets which smelled faintly like clean-picked flax in a dry bin.

Sarah lay for some time, looking at the dark ceiling, unable to feel drowsy in the strange bed, with the window in a strange place, and the faint snow-light coming in from an odd angle.

She thought of Noah, of how much she'd missed him over Christmas, and of how her face had grown hot when she'd looked up and seen him entering the newspaper office, how her pulse had leaped and her hands had gone motionless. She relived the minutes out by the wood-pile before he'd kissed her, all the insurgent feelings that had risen up and deluged her, the wondrous shock when he'd said he loved her and had proposed marriage.

How incredible that she, who in her first twenty-five years attracted no more male attention than a garden scarecrow should, within three months of arriving in Deadwood find herself in love and loved by a man who wanted to spend the rest of his life with her.

"Addie?" Sarah called quietly. "Are you awake?"

"Yes."

"Would you mind if I invited the marshal for New Year's Eve?"

After a pause, Addie answered, "Why should I mind?"

"I just thought I should ask."

"The marshal's a very nice man, Sarah, and I have no claims on him."

Sarah smiled. "We'll make it supper for four then."

On New Year's Eve Sarah closed the newspaper office at four and went by Emma's to pick up bread, and by the butcher shop where, to her great delight, she found a rare supply of beef. Back then to Emma's to find out specifics about how to cook a roast.

At home she entered to find their kitchen transformed.

"You've made curtains!" she exclaimed.

"You like them?"

"Oh Addie, they're wonderful!" They were far less glamorous than any they'd had in Missouri, but so few buildings in Deadwood had curtains that any were a luxury. Addie had simply hemmed long rectan-gles of white sheeting, sewn lace on the fourth side, driven nails into the upper corners of the window frames and draped the curtains over them as swags. Below she'd used flat pieces the size of the window opening with buttonholes worked into the top corners. When Sarah entered, they hung on nails to the left of each window.

"We can cover them at night . . . see?" Addie demonstrated, stretch-ing a curtain across a window and catching the buttonhole on the far nail.

"Ingenious! And ever so much easier than tacking up sheeting every night. And a bouquet, too . . . Adelaide Merritt, what a regular domes-tic you're becoming!" On their blue and white checked tablecloth Addie had put a bowl of pine sprigs.

"I thought we should have something special for tonight."

"You went out," Sarah noted, pleased.

"Just up to the cemetery. Nobody goes up there much in winter."

"It's a start. The kitchen looks lovely, Addie, truly it does. But listen—we must hurry. I've brought a roast of beef and Emma told me just what to do with it."

Sarah showed Addie how a roast is seared, and smothered in onion and bay leaf and covered with its own drippings and baked in the oven. They peeled potatoes and scraped carrots and cobbled up some tinned peaches and left them baking in the oven while they went upstairs to dress.

Addie wore a new dress she'd stitched from the blue wool druggeting. It was simple, collarless, with sleeves gathered onto dropped shoulders and a skirt gathered onto an unadorned bodice. She drew her nickel-colored hair into a tasteful French roll and left her scrubbed face un-painted.

"I look terribly pale this way, don't you think?" she asked, coming around the corner into Sarah's room. "Why Sarah . . ." Addie's face went flat with surprise. "While I'm bleaching myself out you're turning into a butterfly. Where did you get it?" Addie took a turn around Sarah's burnt-orange dress. It was made of silk and had a bustled rear, swagged like the kitchen curtains and gathered up onto three covered buttons at the lumbar bend.

"It's an old one I haven't worn since I've been here. I got it for Christmas two years ago, but I hardly ever had an occasion to wear it afterward."

"And your hair. You've curled your hair?"

"Just a little, with the tongs, yes." Sarah laughed at Addie's astonishment. "Well, I *have* curled it before, you know. And after all, it's New Year's Eve. I wasn't going to wear my leather apron and my sleeve guards."

Addie's expression turned amused. "The marshal's going to drop his rocks."

Sarah laughed. "So is Robert. Your dress turned out heavenly. And wait till he sees your hair."

"Don't change the subject, Sarah. What's going on between you and the marshal?"

"The same thing that's going on between you and Robert—nothing. We're simply going to enjoy a festive New Year's Eve together."

The gentlemen arrived promptly at seven P.M., meeting on the street leading up the hill. Noah bore a bottle of port and Robert another of sherry.

"Fancy meeting you here, Baysinger," Noah said when the two found their paths merging. "Are you going where I suspect you're going?"

"Up to Addie's."

"And I'm going up to Sarah's. Looks like we're spending New Year's Eve together, eh?"

The two had never been cordial, largely on Noah's part, because he'd never lost the suspicion that Baysinger held a great attraction for Sarah. He set his antagonism aside, however, as the two climbed the street toward their destination.

"I was surprised to hear about Addie leaving Rose's. Sarah is pleased."

"So am I."

"You talked her out of there, did you?"

"I did."

"The men of this town won't thank you."

"Does that include you?"

"Not anymore it doesn't."

"That's good, because Addie is an old friend. Her welfare is far more important to me than the whims of a bunch of randy miners."

They reached Mimms' house and approached the door together. Pausing, each allowed the other the opportunity to knock. With a flourish of one hand Noah gave Robert the go-ahead.

His knock was answered promptly by Sarah.

"Hello, Robert. Hello, Noah. Come in."

Robert looked dumbstruck, gazing at her. Up. Down. Up again. At last he moved toward her. "Sarah—you look wonderful!" Without compunction he kissed her cheek, which she willingly offered.

"Why, thank you, Robert."

"I'll double that," Noah put in, swallowing his jealousy as he received only her hand in greeting.

"Thank you, Noah. May I take your coats?" She hung them on brass wall hooks beside the door.

"For you . . ." Noah said, handing her his bottle.

"Also for you," put in Robert, doing likewise.

"My goodness . . ." She lifted the bottles to examine their labels. "Spirits."

"Allowable, I believe, to toast the new year," Robert said.

"Certainly. Thank you both." She gave each a smile. "Addie's still upstairs. She'll be here in a moment." She raised her voice and called, "Addie, the gentlemen are here." And to the men, "Please sit down."

Noah did, on the edge of the divan. Robert, however, took a turn around the room, remarking, "You two have been busy, haven't you?"

"As beavers. What do you think of it?"

"I approve. Ah . . . this looks familiar." He opened the cover of the family Bible which lay on the library table.

"I brought it over from the newspaper office. I thought it belonged in the house."

Noah watched and listened, jealous once more because he could share nothing of Sarah's past as Baysinger could.

"There's your father's writing. Sarah Anne, born May 15, 1851. Adelaide Marie, born June 11, 1855. Ahh, we ate a lot of Mrs. Smith's sour-cream cakes on those days, didn't we?"

Noah had not known until that moment the date of Sarah's birth, much less celebrated it with the sour-cream cake of the revered Mrs. Smith, nor could he recognize the writing of Sarah's father. He wondered if there would ever be, between himself and Sarah, the easygoing closeness she shared with Baysinger.

"Hello, Marshal. Hello, Robert," Addie said at that moment from the doorway.

Robert glanced over his shoulder. The Bible cover fell from his fingertips and plopped shut. For a moment he thought someone else stood at the foot of the steps. Her hair was nearly silver, swept back simply and becomingly. Her dress was dark, with Puritan lines. There was no paint on her face.

"Addie?"

"It's me."

"Your hair . . . it's not black anymore."

"Sarah did it." She touched it, tipping her head. "It didn't get quite as light as we'd hoped, but it'll have to do until it grows out or until some fresh lemons come into town."

Robert went to her, took her by the arms and scrutinized her at close range. "Well, *this* is cause for celebration."

They had a lighthearted evening, enjoying each other's company with increasing relaxedness. Noah found, much to his surprise, that the longer he was around Robert the more he liked him. Baysinger had a ready smile, an artless way with both women, and he laughed easily. To Noah's increasing amazement, he found that the three of them acted like unilateral friends. If there was another side to the relationship of Robert with either woman, it certainly didn't show. They teased one another, told amusing stories about their youth, and, as Noah laughed with them, his jealousy faded.

Supper itself was plain fare, but a joy to eat among the company of friends his own age and in the kitchen with its cheery atmosphere.

"I envy you," Noah said to the three at one point. "Still such good friends after all these years."

"Envy us no more," Robert said, raising his glass. "Join us. To a long and endearing friendship among the four of us! Let tonight be the first of many such nights to come."

"Hear, hear!" Four glasses clinked and they all sipped sherry. When the meal was finished and the dishes set aside, they played Parcheesi. As the competition became good-naturedly cutthroat, the men removed their sack coats, unbuttoned their vests and rolled up their sleeves.

At five minutes before midnight they refilled their glasses and counted down the hour with Noah acting as clock watcher, holding his pocket watch in his hand.

"Five, four, three, two, one . . ."

"Happy new year!" they chorused, exuberantly clinking glasses together, partaking of port before exchanging a round of kisses across the kitchen table.

Robert kissed Addie.

Noah kissed Sarah.

Then Robert kissed Sarah and Noah kissed Addie.

The men shook hands.

The sisters hugged.

"Should auld acquaintance . . ." Robert began, and the others joined in.

When the song ended, the silence was tinged with melancholy.

Robert spoke for of all of them. "We all have old acquaintances we've left behind, acquaintances we miss, but, thanks to all of you, especially you ladies for gathering us all together, it's been the best night I've spent since coming to Deadwood. Here's to a promising year ahead, and happiness for all of us."

"Hear, hear!"

After emptying his glass, Noah drew a deep breath and said, "I'm sorry to break this up, but I promised Freeman I'd spell him at midnight so he can do a little celebrating himself. Walk me outside, Sarah?"

As they rose, Robert tactfully decided, "I think Addie and I will have one more glass of port."

Outside, Noah said, "Thank you. It was fun, and I like Robert."

"I'm glad." She hung her head back. "That way the four of us can do more together. Oh my, look at those stars. Aren't they heavenly?"

"Mmm . . ." He gave them a glance. "What did you tell Robert and Addie about us?"

"Nothing. Only that we're friends." Her head still hung as if on a rubber support. "Heavenly stars . . ." She giggled.

He peered at her more closely. "Why, Miss Merritt, are you tipsy again?"

She drew her head up with a great effort. "Why, I believe I am, Mr. Campbell, and it's quite delightful." Another lilt of mirth escaped her.

"You're giggling!"

"So I am, but it's all your fault. You brought the port."

"So the woman I'm going to marry occasionally overindulges, does she?" He found himself grinning.

"Mmm . . . disgraceful, isn't it?"

"Absolutely."

"So arrest me." She flung her arms around his neck and let her body thump against his. "You've got the gun and the star. Go ahead, arrest me, Marshal Campbell," she challenged, an inch from his nose.

He kissed her, full and hard upon the mouth, and when it ended they were both breathing like stopped trains. Her giggling was gone. His grin was, too.

"It's freezing out here," he said, unbuttoning his sheepskin jacket and holding it open. "Get in here with me."

She had come outside without her coat and went willingly against him, sliding her arms around his trunk where it was warm and the sheepskin furry and his body very solid. He folded his jacket around her shoulders and doubled his arms around her.

"I like this new side of you," he said, the words caught low in his throat.

"I'm shameless."

"Then always be shameless," he replied as his lips covered hers again and he drew her hips flush to his. They tasted port upon one another's tongues, and felt the heat of two bodies straining together in the chill of the night—breasts, bellies, knees—until delightful suppression became agony, and he sensibly broke away.

He groaned a little and took in a big gulp of air.

"I am shameless," she whispered against his jaw, the scent of his leather vest and his skin warm in her nostrils.

"No, it's just the port."

"Something remarkable has happened, Noah."

"What?"

"Anxiety. All the while I sat across the table from you, calmly playing Parcheesi, I was worrying that we wouldn't get a moment alone."

"I was anxious, too, because I brought you something."

"What?"

He produced it from his pocket, wrapped in an envelope of velvet. "To make it official."

"A brooch." She withdrew from inside his jacket, took the brooch and held it up as if to catch the starlight. "My betrothal brooch . . ."

"Yes."

"I can't see it."

"Here." He found a wooden match in his pocket and struck it on his bootheel, then held it cupped in his hands. By the meager light she examined the pin. It was shaped like a wishbone with a rose on its left branch.

"A wishbone . . . it's beautiful, Noah." She had begun to shiver.

"And a rose, for love. I know you can't wear it where Addie can see it, but you'll find a hidden place, I'm sure." The match burned short and he shook it out.

"I will. I'll wear it every day. Thank you, Noah."

"You're shivering. You'd better go in before you catch a cold."

"Yes . . . Addie and Robert will be wondering."

"Thank you for the supper."

"Thank you for the brooch . . ." She smiled. "And the port."

He went away several steps, returned and kissed her softly on the mouth.

"I love you, though it still amazes me."

"I love you, too."

CHAPTER 18

*E*IGHT days later, on a Sunday night, Robert and Noah had supper with the Merritt sisters again, setting a precedent for the weeks that followed. The foursome met often after that, to share a meal, or popcorn, play games or visit. Sometimes they had long discussions that lasted late into the night on such varied topics as true happiness; men's right to expectorate on the street; women's revulsion at men who expectorate in the street; the possibility of raising lettuce in the dead of winter using a cold frame; what makes popcorn pop; and the effect of weather upon human emotions. As the winter advanced, their friendship became cemented, taking the edge off the dreary season with its short days and bleak snows.

Meanwhile Sarah's newspaper reported the events of the new year, 1877. In Washington, a new president and vice president took their oaths of office. In Philadelphia, the U.S. Centennial Exhibition closed down. In Minneapolis the state's first telephone switchboard opened at the city hall. In Colorado a naturalist named Martha Maxwell discovered a new species of bird called the Rocky Mountain screech owl, while another woman named Georgianna Shorthouse was sentenced to three years in prison for performing an abortion. Out of New York came the remarkable news that a woman could detect when she was pregnant by keeping careful daily measurements of her neck, which would swell immediately upon her getting in the family way. Electric clocks, run by batteries, invented by a German named Geist, were beginning to appear in American homes. Throughout all of America, trade in cattle hides had completely replaced that in buffalo hides.

Closer to home, the legislature of Dakota Territory convened in Yankton, the capital, while in Washington the national legislature did the same, their ratification of the Indian Treaty finally and officially opening the Black Hills to legal white settlement. The inclement weather brought a respite from robberies on the Deadwood Stage Line.

In Deadwood itself offerings at the Langrishe changed weekly. Flour was selling for $30 per hundred. A fellow named Hugh Amos shocked the town by committing suicide, apparently due to loneliness. Another fellow named Schwartz slipped and fell on the boardwalk in front of the Nugget Saloon and sued the owner over his broken arm. Local business-men were encouraged to spread wood ashes on their boardwalks to prevent such mishaps from occurring. The females of Deadwood were invited to meet at the office of the *Deadwood Chronicle* to form a Ladies' Society whose functions would be both social and charitable.

The formation of such a group had been on Sarah's mind for some time. Not only did the local women need to socialize; by banding together they could have a domesticating influence on the entire gulch. The town needed a library. Until a school was built, children—and adults, as well—needed a source of reading material. What a wonderful head start a library could give their school when it was eventually built. Sarah saw a women's group as the perfect organization to begin collect-ing and cataloguing books for the cause.

The problem of men spitting on the street was more than aesthetic. Not only did the women's hems trail in the effluvia, it spread disease. Since the smallpox epidemic Sarah had written one editorial about the health hazards engendered by the habit, but she'd seen little improve-ment. A women's group could work on a campaign to educate the men about hygiene and perhaps make anti-expectorating signs and post them around town.

On the social side, the women might discuss books, read poetry, exchange seeds for their spring gardens, plan Fourth of July celebra-tions, perhaps invite a temperance advocate to speak.

It was Sarah's hope, too, that she might use the group to inveigle Addie out of the house and into the good graces of the townswomen. However, on the night of the first meeting Addie refused to go.

"I'm not ready yet," she said.

"When will you be?"

"I don't know. Maybe when my hair grows out." Addie's natural blond was beginning to show at the roots.

"If they see you there beside me, in *my* newspaper office, joining a group whose intent is to do charitable work, who'll cast stones?"

But Addie refused to go and the group was formed without her. At their first meeting they avidly embraced Sarah's suggestion and dedicated themselves to their first project: the collection of books for the Deadwood Public Library. Sarah offered to keep the volumes in the *Chronicle* office and put Josh in charge of lending them out until other arrangements could be made.

The ladies agreed with Sarah that when the town found a schoolteacher he would be overjoyed to discover the citizens had been forward-thinking enough to have already established a lending library. They believed, too, that the building of a school should be of primary concern to all of Deadwood, since it would draw more families to the town, come spring.

Yes, they agreed, the school should come first before a church.

In early February, however, a telegram arrived from a man named Birtle Matheson, who agreed to become Deadwood's minister. He was a Congregationalist and would be arriving in early April.

The news caused a great stir of excitement, not the least of which was displayed by Noah Campbell, who, upon hearing it, went directly to the *Chronicle* office.

"Sarah, can you come with me for a few minutes?"

"Certainly. What's going on?" She got her coat and they headed outside, striding side by side down the boardwalk.

"Deadwood's getting a minister."

She halted in her tracks. "When?"

"The first of April. A fellow named Matheson from Philadelphia. A telegram just came in this morning."

"Well," she said on a puff of breath, leaving an undecided note in the air.

"We can set a date now," Noah said.

"But what about Addie?"

"Addie can take care of herself."

"She still refuses to leave the house."

"Then it's time you force her."

"How?" Sarah resumed walking and Noah stayed with her, step for step.

"Stop babying her. Stop delivering everything she needs to her doorstep. Stop going to the butcher shop, and the grocer's, and Emma's every day for bread. The agreement was that she'd take care of those things for you, but you've continued to do it all and run the newspaper, too. Does she even cook?"

"She tries." Addie did try, but her cooking was abysmal.

"Maybe Robert and I have added to the problem by providing just enough social diversion to keep Addie happy without having to leave the house. Maybe we should insist on the four of us going to the theater sometime instead of holing up the way we do."

"I confess, I'd rather hoped that Robert might ask Addie to marry him and our problem would be solved, but he seems quite content with a platonic relationship. Has he mentioned anything to you?"

"Nothing. Which brings us back to you and me and setting a date."

Sarah was torn. What would Addie do if forced to live alone?

"I feel a responsibility toward Addie."

"And none toward me?" His voice took on an edge.

"I didn't say that."

"You're not her mother, Sarah."

"No, I'm not. But if she had one, chances are she wouldn't have gone astray, so who cares about her? Who helps her? Now that I've gotten her out of Rose's shall I simply abandon her?"

"Living across town isn't exactly abandoning her."

"Living where?"

"I've found us a place."

"You have?"

"Amos's."

"Hugh Amos's?" She came to a stop.

"It's for sale."

"But Noah . . ."

He turned around and went back to her. She wore an expression of wide-eyed repugnance.

"He didn't kill himself in the house, Sarah, he did it out at his mine."

"I know that, but . . ." Hugh Amos had used his shotgun. Sarah had reported the suicide. How could Noah blame her for balking?

He mulled awhile, looking annoyed. Abruptly he grabbed her hand and ordered sternly, "Come with me." They were three doors from his office. He hauled her to it, took her inside and closed the door behind them. At the rear two new jail cells stood empty. A blue granite coffee-pot stood on the chrome fender of a small, oval woodstove. It was warm in the room, and private.

Noah swung around and clamped Sarah by the shoulders. "All right, I want to know the truth. Do you want to marry me or not?"

"It's not that simple."

"Yes, it is that simple. Either you want to or you don't."

"I want to, but—"

"Dammit, Sarah, you find enough reasons to put it off! You won't tell Addie because she might go back to Rose's. You don't want Amos's house because he shot himself. You won't set a date because we don't have a preacher. Well, now we've got one, and I'm asking you to make it official. I want to set a date and tell my family and tell your sister and get on with our lives."

His insistence left her silent. There were times when she recognized in herself hints of dispassion. If not dispassion, certainly a more controlled passion than his, coupled with a reluctance to commit to all that marriage would entail: the sudden overturning of her life, which had just achieved a satisfying orderliness; sexual submission, which filled her with a certain amount of dread; and along with sexual submission, children, whose arrival would signal the exchange of her leather apron for a cotton one; the end of her newspapering—at which she was very capable—in exchange for daily domesticity, at which she was only minimally capable; the relinquishment of her financial independence, which she also found satisfying.

"Do you love me, Sarah?" he asked, sounding a little hurt and confused. "Because some days I'm really not sure. I know it was a little slow in coming—I realize that. Remember the day I first told you I loved you? I asked if there was any possibility that you loved me too, and do you know what you said? Not I love you, Noah, but, I think there's a very good possibility of it. Well, I think it's time we clarify that matter. Granted, I resisted falling in love with you, too, but now I have and I'm not afraid to say it. I love you, Sarah, and I want to marry you and live with you. I'd like to know if you feel the same way about me."

His eyes were dark with intensity, his voice was earnest as he fixed her with an unwavering gaze that demanded the truth. She did love him in return. She *did*. But she had known him only five months and he had to understand that she had accepted his proposal conditionally; that condition was Addie.

"I do love you, Noah." The worry remained in his eyes. "I do," she whispered, embracing him tightly. "And you're right. I'm not Addie's mother. Sometimes I forget that, but I've grown accustomed to mothering her over the years. Please understand that and give me the time I'm asking for. I have to see some progress in her before I walk out of her life, because no matter what you say about living across town, when I leave that house she'll feel abandoned."

He said nothing, only held her.

"Noah," she told him, "we've only known each other since September. Shouldn't we give ourselves a little more time, too?"

He drew back and studied her eyes. His remained somber. She wondered what he was thinking.

He kissed her, holding her by the upper arms, a tender-sad kiss that made her wish she could concede to his wishes and marry him without delay. Because she could not, she put her arms around his neck and gave him a kiss of apology.

In the middle of it, Freeman Block opened the door and walked in. "Well, what have we here?"

"Get out," Noah ordered, keeping Sarah where she was.

"Do I have to? This looks pretty interesting."

"Dammit, Freeman!"

"You forget, I work here."

"Go work somewhere else for half an hour."

Freeman chuckled. "You and Sarah, huh? I told you, didn't I? The day she bought you that hat, I says, Noah, that gal's got eyes for you."

"Freeman, damn your mangy hide!"

"All right, I'm going."

When the door slammed, Noah sighed and released Sarah. "Well, it won't be a secret anymore."

"Perhaps you're right. Perhaps it's time I tell Addie anyway."

"Against your wishes?"

"Let's call it a compromise. I'm not ready to name a date yet, but I'll wear your brooch where it can be seen. Maybe if Addie knows about my upcoming departure she'll prepare herself for it."

Studying her, Noah thought, *She's always so rational, so in control of every situation. I wish sometime she'd lose that control.*

"Now I really must go back to work, Noah. I'll have to write up the news about the new minister coming."

"Should I walk you back?"

"No, you don't need to."

"Let me know what Addie says when you tell her."

"I will."

He gave her a brief kiss, wishing once again that she felt the same reluctance at parting as he. Wishing just once she would fling her arms around him and declare she would miss him, would give anything if they could spend the rest of the day together, the rest of their lives, starting now. But Little Miss Containment had things to do that were probably of equal importance to her as lollygagging with him, so he had to be content with her brief display of affection and the one promising kiss that had been interrupted by Freeman.

When she was gone, Noah went over to the stove and tipped the coffeepot above a white enamel mug, but only a tablespoon of thick black sludge ran out. He lifted a stove lid and tossed the dregs inside. A plume of smoke rose. A hiss. The smell of charred coffee. He stood a long time staring into the coals.

If she loved him she'd want to marry him, it was as simple as that. He loved her and that's what he wanted to do—speak vows, set up a house, sleep together (lord, yes), have babies. That's how it was done, dammit. He didn't understand loving without being impatient for these things. He didn't understand how she could put her feelings for her sister before her feelings for him. It wasn't enough for Noah that Sarah conceded to wear his betrothal brooch only when forced to by Freeman Block's wagging tongue. She should have been wearing it all along in plain sight because she was so excited she wouldn't consider doing anything else!

But it had never been that way with Sarah.

His mother had a theory that in every marriage there was one who loved more. Well, in his it seemed obvious who that one would be.

He put two sticks of wood in the stove and returned to his desk. Five minutes later he'd done nothing but stare at a bunch of papers.

He needed to talk to somebody.

He chose Robert, that night, at a table in a corner at the Eureka Saloon. It was smoky and loud, and somebody nearby had horse manure on his boots. But in all the noise nobody paid them any mind.

"What do you think of Sarah?" Noah asked Robert.

"Salt of the earth. Honest. Moral. Hard worker. Probably the most intelligent woman I know."

"Probably a damn sight more intelligent than me."

"Hell, Campbell, that wouldn't take much."

They laughed good-naturedly. They could do that now.

Noah tipped his chair back on two legs. He studied Robert from beneath his hat brim. "I'm going to marry her."

Robert's cheeks went flat with surprise, then lifted in a smile. "Well, I'll be damned. You've already asked her?"

"Yup."

"And she said yes?"

"Sort of."

"Sort of?"

Noah's chair came down on all fours. "She's not willing to name a date yet. I've given her a betrothal brooch which she's agreed to wear, though."

Robert set down his beer and gripped Noah's hand. "Congratulations! This is good news."

Noah smiled wryly. "I hope so."

"What's the matter? You don't look very excited."

"Oh, I'm excited. Sarah's the one who's not."

"Well, she said yes, didn't she?"

Noah studied the rim of his beer mug, then leaned forward with an elbow on either side of it.

"She's an odd woman, Robert, totally different than Addie. Sometimes I get the feeling that she's so smart, there's so much going on in her head, so much she wants to *do* that she hasn't got time for marriage. It's the *other* thing she'll do when she finally gets time. Sort of takes the edge off the excitement, if you know what I mean."

Robert took a sip of beer and waited.

"There's a preacher coming to town and I want to get married as soon as he gets here but she's dragging her feet. It's as simple as that."

"Hell, you haven't even known her half a year, and half that time the two of you fought like two roosters slung over a clothesline."

"Yeah, I know." Noah sighed and rubbed the back of his neck. "There's something else."

"I'm listening."

Noah studied his beer mug. Scratched its handle with a thumbnail. Met Robert's eyes.

"I think she's scared to death of being touched."

"I told you she was moral, didn't I?"

"It goes beyond that. It's all mixed up with what Addie was. Sarah says, 'I don't want to be like Addie.' "

"Can you blame her?"

"I don't expect her to be. What I mean is I . . . well, I got carried away once. Just once. I tried something with her and she made it very clear she wasn't that kind of girl. So since then I've been what I believe is called a perfect gentleman. I don't even kiss her very often and half the time she acts like she's scared to death to do that. Now, dammit, Robert, that's not natural. Not when two people are supposed to love each other. Saying goodnight should be torture, that's how I see it."

"Are you sure you love this woman?"

"I think about her day and night. She's driving me nuts!"

"But do you love her?"

"Yes. Against my better judgment, yes."

"Then don't worry about it. Women want a marriage certificate first."

"You want to know something funny?"

"What?"

"I thought for a while it was you she loved."

"Me!"

"I was jealous as hell when you first came to town."

Robert laughed. "No, it was always Addie for me. Sarah and I were just friends."

"So what about you and Addie? You got any plans?"

Robert settled back in his chair, drew a huge breath and blew it out with his cheeks puffed. "Addie's still a mess."

"She's scared as hell to go out of that house, isn't she?"

"Not only that. Believe it or not, I think there are times when she misses the whorehouse."

"Oh Robert, come on."

"I know it sounds ridiculous, but think about it. She lived the life for five years. She made good money. All her needs were taken care of. She didn't have to cook, clean, work, worry. The men loved her. I think she was good at what she did—hell, you'd know about that better than I would."

"She was good."

"And *you're* jealous of *me*?" Robert said wryly.

"That was business, Robert. Nothing but, and I gave that up when I fell for Sarah."

Robert took a long swig of beer, studying Noah over his glass. "It's a damned miracle you and I ever got to be friends, you know that?"

Noah answered with a slow grin. When it passed he asked, "So do you love Addie or what?"

"The truth is, I don't know. I care enough about her to want her to have a decent life, but taking on a woman with her kind of past is scary. It makes you wonder if one man will ever be enough for her. Or if one man is too many. Because the odd thing is, though she might miss the life, she hated it, too. She hated the men all the while she pretended to love them, did you know that?"

Noah had never thought about it before. The idea was mildly shocking.

That night after supper while Sarah and Addie lingered over coffee, Sarah said, "I have something to tell you. I hope it won't upset you."

"Upset me? Is it something bad?"

Sarah's smile dawned and set in rapid succession. "No, it's not bad." She leaned her elbows on the table and said, "Noah has asked me to marry him."

Consternation flitted across Addie's features. At first she said nothing, then rose and went to the stove to get the coffeepot.

With her back to Sarah, she said, "My goodness."

"What do you think, Addie?"

"You and the marshal—I don't know what to think."

"Addie, come here. Sit down."

Addie turned slowly and returned to the table, leaving the coffeepot behind. She sat down on the edge of her chair.

"We haven't set a date yet."

Addie nodded, her eyes fixed on her full cup.

"But a telegram came in today with the news that Deadwood will be getting a minister in early April."

Addie's gaze shot to Sarah. "Early April!"

"I didn't say I was getting married then, I said that's when the minister will get here. But Addie, you must face reality. It will happen sometime and when it does, I'll be going to live with him."

"Why can't you live here?" Addie asked plaintively.

Sarah touched Addie's wrist. "I think you know the answer to that."

"Oh." With the quiet word Addie dropped her gaze. "Then what would I do?" she asked forlornly.

"You would make a life of your own. You must start now, Addie, by leaving this house like a normal person, by going uptown and doing the shopping and seeing people again."

"I had a life of my own, but you and Robert took me out of it," Addie retorted with a sudden burst of anger. "If neither one of you wanted me, why did you make me leave Rose's? I was happy there, can't you understand that?"

"Addie, don't say that."

"I *was!* Happier than I am here being a nothing. I can't cook, I can't write articles, I hate washing clothes and blacking stoves! I'm not even good enough to be Robert's wife, because if I was he would have asked me by now. Instead he treats me like a pet sister. Well, I don't want to be his pet sister and I don't want to be your house slave, so just go ahead and marry the marshal and move wherever you want to!"

Like a petulant child Addie ran from the kitchen, up the steps and slammed her bedroom door.

Sarah remained behind, stunned. Of all the ingrateful, self-indulgent, moronic women in the world, her sister took the prize! Addie couldn't see beyond her narrow concerns to what it was she and Robert had done for her. She wouldn't make an effort to become self-reliant, to become proficient at anything that smacked of hard work. Instead she would blame them for not sacrificing themselves further so she could remain in her ivory tower, disdaining the rest of the world.

Sarah rose and clanked her empty cup into a dishpan. She poured hot water from the teakettle, added cold, began washing their supper dishes with enough vehemence to be heard through the ceiling.

Well, let her sit up there and bawl!

Sarah felt like bawling herself. She loved Addie, had left St. Louis for her, had made the fearful trip out here into the unknown, had set up a business and a home and sprung Addie out of Rose's meat hole and all she got for it was blamed!

Well, so be it.

When the preacher came she'd be the first one married and let Addie run back to Rose's and stay there till the syphilis got her out once and for all!

Of course the anger burnt itself out. By ten o'clock, when each of the two women had listened to the house noises for three hours, when their self-imposed exiles had begun to grow lonely, when antipathy lost its buoyancy and became burden, Sarah extinguished the kitchen lantern and felt her way up the stairs. They creaked. At the top she paused to study the thin blade of light showing beneath Addie's closed door. Sadly, she turned to her own.

She had just lit her lantern when Addie's door opened and she came to Sarah's doorway, pausing one step inside.

"Sarah?"

Sarah turned.

"I'm sorry. I didn't mean it."

The two exchanged gazes across the quiet room. Sarah rose and the two rushed together to hug.

"Oh Addie . . . I'm sorry, too."

"You didn't do anything wrong. You have every right to marry the marshal, and you should. I'm just scared is all. I don't know what's going to happen to me."

Taking Addie's hand, Sarah led her to the bed and they sat down.

"You'll be fine," Sarah said.

"How? How can I be fine when no man will have me, not even Robert, who loves me? I know he does."

"Have you ever stopped to think, Addie, that Robert may be waiting to see that you *don't* need him before he decides he *does* need you?"

Addie looked puzzled. "That doesn't make any sense."

Sarah took her hand. "What man would want to marry a woman who believes she's better off in a brothel? You've got to show him, Addie. You say you can't do anything, but that's not true. There *are* things you can do. You just don't want to because most of them are hard work and you've never had to work hard before. You live in a town that's ninety-nine-percent men, for heaven's sake! There are dozens of jobs that women do better than men, or that men wouldn't dream of doing for themselves. You could clean their houses, mend their shirts, launder their sheets, cut their hair—I don't know exactly what it is. You're the one who must decide. But I know one thing: there's enough money in this gulch, and enough womenless men, that any woman has a distinct advantage when it comes to business. If you were to open up a shop and a man opened up the same kind right across the street, he'd probably go out of business because you'd get it all."

It was obvious Addie had never pondered the possibility before.

"I'm asking you to use your head, Addie. Stop hiding behind the excuse that you're not as bright as I am and find something you can do better than me. When you find it, my guess is that Robert will pop the question. He didn't break you out of Rose's for nothing."

"You really believe that, Sarah?"

"Yes, I do. Robert loves you as surely as trees are green. He's just waiting for you to become worthy of him."

"Oh Sarah, I love him so much, but he's never even kissed me since the night he took me out of Rose's."

"Give him time. But more importantly, give him a reason to."

Addie's countenance remained sober. After lengthy thought she said, "All right. I'll try."

It seemed there would be a church raising. The next issue of the *Chronicle* announced not only the hiring of the minister, but the fact that lumber was needed, and each mine- and landowner was requested to donate one tree, delivered to the Beaver Creek Sawmill. The mill donated the cutting time to the cause while the butcher shops donated venison to feed the crew. Teddy Ruckner said he would cook it, and the Ladies' Society, which had already held several weekly meetings, volunteered to serve it.

The event was planned for the first weekend in March.

"Are you coming with me tomorrow?" Sarah asked Addie the night before it.

Addie took a deep breath and answered, "Yes."

Sarah smiled. Addie smiled, though not as confidently as her sister.

The day of the church raising dawned clear and warm. As if the project were blessed by some omnipotent force, the chinook winds came over the Rockies and turned winter to spring. The morning temperature was just below freezing, but by noon it had reached the sixties.

Everyone turned out—merchants, miners, men, women, children and one ex-prostitute, wearing a scarf tied backward over her gray and blond hair. When Addie showed up beside Sarah, she brought more than one person up short. Some of the men, after jolts of recognition, mistakenly greeted, "Hello, Eve," to which she replied, "My name is Addie now." Most of the women stiffened, but out of respect for Sarah offered perfunctory greetings when Addie was introduced. Emma, of course, led the vanguard of acceptance, thumping an arm around Addie's shoulders and ordering, "Come with me. I need someone to help me carry bread over from the bakery."

On their way they ran into Noah, heading toward the church lot dressed in dungarees and a red flannel work shirt, carrying a wooden toolbox.

"Addie!" he exclaimed in surprise. "You're helping today?"

Addie offered a dubious smile. "Sarah talked me into it."

"That's wonderful!" he exclaimed, beaming.

"So you're going to marry my sister."

Emma exclaimed, "What!"

"That's right. Soon, I hope, now that we've got a preacher coming."

"I guess that'll make us relatives."

"I guess so."

"Well, I can stand that if you can."

He laughed. She followed suit, and they stood awhile facing each other in the street, aware that the situation could be awkward if they'd let it, determined they would not let it.

"Congratulations," Addie said.

"Thanks, Addie."

"Why hasn't Sarah told us?" Emma put in.

"It hasn't been official very long. My family doesn't even know yet."

Emma thumped him on the arm. "Well, that's just grand news, Marshal, just grand."

"I think so, too. Well . . . I'd better get up there and lend a hand. I hear hammers pounding already."

They parted, Noah to pitch in with the carpenters, Emma and Addie to get the bread. Upon their return to the church site, Robert found them. He, too, held tools and wore rough work clothing.

"I heard you were here today," he said to Addie. He looked pleased. "You keeping her busy, Emma?"

"You bet. No slackers allowed in Deadwood when there's a church to raise. Where's Sarah?"

"Over there, making coffee."

Emma climbed onto a nail bucket and spied Sarah working with the women while nearby Noah helped the men. Emma formed a megaphone with her hands. "Listen, everybody! Let's get this thing built right 'cause the first ones married in it's gonna be the marshal and Sarah Merritt!"

Sarah and Noah were separated by fifty feet, but their heads snapped around and their eyes met. The resulting hoorah put color in Sarah's cheeks.

"Noah Campbell, you old sonofagun you!" Somebody banged Noah's shoulder blades.

"Had to throw her in an abandoned mine to get her to say yes though, didn't you, Marshal?"

"And she give him a black eye for it, as I recall!"

"I'd treat you better than that, Sarah! You wouldn't have to give me no black eyes!"

The jovial ribbing went on and on until Sarah spun away to help the women make coffee over the open fire.

At midmorning a wagonload of Spearfish Valley farmers arrived, among them Noah's family. They heard the news before they reached the heart of town. Carrie was the first off the wagon.

"Where's that son of mine? I want to hear it from his own lips!" When she found Noah she bellowed, "Is it true? You marrying that young newspaper gal?"

"It's true, Ma."

"Where is she?" Louder she hollered, "Lead me to my future daughter-in-law!"

The crowd produced Sarah, nudging her forward while Carrie bore down on her from the opposite direction with her son in tow.

"Gal, you've made a mother happy! When's the glorious day?"

"I . . . I'm not sure." Sarah barely got the words out before she was enarmed by Carrie and found herself confronting Noah over her shoulder.

"Well, it can't happen too soon to suit me. I'm just mighty happy about the turn of events. Kirk, Arden, here she is!" She heralded them over. "Here's Sarah! And Noah, too!"

Kirk arrived with Arden trailing. Noah's father gave Sarah a bear hug that nearly popped her spleen. "Well, this is something," he said, "this is certainly something. You have our blessings." He released her and shook Noah's hand. "Congratulations, son."

It was Arden's turn. He tried for a smile but it barely bent his lips. "You broke my heart, Sarah," he said, kissing her cheek. "I asked you first."

He did the correct thing, however, with Noah: shook his hand and said for the whole town to hear, "I guess the best man won."

Noah and Sarah found no privacy until sometime later when she came by offering him a cup of coffee. He held a cup while she poured.

"I guess everybody knows now." His statement assumed the unasked question, *And what do you think of that, Sarah?*

She righted the coffeepot, gave him a smile and caught him by surprise by saying, "Then I guess it's time we set a date."

The church went up with the grace and precision of a staged dance. The floor first. Then one wall, and another and two more, followed by the roof joists, white as bone china. On the ground an eight-man crew was designing a belfry with a pointed steeple. At another station a crew was building a pair of matched doors. Nearby some older men were riving shingles while the children bundled them twenty to a pack and tied them with twine for easy lifting up to the rafters. Soon the carpenters appeared in silhouette against the blue March sky, balancing on the skeletal building, plying braces and bits and joining the sturdy structure with pegs. Meanwhile the women kept the coffee coming.

At noon the venison was carved over the open pit where it had cooked, and served with fresh bread, baked beans and corn cakes at tables made of planks and sawhorses. Afterward, the women worked on the cleanup while the men returned to their labors. In the late afternoon, with the structure framed and enclosed, the belfry was hoisted up and set in place to the accompaniment of cheers. At suppertime platters of cold venison sandwiches appeared, accompanied by more hot coffee and dried-apple pies.

At twilight the tools were stored for the night, lanterns came out and a keg of beer was tapped. Someone produced a fiddle, someone else a mouth organ, and an impromptu dance began on the fragrant, freshly milled floor of the church. Every woman was pressed into service as a partner, but still there weren't enough. A number of good-natured men played the parts of women by appropriating the ladies' aprons and tying them on while dancing to "Turkey in the Straw" with partners of their own gender.

There was much laughter and camaraderie. No females were allowed to play favorites, but were whirled and swirled from one man to the next.

Passing through Arden's arms, Sarah heard, "If he doesn't treat you right, you know where to come!"

Passing through Noah's, she heard, "I'm going to walk you home when this is over."

Only one clinker spoiled the night. When Addie was reeling from the

dance floor, breathless, at the end of a number, she was confronted by
Mrs. Roundtree, who hissed in an undertone, "You have your nerve,
mixing with honest, God-fearing folks in *this* building. Go back to the
whorehouse where you belong!"

Sarah overheard and rounded on the woman. "Do you call yourself
a Christian!"

Robert found Addie later, outside, standing apart from the others,
staring into the bonfire, which still burned.

"What's the matter? Why did you leave the dance?"

"There are some who don't want me there."

"Who?"

"It doesn't matter."

"Who?"

She refused to answer.

"Did one of the men say something?"

"No, one of the women."

"The women will be harder on you than the men. It'll take some
time."

"I can't say I wasn't expecting this. It just hurts a little more than I
thought."

"So are you going to knuckle under and hide in your house again?"

She looked up into his face, which was illuminated by the shifting
firelight. "No. I'll be back tomorrow to finish what we started."

He smiled and said, "Atta girl, Addie. Come on, I'll walk you home."

The dancing was short-lived: everyone was tired; they'd worked hard
today. No beer was allowed inside the church, and the single keg that
had been tapped emptied fast. The Spearfish Valley folks went home.
Those with children had packed them off to bed. Robert and Addie had
disappeared. Noah took Sarah's hand and repeated Robert's words.
"Come on, I'll walk you home."

They climbed the steep hill where the day's melt-off was still gurgling
downhill. A half-moon had risen and rimed the gulch with silver. The
night had the raw-earth smell of near-spring. Below, the new church
steeple and rafters stood out like a drawing on a blackboard.

Between Sarah and Noah, everything had changed. Everyone knew.
Soon the church would be complete and there would be a minister.
Sarah had said she'd name a date.

Neither of them spoke until they reached her doorstep. Noah took
both her hands and said a single word. "When?"

She'd expected the question and had prepared an answer on her way
up the hill.

"How about the first Saturday in June?"

His grip tightened on her hands. In the moonlight she made out his swift smile.

"You mean it, Sarah?"

"Yes, I mean it, Noah."

He kissed her in jubilation. Then in speculation, the mood changing as he angled his head and opened his mouth. He drew back, sent a silent message into her eyes and lowered his open mouth to hers once more. She moved against him and opened hers, too, and felt ardor dawn as a wondrous, impulsive force. It fed upon itself and gave way to outright temptation, fueled by the touch of his tongue upon hers and the caress of his hands on her back, her ribs, her breasts. She shuddered once in pleasure, amazed that it should be so, that she could allow the intimacy and revel in it. How different it felt, sanctioned almost, by their plans to be married in a mere two months.

But when his hands moved to her throat as if to free buttons, she halted them.

"No, Noah, we mustn't."

They stood in the grip of the silent impasse with his hands detained by hers. She folded his much longer hands between hers and kissed his fingertips.

"Not because I don't want to," she whispered.

He relented, releasing an unsteady breath against her face.

"I won't apologize this time."

"There's no need to," she replied, and for the first time said the words without prompting.

"I love you, Noah."

CHAPTER 19

THERE was one thing Addie had done since leaving Rose's that had brought her both pride and pleasure: making the curtains. A service with questionable potential, curtain-making, but one she could, in spite of her limited sewing skills, perform with a degree of self-confidence. Why wouldn't it succeed? The womenless men of Deadwood Gulch lived in bare-bones houses, lacking the time and know-how to dress them up. Might they not pay someone else to do so for them? Furthermore, everyone in town was predicting a deluge of settlers when spring came, prompted by the continued excellence of the gold prospect, the presence of the telegraph, daily stagecoach service and now the church, with a school sure to follow by autumn. Deadwood had all the earmarks of a boomtown destined to live on. When the ladies started flooding in, Addie's Window Dressings would be there waiting for them.

From Mr. Farnum's suppliers of yard goods and sundries she ordered a selection of ginghams, poplins and calicos, braiding, tassels and lace. They arrived on True Blevins' first ox train in late March, along with twenty other carts loaded to the heckboards with everything from ice boxes to windowglass to a twenty-four-inch-diameter brass bell for the First Congregational Church of Deadwood. Addie placed an advertisement in the *Deadwood Chronicle*: "Fine quality, hand-stitched curtains made to order for your windows from my large supply of material and trimmings. See Miss A. Merritt, Mt. Moriah Road."

Her first customer was the future Mrs. Noah Campbell, who ordered curtains made for the house she would occupy with her husband, come June.

Her second was the Reverend Birtle Matheson, who arrived by stage-coach in early April.

Addie had finally decided to join the Ladies' Society, who took it upon themselves to outfit the log house and have it all homey when the new minister arrived. They scrubbed and cleaned it, polished its windows, blacked its stove and wove rugs for its floor. Addie, meanwhile, had volunteered to make the curtains.

She got the flu, however, which lasted two days and put her under the weather. By the time she felt well again and completed the curtains, the Reverend Matheson was already installed in his house.

The day she delivered them it was feeling like spring. The sun was bright and the air was filled with the scent of rain-washed pine from the previous night. It was warm enough to leave her coat behind and wear only a fringed shawl over her blue dress. She packed the new curtains into a basket, along with a hammer, hooks and a cluster of dowels to use as curtain rods.

She knocked on the door of the parsonage, expecting a middle-aged man to answer. Instead, the door was opened by a man only a few years older than herself. He wore brown trousers and a white shirt, open at the throat, with the sleeves rolled to midarm. He had attractive eyes, beautiful wavy hair the color of cherry wood and, overall, a set of unexpectedly handsome features.

"Reverend Matheson?" she inquired.

"Yes." He smiled, showing perfect teeth.

"I'm Adelaide Merritt. I'm a member of the Ladies' Society and I've brought the curtains for your house."

"Miss Merritt, come in." He reached out and shook her hand, then drew her up the last step and over his threshold. His door faced south. He pushed it back against the wall, letting the sun flood his front room. He hitched his hands onto his hipbones and stood regarding her in the comfortable, wide stance. "What a beautiful day. And what a beautiful surprise!" She had the startling impression he was not speaking only of the curtains in her basket. He smiled at her with his whole face, raining upon her the considerable force of his attention.

His youth came as a shock. Perhaps it was his name—Birtle—that had led her to believe he'd be old, a widower perhaps, for they'd been forewarned he had no wife. Addie had asked Sarah, who'd already met him, what he was like, but Sarah had only said he was a very nice-looking man.

He was all that and more as he stood before Addie alert and attentive with no cleric collar in sight.

"Curtains, you say?"

"Yes. I've started a business making them, and I volunteered to make yours. I'm sorry they weren't up when you got here, but I had the flu."

"The flu . . . I'm sorry. You're feeling better, I hope."

"Yes. Much."

He smiled at her long enough to make her uncomfortable, then moved abruptly, as if just remembering he hadn't done so for a while.

"Well, come in. Let's have a look." He took the basket from her hands and set it on a square table. "Show me what you've made."

While she took them from the basket he said, "You must let me pay you."

"Oh no, it's my contribution. I'm not much of a cook, so I didn't bring any cakes. And I don't care much for rug-making so I didn't help with those, but curtains I'm getting a little familiar with. I've also brought some things to hang them with."

The curtains were of broadcloth, white on white, with a design of ivy leaves woven within vertical stripes. "The white will show the soot more than a color would, so they'll have to be washed regularly, but this cabin is rather dark. I thought it could use brightening up."

"Indeed, it can, Miss Merritt. It is *Miss* Merritt, isn't it?"

Her glance returned to his Mediterranean-blue eyes. "It's Miss," she answered, and his smile unabashedly doubled in candlepower.

"Miss Merritt," he repeated. A lull followed, charged with his attention and her discomfort at being its object. "Well!" He clapped his hands once and rubbed them together. "Can I help you hang them?"

It was one of the the most bizarre hours of her life. Birtle Matheson acted like no minister she'd ever imagined. He took her shawl and folded it over the back of a chair. In his rolled-up shirtsleeves he stood on a chair and drove the hooks into the window frames where she told him to. He conversed in loquacious fashion, punctuating his speeches with frequent laughter, asking her a hundred questions about herself and the town, supplying information about himself. He was fresh out of the seminary and determined to do well in this his first assignment. His father was a minister in Pennsylvania, his mother was dead—her maiden name had been Birtle—and he had two sisters back east, both older and married. He had once had ringworm and lost half his hair and promised God that if he'd just let it grow back, he would follow in his father's footsteps and become a minister. He had answered the Deadwood advertisement because he saw it as an opportunity to build a church from the ground up and form a strong bond with his congregation. He liked to fish, read Dickens, sing and watch sunsets.

"You won't be able to watch sunsets here," she told him.

"Of course I can. They just happen a little earlier."

He had a contagious optimism and when he rested his unsettling eyes on her she found it difficult to look away.

"Perhaps sometime we can watch one together," he suggested, again facing her directly with his hands on his hips.

"I don't think so." She handed him a curtain shirred on a dowel.

He stepped onto the chair, hung it and stepped down, resuming his forthright stance—a stance with which she was rapidly becoming familiar. "Why not?"

"Ask anyone in town," she replied, turning away, heading to retrieve her basket and shawl now that the last curtain was hung.

He followed, said at her shoulder, "I've been unpardonably rash. Forgive me, Miss Merritt. Now you're running away."

She flipped her shawl around her shoulders, put her hammer in the basket, the basket over her arm and turned to face him.

"You're forgiven," she said. "And I'm not running away. The curtains are all up. I must be going now."

"You're sure you're not running?"

She was, but lied. "I'm sure."

"All right. Then thank you, Miss Merritt," he said, detaining her by offering his hand for shaking. She obliged. He squeezed her hand hard, his smile entering her eyes like rays of blue sun. "Will I see you tomorrow at services?"

"Yes, I'll be there."

"Till tomorrow then."

She went away feeling stunned. A minister! And a bold, young, attractive one at that. It had been so long since an ordinary man had shown an interest in her. It felt very good, being admired and wooed, exchanging repartee with a man the way young people were supposed to. It was a part of life she'd missed. Of course, he had no way of knowing her past. He'd find out soon enough.

The following morning, Sarah and Addie attended church with Noah and Robert, a prearranged plan. When they arrived, Reverend Matheson was standing out in front shaking hands with his new congregation.

"Ahh, Miss Merritt," he said, shaking Sarah's hand first, recalling her from earlier. Likewise Noah, whom he greeted by name. "Soon to be my first nuptials. How nice to see you here together." They moved on. "And the other Miss Merritt, who brightened my house yesterday." There was no denying he retained his hold longest on Addie's hand, and his smile was specially bright and steadfast upon her. In his black suit and white cleric collar he was an eye-catching sight. The sun radiated off his auburn hair and his perfect teeth. "The curtains add a real touch of hominess. Thank you again."

"You're welcome."

Behind Addie, Robert observed, feeling a riffle of annoyance at the man's undisguised interest in her.

"I thought perhaps one day soon I might call on you and your sister, pay an official greeting, as it were, on the founders of the women's group, which I'm sure will play an important role in both the charitable and social future of our church."

"Sarah founded it, I didn't."

"Have I your permission nonetheless?" he inquired.

"Yes, of course. We'd be happy to receive you. May I introduce you to our friend Robert Baysinger?"

Matheson shook Robert's hand firmly and offered a smile, but Robert's smile was a veneer, short-lived, scarcely touching his eyes.

"Reverend Matheson," he said.

When they moved on, Robert spoke quietly at Addie's ear. "Seems you've made an impression on our new minister."

"All I've made, Robert, are his new curtains." They entered the church at that moment, cutting off the possibility of further exchange.

Matheson gave a thumping, exuberant speech—hardly a sermon— thanking the town for their rousing welcome, Mr. Pinkney for the donation of the land, the men for the spanking new church, the women of the Ladies' Society for his comfortable house, and especially Miss Adelaide Merritt for his new curtains. He gave a thumbnail sketch of himself, gaining a round of laughter (from everyone except Robert Baysinger) when he told the story of how he was drawn to the ministry by a case of ringworm. He announced plans to begin a children's Bible study class immediately, and to visit the homes of the townspeople and even venture out to the mines to personally invite those outside the town limits to join the parish. He invited the Ladies' Society to affiliate themselves with the church and use it for their meetings. He announced a hymn, then led all in a voice so true and enthusiastic, the combined chorus fairly loosened the pegs holding the building together.

After services, Matheson again took up his post at the church door. Robert, however, steered Addie around him without pausing.

She pulled her elbow free and remarked, "Robert, how rude!"

"You keep away from that man!" Robert ordered.

"Ro-*bert!*" Indignant, Addie drew to a halt. "He's a man of the cloth! And furthermore, I don't take orders from you!"

Robert appropriated her arm and forced her on. "Keep walking, Addie. People are staring."

"I don't doubt it, with you storming out of church and giving the minister the cold shoulder on his first Sunday in town! Let me go! I'll walk on my own."

She did. All the way home. While Robert stalked along beside her, glowering. When they reached the house she stopped on the doorstep and turned to him, plainly to prevent him from following her inside. "I don't like your proprietary attitude, Robert. Thank you for walking me home, but you don't need to do that anymore either if you can't be civil to the people who are civil to me."

She turned and entered the house, leaving him simmering on the step. He spun and marched down the hill, meeting Sarah and Noah coming up.

"Robert?" Noah said as the other man strode past with a stormy expression on his face. "Hey, Robert, what's wrong?"

Robert spun around and ordered Sarah, "Tell your sister, *Fine!* If that's the way she wants it, that's fine by me!"

Executing a brisk about-face, he stalked away.

Sarah gaped at Noah. "What do you suppose that was all about?"

"Probably the new minister. He seems a little moonstruck by Addie."

Birtle Matheson came to call that very afternoon. Addie answered his knock and had difficulty hiding her shock. "Why, Reverend Matheson!" He was dressed in his black suit with the white cleric collar. His eyes were quite as blue as the sky behind him, and his eyelashes were the kind that make old ladies say, he should have been a girl.

"It was a little lonely in my house all alone. I hope you don't mind that I came unannounced."

"No, not at all."

"May I come in?"

"Sarah's not home. She and Noah have gone over to their house to do some cleaning."

"Perhaps we could walk then."

"Walk?" Wouldn't Mrs. Roundtree have a field day with the news that Eve, the ex-prostitute, had spent her Sunday afternoon walking with the new Congregational minister?

"It's a lovely day." He squinted at the sun. "Feels like spring. I think I heard some peepers down by the creek." He transferred his most convincing smile to her.

"I think not," she answered.

"Why?"

"It wouldn't be good for you."

"Let me be the judge of that."

"Please, Reverend Matheson, I cannot walk out with you."

"Because you used to work at Rose's?"

Addie's face paled. She stood stalk-still, waiting for the blush that was sure to follow. Not a reply came to mind.

Birtle Matheson put his hands on his hips, caught one shoe on the threshold. "I did some inquiring after your remark yesterday afternoon."

"Then you know how inappropriate it would be for the two of us to be seen together."

"Not at all. Judge not, lest ye be judged."

She studied him in amazement. "You're crazy," she whispered.

"I think you're a very pretty lady, Adelaide Merritt, and you're single, and I'm single, and it's a beautiful spring day and I should very much like to take you for a walk. Now what's crazy about that?"

She stared at him, speechless. She no longer thought of herself as pretty. When she looked in a mirror she saw an ex-prostitute who'd known for years she was fat, who had shorn her hair to an unfashionably short boyish cap of blond curls to get rid of the last of the gray, who wore high-collared plain dresses and could not get the man she loved to propose marriage.

When Birtle Matheson looked at her he saw a woman whose white-blond hair puffed around her face in the unspoiled, slightly curled fashion of a child's. He saw a woman who had been eating her own terrible cooking for four months and had trimmed to an attractive silhouette. He saw clear skin, clear eyes, and clear amazement that he should find her attractive, the latter which attracted him even as much as her considerable physical attributes.

"A simple walk," he reiterated.

They went on a walk, heading away from town, following the creek for a while, then heading into the woods, over hills and along tributaries swollen with melted snows, where wild creatures were nesting in the banks and willow branches had turned brilliant red in preparation for leafing. They spoke about the town, its people, the haunting Christmas triangle concert, about Sarah and Noah and their rocky beginning, about nature, the possibility of there being trout in the mountain streams. They sat on a sandstone outcropping in the pleasant afternoon sun and watched a water ouzel walk underwater as it fed. Birtle said, "Tell me about this Mr. Baysinger who accompanied you to church this morning."

She told him, "Robert is our friend from back home. I've loved him since I was a girl."

Birtle remained silent a long time. Somewhere in the trees behind them a chipmunk clucked. "All right," he said at length. "Now I know what I'm up against."

Meanwhile, Noah and Sarah were busy at the house they would share as husband and wife. In the yard, Noah knelt, running a brush through the black stovepipe while a black-billed magpie looked on and cocked his head in curiosity, then rose in a flash of white to a better vantage point. Above him, Sarah finished washing an upstairs window, lifted it and knelt with her elbows propped on the low ledge, looking down on Noah. She was dressed in a brown muslin skirt, a white blouse with the sleeves rolled up and a bibbed apron.

Noah sat back on his heels and looked up. "All done?" he asked.

"With the windows. But I'd like to turn the mattress over."

"Hold on till I finish this and I'll be right there."

He went back to work while she remained at the sill in the warm sun, watching the magpie, who was soon joined by another; smelling spring lifting from the warming earth; glancing off toward Elizabethtown where the willow trees looked swollen with buds. She turned her gaze on Noah, watching his russet head bent over his work, his shoulders flexing as he plied the brush and lifted the pipe to peer inside. He set it down, got to his feet and washed his hands in an enamel bucket, dried them on a rag from his hind pocket and entered the back door.

She heard him come up the stairs and rose from her knees.

"Here I am," he said, coming around the corner into the room. "Let's turn that mattress." He wedged between the bed and the wall and together they flipped the mattress end over end.

"Feels heavy as a bag of oats," he said.

"Cotton batting," she explained, leaning over to whack at the rope marks on the blue and white ticking.

He circled the foot of the bed and stood behind her. "We'll need sheets and blankets."

"I'll take care of that." She whacked the mattress again.

"And pillows."

Whack! Whack! "I'll take care of those, too."

He glanced down at her backside while she thumped the mattress and made her skirts stir. "And a coverlet."

She glanced back over her shoulder and quickly straightened. "Noah," she reprimanded.

He looked up and grinned. "On the other hand, who needs sheets and blankets and pillows."

She was on her back beneath him so fast the mattress bounced. Dust motes rose around them. Outside, the magpies chattered quietly while inside all was still. His eyes, above hers, were dark with mischief that slowly faded, replaced by a certain kindling as he braced on his elbows and considered her facial features in turn—eyes, nose . . . mouth.

"Noah, we—"

"For once, Sarah, don't say it. I know what the rules are."

He leaned down and kissed her once, lightly, an unhurried sample and warning before lifting his head to meet her eyes briefly. Dipping down again, he toyed with her lips, nipping first one, then the other, leaving touches of dampness and the faint whisk of his mustache before settling, eventually, at an angle, kissing her with deliberate voluptuousness.

In time he raised his head and let their gazes meet while his fingertips grazed her neck and they considered where this could lead. Where it must not lead. Her lips were open and wet and she was breathing fast. The next kiss was unrestrained, his mouth wide and his arms surrounding her as he rolled them to their sides. He kissed her as if there were no rules. Kissed her the way young swains have been kissing their maidens in springtime since there has been a springtime. Kissed her until they felt like the buds on the willows outside.

It became an ardent battle, each of them fighting for a fuller, wetter, warmer fit. With their mouths locked, he found her breast within her blouse and apron bib. He caressed and reshaped it, raising a pleasured sound in her throat. He pressed a knee high within her skirts and went on petting her until petting would no longer suffice. The ropes gave a single creak as he fit their bodies together and held her with an arm across her spine. They stopped kissing and lay entwined, breathing on one another's faces in labored puffs.

Finally they fell apart, distancing themselves enough to regain composure.

"Oh Noah," she whispered, "you make it so difficult."

"Do I?"

"Oh yes."

"It's never seemed difficult for you before."

"It's difficult today."

He smiled and touched her chin. "That's what I've been waiting to hear."

They lay awhile, enjoying each other's eyes, the warmth of the sun as it crept another inch up their bodies, the simple linking of their hands between them. Once she touched his mustache. Once he tucked a strand of hair back from her temple.

Finally they fell to their backs, hands upthrown, and studied their ceiling.

He rolled his head to look at her. "I'd better get that stovepipe back inside," he said.

"And I'd better get some sheets on this bed."

They smiled and he sat up and tugged her after him.

The Reverend Birtle Matheson's immediate pursuit of Addie Merritt had the town buzzing. Everywhere Robert Baysinger went, he heard murmurings behind his back or was asked outright questions about it: "Is it true he's sparking her? What's between you and Addie? Folks figured the two of you for a pair after you took her out of Rose's. Doesn't seem right, a minister and a soiled dove."

His hackles rose at each new comment he heard. He grew irascible with the world. At the stamp mill the men remarked grouchily that the boss must've breathed too much mercury vapor and it had poisoned his system. Robert even snapped at Noah one noon when they were eating dinner at Teddy Ruckner's together and Noah mentioned, "I heard Matheson's planning some kind of spring fair to raise funds for hymnals and pews."

Robert thumped a fist on the table and barked, "Goddammit, Noah, do I have to hear that man's name everywhere I go?"

Taken aback, Noah replied cautiously, "Sorry, Robert. It was just an innocent remark."

"Well, *don't* make any more innocent remarks, not about Matheson! He's nothing but a goddamned lecher!"

Noah waited a while, ate a hunk of venison chop, drank some coffee, cut another piece of meat, watched Robert chew his as if it wasn't dead yet.

At length Noah took another swallow of coffee and asked, "How long since you've seen Addie?"

"What business is it of yours?"

"How long?"

Robert glared at Noah and said, "Three and a half weeks."

"Three and a half weeks." Noah paused. "You gotten any smarter?"

Robert's eyes flashed to his friend's. He threw down his fork. He pointed a finger. "Listen, Campbell, I don't need any lip from you!"

Noah affected an expression of righteous astonishment. "You need it from somebody! Everybody in town is talking about how you're growling at them when they so much as say hello on the street. Half the men at the mill are ready to quit because you've been such a damned bear to live with. I'm ready to kick your ass clear up to your armpits.

Don't you know what's wrong with you, Robert? You're in love with Addie."

Robert stared at him.

"You've been in love with her since you were fifteen years old, and you're so damned scared to admit it you're willing to let Matheson sashay into town and sweep her off her feet, and never go banging on her door to call a halt to it."

"She told me not to bother her anymore."

"Hell yes, she did, after you acted like a horse's ass that first Sunday Matheson was in town. Why do you think she did that?"

"How am I supposed to know? Who the hell can figure out the woman?"

"You don't suppose she was trying to scare you into something, do you?"

"Noah, she told me point-blank she didn't want to see me anymore."

Noah threw up his hands. "You're so damned ignorant. Open your eyes, man! The woman loves you!"

Robert glowered while Noah preached on.

"Why do you think she left Rose's? Why do you think she let her hair go blond? Why do you think she started sewing curtains and joined the Ladies' Society and became respectable again? To be worthy of you, only you're so dim you can't see it. Have you got any idea how much courage it took her to do any one of those things in this town? Everywhere she goes she runs into men she's been in bed with and women who know it, but she's willing to face them down and say, that's over, I'm changed, I want a decent life now. So are you going to let her have it or what?"

"I think she wants it with Matheson."

"Bullshit." Noah threw down his napkin. "But if you're not careful, she will, because that man's showing her some fevered pursuit, and her head's likely to be turned by it sooner or later. Especially given the fact that he's the minister. Why, can you imagine what a victory it would be for a woman like Addie to marry such a man after what she was? She could thumb her nose at the entire town."

"Addie wouldn't thumb her nose at anybody. She's not that kind."

"There! You see? See how well you know her? See how you jump to her defense?"

Robert thought awhile, then shook his head. "I don't know, Noah. She dropped me flatter than a stove lid the minute she laid eyes on him. That hurts."

"Well, maybe it does. Maybe she hurts, too, you ever thought about that?"

When Robert refused to answer, Noah leaned forward, resting his forearms on the edge of the table. "Remember once I told you I was jealous because I thought there was something between you and Sarah? Do you remember what you said? You said it had always been Addie for you. So put your claim on her, man. What are you waiting for?"

Robert slept little that night. He thought about Noah's words. He thought about how pretty Addie looked with her hair back to its natural color, and how slim she'd gotten since she'd left Rose's, and how she dressed as normal as any housewife, and how she'd overcome her fear of leaving the house, and had started up a perfectly respectable business.

What man wouldn't sit up and look twice?

Noah was right. If he didn't move fast he was going to lose her, and the idea was unthinkable!

The following afternoon at quarter to four Robert stood before the shaving mirror in his room at the Grand Central Hotel. He had just returned from the bathhouse and Farnum's store. Every garment on his body was brand spanking new. His beard and mustache were neatly trimmed. His hair was slick as an otter's. He smelled like geranium vegetal.

He used a sharp-toothed comb on his beard, mustache and eyebrows. His mustache again. He dropped the comb, tugged at his waistcoat, frowned at his reflection, drew a great breath, blew it out, adjusted his new lapels, his starched wingtip collar, his gray and maroon paisley tie and finally dropped his hands to his sides.

Go ask her, Robert. Before that preacher does.

He donned his beaver bowler, left his cane but took a clump of blue flag—wild iris—out of a glass of water and left the room.

Outside it was one of those balmy days that come along maybe twice in a springtime, the kind you wish you could bottle and keep, so still a man could hear his own whiskers growing, so perfectly temperate it was hard to resist flopping down beneath a tree and looking for pictures in the clouds.

He'd chosen the time carefully—four o'clock when Sarah would still be at the newspaper office and Addie would have the bulk of her day's work done.

On his way up the hill he rehearsed what he would say.

Hello, Addie, you look lovely today. How perfectly transparent. He'd have to do better than that.

I've come to apologize, Addie, and to say you've been brave and wonderful and I've been a perfect fool. No, that sounded silly.

Hello, Addie. I've come to see if you'll go for a walk with me. (She must love walks; she'd been taking enough of them with that preacher!) But he didn't want to run the risk of being interrupted by people, so a walk wouldn't do.

Hello, Addie. I've brought you some wild irises. The men found them up in the creek this morning.

The door was wide open when he approached it, with sunlight angling across the floor inside. He could smell supper cooking but not a sound came from inside. He knocked and waited with his heart in his throat.

He heard chair legs scrape and in moments her footsteps approaching on the pine floor.

After all the rehearsal, upon seeing her again the prepared words fled.

She appeared before him wearing a blue and white striped skirt and solid blue shirtwaist with a high white collar and deep starched cuffs, also of white. Over this she wore a white bibbed apron tied at the back, with some fancy stitching across the bib and pocket. On her right middle finger she had a silver thimble. Her white-blond hair curled softly around her face, only a finger-length long. Her face was thinner and her curves had returned, accented by the waistband of the apron and the gentle swell of the bib above. She stopped on the threshold and stood very still.

"Hello, Robert," she said quietly.

He removed his hat. "H——" He cleared his throat and tried again. "Hello, Addie." The words sounded wheezy and unnatural.

She waited without fidgeting. Her skin was very fair. It was easy to see the faint blush that rose to her cheeks. Ruler came padding from somewhere and sat down in the sun to look up at the two of them.

"What are you doing here?" she asked.

"I came to see you," he replied stupidly.

"Yes, I see that. Is there something you wanted?" She was so calm, so quiet-spoken.

"Yes, to apologize, first of all."

"There's no need to apologize."

"The last time I saw you I was very upset. I was rude to the minister and sharp with you. I'm sorry."

"You're forgiven."

He stood in the spring sun, she in the shadow of the doorframe with the sun slicing across her right shoulder and down her skirts. Seconds ticked by and neither of them said anything.

Finally she glanced down. "Are those for me?"

"Oh . . . yes!" He handed her the flowers. The stems were crushed. His palm was green. "From up in the stream above the mill. They grow wild up there."

"Thank you. They're very beautiful." She lowered her face to smell them while he watched the sun glance over her shining hair for a second. When she lifted her head her upper body again retreated to full shadow. "I should put them in water. Come in, Robert." She turned and walked sedately away.

He followed, feeling callow and earnest and wistful, past two patches of sunlight that fell through her curtained windows, into the kitchen, where her stitchwork was lying on the bare table beside a pincushion and a cup half-filled with coffee. Ruler watched them go, then padded slowly after them and took up a post near the range. Addie poured a dipperful of water into a clear glass and put the irises in it and brought them to the table.

"Sit down, Robert. Can I get you some coffee?"

"No. No coffee."

He sat and she sat, at right angles. He laid his hat on the table beside her closework. A fly came in and landed on the edge of her cup and she waved it away, again with the collectedness he found so terrifying. After a vast silence he asked, "How have you been, Addie?"

Their eyes met. "Fine . . . just fine. Busy. I've gotten a lot of orders."

"Good."

"Yes, it is. Better than I ever imagined. Would you mind if I keep sewing while we talk?"

"No, go right ahead."

She picked up her work, draped it across her lap and began stitching. So calm, so remote, so indifferent it made a lump form in his throat. She was treating him exactly the way he'd treated her since she'd lived in this house. How stupid he'd been!

"You look very good."

Her eyes flashed up, returned to her work. Stitch. Stitch.

Good? She looked incredible. She made the flowers look garish, the sunlight wan. He couldn't peel his gaze off her.

"Are you still seeing the minister?"

"I have been, yes."

"Do you have feelings for him?"

She gave him another glance, the duration of one stitch, then dropped her eyes. "I consider that private, Robert."

"What I mean to say is . . ."

Stitch. Stitch. Her needle went on tunneling.

"What I mean to say is, do you have any feelings for me?"

She stopped stitching. Her eyes remained downcast. The needle moved on.

"I've always had feelings for you, Robert."

"Then would you . . ." He reached over and covered her right hand to stop it. "Would you look at me, Addie?"

She wouldn't. He waited several seconds, but she wouldn't. He left his chair, removing the work from her hands, placing it on the table before going down on one knee beside her chair. He took both her hands and looked up at her beautiful, pale face.

"Addie, I came here today to tell you I love you. I've loved you for so long, I don't remember a time when it wasn't true."

She lifted her beloved green eyes. They were brimming.

"You do?"

"Yes. And I want to marry you."

She swallowed once, trying very hard to hold her tears in check. "Oh Robert," she whispered, "what took you so long?"

Their reunion was swift and fierce. He caught her hard against him, so hard the impact sent her tears spilling. Her arms doubled around his neck and for a moment they merely clung, their eyes closed, his bearded cheek pressed against her pale jaw. At length he drew back and lifted his face to kiss her, kneeling yet with his trousers lost in the folds of her white apron. She held his face in both her hands, forgetting she still wore the thimble on one of them. What a long, long, long-awaited kiss, flavored of coffee and geranium vegetal, open and wet and tempered by all those years, and all that history that had brought them to this moment of truth. When the kiss ended he laid his face against her apron bib and breathed, "Oh Addie, I love you so much. I've been so miserable these last three weeks."

"So have I." She continued caressing the back of his head, his neck, his shoulders, while he pressed kisses wherever his lips touched her starched clothing. "I thought I'd have to marry him to finally get you to realize you loved me."

"You've known it?" He drew back to see her eyes.

She nodded, stroking his hair back from his temples, the expression in her eyes loving and uncomplicated for one of the first times in their lives. "For quite some time."

"Noah gave me a good talking-to yesterday. He told me I was going to lose you if I didn't pull my head out of the sand."

"Hooray for Noah," she replied softly.

They kissed once more, Robert still kneeling while Addie's palms covered his silken beard. They tasted each other shallow and deep, letting time drift by unheeded. When the kiss ended he remained for a while with his forehead against her chin, her left hand softly skimming his shoulders while he held her right and discovered the thimble still on it.

He sat back and looked down at it, fitting and refitting the thimble on the tip of her finger.

Finally he looked up into her eyes. "You haven't said you love me."

"But I do."

"I want to hear you say it."

"Oh Robert, in all my life I've never loved another man but you."

"Then you'll marry me?"

"Of course."

"Even though Birtle Matheson will have to perform the ceremony?"

"Even though."

"He won't like it."

"He knew all along how I felt about you. I told him the very first day he took me out walking that I loved you."

"You did?"

She nodded, lifting one hand to sculpt the hair above his right ear, following its contour with her fingertips while his face was lifted to receive the love in her gaze.

"We've come through some hell to get here, haven't we, Addie?"

"That's all over now." She kissed him as if to promise only heaven ahead, leaning down and slanting her mouth over his, running her palms over the scratchy new wool covering his back. He rose, drawing her to her feet, fitting their hips together and holding her close while his head tipped and their open mouths joined. He made a sound, throaty and passionate, an ode to the end of their separateness while he locked her ever tighter to his mouth and body.

The thimble dropped to the floor. Ruler shot out from beside the stove and batted it against a chair leg while above her the man and woman went on kissing. On and on the thimble rolled—across the bare floor, against a mop board, across the floor again—creating the only sound in the otherwise quiet room.

In time Robert lifted his head. His face was flushed and his breath sketchy. He touched Addie's face—as flushed as his own—and, looking into one another's eyes, they laughed.

In joy.

And wonder.

And relief.

"Won't we have some stories to tell our grandchildren?"

"Robert, you wouldn't."

"Maybe I wouldn't. But it would be a convenient threat to keep you in line with."

"You won't need to keep me in line. I'm in it and I'm staying."

"We should tell Noah and Sarah."

"They'll hardly be surprised."

"Did everybody in this town know how I felt before I did?"

"Just about."

"Should we tell them tonight?"

"Let's. I'm trying not to ruin an elk roast. Why don't you run and find Noah and ask him if he can come up here for supper and we'll tell them then."

He beamed, happier than he had ever imagined being.

"Don't worry. I'll find him."

CHAPTER 20

ROBERT brought champagne, which was plentiful, given the number of saloons and the amount of wealth in town. Addie's elk roast turned out passably good, accompanied by roast potatoes and carrots and surprisingly light cornbread. The mood around the supper table was festive even before the announcement was made. The foursome had spent many hours together before Robert and Addie's rift, making the reunion in itself cause for celebration.

When their plates were full and the meal in progress, Robert refilled their glasses and lifted his own in one hand while capturing Addie's hand on the corner of the table.

"Addie and I have an announcement to make, though it may not come as much of a surprise to either one of you. But we wanted you to be the first to know . . ." His eyes lit on Addie and stayed.

"We're going to be married," she finished.

Sarah and Noah spoke at once.

"Oh Addie . . . Robert . . . this is wonderful!"

"Well, it's about time!"

"Congratulations! I couldn't be happier." Sarah rose and circled the table to hug them both.

Noah followed suit. "The same goes for me. I spread it on a little thick yesterday, Robert. I figured I'd either lose a good friend or shock some sense into your head. So when's the big day?"

"When *is* the big day?" Robert asked Addie. "We haven't had a chance to talk about it yet. We just decided three hours ago."

"Soon." Addie smiled. "I hope."

"So do I," Robert seconded.

Sarah said, "You're going to be married in the church, I suppose."

"Yes."

"By Matheson?" Noah asked.

"He's the minister," Robert replied.

"Well, I propose a toast." Noah lifted his glass. "To Robert and Addie, who absolutely belong together if ever two people did. May your wedding day be sunny and your lives be the same."

They had a lot to talk about—two weddings, two homes, four futures which would be inexorably entwined, to the delight of all. They discussed dates and celebrations and the disposition of the house in which they presently dined, deciding it would work out beautifully for Robert and Addie to be married the week following Sarah and Noah's wedding and make this their home after Sarah moved out.

They laughed about Robert's stubbornness, and how long it had taken him to pop the question to Addie. They speculated on what Birtle Matheson's reaction would be when asked to perform the service for the girl he'd been sparking. They even talked about Rose's—all of them felt it was a healthy sign they could do so—and the possibility of inviting some of her girls to Addie's wedding. Wouldn't all those doves have stars in their eyes? Wouldn't Mrs. Roundtree have venom in hers?

Their meal was long finished, the dishes removed to the dry sink, awaiting washing, and the four of them were still lolling at the table sharing lazy and pleasant conversation, winding the evening down. Robert leaned forward, half-sprawling on the table, his jaw propped on the butt of one hand, comfortable and relaxed with his friends. He turned his glass round and round with his fingertips, watching it catch the tablecloth and drag it into a pinwheel.

"What you said is true, Noah. I can't think of another couple who belong together the way Addie and I do. We've been through it all and put it all behind us—her running away, her working at Rose's, what her father did to her—what could be tougher to face than all that? But we did it, and the way I see it, after overcoming all those hurdles, marriage will be a breeze."

Into the silence that followed, Sarah spoke with an edge to her voice. "What her father did to her?"

Robert gave up his preoccupation with the glass and lifted his head off his hand. Addie was making surreptitious shushing motions, a horror-stricken expression on her face. He straightened slowly.

"What did her father do to her?" Sarah asked Robert.

He glanced from one sister to the other. "Doesn't she know?"

Addie's face had gone ashen. "Let's just forget it, Robert."

"Know what?" Sarah's glance darted between her sister and Robert.

"Nothing," Addie said, reaching for her dirty cup and saucer and jumping to her feet.

"Addie, sit down," Sarah ordered quietly.

"The dishes are getting all dried on."

"Addie, *sit down.*"

Noah sat unmoving, wondering what the hell this was all about.

Addie returned to her chair, set down the cup and saucer and fixed her eyes on them.

"Would you care to explain?"

Addie said, "This is something between Robert and me. He shouldn't have brought it up."

"But he did. Now I want to know what it's all about. What did Father do to you?"

Addie's eyes grew glittery. She banged a fist on the table, making the cup and saucer dance. "Robert, damn you! You had no right!"

"Addie, I'm sorry. I assumed you told her a long time ago, right after you told me. Why, hell, if she doesn't know, how could Noah have found out?"

Noah spoke up. "I'm afraid I don't know what you're talking about."

"Of course you do. You alluded to it one night when you told me you were going to marry Sarah, remember?"

"No, I don't, Robert, I'm sorry."

"You told *Noah?*" Addie cried, aghast.

"No, I didn't tell Noah. I thought he knew! I thought Sarah had told him. We were talking about you women, that's all."

"Enough of this!" Sarah put in. "I want to know what it was Father did to you that's causing all this distress!"

Addie pinched her folded hands between her knees and dropped her eyes to the cup and saucer. "You don't want to know," she whispered.

"Robert?" Sarah snapped officiously.

Robert said quietly, "I can't tell you. Addie has to."

"Very well then, Addie."

Addie continued staring at the tabletop with tears lining her eyelids. Noah sat with his arms crossed, an innocent observer.

"Will somebody tell me!" Sarah shouted, again banging a fist on the table.

A massive silence followed.

After several seconds Robert's contrite voice broke it. "This is my fault, Sarah. I'm really sorry. Please, just let it ride."

"I cannot any more than you could if it were your father being discussed in such dire tones. Now what did he do?"

Robert reached over and squeezed Addie's shoulder. "Tell her, Addie. Tell her and be done with it."

Noah began to rise. "If you'll excuse me, this seems like a family matter."

Addie caught his arm. "No, stay. If we're all going to be related you might as well hear it, too."

Noah glanced at the faces around the table—Sarah's, looking pinched with displeasure as she stared at Addie; Robert's, looking penitent and concerned for his fianceé; Addie's, looking sad while asking him to remain. He sank back to his chair.

Addie rested her forearms on the table and wrapped both hands around her empty cup. There was a silvery track from a tear on her right cheek, but she was no longer crying. She appeared outwardly calm, resigned, studying the cup. "When Mother ran away, Father forced me to take her place . . . in bed."

Robert laid a hand on Addie's wrist and stroked it with his thumb.

Noah spread a hand over the bottom half of his face and gripped the hollows of his cheeks.

Sarah gaped at her sister.

"I don't believe you!" she whispered at last.

Addie met her eyes for the first time. "I'm sorry, Sarah. It's true."

"But . . . but you were only three years old!"

"That's right," Addie said sadly. "I was only three years old. And then I was four, then five and ten and eleven and twelve. And when I was sixteen I knew I couldn't stand it anymore, so I ran."

"But our father was a good, wholesome, God-fearing man. He wouldn't do such a heinous thing."

"He was a good, wholesome, God-fearing man around you, but he had two sides, Sarah. You only saw the one he wanted you to see."

Sarah shook her head, her eyes wide with shock. "No. I'd have known, I'd have . . . you'd have . . . ."

"Given it away somehow? He made me promise not to at first and later I was too ashamed to."

"But how could he . . . ." Sarah's lips hung open. She seemed to be silently begging for help.

"He pretended he was just comforting me because I missed Mother so much. He said it was our little secret and I must not tell anyone. He made you believe he was moving me into a room of my own because

I was wetting the bed, but the real reason was so he could slip into my room without being suspected. Why do you think he never let Mrs. Smith live in with us? She would have—"

"No!" Sarah screamed, leaping to her feet. "I won't listen to any more! You're lying!" Tears rained down her face. Her eyes were wide, her face blanched. "Father wouldn't do such a thing! He loved us and took care of us! You're . . . you're defaming him and he's not here to defend himself!" She was sobbing as she ran from the room up the stairs.

"Sarah!" Noah ran after her, taking the steps two at a time, ignoring the fact that he was trailing her to her bedroom. He followed the sound of her weeping and found her in a room to the left. She had thrown herself across the bed in the dark.

"Sarah," he said gently, sitting down beside her.

"Get away!" Twisted at the waist, she struck back at him blindly. "Don't touch me!"

"Sarah, I'm sorry . . ." He found her shoulder and tried to turn her over so he could take her in his arms.

"Don't touch me, I said! Don't you ever touch me again!" she screamed. He withdrew his hand while she sobbed into the mattress and made the entire bed tremble. He remained awhile, uncertain, aching for her, wanting to hold her and help her through this ordeal.

"Sarah, please . . . let me help you."

"I don't want your h–help. I don't w–want anything. Just leave me alone!"

He rose and stood looking down at her dim form while she wailed and sobbed by turns. He went and stood by a window, looking out at the night, feeling bereft and helpless and shocked himself. Her father, sweet Jesus, her father. The man she'd patterned her entire life after, the man she quoted and imitated and adulated. He'd been more than a parent to her, he'd been her mentor and emancipator as well. Not only had she learned his trade, she had adopted his strict code of morality in that trade—she thought.

My God, how devastated she must be.

He thought of Addie, below. Poor, beautiful, abused, unbright Addie, who had carried that knowledge all these years and protected her sister from it. She had run from a father into a life of degradation and he, Noah, had been one of the men who'd compounded her self-abasement. What should he say to Addie when he went downstairs?

And to Robert, who unwittingly had uncovered this nest of maggots? Robert was a man who would not knowingly hurt a soul.

Noah wanted to remain here in the dark until harmony had been restored and the sorrow in this house had been eased, but what kind of friend hides in times of need?

Sarah's keening had become high and grieved and had begun a queer, resonant quaking in his stomach.

He tried again. "Sarah," he said, returning to the bed, sitting beside her and touching her heaving back. "Sarah, what he was to you can never be changed."

She shot up, swinging on him, screaming, *"He was my father, don't you understand! He was my father and he was a liar and a filthy hypocrite! An animal!"*

He didn't know what to say, so he sat on the bed and tried to put his arms around her.

"Get out!" she screamed. *"Le . . . ea . . . eavvve . . . meeeee allllooooone!"*

Her vehemence abashed and terrified him. He withdrew and stood uncertainly beside the bed while she sat on the edge of it with her entire body drooping and her frame convulsed by great heaving sobs.

"All right, Sarah. I'll leave. But I'll come by tomorrow and see how you're feeling. Would that be all right?"

His only answer was her continued weeping.

"I love you," he whispered.

She remained as before, drooped and crying as he left the room.

Downstairs, Addie was huddled in Robert's arms near the dry sink with the dishes forgotten beside them. A dish towel was slung over Robert's shoulder as the two exchanged murmured conversation. When Noah entered the kitchen they turned to watch him cross the room but remained linked with their hands upon one another, as if afraid to break apart.

Noah stopped near them and the three stood in a tangled silence.

"She's in a bad state," he said quietly.

"Let her cry for a while and then I'll go up to her," Addie said.

"She won't let me touch her."

"She needs to be alone awhile."

Noah nodded, then stood forlornly. "Addie, I'm really sorry," he finally said.

"Well, who isn't, but what can we do about it except try to overcome it and make our lives happier?"

"I never knew . . . I mean, when I used to come and see you up at Rose's . . ." His eyes flashed to Robert, back to Addie. "This is awkward, but I figure it needs saying. I wouldn't have come there if I'd known. I thought you girls were . . . well . . . I thought . . ."

She took pity and touched his arm. "Yeah, that's what everybody thinks. That we're just crazy about it. But listen, Noah, it's not your fault, what the old man did to me. I don't want you feeling guilty about it, too. I think there's been enough guilt around here for one day."

Noah shifted his eyes to meet Robert's.

"Robert," he said, and paused, searching for words.

Robert said, "Some big mouth I've got, huh?"

"Hell, you didn't know."

"That doesn't help Sarah any though, does it?"

They stood awhile, quiet, until Noah put one hand on each of their necks, forging them into a circle.

"You two are good people. You're going to be happy, I know it. And Sarah and I are going to be happy, too. We'll all get over this and be two old married couples who play cards every Sunday night."

They narrowed the circle and stood with their heads touching in a clumsy three-way embrace. Noah broke it up.

"Listen, I've got to go. Tell Sarah I'll be by tomorrow. You'll go up to her soon, won't you, Addie?"

"Yes, I promise."

He nodded and gave her a little smile of gratitude.

"Robert," Noah said by way of parting.

The two clasped hands, necks—a silent communion, gripping each other, reluctant to let go. Finally they parted, clearing their throats. There'd been more emotion expended in this house tonight than any of them were comfortable with.

"I'll see you both tomorrow."

Up in her room, Sarah lay lifelessly on her side, her hands limp, one of them holding a damp handkerchief. Her lips felt puffed and glossy. Her eyes hurt. Her body was inert but for an occasional residual sob that shuddered through her.

The pieces all fit now. Everything.

Father, abandoned by his wife for another man, never marrying or even seeing other women. Addie, after Mother left, inconsolably sad, wetting the bed, getting a room of her own but growing sadder as the years advanced and she should have gotten over Mother's absence. Father's first approval when Robert entered their lives, his later antipathy when Robert reached puberty and began noticing Addie as a girl. Addie's disappearance followed by Father's immediate failing. Addie, taking up the oldest profession as an extension of her role at home; her adamant refusal to speak of their father or accept any inheritance money from him. Even Addie's being excused from having to work at the newspaper office the way Sarah had. Sarah understood now the true reason.

How lucky she'd been.

Sarah, the smart one.

Addie, the pretty one.

She groaned and dragged one heavy arm closer to her face, guilt-struck because she'd complained about Addie not having to help the way she did. Ruler appeared out of the darkness, jumping up behind her with a soft "Mrrr?" as if asking what was wrong. She reached an arm back and hauled her over her hip, settled her in a silky, vibrating curve against her stomach. Funny how when she really needed her the cat stayed, even though her first loyalty was to Addie.

For a while Sarah erased tonight's revelation from her mind, concentrating on the cat's purring, the warmth of her body, the milky smell of her fur, the comfort of having her close, just as Addie must have been comforted by her when she worked at Rose's.

Rose's.

Father.

The ugly truth returned, bringing a shudder that closed Sarah more tightly around the cat until her mouth touched her head.

Was this how Addie had felt, night after night, alone and wretched after their father had done his dirty work?

No. Much worse . . . immeasurably worse. Guilty and frightened and filled with hatred and despair and helplessness, for whom could she have turned to? Who would have believed a child so young, given the sterling reputation of Isaac Merritt, who was respected from one end of St. Louis to the other?

The faint light from the lower level went out and footsteps came up the stairs in the dark . . . into Sarah's room . . . to the bed. Sarah remained silent, facing the wall. Addie lay down behind her, matching the curves of her body to those of Sarah's, hooking an arm around her waist and finding Ruler on the far side, then locating the back of Sarah's hand. She fit her own over it and squeezed hard, her fingertips digging into Sarah's palm, the younger sister now succoring the older, protecting her from what she herself had never had protection from.

Sarah's tears came again, stinging her sore eyes. She felt Addie's face pressed between her shoulder blades. They lay motionless a long time, like twins in a womb, until Sarah could contain her despair no longer.

"All this time," she said in a croaky voice, "I thought it was something I'd done that made you run."

"No. Never you. You were my bulwark, didn't you know that? You still are."

"Some bulwark. I feel like I've been struck by a big fist right here where Ruler's lying against me. I'm unable to move or to . . . to reason."

"Maybe it's better that you know."

"It doesn't feel better."

"I know it doesn't right now, but in the long run."

"Now that I do, I'm surprised it took me this long to figure it out except I . . . I never knew . . ." Sarah swallowed a new lump forming in her throat. "I never knew f–fathers . . ." She couldn't finish.

"Shh . . . don't cry anymore." Addie petted Sarah's hair. "It's not worth it. It was over a long time ago and I've come through it all right. Look, we all have. Like Noah said, soon we'll be two old married couples playing cards on Sunday night."

Sarah touched her knuckles to her lips, her eyes still streaming.

After a while Addie said, "Robert said to tell you he's sorry."

Sarah made an effort. She blew her nose. She took a deep, shaky breath, turned to her back and settled Ruler between herself and Addie.

"Dear Robert . . . how he must love you."

"He loves you, too. He felt terrible about hurting you."

"How long ago did you tell him?"

"Christmas Eve."

"Christmas Eve . . ." The night things had started between herself and Noah.

"It was a terrible night. He came to Rose's wanting to hire me for the night, but in the end he couldn't make himself do it for money. I ended up crying and telling him about Daddy and that's when he made me leave Rose's. He said I should tell you then. He thought you should know, but I didn't see any reason. You always loved Father so much and thought he was some kind of a god. I knew this would happen when you found out. But Sarah, you have to forget it. If I can be happy with Robert, that's all that matters."

"It's not all that matters. It matters that my father was a hypocrite, preaching one thing and living another, that he was a filthy bestial criminal, preying on his own daughter and ruining her life. I feel so guilty, Addie, for not knowing, for not helping, for . . . for criticizing you because you never had to go to the newspaper office and help." Sarah rolled to her side, facing Addie. "Don't you see, Addie? He took everything away from you and gave me everything. How can I live with that?"

"By remembering what you did for me. You came here to find me, you brought me Robert. If it wasn't for the two of you I'd have died in that whorehouse thinking that I wasn't worthy of anything better, because all those years I thought I was a low, foul person, the scum of the earth. I thought all I was good for was that one act. But Sarah, I don't think that anymore. You and Robert have given me back my self-respect."

They lay awhile in silence, thankful for the dark, each with a hand on the cat's fur, linked by her comforting presence.

"Addie, did Father . . ." There were so many questions Sarah wanted to ask, needed to ask, was afraid to ask.

"You can ask me, Sarah, if you want. Anything. I'm not ashamed anymore because I know now I was innocent. But what good will it do you to hear the truth? I'll tell you this much. The real stuff didn't start till I was thirteen. Till then it was a lot of him touching me and kissing me. Now think good and hard before you decide to ask me more."

The room remained quiet a long time, the darkness impacted with unwanted visions. Finally Sarah replied, "All right, I won't ask, but I have one more confession to make. May I?"

"What could you have to confess?"

"I was always jealous of how beautiful you were."

Their fingertips touched on Ruler's fur.

"And I was always jealous of how smart you were. I used to think if I could just get smarter he'd let me go to the newspaper office the way you did and he wouldn't need me for that other reason."

"Oh Addie . . ." Sarah reached up and put her hand around the back of Addie's head and drew it near so their foreheads touched.

"The world's not a very perfect place, is it?" Addie said. After her staunchness through Sarah's weeping, she now sounded on the verge of tears herself.

Sarah became the strong one. She patted Addie's short, silky hair and left her hand curved protectively around Addie's nape. "No it isn't, dear one. Far from it."

They fell asleep where they were, fully dressed and exhausted from the surfeit of emotion. In the deep of night Addie awakened, removed her shoes and those of Sarah, who mumbled, "Addie? . . . whm . . . ?"

"Get under the covers and go back to sleep."

The next morning Sarah overslept and arrived at the newspaper office late, her face looking like an overstuffed pillow. Patrick glanced at her sideways and took a swig from his flask. Josh stared at her head-on and said, "You look pure awful, Sarah! Are you sick?"

Her head felt like she'd boiled it. Her eyes ached and her nose was swollen. Concentrating was impossible. She stayed until nearly eleven A.M., when she finally gave up and went back home to bed.

Addie came to her room much later and gently shook her shoulder. "Sarah, wake up."

Sarah opened her bleary eyes and tried to recall why she was in bed in the middle of the afternoon.

"Ohhh . . ." she groaned and rolled to her back with a hand covering her eyes.

"Noah is here." Sarah struggled to become lucid. "You've been sleeping four hours already. It's the third time he's been here and I thought I should wake you. Do you want to see him?"

Sarah pushed herself up shakily. "No, not really." She scraped a hand over her tousled hair and glanced around, orienting herself. The sun was on the windowsill. Ruler was near her feet. At her desk her journal lay closed and the crystal penholder sat beside it.

"What time is it?"

"About quarter after three."

Sarah boosted herself to the edge of the bed and dropped her feet over. "How are you today?"

"I feel wonderful, actually. What shall I tell Noah?"

"Tell him I'll be down in five minutes."

"All right." Addie swept toward the door. She pointed to the pitcher and bowl. "I brought you some warm water."

Sarah rose, feeling unsteady as a newborn colt. She washed her face, combed her hair and winced at her reflection in the mirror. She looked no better than she had this morning. Her eyes were bloodshot, her skin saggy and purple around the eyes. Even her lips looked swollen. Yet Addie seemed revitalized. Perhaps Robert had been right: revealing her secret, Addie had at last become free of it. If so, Sarah felt as if the burden had been transferred to her shoulders.

She changed her wrinkled dress and went downstairs to face Noah. He was sitting on the parlor settee wearing his work equipment—gun, holster, brown leather vest and star. He held his hat in his hands—the one she'd given him—and rose immediately when Sarah entered the room.

"Hi," he said with an uncertain pause. "How are you?"

"Puffy and shaky and a little incohesive."

"I was worried when I went to the newspaper office and you weren't there."

"It was a bad night."

"I imagine. You and Addie talked?" Addie had retreated to the kitchen to give them privacy.

"Yes."

Noah left his hat on the settee and went to her, taking her by the upper arms while she crossed them and fixed her eyes on an armchair to her left. Neither of them spoke.

At length, she pulled back so he was forced to release her. "I'm not very good company today." The damnable tears threatened once more and she turned away to hide them. "I'm sorry. I know this must seem bizarre to you. It does to me, too. I'll need a little more time to get my emotions in order."

"Of course you will," he said quietly. "But don't worry about me. I've got plenty to keep me busy at work. When you're rested up and want to see me, let me know."

"Thank you, Noah, I will."

She recognized the coldness in herself immediately—her unwillingness to meet his gaze, a reluctance to be touched by him, relief when he dropped his hands. His visit was absolutely correct, even thoughtful, yet she could not conjure the slightest sense of gratitude for his attempt at comforting her.

Rebuffed, he withdrew, collecting his hat and leaving the house with the careful footsteps of one retreating from a wake.

When he was gone, Sarah sat on a stiffly upholstered side chair, her eyes closed, her arms crossed, imagining this must be what it felt like to be in a coma, chilly and removed from the life around you, hearing it but not heeding it.

In the kitchen Addie clamped a handle on a hot iron and laid it on a damp cloth over a curtain-in-progress. It sizzled. Out on the back doorstep Ruler meowed to get in. Addie went to the door, opened it and said, "Well, are you coming in or not?" The door closed and the iron clanked again, hitting the stove. Outside, a wagon passed on the road, rearranging the gravel. Some birds chirped.

The way you treated Noah was unpardonable.

I am suffering.

Maybe he is, too.

His suffering, if it existed, was of little import to Sarah beyond that brief thought. She struggled to merely open her eyes, to rise from the chair, to proceed with normality. How could Addie be ironing curtains in the kitchen as if the axis of the world had not tilted?

Sarah moved to the kitchen doorway. Addie looked up.

"Noah has gone?"

Sarah nodded.

"He's very worried about you."

"Is there any coffee?"

Addie blinked in surprise at Sarah's response. "Yes, I believe so."

Sarah poured some and took it upstairs without a further word about last night or about Noah. Leaving the kitchen, she only said, "I'm not very hungry tonight, so don't fix much for supper."

She returned to work the next day, submerging herself in daily duties and trying to keep unwanted images from her mind, but they persisted, horrid vignettes of her father hunkering over Addie. They came at frequent intervals and Sarah would snap from her involvement with them to find her hand clenched on a pen and her stomach muscles quivering. Though she was ignorant of the machinations of copulation, she had once seen a pair of dogs mating. A woman had run out of her house with a broom and had beaten on the male, shouting, "Get off her! Get off her, you big thing!" to no avail. The two had remained sealed together for an ignominiously long time in the woman's front yard, until every child in the neighborhood had witnessed the spectacle.

Sometimes Sarah imagined herself with the broom in her hand, flailing her father, whom she pictured in the pose of the male dog. The image might have lasted only a second or two, but it would leave her feeling soiled and shaken.

It persisted at night, too, before sleep came, while she lay in the room next to Addie's and nursed an anger for her father that grew to immense proportions. She began having nightmares, awakening from them with her heart hammering and the visions from her dream already evaporated before she could see them.

Four days passed and she had not seen Noah. Five, and she still hadn't seen him. Six, and he appeared beyond her window glass, standing outside the newspaper office, raising a hand in silent hello. She raised hers, too, but returned to work without going out to invite him in.

A week after that fateful betrothal supper, he came to the house while making his early-evening rounds.

Addie answered his knock. She and Robert had been sitting on the settee making wedding plans while she stitched her own bridal dress.

"Noah!" Addie exclaimed happily, "come in!"

"Noah!" Robert jumped up from the settee and came to greet him with a handclasp. "Where have you been? We were just talking about you."

"I've been keeping out of Sarah's way. How is she?"

"Remote."

"From you too?"

"From all of us, I'm afraid."

Noah sighed and looked worried. "Is she here?"

"I'll get her," Addie said.

Sarah was sitting at her desk writing when Addie announced from the doorway, "Noah is downstairs. He'd like to see you."

Sarah looked over her shoulder. She was dressed in a white long-sleeved nightgown topped by her old pumpkin-colored shawl. Her hair hung in a loose braid down her back. Some seconds passed while she contemplated. Finally she answered, "Tell him I'll be down."

Five minutes later she emerged from upstairs wearing a wine-colored dress and high-button shoes with her hair secured in a fastidious bun at the back of her head. When she entered the parlor all conversation ceased. She stopped near the foot of the stairs and returned the regard of the other three, who were seated on the settee and an adjacent chair.

Noah rose, holding his hat.

"Hello, Sarah. I haven't seen you in a while."

"Hello, Noah."

Neither of them smiled.

"Could I talk to you a minute?"

"Surely."

"Outside," he suggested.

She led the way, stopping perhaps ten feet from the door, which Noah closed. He stopped behind her and replaced his hat on his head. It was dark; no moon, only the light from the windows falling across the rocky surroundings of the house. The faint tang of dying wood fires lingered in the air from the nearby chimneys. Down below, the lights of the saloons along Main Street created a faint glow.

He didn't know how to begin.

"I thought I'd hear from you," he finally said.

She made no excuses, said nothing at all.

"Addie said you've been quiet, not talking to her either."

"Addie's been with Robert a lot."

"That's why you're not talking to her? Because she's been with Robert?"

"I've been . . . evaluating, let's say."

"Me?"

"No, not you. Life."

"And what have you discovered?"

"That it is fickle."

"Sarah . . ." He touched her shoulder but she flinched away. Hurt, he withdrew his hand and waited. When she refused to face him he walked around her and confronted her face to face.

"Why are you shutting me out?"

"I'm not shutting you out."

"Yes, you are."

"I'm healing."

"Let me help you." He reached for her, but she squirmed away and held up both hands.

"Don't!"

"Don't?" he repeated sharply, hurt by her continued rebuffs. "I'm supposed to be the man you love and you say don't when I try to touch you?"

"I simply can't stand it right now. All right?"

Noah considered, then said, "I'm not him, Sarah, so don't blame me for what he did."

"You don't understand! What he did was monstrous. I cannot simply blink my eyes and get over it. I loved him unquestionably all those years, then in one moment my illusions about him were shattered. If I need time to get over that, you'll simply have to understand."

"Time? How much time? And while you're getting over it, do you intend to keep pushing me away?"

"Please, Noah," she whispered.

"Please what?" he snapped.

She hung her head.

"Please don't touch you? Please don't kiss you? Please don't marry you?"

"I didn't say that."

He studied her downcast face, his mouth small, his throat constricted, so confused and hurt he didn't know what more to say to her.

"Matheson wants to talk to us about the wedding."

She looked off into the distant dark. "You talk to him."

He let out a chunk of sound resembling a laugh, only short and hurt. It shot into the night like a knife thrown into a tree. He turned away, stood facing the town, sensing only doom ahead.

"Do you want to call it off, Sarah?"

It took her some time to answer. "I don't know."

"Well, you'd better decide, because it's only two weeks away."

She stepped near him and laid a hand on his shoulder blade.

"Poor Noah," she said. "I know you don't understand."

"The hell I don't," he said deep in his throat and stalked away, leaving her standing alone in the night.

He told Robert, who told Addie, who talked to Sarah the next night.

"What are you doing, Sarah? You love Noah, you know you do!"

"Nothing's been decided yet."

"But he told Robert you wouldn't go talk to Birtle Matheson about the wedding."

"That doesn't mean I'm not marrying him."

"Are you then?"

"Quit badgering me!"

"Badgering you!" Addie plunked down on the edge of Sarah's bed and pushed down the book Sarah had been reading, forcing Sarah to meet her eyes. "You know what you're going to do? You're going to let our father ruin your life next. Nobody that wicked should have so much power over another human being, especially not from his grave."

Without a further word she left the room.

Two days passed. On the third, Noah sent a note via Freeman Block.

> Dear Sarah,
>
> Could I take you out to supper tonight? I'll come to the house to get you at seven o'clock.
>
> Love, Noah.

"Tell him yes," she said to Freeman.

Sarah had thought about what Addie said. Her father should *not* have the power to ruin her life, especially after he'd ruined a good portion of Addie's.

She dressed in a fine lawn dress of solid white, with two lace-trimmed petticoats underneath and her engagement brooch pinned at her throat. It was a stunning May evening and she wanted to please Noah, and be unflinchingly in love again and feel exhilarated by the sight of him, and revel in the innocent kisses and caresses that she'd come to enjoy only days before this disaster had befallen.

He wore the new suit he had bought for their wedding, crisp and black and proper with a winged collar catching him high beneath his chin, and a silvery-gray tie as wide as an ascot, stuck through by a pearl pin. On his head, not the Stetson, but a flattering black topper with a bell-shaped crown.

When she saw him on the doorstep her heart fluttered. When he spoke, the words sounded tightly controlled, as if he were afraid to release them from his throat.

"Hello, Sarah."

"Hello, Noah."

"You look pretty."

"So do you."

They smiled stiffly.

"Are you ready to go?"

"Yes."

They walked down the hill, looking straight ahead, without bumping elbows, exchanging only the most stilted dialogue. They dined at the Custer on the finest fare the town had to offer—deviled clams, pheasant in claret sauce, parsnip fritters and that rarest of delicacies: fresh, cold glasses of real cow's milk. Though each of them relished every drop of their milk, neither ate more than half the food on their plate.

After dinner he took her to the play at the Langrishe. It was a farce called *Hanky-Panky,* which elicited great laughs from all the crowd. They sat through it without even registering what was happening on the stage.

Afterward, he walked her home through the pleasant spring night. A slim crescent moon had cleared the mountains, and above the ravine a corridor of stars glittered. When they reached the house, the windows were dark, the door closed. They stopped before it and Noah turned toward Sarah.

"I realized tonight that we haven't done much of this."

"Of what?"

"Courting. The real thing—me inviting you and coming to pick you up and the two of us fussing up for each other. It felt like this is the way it's supposed to be."

"Yes, it did."

"You felt comfortable with me?"

"Yes, I did."

"And if I kiss you? Will you still feel comfortable with me?"

She had known it was coming, had been preparing herself all night. How intimidating that she'd *had* to prepare herself for it. What had happened to the woman who'd lain on a newly turned mattress in the sunlight and enjoyed this man in a wholly physical way? Why, as he stepped nearer, did her heart clamor with unreasonable fear? He was gentle, understanding, patient, and she loved him. How confusing: she truly loved him . . . as long as he kept his distance.

In the shadows beside the front steps, he rested his hands on her shoulders, giving her fair warning. She knew full well that all his preparations for tonight—his written invitation, all their finery, the meal, the play—had been merely a prelude to this moment of truth.

"You're not Addie and I'm not your father. Think about it."

He laid his mouth upon hers very lightly. She felt smothered but waited for the sensation to recede. Instead it advanced, taking on magnitude as the kiss became fully realized. She submerged her resistance and saw it through, put her hands on his breast and opened her lips when his tongue touched them, and tipped her head aside in response to his head tipping, and tried to recapture the innocence and trusting they'd built between them.

It didn't work.

She felt a sob building deep within, pushing panic along before it. When it erupted she pushed him hard with the butts of both hands, and he stumbled back.

"I can't!" She was breathing as if chased, gulping air and crying. "I can't," she whispered, spinning away, clamping a hand over her mouth, terrified and abashed because she was humiliating and hurting him. What should she do? How could she cure this ungrounded fear? How could she love him and be repulsed by him? She understood clearly, he was not her father, he would not hurt or abuse her, yet she could not control her revulsion at even this simplest intimacy.

"Damn you, Isaac Merritt!" she shouted. "Damn you to eternal hell!"

Her shout echoed once from the wall of Mt. Moriah above them and left an awful stillness afterward.

Noah stood behind her, out of his depth. She had annihilated all hope for them. Who was to blame?

"I'm so afraid," she said. She was not crying but her voice quivered.

"There's nothing to be afraid of anymore."

She turned, her hands still at her chin. "You're leaving me."

"No, you left me. The minute you found out why Addie ran away from home, you left me."

"I didn't mean to . . . I couldn't . . . it was . . . oh Noah, I don't want to lose you."

"Yes, you do. You've been fighting your feelings for me since the first time I kissed you. Well, now I know, and maybe I'm a little relieved. It's not any fun being the one who's always asking for affection. When it really works, it's supposed to flow both ways. So let's just put an end to this misery, okay, Sarah? I don't think . . ." He paused, sighed, raised his hands and let them drop. "What difference does it make? We could never make this work."

She stood mute while her future withered.

"Do you want to cancel things with Matheson or should I?"

"Noah, maybe if I . . ." She had no further words, no idea how to help herself or him.

He said, "I'll tell Matheson." After another silence he added, "Well, I guess this is it then. I want to say good luck, but the words stick in my throat."

"Noah . . ." She reached out one hand.

He turned and walked away. She watched the weak moonlight pick out the rim of his new top hat, his shoulders which dropped away from her with each downhill step he took. At the bottom of the path he stopped dead still for a full fifteen seconds. As if losing a battle with himself, he turned and called quietly, "Good luck, Sarah," before resuming his walk out of her life.

CHAPTER 21

AND so it was that Adelaide Merritt and Robert Baysinger were to be the first ones wed in the Congregational Church of Deadwood. Their wedding day dawned cloudy, but by nine o'clock the blue sky had broken through, reminding Sarah of Noah's toast on that evening before her world had crumbled. *May your wedding day be sunny and your lives be the same.*

She would see him today. The two of them would be standing up for Addie and Robert while the entire town wondered why their own engagement had been canceled. She had carefully tucked away her betrothal brooch between layers of cotton in a tiny inlaid box of tulipwood which she kept on her desktop.

Addie's wedding was scheduled for ten A.M. Shortly after nine Addie came into Sarah's room carrying her curling tongs, dressed in her chemise and petticoats.

"I want to fix your hair."

"I should be fixing yours. It's *your* wedding day."

"I'm better at it. And besides, mine's all done."

"It looks beautiful."

"I know it does. Sit down."

"But Addie—"

"Don't but Addie me. I'm going to make you ravishing."

"An Eleventh Commandment couldn't make me ravishing."

"Sit down, I said."

Sarah sat. "I know why you're doing this, but it won't work. It's over between Noah and me."

"I once thought it was over between Robert and me, but look where I'm going today. Just sit still so I don't burn you, and tip your head when I say tip." She removed the lamp chimney, struck a match and began heating the tongs.

Twenty minutes later Sarah's hair was drawn to the crown of her head, secured by a wide mother-of-pearl barette, and cascaded past her collar in a froth of springy ringlets.

"Oh Addie, it's so obvious!"

"It's your sister's wedding day. You're expected to primp."

"But what will Noah think?"

"He'll think exactly what I *want* him to think. That he'd better think again!"

"Addie." Sarah turned and caught Addie's arm. "You don't need to try to make amends. It was Noah's and my decision to break off our engagement. You're not responsible."

Addie saddened. "I know. But Robert and I feel so awful about it."

"Enough about that. It's your wedding day. I won't have you spoiling it by getting blue. Now let's go to your room and I'll help you into your dress."

Addie's dress had its flaws—stitching together gussets and tucks was more difficult than making flat curtains—but what the garment lacked in perfection it made up in flattery. High-necked, V-waisted (front and back), with corkscrew sleeves and a brief pleated train, it gave Addie a fairy waist. Its whipped-honey hue nearly matched her hair, into which she had pinned some wild plum blossoms which matched those she would carry along with six red tulips from Emma's yard.

When the last wrist button was closed, Sarah offered a moment of silent adulation before kissing Addie's cheek. "In spite of what you think, this is one of the happiest days of my life. Noah was very right when he said you and Robert belong together. You truly do."

Noah came to collect the women in a rented rig. When he knocked on the door Sarah's duty, as handmaiden to the bride, was to answer. She calmed herself, pressed a palm to her stomach and approached the door with careful control and a cardboard smile.

"Hello, Noah," she said as if his appearance had not created a rent in her heart. He was dressed in the black suit he should have worn for their own wedding. His cheeks were shiny, his mustache neatly trimmed, a rich dark wing above his familiar mouth. The sight of him made her tongue dry.

"Hello, Sarah. How have you been?" So proper it was numbing. No smile, no second glances.

"Fine." Proper, too. "I believe Addie is all ready. I'll get her."

They rode to the church in a carriage for four, with Addie insisting on sitting in the backseat alone. Proximity, however, had no effect on the estrangement of the two up front. They rode as if a great-aunt sat between them.

At the church Robert waited, dapper and smiling, reaching up to help his betrothed alight from the carriage, to accept a touch of the cheek from his future sister-in-law, a handshake from his friend.

To Noah, aside, he said, "Take notes today. You're going to need them, mark my words."

The wedding was short and simple. Birtle Matheson carried it off in a manner that gained him only further respect from his new congregation, who knew he'd had eyes for the bride himself. The attendees packed the church and included three of Rose's girls, who watched the proceedings with bald yearning in their eyes; many single businessmen in town who chided themselves for never seeing the possibilities in the woman they'd known as Eve; Patrick Bradigan, who was sober for the occasion; the Dawkins family and more.

When Robert spoke his vows he clutched Addie's knuckles so tightly white rings appeared below his thumbs.

"I, Robert Baysinger, take thee, Adelaide Merritt . . ."

Sarah stood behind them, painfully conscious of Noah, six feet away, his hands linked, standing straight and still as an obelisk, watching the proceedings.

It came Addie's turn.

"I, Adelaide Merritt, take thee, Robert Baysinger . . . to be my wedded husband . . ."

Addie displayed a smile of singular radiance as she looked into Robert's eyes. A tear formed in Sarah's, and as she lifted a handkerchief to wipe it away, Noah turned his head to watch. His glance lasted no longer than it would have taken the tear to fall, but in that moment when their gazes met she saw that it was no more over for him than it was for her.

The ceremony ended. Addie walked down the aisle on Robert's arm. Noah took Sarah's. For the duration of the exit they touched, but it was the only contact they shared that day. At the church door he released her. Throughout a dinner in the churchyard and a dance beneath the June sky they remained carefully aloof. Through the thousands of touches and words exchanged with familiar people, they exchanged none with each other. Sometimes, across the crowded yard Sarah would see him, drinking beer or talking, dancing with Emma or Addie, but if their eyes chanced to meet they parted in the same breath.

Once he danced with Geneva Dawkins, who wore a profuse blush, and once with one of Rose's girls, whom he seemed to find highly amusing. He threw his head back and laughed at something she said. How excruciating to watch the play of sun on his hair and mustache, to relive moments when his laughter had been shared with her, to realize it would not be again. *Who knows? He might even start frequenting Rose's again.* The possibility brought Sarah an actual physical pain.

For a while he watched a game of mumbletypeg whose knife-flippers were all lads Josh's age. When he glanced up and saw Sarah watching him, she turned away.

The town had grown. Unfamiliar faces dotted the crowd. She put her time to use introducing herself to each one, taking down names for the "Welcome" column of the *Chronicle,* inviting the new women to join the Ladies' Club, the new men to attend the town meetings. But her zest for the work seemed a thing of the past.

Near the end of the afternoon, Sarah searched out Emma.

"I have a big favor to ask you."

"Ask away."

"I need a place to stay tonight."

"You've got it."

"A pallet on the floor will do. I know your place is crowded."

"You've got it."

"I thought I should leave the house to Addie and Robert. You see, the original plan was that—"

"I know what the original plan was."

"I'd rent a hotel room for the night, but they're full and—"

"Are you going to quit apologizing? We're your friends. You'll stay with us and no questions asked."

She found Addie and told her. Addie said, "I feel like I'm putting you out of your own house."

"It's your wedding night. If we had a train, you'd be on it, heading somewhere for a honeymoon. Since you can't be, I'm going to Emma's."

At Emma's, after all the others had retired for the night, the two women sat in the kitchen, sipping something Emma called "teakettle tea," little more than weak tea diluted with a lot of hot milk.

"It was a nice wedding," Sarah said.

"Yup."

"And Addie was a beautiful bride."

"She was that."

"Matheson didn't bat an eye."

"No, he didn't."

"I've never seen Robert so happy."

"We going to chitchat all night about junk like that or are you going to spill what's on your mind?"

"You know what's on my mind . . . Noah."

"I thought that was over."

"It's supposed to be, but I still love him."

"I saw him staring at you a time or two when you weren't looking, too."

"You did?"

"Me and about five hundred others. So what happened between you two?"

"Oh Emma, it's so complicated."

"I'm not simple, you know. I might be able to shed some light if you give me a chance."

Sarah considered, sipped her teakettle tea. She wanted to confide in Emma, but now that the opportunity presented itself, she wondered about loyalties.

"I'd be telling you without Addie's permission so I must have your word of honor it'll go no farther than this."

"You got it."

Sarah told the entire story. When she reached the part about Addie and their father, Emma put a hand over her mouth and squeezed hard. Above it, her eyes seemed incapable of blinking.

". . . and so ever since then, every time Noah touches me . . . I don't know . . . something happens inside me and I stiffen up. I know he's not my father, I *know* that, but somehow I feel threatened and I freeze up and . . . and I feel so stupid and guilty and . . . Oh Emma, what am I going to do . . ." Sarah was in tears as the last word wailed through the kitchen.

Emma, appalled and out of her depth, found it easiest to draw Sarah from her chair and clamp her in a hard embrace to avoid meeting the younger woman's eyes. A father and his own daughter. Dear lord, in all her born days she'd never heard of anything so vile. Poor Addie, and this poor one here, worshiping the damned old swine all those years. Who could blame her for backing off from anything wearing pants after getting a shock like that? But what should she tell her? How should she comfort her when Emma's own reaction was so horrified she was having trouble coming to grips with it herself.

Sarah sobbed and clung as she would to a mother. Emma patted and rubbed her shoulders.

"Oh, my dear, dear girl, what a terrible thing for you to go through."

"I love him, Emma. I want to be married to him, but . . . Oh Emma, how can I change . . . ?"

Emma had no notion what to advise. Such convoluted relationships were beyond her scope of experience. She had fallen in love with a plain man, married him, had his children, worked hard and lived by the Good Book. She'd thought that's how most lives worked. This disgusting story though . . .

"You've got to give it some time is all. Isn't that what they say heals all wounds?"

"But I hurt Noah so. I pushed him away when all he wanted to do was help me. He'll never come back."

"You don't know that for sure. Maybe he's just giving you some time to heal."

"I don't want time. I want to be married to him now and be as normal as everybody else."

Emma patted her some more, rubbed her shoulders, felt like crying herself, but could think of not one word to ease this pitiful creature.

"Oh me," she sighed. "I wish I could help you."

Sarah dried her eyes and Emma refilled their cups. When the two women were reseated, Sarah spoke, gazing forlornly at Emma.

"He danced with that girl from Rose's today. I saw them laughing together."

Emma could only squeeze her hand in silence.

In the house on Mt. Moriah Road, the bride and groom entered their bedroom. Robert set the lantern down, closed the curtains and returned to Addie. He smiled, reaching to the top of her head. "Your flowers are wilted." He took the plum blossoms and put them beside the lantern.

She rolled her eyes up and touched her hair self-consciously. "I'm surprised they didn't fall out. There's hardly enough hair to hold them."

"There's enough," he said, drawing her hands down, keeping them.

They had been among a crowd for ten hours, jovial, smiling, celebrating, while this singular hour waited like winter-locked violets await the spring.

"How do you feel?" he asked.

"Nervous."

He laughed. "Why? We've only waited six years for this, or is it seven?"

"More like twelve," she said. "Since we were children."

"Very young children, and I came to your door begging for fat drippings and thought you were the most beautiful creature God ever put on this earth." He took her face in both his hands. "I still think so."

"Oh Robert." Her glance dropped.

How amazing, he thought, *she's timid with me.*

He dropped his hands to her shoulders.

"Mrs. Baysinger," he said, as if the word had some new, exotic flavor that he was testing on his tongue.

"Yes, Mr. Baysinger?" She looked up.

"Shall I kiss you first or unhook those fifteen hooks down your back?"

"How do you know there are fifteen?"

"I counted them today."

Her face lit with surprise. "How could you have counted them? They don't show."

"I can see I'll have to prove it. Turn around."

She turned, smiling at her window curtains while he counted aloud.

"One . . . two . . . three . . ."

"Robert?"

"Four . . . five . . ."

"How could you have counted them?"

"Your stitches show. Six . . . seven . . . eight . . ."

"Robert?"

"Ten . . . eleven . . ."

She waited through numbers twelve and thirteen before admitting, "I thought today would never end."

At *fifteen* the room fell into a vibrant silence, broken only by their breathing. The dress was open to her hips. He slipped his hands inside and rested them on her waist. He leaned down and kissed her gently between the shoulder blades, lingering, breathing her scent, while his pulse felt like hammerblows in his throat.

"I think I deserve a medal," he whispered, "for all the times I wanted to do this and didn't." At her waist his grip tightened. He straightened, drawing her back flush against him, speaking near her ear. "In that hotel room on Christmas Eve, and here in this house on a hundred occasions since then, when I sat across the table from you playing Chinese checkers, or eating apple cobbler, or listening to Sarah talk. Sometimes in the kitchen when we'd be doing dishes or you were sitting at the table stitching a curtain and I'd look at you and watch your hair change from gray to blond, and realize that I'd loved you since I was twelve years old and no other man in this world had as much right to you as I."

"Is that what you were thinking?" Her voice sounded breathy.

"I wanted you so much I felt pagan."

"And I thought it was just the opposite. All these months since you took me out of Rose's I thought you were remembering my past and trying to get beyond it."

The butts of his hands pressed down upon her hipbones, then rode her ribs to the hollow below her breasts before starting back down. "How could you think that? I've wanted you, wanted this since I was eighteen and I went to your father to ask his permission to marry you. And since Christmas Eve when I made the worst blunder of my life by offering you money. Addie," he whispered, "can you forgive me for that?"

She turned, forcing his hands to divert to her elbows. Fixing her shining green eyes on his, she whispered, "I will forgive you, Robert, if you'll end this torture and make me your wife."

The wait was over. He kissed her wholly, reaching deep around her until their bodies coiled like vines and his hands were inside the back of her gown, skimming her shoulders, waist and spine, sweeping lower still, filling with her petticoats and—faint within them—the swells of her flesh. Through tier upon tier of cotton, he learned her shape, moving the fabric and himself against her while their kiss became grand and avid.

When he lifted his head they were both breathing like runners. Her lips glimmered wet in the lamplight, her eyes were wide, the pupils dilated, fixed upon him. He gripped her right hand, hard, and kissed the butt of it with his intense gaze riveted upon hers. Brief as an exclamation point, that kiss, before he dropped her hand and stepped back.

"Don't move," he ordered; fiery-eyed as he began stripping off his jacket. "Don't touch a thing. I haven't waited all these years to watch you take your own clothes off."

"My shoes . . ."

"All right, your shoes."

She sat on the edge of the bed with a buttonhook while he rid himself of jacket and vest, then sailed his shirt toward a chair. It fell on the floor as he sat on the bed beside her and bent to his own shoestrings. Removing their footwear, they exchanged ardent glances, then he stood, shucked off his trousers, flung them aside and reached for her hand. "Come here," he said huskily, standing before her in his short-legged cotton union suit. She gave him her hand and let herself be drawn to her feet.

"Now I'm going to see you," Robert said.

He turned down her dress, unbuttoned the waist of her petticoat, freed her corset hooks and stripped the whole works to her feet, shucking garters and stockings along the way. He rose, offered his hand, and she stepped from the blossom of clothing, naked.

He let his eyes rove, let a smile put a single shallow wrinkle beside his mouth and said, "Aren't you the prettiest thing I ever saw."

He lifted his eyes to her face. "Why, Addie, you're blushing."

"So are you."

The smile reached his eyes. "Well, isn't that nice."

She touched the buttons at his chest and asked, "May I?"

He raised his palms and let them fall.

A moment later their blushes intensified.

He touched her the first time with four fingertips, just below her throat, on the firm, pale place above her breasts, as if to confirm her reality. From there straight down, over the tracery of lines left by her tight undergarments, then circling the perimeter of each full breast with a touch as faint as a dropping leaf.

As her eyelids closed he gently put his mouth on hers and murmured against her lips, "You're so beautiful," then picked her up and laid her on the bed.

The lantern light angled across her face as he braced on an elbow above her. It gilded her skin and sketched her eyelashes as sweeping dark curves that followed the line of her cheek, just as his hand followed the line of her breast and ribs.

"I love you, Addie," he whispered.

"Oh Robert, I love you too . . . so much."

He opened his hand on her stomach. She might never have been touched before, so fervid was her reaction, a shudder and soft gasp as she drew his head down and claimed his mouth with hers. Silence passed, a long, rich silence, while they became two in love, exalted by it.

He touched her low, made her lips part and her breath cease.

She took him in hand, made his eyes close and his heart plunge.

They opened their eyes and breathed once more, taking each other back to the beginning . . . Robert and Addie, children again, innocents, trudging through the days of acquaintanceship. Robert and Addie, adolescents, studying each other with changed eyes, imagining this day. Robert and Addie, husband and wife, pure in intention, taking their due, sharing an imperfect love made perfect by forgiveness.

It was, for Addie, all she had missed, and for Robert, all he had dreamed.

When their bodies joined it became triumph. He was kneeling with her folded around him—a damp leaf around a stem—her arms crossed upon his shoulders, his caught below her hips.

Pressed together wholly, they stilled in wonder. He lifted his face and met her lambent gaze. All those years . . . how incredible that they'd never before known each other this way. How perfect that nature had provided this accolade for two who loved as they did.

They kissed. And created motion. And made it lithe and graceful as flight.

In time her head hung back and she shuddered, calling out his name . . . half of his name . . . the remainder drifting off into infinity.

He took her down beneath him, beat an ardent rhythm upon her and watched her eyes adore his countenance, watched a smile steal upon her face as his left to make way for the clench and flush of climax.

Afterward, he rested upon her heavily.

The hair on his nape was wet. His limbs were sapped and lifeless. His breath was sketchy. Onto their sides he rolled them, keeping her close with one heel, then folding an elbow beneath his ear. He touched her nose with a fingertip and let it trail over her lips and chin.

"How do you feel, Mrs. Baysinger?"

She smiled and closed her eyes. "Don't make me say it."

"Say it."

She opened her eyes; in them, quiet satisfaction. "Like it was my first time."

He waited, thought some about what to say, drawing patterns on her throat. "It was," he said, and sketched a grapevine around her left breast.

They loved with their eyes, and after a lengthy spell of silence she said, "Robert?"

He was too content to reply.

"There's something I must say. It's about my other life."

He stopped sketching grapevines. "Say it."

"Just this once, and then I'll never talk about it again."

"Say it . . . it's all right."

"When I was with others," she told him, looking squarely into his eyes, "I had this place I escaped to, this other person I became. I was Eve, and being her was the only way I knew how to survive. But tonight, with you, I was Addie. For the first time in my life I was Addie."

He clasped her to himself full length, his chin caught on her shoulder, holding her strong.

"Shh."

"But you have to know, Robert, how much I love you for giving me back to myself."

"I know . . ." he whispered, pulling back to look into her eyes. "I know."

"I love you," she told him once more.

He accepted her statement without diluting it by returning the words. And anyway . . . she knew. She knew.

She surprised him by declaring next, "I want to have your babies."

He asked, "Can you?"

"Yes, I can."

"I didn't know for sure. I supposed there must have been something you did to prevent it all those years. I didn't know if it was permanent."

"No, it wasn't."

He kissed her, taking her neck in his hand and petting her hair afterward as if it were a scarf upturned by the wind.

"Robert?"

"Hm?" He continued smoothing her hair.

"I want a lot of your babies. More than this house will hold."

He smiled and boosted himself above her. Just before their lips met he said, "Then we'd better get busy making them."

CHAPTER 22

WITH the loss of Noah, the fervor had gone out of Sarah's life. Always, before his advent, she had enjoyed a passion for her work that energized and drove her. Whatever the demand placed on her by the exigencies of newspapering, she placed an even greater one upon herself. She had been a fomenter, an inciter, a zealot who oftentimes charged in with horns lowered, her enthusiasm stemming from some source she had not questioned, had not actually known she enjoyed until it disappeared.

In the weeks following the wedding, she lowered her horns no more. She went to the newspaper office each day, but her work there seemed of little consequence. She composed articles, set type and proofread, but her labors seemed trite if not pointless. She scouted news, sold advertising and reviewed plays but admitted that in the long run what she did made very little difference in the grand scheme of the world.

At home she retired early to her room, feeling like an interloper downstairs where Addie and Robert, paragons of marital bliss, snuggled on the settee, held hands and sometimes dropped quiet kisses upon one another. Though she rued them none of their happiness, witnessing it left her feeling bereft.

In her room, she began articles that often lay unfinished while some transient memory would bring forth a line of poetry. Sometimes she composed an entire poem, other times only the one line; sometimes she poured out her loneliness in her personal journal, other times stared at the grain of the tulipwood box until her hand reached out and opened it, removed her engagement brooch and held it, rubbing it with her thumb. Afterward, she would cover her face with her palms and dwell upon her shortcomings as a woman.

Who would ever love her, a frigid shell unable to accept human warmth? If she could not accept it from a man she loved, what hope was there of overcoming her disastrous strait? Sometimes she imagined herself going to Noah and instigating a liaison, carrying it through to its end, simply to test herself. But she was too ignorant to visualize such endings, and after recounting what little she did know of sexual encounters, she would always emerge feeling guilty and dissolute.

How ironic that once she had pushed Noah away, crying, "No! I will not be like Addie!" while now she prayed to become more like her, only to find herself instead an aberration, a freak. It seemed the greatest of cruelties that nature had given her the need to be loved while robbing her of the ability to accept its most profound manifestation.

Often she damned her father, that once-admired pillar of propriety, whose licentious acts had brought her to this impasse. Despising his memory only added to her grief, turning her lonelier and more retiring at home, more bitter and fault-finding at work, where, daily, she was forced to touch the tools she had once so valued for having been Isaac Merritt's.

One day in mid-July when the newspaper office was hot and pervaded by the smell of animal dung from the street, she made a regrettable scene. She had been counting the number of times Patrick got out his hip flask and tipped it up. She'd also been listening to the speed with which the type clicked into the composing stick. It seemed to have gotten slower as the afternoon progressed. A clunk and skitter sounded behind her, followed by a curse. She looked over her shoulder to find Patrick mumbling under his breath and perusing pied type that was scattered over the galley tray. Rather than begin sorting it, he reached for his flask again. She swung about and knocked the flask from his hand.

"That's right! Drink some more! That'll fix the pied type, won't it!" she shouted. On the floor the flask whirled twice and gurgled out its contents.

Patrick tipped back on his heels. His cheeks were flushed and his gaze somewhat glassy. " 'M sorry, Miss Sarah. Didn't mean t——"

"*You didn't mean,*" she scoffed. "You poison yourself day after day with that . . . that *swill* while it slows down your work and fills the very air with fumes! Well, I'm sick of it, Mr. Bradigan, do you hear me! Sick of it and of you stumbling around here inept in the afternoons!"

Her shrill words echoed in the room as she spun and stormed out the door, leaving Patrick and Josh staring after her. The puddle of liquor was soaking into the floorboards. The bottle had stopped gurgling. Josh crossed the room and picked it up, handed it to Patrick apologetically.

"She didn't mean it, Patrick."

"Yes, she did." Patrick studied the bottle in his thin, knobby hands. He sniffed loudly. "I drink too much and I know it."

"Naw. You do all right. You set type faster than anybody she's ever seen. She's told me so."

Patrick shook his head abjectly, staring at the bottle. "No . . . she's right. I'm nothing but a rock around her ankle."

He looked so forlorn Josh didn't know what to say by way of comfort. "Come on." He draped an arm over Patrick's back. "I'll help you pick up the type. We'll have it all sorted by the time she gets back."

Sarah, however, did not come back before closing time. When Josh and Patrick left for the day they locked the door.

She returned shortly after six P.M. to find the pied type straightened, the galley meticulously filled and lying on the composing stone with the furniture locked into place around it, ready to be printed.

The room smelled of turpentine and was stiflingly hot, the back door closed, cutting off drafts. The front door was open to the street sounds that seemed remote and lonely. Sarah stood beside the printing press feeling as if the platen had just been lowered on her chest. She had lashed out at Patrick when it was not he with whom she was displeased, but with life. She had treated him unforgivably, and had no excuse. Granted, Patrick drank, but he managed his work in spite of it, and pied type only rarely. *Anyone* who worked around type long enough would pie it occasionally: this afternoon's spill could have been caused by Josh or herself as easily as by Patrick. The three of them had established a wonderful working relationship. If anyone was threatening it lately it was she, not Patrick; she with her quick temper and sullen moods and her inability to be pleased, no matter how the others tried.

She dropped to her chair, let her head fall back against it and closed her eyes.

Oh Noah, she thought, *I'm no good without you.*

The next morning Patrick failed to show up. Sarah's apology waited on her lips, but by eight-thirty, when no Patrick appeared, she suspected she'd have no opportunity to express it. She looked up often, watching figures passing on the street, but by nine o'clock he still hadn't arrived.

She took the broom and went out to sweep her boardwalk, pausing several times to gaze up the street in the direction of the hotel, hoping to see his tall, curved frame come shambling toward her. Still no Patrick.

She went inside and asked Josh, "What did he say yesterday?"

Josh shrugged and studied the toes of his boots.

"You can tell me, Josh. I know I was in the wrong and I'm very sorry for it. I only hope I get a chance to say so to him. What did he say?"

"He said he knows he drinks too much and that he's a rock around your ankle."

Sarah bit her lips to keep them from trembling, turned toward the window and murmured affectionately, "Oh Patrick."

By noon, when he still hadn't appeared, she knew he was gone, knew even as she hustled over to the Grand Central Hotel to ask Sam Peoples if he knew where Patrick was.

"He paid up this morning and left," Sam told her.

"On the stage?"

"I'm afraid so, Miss Merritt."

She turned away quickly to hide the tears that sprang to her eyes. *Patrick, come back. I didn't mean it. You were always so good to me, from the first night I came to town when you laid down your gold for me right here in this lobby and paid for my room. Please, Patrick, I'm so sorry.*

Patrick didn't come back of course. He had vanished the way all tramp printers vanish, as she had early on expected him to, but as she had in later months believed he never would, for she had come to rely on him so completely she'd been unable to imagine running the paper without him. He'd been there at its inception. He'd set her first type and run her first copies under the big pine tree the day she'd been locked in that mineshaft. He'd been around here for months, singing amusing Irish ditties, training Josh—and a patient teacher he'd been—and manning the office whenever Sarah left it. And once he had even kissed her and asked her to marry him.

One didn't lose a friend like Patrick without regrets.

Summer advanced and August came on—hot, dusty and dry. The underground quartz mining bore immense riches not only in gold, but in silver as well, while the prospect in placer mining continued at record highs. The shipments leaving Deadwood were valued in the tens of thousands of dollars. The James gang was raiding all over the upper central corridor of the country, and a kid named Antrim chalked up his first victims down in Arizona. Then one day in late August, a Deadwood freight wagon was found ten miles southwest of town with its driver and guards all dead and its thirty thousand dollars' worth of gold and silver gone.

Within an hour after the news reached town, Noah Campbell mounted a buckskin gelding in front of his office, signaled to the men who'd volunteered to ride with him and dug his heels into the horse's sides. A cloud of dust rose as the riders galloped down Main Street with guns strapped to their hips, rolls behind their saddles and their buckskin bonnet strings cinched up tightly by wooden beads.

The street was crowded with people who'd heard the news and had gathered to watch the posse off. Noah rode through them with his eyes leveled on the horizon and his expression grim. His glance shifted only once, when he passed the office of the *Deadwood Chronicle,* where Josh Dawkins, Addie Baysinger, Sarah Merritt and her new printer, Edward Norvecky had gathered to watch the departure. Of the four, he saw only one, Sarah Merritt, dressed in her leather apron with her arms crossed tightly over the bib of it and her eyes following him, only him, intent and worried as he shifted his eyes from her and riveted them straight ahead as he galloped past.

Robert rode with him, and Freeman Block, and Andy Tatum and Dan Turley and Craven Lee, and a delegation of three miners, plus an ex-army tracker who went by the name of Wolf. They rode out toward Lead, across the forested hills of Terry Peak, through the limestone plateau, a high escarpment of buff and pink rock and invariable ponderosa pine. They spent their first night in a cave at the foot of the cliffs, continuing the next morning across "the racetrack," a red valley of sandstone, clay and shale that entirely circled the hills, its soil so salty and dry no tree could survive in it and no man wanted to. Across the barren racetrack to the hogback ridge—the outer rim of the hills—traveling through eerie graveyards of petrified wood that dropped eventually to the arid stretches of the Great Plains beyond. And so into the plains themselves where water was scarce and food scarcer.

The August sun scorched their skin. The wind dried their eyes. Their tongues felt swollen. Their mounts plodded listlessly, and they stopped often, pouring water from their canteens into their hats to water their horses, drinking sparingly themselves, gnawing on jerky to replace the salt in their systems, redonning their hats to feel the welcome coolness on their heads dry within minutes as they pushed on again.

A hundred and fifty miles to the west lay the Bighorns, the probable destination of their prey, but little more than a blue haze on the horizon. The men plodded toward it. Their lips cracked. Their beards grew. Their skin stank. It became difficult to recall why they were out here in this purgatory.

Their fourth night out they camped in the open on hard earth, saddle stiff and disheartened, with prickly pear and yucca for company.

When they were bedded down on their comfortless bedrolls with their heads on their saddles, studying the stars, Robert said, "What's wrong, Noah?"

"We're never going to catch those murderers. The sonsabitches are gone and they left three dead men behind."

"No, I mean, what else is wrong? You've ridden for four days and haven't said a dozen civil words to anyone."

"It's too goddamned dry out here for talking."

Robert let that pass. "They say in town you've gotten sour and heartless, that you'd as soon throw a drunk in jail as point him toward home. You never used to be that way."

"If you don't mind, Robert, I've got some shut-eye to catch."

"It's Sarah, isn't it?"

Noah snorted. "Sarah . . . shit."

"She's just as bad as you. What the hell are the two of you trying to prove?"

"Robert, shut up, will you? When I want your advice I'll ask for it."

"You saw her out there in front of her place when we rode out, worried sick about you, don't pretend you didn't. Are you two going to stay stubborn for the rest of your lives?"

Like a spring, Noah sat up. "Robert, goddammit, I've had about enough of you! Sarah Merritt is out of my life, and I'll run my jail any way I see fit, and I'll run this posse any way I see fit! Now shut the hell up and leave me alone!"

With an angry lurch, he flung himself on his side and yanked his blanket to his shoulders, turning his back on his friend.

That night while Noah slept, something bit him, some crawling creature, no doubt—a spider maybe, Doc Turley said, examining the welt in the morning. Turley broke a yucca spine and smeared some slimy juice on the bite, but it remained scarlet and swollen and left Noah feeling dizzy and fevered. Wolf, the tracker, returned from a brief scouting trip and said it was no use going on, they'd lost the trail. The murderers were on their way to the Bighorns while the posse was exhausted and hungry and sunburned. It was time to go home.

The whole town saw them return, looking like a bunch of convicts, drooping in their saddles, with scraggly beards and dusty clothes and no prisoners in tow. Sarah went to the window of the *Chronicle* office and watched them ride by, relief slumping her shoulders. The hat she'd given Noah looked as though it had been sifted with flour. A dirty handkerchief hung around his neck, and his eyes, fixed straight ahead, appeared small and wincing in his sunburned face while his hands rested on his saddlehorn.

"Looks like they didn't catch 'em," Josh said, at her side.

"No."

"They look pretty rough, don't they?"

"Eight days is a long time."

"You going to interview the marshal about it?"

More than anything in the world, Sarah wanted to be that close to Noah once again, if only to ask him questions. The posse rode out of sight. Sarah drew a deep breath and turned to Josh. "If I draw up a list of questions, how would you like to do it?"

Josh's eyes bugged. "Really?"

"You've got to start sometime."

"Well, if you think I can."

"You interview the marshal, then we'll work on the story together."

"Gosh, thanks, Sarah!"

That night at supper, Robert supplied the story in its entirety, while putting away enough food for two men.

"Noah's changed," he remarked at one point.

Sarah refused to ask. Instead she waited for Addie to do so.

"He's got the disposition of a wounded boar," Robert said. "He's surly and silent most of the time, and when he does talk everybody wishes he wouldn't."

Sarah decided it was time she left the table. "Well . . . I've got some words to get on paper. Thank you, Robert, for filling me in."

"Sure."

When she had escaped the room Robert and Addie looked at each other and Addie asked, "Do you think either one of them will ever break down?"

"Hell, I don't know. I took enough abuse trying to talk some sense into him without getting into it with her, too."

Over the summer the town's population had leaped, as predicted the previous fall. It was no longer an uncommon sight to see women, even single ones of marriageable age, on the street. The arrival of women brought the arrival of the first ready-made clothing store for them, its first milliner, its first sidesaddles, its first sewing machine, which was purchased by Robert Baysinger for his wife's curtain-making enterprise.

Sarah Merritt had inaugurated a women's column in the *Chronicle.* It seemed there was never a shortage of news.

A schoolteacher named Amanda Searles was hired and would begin teaching in September. An assayer from the Denver mint, named Chambers Davis, opened a full metallurgical laboratory with one furnace for the melting of gold dust and two for crucible assays of ore. In the same building the town's second stamp mill opened for business along with the first bathing arrangement with both hot and cold running water—the latter at the encouragement of Davis's well-liked, socialite wife, Adrienne. A man named Seth Bullock, who'd run for sheriff in the fall and lost, was appointed to the position by Governor John Pennington. The Deadwood Post Office was established and the town was named the county seat. A judge named Murphy moved to town and built the first brick house in all of the Black Hills. The nearby village of Gayville was destroyed by fire, prompting the organization of the Pioneer Hook and Ladder Company—again, the first in the hills. A bigamist and soiled dove named Kitty LeRoy was shot and killed by her fifth husband, a faro dealer named Sam Curley, who then turned the gun on himself.

Beyond the hills, the national bicycle craze took fire in the East with the first mass production of Colonel Albert Pope's "Columbia" safety bicycle. Cycling clubs formed everywhere and started badgering for better roads, begging the newspapers to back them up in their efforts. Adrienne Davis had a bicycle shipped into Deadwood and stopped traffic everywhere when she was seen riding it in skirts shorter than her ankles.

Meanwhile, James J. Hill was busy buying up land to lay down the foundations of his railroad empire while President Marvin Hughit of the North Western Railroad assured the mayor of Deadwood that the rails would head their way as soon as the survey showed it to be practical.

By the end of August the grasshoppers left Minnesota.

In September child labor became an issue in Massachusetts.

In October the Evans and Hornick ox train arrived in Deadwood from Fort Pierre with a record-breaking 300,000 pounds of freight.

Over the stretch of that summer and autumn the face of Deadwood changed dramatically. The brush wickiups were replaced by frame buildings, many of them sporting exterior paint. Through their windows curtains could be seen. The flowers planted by the incoming women trimmed yards and fences. The town now employed a lamplighter/ street cleaner who made the main thoroughfare a more pleasant place by both night and day. A new school building was erected. Children were seen walking to it in the mornings and from it in the afternoons.

Deadwood had been domesticated.

So had Addie Baysinger. One evening in late November, with supper over and her hand tight in Robert's beneath the table, she smiled at Sarah and said, "We're going to have a baby."

Sarah's coffee cup never made it to her lips. It clicked onto her saucer as her eyes went round. For moments she only stared. At last she found her tongue.

"Oh Addie, how perfect."

"We're so happy. Aren't we, Robert?" Addie turned her adoring gaze on Robert, who brought her hand from beneath the table and kissed her knuckles.

His smile verified it even before he spoke. "Absolutely happy. We want a boy."

Sarah covered their joined hands with both of her own, squeezing hard. "This is wonderful news. I'm so happy for you. Congratulations." Their countenances radiated such uncomplicated joy, the sight of them beaming at one another gripped Sarah's heart. Her little sister and dear, kind Robert—they'd weathered every setback and emerged victorious.

Truly, their happiness was a victory. Living with them, Sarah had observed its effects firsthand as the two of them settled into the routine of married life like contented birds building a nest. Now that nest would be filled, and it was time—Sarah realized—that she herself moved out of it.

"When is the happy event?"

Addie shrugged excitedly. "I don't know for sure. Sometime in late spring, I think."

"The perfect time. Warm days and cool nights, and a while before the worst of the mosquitoes come out."

"As far as I'm concerned, any time would be the perfect time," Addie said.

"Also the perfect time for me to move out," Sarah added.

Addie's brow furled. "But Sarah, we have plenty of room. Why, this little feller won't need more than a clothes basket to sleep in."

"It's time," Sarah said simply. "I've been thinking about it for a couple of months already. I appreciate your letting me live with you for as long as I have, but this is *your* home, and it's time I left it to you."

Addie and Robert spoke together.

"But Sarah—"

"You know we don't—"

Sarah held up her hands. "I know." She rested them on the table. "You would allow me to stay until I grew too old to climb the stairs if I were silly enough to put you out that long."

"We love you, Sarah," Robert said earnestly. "We don't want you to leave."

Sarah smiled at him tenderly and squeezed the back of his hand once more. "Thank you, Robert, but *I* need to go. I need to have a place of my own, roots of my own, some sense of belonging somewhere for life."

"But the house is yours as well as mine," Addie said.

"It was bought with Father's money, but so was the newspaper office. So we're even, aren't we? Now, I don't want to hear any more about it." Sarah rose, collecting empty coffee cups. "I've decided I'll start looking immediately and will hope to have a place of my own by the first of the year. I'll stay here through Christmas, but that's all." As she carried the cups away, Robert and Addie exchanged glances that admitted, while they were reluctant to see Sarah go, the idea of living alone was undeniably inviting. Robert rose and followed Sarah to the dry sink where she set the cups down. He took her by the shoulders and turned her to face him.

"As long as you know you're always welcome here."

There was no question in Sarah's mind. She also knew as she looked into Robert's eyes that he still felt guilty for causing the breakup between herself and Noah, and that, as penance, he would keep her beneath his wing forever if she would let him.

"I know, Robert. I'll only be across town somewhere, and I'll come back often to see that little boy of yours. I'll probably spoil him silly."

He squeezed her arms and kissed her cheek. The touch of his mustache brought the memory of another and made Sarah already feel like a lonely maiden aunt.

Shortly thereafter, Addie began wearing loose-fitting dresses without waists. She was the healthiest expectant mother imaginable, with a new glow in her normally pale cheeks, her gold hair shiny and grown to collar length, and a contentment level that sometimes brought Sarah a pang of envy. Having grown up as she had in a motherless home, Sarah had never witnessed marital bliss. During those winter days while Christmas approached—short days when dark fell early and the favorite place was near the kitchen range—both she and Robert took to coming home earlier. He would enter the house smiling and go directly to Addie, wherever she was, whatever she was doing. He would kiss her forehead, mouth or ear and ask how the little fellow was doing in there, and would glance lovingly at Addie's round stomach. She would show him the tiny clothes she'd made—the sewing machine was constantly clunking—or exclaim that she'd read in *Peterson's Magazine* some tidbit about the preparation of baby foods or diaper care or teething. Once Sarah found them standing facing a kitchen window at dusk with Robert behind Addie, his chin on her shoulder and his arms doubled around her midriff below her breasts. Addie's arms covered his and her head was tilted to one side. Neither of them spoke, only rocked blissfully left and right. Sarah watched them for some time, then tiptoed away, leaving them undisturbed to stand by herself at the front-room window and stare out at the dusky tones of twilight, thinking of Noah and aching for all they had missed.

Addie and Robert were painfully aware of Sarah's increasing despondency and withdrawal. At night, in bed, they whispered about it and wondered how to help her.

One night in December, when supper was over and Sarah had retired early to her room, Robert went to Addie where she sat stitching in the parlor in a straight-backed side chair which had grown more comfortable as her girth increased. He bent down and braced his hands on the arms of her chair and said, looking into her eyes, "I'm going to Noah's."

When they had exchanged a prolonged gaze she somberly touched his cheek and said, "Good luck, dear."

It was almost eight-thirty by the time he approached Noah's kitchen door. Noah answered his knock and for moments neither man spoke.

Finally Noah said, "Well, this is a surprise."

"You still pissed off at me?" Robert asked, point-blank.

"No. I got over that long ago."

"Am I disturbing anything?"

"Hardly. Just having a late supper. Come on in."

Inside, Noah said, "Take your coat off, sit down."

The room looked barren and lonely but for the yellow flowered curtains that Addie had made last spring, the only woman-touch in the room. Noah's interrupted meal consisted of beans and bread on a blue enamel plate. The table had no cloth; the room no pictures on the wall, ivies at the windowsill, nor rug beneath the table. Noah's boots stood by the woodbox, his hat lay on the table, his gunbelt hung on the back of his chair and his heavy leather jacket hung on a peg by the door, alone. It wrenched Robert's heart to see his friend so lonely.

"So how've you been?"

Noah shrugged. "Oh, you know. Same as always." He sat down and resumed his meal. "I hear you and Addie are going to have a baby," he remarked.

"That's right. Sometime toward spring. She's one happy woman."

"I hear you're one happy man, too."

"That's a fact."

"Well that's good. I'm damned happy for you both."

Silence fell. Noah ate a forkful of beans. Robert sat back in his chair with one elbow on the table and his ankle over a knee, studying his friend.

"How come we never see you up at the house anymore?"

Noah stopped eating. "You know why."

They measured each other awhile. "So," Robert said, "you avoid her and you avoid us, too."

"It's not intentional. I figured you'd know that."

"Well, for what it's worth, we miss you around there."

Noah set down his fork and studied it in silence.

"I came over here to tell you something."

Noah met Robert's eyes and waited.

"Sarah says she's moving out the first of the year."

Noah's eyes remained expressionless while he absorbed the news. "So?"

Robert spoke with fire. "So she's going to find some house and live in it alone, and you're going to sit up here eating your beans alone at eight-thirty at night and it makes no goddamned sense at all!"

"She doesn't want me."

"She wants you so damned bad she's dying inside."

Noah snorted and looked away.

"Jesus Christ, man, she had a shock. I know because I'm the one who gave it to her. And, yes, she needed some time to get over it, but not the rest of her life!"

Noah snapped a look at Robert. "She wrote me off and I'm not crawling back to her to get kicked in the teeth again. Twice is enough!"

Robert studied Noah awhile and asked quietly, "You love her, don't you?"

Noah threw his head back, pushed away from the table edge with both hands and exclaimed to the ceiling, "Sheece!"

"Don't you?"

Noah leveled his chin and shot a withering glance at Robert from the corner of his eye.

"So how many other women have you been seeing lately?"

"How many other men has she been seeing?"

"None. She sits in that house at night watching Addie's stomach get bigger and tiptoeing around to try to keep out of our way, and I never saw a lonelier sight in my whole life than her trying to pretend she's happier without you. Unless, of course, it's you up here with your beans, trying to pretend you're happier without her."

Noah tipped forward, clunked his elbows on the table, joined his hands in a hard knot and pressed them to his mouth, staring at an empty chair on the opposite side of the table.

Robert let the silence go, let Noah stare and think awhile. On the stove a teakettle sizzled. In the firebox a coal popped. Noah's eyes got suspiciously glisteny. He held them wide, careful not to blink.

Finally he closed them, dropped his forehead to his thumb knuckles and whispered, "I can't."

Robert reached out and put his hand around Noah's forearm. "I know," he said softly, "it's hard. But it's hard for her, too." He let some seconds pass before adding, "Chambers and Adrienne Davis have invited Addie and me to their place for dinner next Saturday. We'll be leaving the house at seven o'clock." He squeezed Noah's arm once, let his hand fall away and rose, buttoning his coat.

Noah lifted his head and stared at the chair as before. Robert put on his hat and gloves.

"Sometimes a person can suffocate on his own pride," he said, then left his friend sitting there in his silent kitchen with his elbows braced on either side of a plate of cold beans.

When Robert was gone Noah remained at the table a long time, his wounds freshly opened. The last seven months had been hell: lonely, painful, tormented. She had rejected him, emasculated him, and left him still loving her. Love? Was this love? This colorless movement through days that seemed to have neither crest nor trough but rolled along doldrum-flat? This searching the faces on the street for a glimpse of her, then crossing to the other side if she appeared up ahead? This dwelling on the memories he had of her instead of making new ones with someone else? This wanting, one minute, to go to her and shake her till her head snapped, the next pitying her to the point of misery?

He had moved through his first twenty-six years with relative clear-mindedness, quite sure of himself, his motives, his desires, his goals. Since Sarah Merritt had come into his life and left it, he had become like the habitual drinker who says, I can quit anytime I want to, then gets drunk by noon every day. She was his liquor, the thing he declared he could live without, but dwelled on with debilitating regularity.

Perhaps this was true because he was the spurned one and his ego was wrinkled. But if that were the case, he would have hied himself over to Rose's and gotten his ego starched months ago. Instead, he had felt no predilection toward that pastime in which he'd once so blithely indulged; the revelations about Addie's sorry past had taken care of that.

There were other women in Deadwood now, decent women he might have pursued, but none seemed to appeal, nor could he shake the feeling that he still owed monogamousness to Sarah Merritt, broken betrothal or not.

He wondered if he would go through life without ever marrying, one of those pitiable creatures about whom the locals, when he was seventy and bent, would say, he never got over his broken heart, just holed up there in that house they bought together, and let those yellow curtains she'd put up hang there till they were nothing but holes, and ate his meals alone.

Robert was right, eating his beans alone was one of the most apathetic rites he'd ever experienced. Why did he do it? Why didn't he go up to Teddy's and have supper with people? Why didn't he say, to hell with Sarah Merritt, I have some living to do?

Because he'd been waiting for her to heal, to knock on his door and walk into this kitchen with regret in her eyes and say to him, Noah, I'm sorry. Noah, please take me back. Noah, I love you.

But would she? Could she? Or was he pining away for something she was incapable of doing?

He could go to her and do the pursuing once more, might even get her to say she'd marry him, but what then? An attempt at seducing her before marching her down the aisle was unthinkable. She had made it abundantly clear she would not abide it—and, hell, to tell the truth, the thought of laying a hand on her terrified him by this time. So . . . let Victorian mores dictate that she approach her wedding bed a virgin? But supposing she froze up on him then too? Supposing he took the jump and found himself committed to a lifetime of living with a frigid woman.

Noah Campbell sat with his elbows beside his beans, beleaguered by the dozens of unanswered questions that felt like hammerblows as they clanged through his head.

So what're you going to do when Saturday night comes, Noah?
I don't know.
You gonna go over there and let her turn you away again?
She might not.
That's right. She might not, but then again she just might.

CHAPTER 23

ON Saturday night Sarah watched Addie bustling around the house getting dressed for her first social invitation since she'd married Robert. She pinned her hair up in a neat gold crown, polished her lips with petroleum jelly and donned a maternity frock covered by a hooded cape of periwinkle blue. Dressed totally respectably, she nevertheless stood before Sarah looking doubtful. "I wonder if Adrienne Davis knows about my past."

"My guess is she does, but she's willing to overlook it. She's a natural-born social leader, and tonight is going to be your ticket into acceptable society."

"Do you really think so, Sarah?"

Sarah kissed Addie's cheek. "You're Mrs. Robert Baysinger now." She tipped her chin up. "Be proud, and don't let the past matter."

When they left the house, Addie looked proud indeed, holding Robert's arm, excited and anticipatory. Sarah watched them go, feeling wistful and a little envious of their happiness.

When they were gone the house felt mournful. She wandered around listlessly, watered some houseplants, went up to her room, removed her shoes and replaced them with maroon felt carpet slippers. She pulled the combs from her hair and let it trail down her back, too lonely to care about brushing it. She released her throat- and cuff-buttons, wrapped in her favorite ugly pumpkin-colored shawl, took out her engagement brooch, placed it before her on the desk, donned her spectacles and got out her journal. In time she got chilled and found herself staring into the cubbyholes of the desk, writing little.

Around eight o'clock she took her writing materials downstairs. There was a Christmas tree in the parlor, but the room was dark as Sarah crossed through it on her way to the kitchen where she arranged her things on the table, the brooch within easy reach beside the journal with its marbelized cover and unlined white pages. She added two logs to the fire, poured herself a cup of leftover coffee and sat down once more to write.

The sounds in the kitchen—homey in times of fulfillment—tonight seemed lonely, and intensified Sarah's sense of solitude: the hiss of the teakettle in its customary nighttime spot at the cooler end of the range; the soft pop of the fire as it subsided to glowing coals; the creak of her chair as she leaned over the table; the scrape of her pen on the paper; the hiss of the lantern while she sat staring at the brooch, waiting for words to form in her mind; the quiet thump as Ruler jumped from a chair and stretched with her hindquarters raised.

Sarah sat back. "Hey, Ruler, come here," she coaxed, dropping her hand with the fingers pursed.

Ruler finished her stretch, seated herself in the curl of her tail and blinked at Sarah from five feet away. She studied the cat awhile, wishing she would leap up to her lap—a warm, living solace—but Ruler had other things to do. She started giving herself a bath.

It'd be nice to be a cat. All you'd have to be concerned with would be eating and sleeping and preening. There'd be no such thing as regrets or wishes or broken engagements. When the spirit moved you, you'd go out and hunker down and growl for half an hour, nose to nose with one of your ilk, and howl a little bit and leap around in the moonlight in the tall grass or the crusty snow, and when the moment was right, couple with your lady love, and the next day have no concern or memory of it.

Ruler moved farther away, leaped onto the rocking chair seat where she settled in the shape of a muff with her front paws hidden.

Sarah dipped her pen and wrote, "I wonder what it would feel like to be expecting a child, to don my cape over my bulging stomach and leave the house on Noah's arm, heading for a dinner with Chambers and Adrienne Davis, to be at last a part of the world that moves two by two." She dipped her pen again and held it above the page, staring at its black nib until the ink started drying, creating a marbleized design of peacock and copper on the curved metal.

In the front room, some needles fell from the Christmas tree onto the bare wood floor. Ruler's ears twitched, her pupils dilated, and she glanced sharply at the doorway.

Sarah sat watching her absently until Ruler settled back into a furball and squinted her eyes. Sarah turned her regard to the brooch, reached out and touched it with her fingertips, as lightly as if inspecting it for fine cracks.

In time she sighed, dipped the pen and wrote on. "I find myself fantasizing about Noah so often, picturing what it would be like if I were like Addie and could—"

A knock sounded on the front door.

Both Sarah and Ruler shot startled glances through the doorway. Sarah sat unmoving until it sounded again, then pushed back her chair and removed her glasses, leaving them behind as she gripped her shawl and headed for the dark front room. With one hand she clustered her disorderly hair at her nape, then let it spring back into disarray as she opened the door.

Noah stood on the step.

For seconds neither he nor Sarah spoke. Or moved. He studied her from beneath the brim of his brown Stetson, his hands at his sides, his features only a suggestion in the faraway light from the kitchen lantern. The lines linking his nose and mouth were deep grooves, disappearing into his dark mustache. His somber eyes were mere pinpricks of light.

She stood on the threshold above him, one hand gripping her aged shawl, the other, the doorknob, while only the ragtail outline of her hair was lit from the light behind her.

"Hello, Sarah," he said finally in a voice that sounded weary beyond belief.

"Hello, Noah."

Silence abounded while they waited for a miracle to bring ease between them.

"I think we should talk. Could I come in?"

"Addie and Robert aren't home. They're gone to the Davises'."

"Yes, I know, Robert told me. That's why I came."

She hid her surprise and said, "What good will talking do?"

"I don't know . . ." He dropped his gaze to the threshold and shook his head forlornly. "I don't know," he repeated, quieter. "I only know we've got to because we can't go on like this anymore."

She stepped back and freed his way. "Come in then."

He moved the way a farmer moves through his fields after they have been leveled by hail, entering the front room with its scent of pine and its total familiarity, even in the near dark. She left the door for him to close, placing herself a goodly distance away, waiting with her arms crossed, wrapped so tightly the weave of the crocheted shawl became distorted.

"I'll light a lantern," she said, heading toward a round parlor table between two chairs—three amorphous shapes in the dark.

"No, don't. The kitchen is warmer anyway." He moved toward it as if homing to some force beyond his control. In the doorway he paused, studying the room where he had shared meals and felicitations, laughter and games, and friendships whose absence had left a void in his life. Sarah had been writing: her things were scattered on the table. The room emanated a melancholy that struck him deep—the cat curled up on a rocking chair by the stove, the evidence of Sarah's singular occupation on a Saturday night when the others were off to happier pursuits, the betrothal brooch he had given her resting among her writing materials like a sad, powerless talisman. He stepped near the edge of the table and looked down at her empty coffee cup, the brooch, her glasses, the open book with her effortless angular writing, so different from his own labored scratching that never seemed to follow the horizontal line of the page. He touched the book, read the last sentence she had written and felt a great pressure in his chest.

From the doorway she watched him and remarked quietly, "It's not polite to read other people's journals."

He looked over his shoulder, studied her tightly crossed arms and smileless face. "You don't have any secrets from me, Sarah. Everything you're feeling, I'm feeling. I'd say we're a couple of pretty miserable people."

"Sit down." She came into the room and closed the book, set the penholder atop it and left the brooch where it was. He hung his jacket on the back of a kitchen chair, took off his hat, scooped the cat off the rocker and dropped to it himself while Sarah resumed her place at the table.

Ruler stayed on Noah's lap where she'd been put, giving their eyes a focal point while Noah scratched the creature's neck and head. In time he lifted his gaze and asked wearily, "So what are we going to do, Sarah?"

She put her elbows on the table, wrapped one hand loosely around the other and rested her cheek on them. "I don't know."

Some time passed before he said, "I missed you."

A smile touched her lips, then fled: her only reply.

"Say it," he said.

"I think it's better if I don't."

"Say it anyway."

"I missed you, too."

For a while they simply looked at each other, allowing the loneliness of the past months to show in their faces. Ruler began purring. Noah kept scratching.

"I've done some tough things in my life, but coming here tonight beats them all."

"So why did you?"

"Because I've been going through hell and hell's not my favorite place to be going through. How about you?"

"Yes. The same."

"This town's got some nice decent women now, but I'd as soon eat a dish of mud as take one of them out. Damn you for that, Sarah Merritt."

Her smile glimmered again, as sad as before.

Noah drew a deep breath, let it out with a faint shudder and dropped his head against the back of the chair. His eyes closed. He set the rocker in slight motion and breathed, "I'm so damned tired."

An urge flooded her as she studied him: to rise and cross the few feet that separated them, line his cheeks with both her palms and kiss his closed eyes, then rest her jaw against his forehead.

She rose instead and refilled her coffee cup without offering him any. "I suppose you've heard Robert and Addie are expecting a baby."

"Yes, I heard."

"Ironic, isn't it . . ." She stood facing the stove, a finger in the cup handle, without drinking. ". . . that I wish it were me."

He opened his eyes and studied her long back with the latticework of ugly pumpkin-colored knit covering her brindle-brown blouse, and her hair streaming over both, in bad need of combing.

"Do you?"

"Yes, very much. I envy them."

"That surprises me."

"Me, too. I always thought my newspapering was enough to keep me happy."

"And it's not?"

She refused to answer.

He sighed.

A long time went by before he asked, "Could we talk about your father, Sarah?"

"My father is no longer mentioned in this house."

"Your father's been mentioned in every word that you and I have spoken since that night you found out about him."

"I loved him more than any person on this earth and he betrayed that love in the most unforgivable way possible."

"And now I pay for what he did to Addie. How much longer?"

"Why don't you just go to one of those other women? It would be so much simpler for you."

"Because you're the one I'm stuck on. I told you that before. I stayed away from you for better than half a year hoping I could get over you but it didn't work. I still love you."

He watched her from behind, gauging her minute motions, the slight drop of her chin, the way she held the cup without drinking from it. She took it to the dry sink and set it down, untasted, then returned to her chair and her former pose with her cheek resting on her loosely joined hands.

"Marrying you would be sheer stupidity."

"But you want to, don't you?"

"Yes."

"What if I came over there and kissed you and touched you in a less than brotherly way, what would happen?"

She laughed ruefully, put ten fingertips over her face and wobbled her head left and right twice.

"See?" he said. "That's what I mean when I said coming here took some nerve. If you turned me away again it would be the last time. I could never come back again."

"I've had the most preposterous thought these last few months," she admitted, regarding him again over her joined hands. "It's absurd, sinful even, but I've had it nonetheless, during my weaker moments when I've missed you so much I wondered if I might die of it. I've thought, why couldn't I marry Noah and we would silently agree that he could continue going to Rose's as he did when I first met him? There. Now you know what kind of woman I am."

The corners of his mouth tipped up sadly. "Lonely, scared . . . just like me."

They studied one another while the lantern hissed and the stove radiated warmth, finding their point-blank honesty at once disconcerting and relieving.

"Now I'll tell you a deep, dark secret of my own, something I've imagined since we've been apart—coming here and hauling you upstairs and taking your dress off and kissing you in ten places and showing you that when you care about someone the way we care about each other, that's a natural part of it. Do you want to try it?"

She laughed aloud, briefly. "Of course not."

"No, of course not. If you'd said yes, you wouldn't be Sarah and I wouldn't love you and we wouldn't be sitting here across the room from each other, hurting this way. So what should we do?"

Her mouth got the tortured look that precedes tears. Her only answer was a shake of the head: I don't know, I'm so afraid.

He put his feet flat on the floor and leaned forward, scaring the cat away. Resting both elbows on his knees, he fixed his eyes on Sarah's. When he spoke his voice sounded constricted and unnatural.

"Did you really miss me so much you thought you might die of it?"

"Yes," she whispered, feeling her chin grow hot where her joined hands touched it.

"Then meet me," he said and pointed at the floor halfway between them. "There."

She felt adhered to the chair, studying his earnest eyes, the slope of his shoulders leaning toward her, his squarish hands curved one around the other as he waited for her response. She had only to rise to be in his arms again and face the moment of proof. Her only other choice was to watch him walk out that door, never to return, to relive the purgatory she had suffered since they'd parted ways.

She had moved in a colorless, tasteless void these past seven months without him, but tonight he had merely to appear before her and she came back to life. He stepped into a room and her apathy vanished like frost from a lighted windowpane; she *felt* again.

To maintain this distance from him was agony. To watch his face reflect the torment on her own filled her with anguish. Was this passion? She so wanted passion, not for its own sake, but because without it she was doomed.

"Meet me," he repeated.

She swallowed the tears that were on the verge of forming and pushed back her chair, fear and want crushing her like a great hand that would prevent her from rising. She pressed her palms to the tabletop and rose against it.

He got up from the rocker and waited.

"I wish I were Addie," she whispered as she began to move toward him.

"No, you don't," he replied, moving, too, "because then there wouldn't be you and me."

They met at the corner of the table, pausing before one another before stepping into a tenuous embrace. They held each other loosely, acclimating to the tumult of feelings before he drew back and offered his eyes, then his mouth, softly. The great weight of loneliness lifted, and the kiss became a twining, the embrace a reclaiming of what each had given up. She put her arms about his neck and he drew her full-length against him. Heart to heart, they rested, their eyes closed, their fear of missteps dissolving in the grand rush of reunion. They kissed unbrokenly, testing each other, and themselves, letting the contact heat at will until their mouths opened and their tongues met. She made a small, pained sound in her throat and he replied with a tightening of his embrace. Suddenly their restraint vanished and their kiss became urgent, their bodies taken fire from the taste and touch of one another after the months of self-denial. He made a throaty sound, too, neither sob nor groan, but an agonized end of agony while their fists searched for a grip—his on the woolly weave of her shawl, hers on the smooth leather of his vest.

In time they halted to hold each other fast and let the torrent of feelings rush out.

"Oh Noah, I love you," she said. "I missed you, I was bereft without you."

"I love you, too. Tell me again."

"I love you, Noah."

He held her so tightly her heels left the floor. "I never thought I'd hear you say it again."

"I was always so stubborn about saying it . . . I'm sorry, Noah, but I do love you, I do, only I never thought falling in love would be so terrible."

"Or so wonderful."

"Or so frightening."

"Or so lonely. A hundred times a day I had to stop myself from walking past your newspaper office."

"I kept looking out the window, hoping to see you pass."

"And then we'd meet on the boardwalk and act like we didn't know each other."

"Nobody could live with me."

"Me either. I was angry at the whole world."

"I snapped at everybody and got so irritable and fault-finding. I scared off Patrick with my temper, and I miss him so much. And poor Josh— I've been awful to him, too. Nothing seemed right without you, nothing."

They kissed again, incautiously and deep, searching for motions to reiterate all they felt. When it ended he had a two-handed grip on her hair, tipping her head back with the faintest tug on her scalp.

"I never want to go through that again," he said fiercely.

"Neither do I."

They let their eyes rove each others' faces, sharing a very small space on the kitchen floor, with her maroon carpet slippers planted between

his scuffed brown cowboy boots. He released her hair and began stroking it back from her temples.

"How do you feel?" he asked.

"As if I've been living underwater for a long long time and have just
come up into the air."

"How else do you feel?"

With her head thrown back and her throat arched, the words came
out strained. "I want you."

His hands stopped moving. "I'm going to do something. Don't be
scared." He lifted her in his arms, threshold fashion, and ordered,
"Turn off the lantern."

She reached and adjusted the ribbed brass screw, bringing darkness
descending over the room, then linked her arms around his neck. He
carried her to the rocker and put her on his lap with her legs draped
over a wooden arm of the chair.

"Say my name," he whispered.

"Noah."

"Say it again."

"Noah."

"Yes, Noah . . . and I still want to marry you." He set the chair in
motion, rocking gently, and resumed stroking her hair back from her
left temple while his other hand curved up her back and closed lightly
around her neck, toying with it beneath her hair. He kissed her mouth
softly . . . softly . . . and went on rocking her, easing her, touching his
lips to other fine places—her cheek, her eyebrow, her chin. He nuzzled
her throat, felt her head hang back and the warmth of her hair leave
his left hand. He touched her breast the way he had touched her hair,
a finding in the dark, a mere grazing without demand. He heard her
breath catch and went on caressing her with faint strokes of his thumb
while his forearm rested along her stomach.

"I love you, Sarah," he whispered.

He felt tremors begin deep within her. They shimmied up through
his arm as he caressed her breast and felt it bead up. She murmured
something—a wordless sound that needed no words, sliding from her
throat as she covered his hand with both of her own and clamped it
tightly against herself. She drew her head up with an effort and brought
his open hand to her face and kissed it in three places, then replaced
it on her breast. She closed her eyes and sat very still, letting his hand
play over her. When he found her mouth again, her lips were open, the
breath hurrying from them in wonderful, soft gusts.

As the kiss ended, she whispered in wonder, "Oh Noah . . ."

His hand departed her breast and settled her in the curve of his shoulder with her forehead on his jaw. The rocking chair resumed its faint, rhythmic ticks agains the floor.

"Oh Noah," she repeated, her breath warm against his neck.

In the darkness he smiled and continued rocking.

"So will you marry me, you stubborn woman?"

"Yes, I'll marry you, you incorrigible man."

"I won't go to Rose's."

"I don't think you'll have to," she replied.

He stopped rocking and kissed her—much less desperately than when they'd been on their feet, but leaning forward and coiling around her until his leather vest creaked. He kissed her in myriad soft ways, and, parting, let his lips linger.

"Did I see that betrothal brooch on your kitchen table?"

"Yes, you did."

"Do we have to light the lantern to find it?"

"No, of course not, I can find it in the dark. I've done it many times." She left his lap, retaining a fingerhold on one of his hands while reaching for the tabletop. Momentarily, she returned, and, sitting upright on his lap, pinned the brooch to her blouse, directly over her heart.

"There," she said, settling into the lee of his shoulder once more. "Everything's where it should be."

"Let's see," he whispered. He found the brooch, and if in finding it he touched her breast again, she objected no more than she had the first time.

Minutes later she whispered, "Noah?"

"Hm?"

They were rocking again, wishing Addie and Robert would never come home.

"That feels wonderful."

He chuckled and kept on rocking.

They were married on Christmas Eve at five P.M. by Birtle Matheson in a brief, quiet ceremony with only Addie and Robert as witnesses. Sarah wore a simple dress of ivory satin—made by Addie—and carried a tiny ivory Bible festooned with matching ribbon. Her hair was upswept in a modified pompadour—again by Addie—trimmed by a tiny spray of seed pearls, and her lips were painted, for the first time in her life, with a touch of coral.

Noah wore the black suit he'd bought months ago for this occasion, with its double-breasted vest, a white shirt with a wing-tipped collar and a black four-in-hand tie.

After the ceremony the four of them had supper at Addie and Robert's house, accompanied by champagne and a fancy ribbon cake baked for the occasion by Emma, who had gracefully accepted the news that the wedding was to be private and small, so small she herself would not be invited.

"You do it your way, Sarah," she had said, "and blessed be the day."

On her way home from Addie's, Sarah was thinking, . . . *and blessed be the night . . . please, oh please.*

The house where she would live as Noah's wife was as she remembered, plain and only partially furnished, awaiting her choices on what remained to be bought. Entering the kitchen, she exclaimed, "Why, it's warm in here."

"I hired Josh to come and stoke the fire."

"Oh, how thoughtful, Noah . . . thank you."

The lantern flared, then Noah came up behind her and took her coat from her shoulders. He hung it, along with his own, and his hat, then returned to her.

"I have another surprise for you. Come." He took her hand, and the lantern, and led her straight up the stairs to their bedroom, where he stepped back to let her enter first. In one corner, in a pail of sand, trimmed with embossed cardboard cutouts and red wax candles in tin clips, was a fragrant spruce tree.

"Oh Noah!" she exclaimed, delighted. "When did you do this?" She had been here earlier to bring her belongings, and the corner had been bare.

"This afternoon after you left. I'll have to confess, I hired Josh to go out and find it."

"It smells delicious. Can we light the candles?"

"Of course. But I'd better get some water up here first, just in case." He set the lantern on the dresser, took the pitcher from the bowl and said, "Be right back."

While he was gone, she put her hands to her cheeks and glanced at the bed, trying to be calm.

Noah returned in minutes with the full pitcher and some matches. He struck one on his heel and touched the wicks of ten miniature candles. The shadows of the pine needles danced on the ceiling and walls. They studied the flames in silence before he turned to look at her and said quietly, "Merry Christmas, Mrs. Campbell."

She looked into his eyes and replied, "Merry Christmas, Mr. Campbell." His thumb stroked hers . . . once, twice . . . then they prudently returned their gazes to the tree. Already the candles were dripping red wax onto the lower branches, and it was beginning to tick onto the floor.

"I'm afraid we'll have to blow them out."

"They were lovely while they lasted."

She blew out all ten flames and stood amidst the scent of smoking wicks. "You made us a beautiful memory, Noah. Thank you."

He retreated and she heard movement behind her. She turned to discover he had removed his jacket and was loosening his tie.

"You'll need help with your buttons," he said.

"Oh . . . yes." She turned her heated face away, presenting her back, and he stepped behind her to do the honors.

"Thank you," she whispered when the last button was freed.

He cleared his throat and said, "I have to step out back and put a couple more pieces of wood in the stove." At the sound of his retreating footsteps she glanced back over her shoulder. He paused in the doorway, said, "The water in the pitcher is warm," and disappeared without even taking the lantern.

She was so relieved her breath swooshed from her like a passing gale. He had said he'd visualized taking her dress off and kissing her in ten places, and she'd supposed that's how this interlude would begin, and in spite of the episode on the rocking chair, when her clothing had remained intact, she had worried that at the last minute she would be terrified and stiffen up and would ruin her wedding night. Instead, he proved himself romantic and considerate beyond her dearest hopes.

He gave her more time than needed. By the time he returned, her nightgown was buttoned up the front and tied at the throat, her face was washed and she was brushing her hair before the dresser mirror.

She glanced at the doorway the moment he stopped in it, and tried to hide a smile: he was wearing a red and white striped nightshirt.

"It's all right, you can laugh," he said, lifting his arms and glancing down. "I've never worn one of these things before. I thought you might appreciate it, but I feel like a damned sissy."

A sudden laugh doubled her forward with the back of the brush against her mouth. In none of her preconceptions had she pictured herself laughing on her wedding night. When she straightened, he was chuckling, too, studying his bare feet and rather skinny ankles.

"Good God," he muttered, then stood straight and jabbed a thumb at the bed. "Would you mind getting in there so I can pile in behind you and hide?"

She scrambled into the bed, still smiling, establishing her place closest to the wall. He *did* pile in right behind her, leaving the lantern lit and pulling the covers to their waists.

Settling onto her back, she thought, *He's wonderful. He knows how nervous I am and he's doing everything he knows to make this easy for me.*

He settled on his side, braced his head on one hand, and immediately found her hand, fit his fingers tightly between hers, closed them hard and kissed her knuckles.

"I know you're scared, but there's no need to be."

"But I don't know what to do."

"You don't need to know. I know."

He had ways, oh, he had ways. He used them, one upon the other, gentling her with a first tender kiss, sweet and moist, while finding her bare foot beneath the blankets and covering it with one of his own. His head swayed, and the smooth sole of his foot rubbed the top of hers, then hooked her leg from behind and held it captive. The kiss ended and he nuzzled her jaw, the soft hollow beneath it.

"How can you smell like roses in the dead of winter?" he asked.

"I put on some rose water while you were downstairs."

"Oh, you did?" He backed up and smiled, only inches from her face, and brushed her cheek with a knuckle.

"Did you put some roses here, too?"

She blushed brighter. "Do men always tease women when they're doing this?"

"I don't know. This one does. Does it bother you?"

"It's unexpected . . . it's . . . I . . . I'm not used to blushing."

"It's very becoming, though. I think I'll make you do it often."

"Oh Noah . . ." She dropped her gaze demurely.

He lifted her chin and kissed her so very lightly his shadow never fully darkened her lips. Then again, to one side of her mouth . . . and the other . . . then on her chin . . . and on her throat.

"Mmm . . . I remember this smell. You smelled like this one year ago tonight."

"And you smelled like this across the breakfast table at Mrs. Roundtree's every morning after you'd shaved."

He lifted his head, smiling. "I didn't know you noticed."

"I noticed a lot of things about you. I memorized every shirt you owned, and your favorite foods, and a lot of little mannerisms you have. But mostly I noticed your hair . . . I so love your hair, Noah."

He went perfectly still, fixing his gray eyes on her beautiful blue ones, leaning on one elbow, motionless above her.

"Touch it," he whispered.

She raised both hands and threaded them through his thick, lush hair, ruffling it, mussing it, living out a fantasy as his eyelids slid closed and he lowered his face to the eyelet lace between her breasts. While

her hands continued moving, his breath warmed her, his mouth opened
and he caressed her with it alone, nuzzling the inner swells of her breasts
within her lace-trimmed gown.

Her eye drifted closed, too, and her fingertips relaxed in his hair,
becoming still as he found and covered the fullest part of her breast.
"Ohh," she breathed, surprised by the swift sensation and her response
to it. Her hands clasped his skull, drawing him more fully against
herself, first one breast, then the other, where he bit her—bit her!—and
sent a wondrous recoil clear to her toes.

Abruptly he rose, rushing up like a swimmer out of the deep, meeting
her waiting mouth with his, matching their bodies while everything
became urgent. Tangled in two nightgowns, they pressed as close as the
folds of cotton would allow.

Suddenly he broke away, ordering, "Sit up," doing so himself, drawing her after him, scraping her pretty white nightie up until it caught
beneath her hips. "Up again . . ." And with a shift and lift, she felt the
garment swept away. It sailed over her head and landed on the floor,
followed immediately by his own, and before the two had become a
motionless puddle, his arm took her down with him, onto their sides,
and his foot scooped her close once more.

They fell to the pillows with their eyes wide open, pressed skin to
skin, with her left breast caught up high by his wide hand. When he
spoke, his voice sounded gruff.

"If anything hurts, you stop me."

She nodded her head twice in rapid succession, wide-eyed and breathless.

Then he released her breast, and found her hip, and curved his hand
behind to hold her while teaching her motion—fluid and rhythmic and
altogether tempting. They kissed, all lush and lusty, propelled by the
relentlessness only first times can bring. He caught her knee and drew
it over his hip, and touched her intimately for the first time.

"Oh!" she cried, and "Oh" again, as she twisted her face against the
pillow. In time he captured her hand, whispering, "Here . . . like this."
And all she had thought to be sordid became exalted.

Wily, wonderful man, he had her welcoming him at the moment of
union. And later, crying out aloud with her throat bowed. And later
still, gripping his shuddering body with her heels.

When it was over they lay twined, depleted, breathing the scent of
each other's dampened skins.

She laughed once in celebration, with her eyes closed and her face at his chest. He took her head in both hands and tipped it to a better angle, rubbed his thumbs near the corners of her eyes and said, smiling, "There, now you know."

"All that worry for nothing," she said.

"Nothing!" he exclaimed, lifting his head off the pillow until she laughed and he let it back down.

They rested awhile, replete.

"Noah?" she said, in time.

"Hm?"

"You said ten places. You owe me seven."

A chortle started deep in his chest and rumbled its way up his throat. "Ohhhh, Sarah Campbell, I can see I've started something."

He had. Furthermore, he had to finish it more than one time that night.

At midnight they were still awake, too enchanted to waste time on sleep. She was lying in the crook of his arm when she lifted her head sharply and said, "Listen, Noah!" Then, "Open the window!"

"What?"

"Open the window . . . hurry! I think I hear the chimes."

He obliged her, turning off the lantern first, then opening the curtains and raising the sash. When the chill air rushed in he scampered back to bed, leaped in and yanked the covers to their necks before curling her against him again.

"Oh Noah, listen . . . 'Adeste Fideles,' just like last year."

He began singing it, softly, at her ear.

She joined him, so quietly some words were whispered.

When it ended, they lay content.

"Funny," he said, "I never considered 'Adeste Fideles' a love song before."

"Let's make sure we sing it every Christmas night, to celebrate our anniversary."

"With or without the chimes," he added.

They thought about it awhile, about all the Christmases to come, all the years of happiness piling one upon another while they told their children the story of their rocky beginning and their wedding on Christmas Eve, and the sound of the chimes coming in through the window.

Later, when they'd heard a lot of carols, and the room had grown arctic, and they had closed the window and were trying to warm one another, he fit himself against her like one open page behind another and said, "We're going to be happy, Sarah."

"Mmm . . . I think so," she replied sleepily.

He closed his eyes and sighed against her shoulder blade.
"I love you," he murmured.
"I love you, too," she mumbled.
And they slept, delivered.